THE MIDNIGHT MAN

BOOK 1

THE CLAPHAM TRILOGY

JULIE ANDERSON

This edition produced in Great Britain in 2024

by Hobeck Books Limited, 24 Brookside Business Park, Stone, Staffordshire ST15 0RZ

www.hobeck.net

A CIP catalogue for this book is available from the British Library.

ISBN 978-1-915-817-36-5 (pbk)

ISBN 978-1-915-817-35-8 (ebook)

Cover design by Jayne Mapp Design

Printed and bound in Great Britain by Clays Ltd, Elcograf S.p.A.

For all those women

PROLOGUE

The blackness was complete.

She closed her eyes, then opened them again. It made no difference.

There was no light at all; no paler black, no grey, no moon or starlight encroaching on the dark. Nothing.

As she clenched her fists to halt the rising wave of panic, her nails dug into her palms. That hurt.

So, she was still alive.

But where was she? Inside – it wasn't cold. And somewhere completely without light. A total blackout.

She felt rough fabric beneath her hands; she was lying on it. Tentative, afraid of what her fingers might find, she explored each side of her. Her left hand hit an obstruction, a wall. Not rough brick, but smooth and cold. Stone? Her right hand came to the edge of what she realised must be a bed, a camp bed, a thin mattress lying on a metal frame supported by springs.

She raised her right arm and, feeling nothing above her, sat up.

Too quickly.

Her head thudded and bile rose into her throat. For a second, she thought she would collapse, but she took deep breaths and waited for the pain to recede. What was going on? Had she been knocked out? Her seeking fingers could find no headwound. She couldn't remember what had happened.

She swung her feet around and over the edge of the bed. They scuffed the ground; the bed was a low one. Maneuvering onto all fours on the floor, she swept her hand in an arc around her. The surface was hard and dusty, probably concrete. There was a staleness to the air, too. Wherever she was, it had been closed up for a long time. Slowly, she began to crawl forwards, her hands feeling the way.

She tried to recall the series of events before she got here. She remembered finishing work and leaving the hospital, but she didn't go to her lodgings, she was sure. So where did she go? And why? She had a vague memory of a train then... nothing. She had no idea how she'd got to this place.

What was that?

She paused. A noise in the distance. Traffic?

No, it was a continuous sound; a growling, rumbling, growing louder, coming closer. Then it ceased. She held her breath and waited for the noise to begin again, but all was silent.

Machinery?

Maybe. She continued onwards.

Ow!

She recoiled; she'd hit her head. Smacked up against something flat. Her fingers touched a metal thing, with a slit down its centre. Laying her palms flat against it, she stood. There were handles, it was a cupboard. Locked. There was another to the left of it and one to the right. A row of cupboards. She could be in a storeroom.

A flash of memory.

She was crossing Balham Hill, towards the Odeon Cinema. *Terror by Night* was this week's film and it had a train on the poster; that was why the train was in her mind. But she couldn't remember seeing the film.

There was nothing to the left of the final cupboard, only more wall, but... a pole. No, a broom handle. This *was* a storeroom. Grasping the handle she waved it out to her right. It hit an obstruction and she reached out; it was a wall, like the other. When she waved it left, there was nothing there.

So, the place she was in was long and narrow. She banged the tip of the broom on the floor, listening. The concrete absorbed the sound, but she thought there was a suggestion of an echo. Using the broom held out like a blind man's cane, tapping it on the floor, she walked forwards a few steps, then some more, slowly waving her left arm, hand extended, cautious. She kept feeling for the wall to the right of her with the broom, making sure it was there.

How had she got here? What had happened after she crossed Balham Hill? Her brain wouldn't work; she couldn't remember.

The wall stopped. So did she. She prodded the air with the broom, where the wall should be. She had reached a corner; her hand found the angle of the wall. It was metal, not stone.

What was this place?

There was more of an echo here, she thought and the faint suggestion of movement in the air. No, more than a suggestion, there was a cooling on her skin. She waited, but the air was still again. Had a window been opened somewhere nearby, then closed? Or a door?

Encouraged by the thought of finding it, she walked onward in the direction of the tiny gasp of air, keeping the wall to her right. The floor was even beneath the broom, she was sweeping it from side to side and moving less carefully.

She'd been going to see that film, *Terror by Night*. That was it. But she couldn't remember any more.

What was that? Was it... a small speck of light in the distance?

For a few heartbeats she didn't really believe it existed, it was her eyes playing tricks, seeing something that wasn't there. She blinked, screwing up her eyes. It wavered, but it didn't disappear.

'Hello?' Her voice echoed, but dully, absorbed by the darkness. 'Hello, I'm here!'

The light moved. Could it be someone carrying a lantern?

She hurried forward. The light was coming towards her, she

could see a yellowish tinge to it and a moving pool of grey light preceding it on the floor. It was a torch.

She drew breath to shout again but stopped. She backed against the wall and began, moving as silently as possible, to retrace her steps.

Suddenly, it all came back to her.

She remembered.

SUNDAY

1

FAYE SMITH

The woman didn't belong.

Faye noticed her as soon as she walked into the canteen. She was tall and very pretty, wearing an expensive-looking greatcoat. She entered with a crowd and took a seat at the table furthest away from the serving counter.

Cold November light filled the large windows. The clatter of plates and the chatter of diners echoed from the high ceiling and tiled floor as tables were taken and queues formed. Sunday lunch was always popular. A covey of laughing nurses was blown in through the doors on a gust of icy wind, their navy capes flapping. They dumped their things on the big, round table in the corner and joined the snaking line leading to the servery.

Faye stood at the lectern beside the counter. She stamped the ration books of those who offered them and checked names on a list of those staff who had yielded up their books and took all their meals in the canteen. A lot of people had – the war was over but rationing continued and the food at the South London was better than in most places. Hospitals got a wider range of foodstuffs than was in the shops and Cook was a genius when it came to making tasty meals from nothing.

Two women in pale green uniforms, hairnets beneath peaked

hats, ladled soup into bowls or piled vegetables on to the heated plates handed to them by diners, plates that already held small helpings of meat. Portions of corned beef sat, unchosen, at the end of the counter. There'd be corned-beef-hash tomorrow.

The room hummed with disciplined activity; everyone knew their job and how to do it. Faye could almost feel the clicking tremor of a smoothly running machine, cogs turning, crankshafts rising and falling; this was how it should run.

Crash!

A tray loaded with lunch hit the floor, silencing everyone.

Seconds later the chatter resumed. The tray's owner looked around for the means to clean up the mess, wincing in apology. Faye stepped out from her place. They'd been short-handed since Margaret had gone to the maternity ward, the third employee in the last six months to give birth and return to hearth and home. The queue would have to wait; someone would have to help clear things up.

'Stay there, I'll help, I've finished,' a porter, a small woman in brown overalls, called.

Faye returned to the lectern and the queue began to move once more. Kitchen staff replenished empty serving dishes. Flat oblong tins of sponge and fruit crumble and large metal jugs of custard were placed at the other end of the counter.

There was a subtle shift in atmosphere, the general hubbub reducing, as a diminutive figure clad in a navy uniform, white piping round the collar, strode through the doors.

'Matron,' Faye greeted her.

'Miss Smith, busy as ever, I see.'

'Sunday lunch always is,' Faye replied. 'Morning, Sisters.' She welcomed the three women following in Matron's wake. Near the far end of the counter a table which had been occupied a moment earlier was being vacated at speed. It was well-known that Matron liked to sit there.

The canteen was full to bursting, noisy with high-pitched clamour, yet already the earlier diners were leaving, depositing used trays on the tall racks provided. Their places were quickly taken and the queue, which had stretched beyond the doors and down the chilly corridor, was dwindling. Faye signalled to the servers to begin clearing away behind the service area. The litter and debris on the dining tables would have to be cleared too.

The mystery woman was still sitting over by the windows, with a cup of tea and a half full rack of toast in front of her. All employees and business visitors to the hospital were entitled to eat in the staff canteen, but this woman was neither, Faye was almost certain. She hadn't shown a ration book or other identification because she hadn't been up to the counter. Her companions had vanished. It was strange, especially on a Sunday.

Faye studied her.

She appeared to be around Faye's age, in her late twenties, with glossy dark hair falling to her shoulders in waves which were either natural or very expensively purchased. A peaches-and-cream complexion in a heart-shaped face, with a high forehead and full lips painted scarlet. Neat, pearl earrings added to a refined, even glamorous, appearance. No wedding ring. She sat erect, shoulders back, wearing civvies, a simple woollen sweater over a pale blouse with the thick greatcoat folded over the back of her chair. Money written all over her.

Whose money? Faye wondered. Parts of Clapham, the Old Town in particular, were known to be where Brigade of Guards officers set up their girlfriends and mistresses. Chelsea Barracks wasn't far across the river, making Clapham handy to visit when wives and children were in the country. Could she be one of those women and, if she was, what was she doing here?

Her eyes were cast down, yet there was something in the woman's posture that suggested she was alert and watchful, ready to bolt in a moment.

She didn't belong. She wasn't eating lunch and, apparently, had no business at all in the canteen.

Faye prided herself on not being taken for a ride. Not that she was about to judge anyone, but she was always careful, especially in doing her job. She wasn't going to let anyone take advantage of the South London and there were plenty who'd tried, during the war and afterwards.

'Can you take over here, please?' Faye called over one of the servers at the counter.

She threaded her way across the room, replacing chairs under tables, picking up discarded serviettes. When she reached the stranger's table, she drew out the chair opposite her and sat.

'Enjoyed that, did you?' she asked, indicating the now empty toast rack. 'Bread's rationed, you know. We don't throw it away; we use it to make puddings.'

The woman said nothing. She met Faye's gaze with a level stare and pulled a teacup towards her, her fingers wrapping around it. Her eyes were a vivid violet blue.

'Not the best cup to choose.' Faye pursed her lips and raised one eyebrow. 'The last person who drank from it was wearing "Baby Pink" and I'd say your lipstick's closer to "Pillar Box Red". It's not your cup.'

The marks on the rim of the teacup were damning. She might look like Lady Muck, but the mystery visitor was trying to pull a fast one, she was eating leftovers, cadging food. Like any street urchin or tramp.

The woman's shoulders sagged, as if someone had let the air out of her. The blue eyes were filling rapidly with tears, but she blinked them away.

'You're not very good at this are you?' Faye said with a cold stare. 'I'll bet you don't have any business here at all? You'll have to pay for what you've had.'

She expected a response.

The silence lengthened, but she could wait.

'I don't,' the woman eventually conceded, in a clipped, refined accent. 'And I—I can't pay.'

Faye expelled air from her long nose in derision. The woman's clothes were quality and those earrings didn't look like paste. Who was she trying to kid?

'This is *stealing*.' Faye emphasised the final word, giving the woman a contemptuous glance. 'I should report you to the police. You can get a meal for ninepence at the British Restaurant in the school along the South Side; you don't have to steal.'

'Oh. I—I didn't know; I'm not from round here.' The end of the sentence was bitten off, as she pressed her lips together. The tears threatened to return. 'I'll go there then.'

The woman fumbled behind her, reaching for her coat and began to rise. Faye watched as she gathered up her things, seeming genuinely distressed and trying to hide it. Probably a performance to avoid getting reported.

A single tear ran down the woman's cheek and she dashed it away, frowning. She had, it seemed, some pride left. Faye's compassion, and her curiosity, was stirred. What had brought a young woman like her, well-spoken and obviously from money to this?

Faye made a decision.

'Hold on,' she said, sharply.

The woman froze, a fearful look on her face.

'We're short-handed today, if you help clearing tables and cleaning up, I'll see you get a decent meal at the end of the shift and I won't report you. How's that for an offer?'

After a moment's hesitation the woman said, 'Thank you, yes, it would suit me very well. Shall I start straight away?'

'There's no time like the present.'

'Right. I can work for as long as you like.'

No surprise. It was bitterly cold outside and the canteen was warm and welcoming.

'Why?'

The woman opened her mouth to reply; she blinked hard as tears welled again.

'I d—don't have anywhere to stay. I need to find a place for tonight.' She pulled herself together, chin jutting out. 'Is there a cheap guest house round here, d'you know, that'll take me on trust and let me stay for a night?' Her face blanched. 'Or a—a hostel?' She swallowed hard. 'I don't have any ready cash and the banks aren't open till tomorrow. I can get some then.'

Now why would that be?

'None immediately spring to mind, but I'll give it some thought while you're cleaning,' she said and rose to offer her hand. 'Faye Smith, canteen manager.'

'Ellie Peveril.' They shook hands. 'I'm a legal clerk, just returned from Nuremberg and currently unemployed.'

Why are you here, Ellie Peveril? Maybe you're a rich man's mistress, maybe not, but you're hiding or running from something. Or are you in a different kind of trouble?'

Covertly, Faye eyed the mysterious stranger, looking her up and down. The woman didn't look pregnant, but appearances could deceive. There were a lot of babies on the way now the men had returned, not all of them made within wedlock. It was one possible reason why an apparently well-bred young lady was cadging left-over food in a hospital canteen on Clapham South Side and trying to find a cheap room. If she was expecting, she might think a hospital was the place to find something or someone to help rid her of her baby.

She'd be disappointed if she was looking for that at the South London. Abortion was a crime and SLH doctors could only perform the procedure under the strictest of circumstances, regardless of what they thought about the law.

'This way.' Faye waited while the woman gathered up her coat and a faded rucksack. 'Nuremberg, you say. The tribunal? I'd like to hear about the trials, that would be worth a meal.'

Like many others, Faye had seen the newsreels and pored over the reports in the newspapers.

If, she thought, you're telling the truth.

She beckoned Ellie behind the counter and took a nylon uniform coat from its peg. 'Stow your things in the back, put this on and get to work and we'll see what we can do.'

2

FAYE SMITH

The slap and clang of a mop and bucket echoed around the empty canteen.

The newcomer mopped, stacking chairs, or putting them on tables. Her hair was tied up in a high ponytail and the lipstick was long gone, yet, somehow, even in a staff uniform, she managed to look sleek and glamorous. The uniform coat was tight fitting and there was no sign of a bulge that Faye could see.

Ellie Peveril had put in a full afternoon shift and, Faye had to concede, she'd worked hard. The place shone and sparkled. Better than when Margaret cleaned it.

'You can knock off now,' Faye called, as she began to place chairs beneath the tables. 'We're open again at four, so put the chairs down. Would you like something to eat?'

'Yes, please!'

'Come through to the staff-room and Cook'll give you a meal.'

After ten minutes, Faye went to join her.

The empty plate at the woman's elbow showed she'd already polished off at least one portion of corned beef and was now attacking a large bowl of pudding and custard. Was this ordinary hunger, or was she eating for two?

Faye sat in one of the shabby armchairs.

'So how did you end up in Clapham, Ellie?' she asked, watching her eat.

'It's a long story,' Ellie answered between spoonfuls. 'I've not been back in the country a week.'

'From Nuremberg, you said. Did you attend the war trials?' Ellie nodded as she chewed. 'What was it like?'

'Horrible, but impressive too.' The spoon was poised in mid-air. 'Over a thousand people were working on them, with judges and lawyers from all the Allies and from Germany.'

'Hmmm. Why were *you* there? Were you working? You're a legal clerk, you said?'

'Sort of. My friend, Moira Shawcross...' The newcomer hesitated, then explained. 'She's the niece of Sir Hartley Shawcross, who was the judge in charge of the British delegation. She's training as a lawyer and accompanied her uncle. We were at school together. She asked me along for company and to be a clerk. I ran my uncle's solicitors practice during the war.'

Faye knew who Sir Hartley Shawcross was but she wasn't about to let Ellie Peverill know that. Better to keep her cards close to her chest and play dumb. If Ellie Peveril was as well connected as she claimed to be, why was she scrounging food from a south London hospital, with no money and nowhere to stay? Curiouser and curiouser.

'And what about the Nazi commanders?' Faye asked. 'Did you see them? Were they ashamed?'

'They were in court, except for Hitler of course. In the dock. Some of them expressed remorse and repentance, some didn't. They looked... ordinary, like anyone else,' Peveril replied. 'Like you and me.'

'I suppose that's what's so frightening,' Faye said. 'What ordinary human beings are capable of.'

'There were things in evidence – terrible, shocking things – you wouldn't believe. You wouldn't *want* to believe. The things one human being could do to another and, sometimes, on a massive scale. Even learning about it was difficult to cope with. One couldn't imagine what it must have been like...' She shuddered and her gaze was far away before returning to the rest room. She placed the spoon into the empty bowl. 'But the individuals were an odd mix. I think Hitler *must* have been mad to surround himself with people like that.'

'Like what?'

'Some of them were chancers, bullies and criminals; gangsters who'd never have got away with it in normal times. Like any gangster, they were in it for themselves. Others were worse – true believers in the purity of the Aryan race, in their right to use and destroy any who they regarded as lesser beings. They were the frightening ones. Put the two types together and...'

'I saw the pictures of those camps on the newsreels, where they put the Jews. They were horrific.'

'Not only Jews; gypsies, workers' rights organisers, anyone who dared oppose them. Anyone who the Nazis claimed didn't belong, who was in any way different. Do you have patients here who were crippled at birth or by accident?'

'Of course.'

'They would've been killed in Nazi Germany, though only after they had been used for medical experiments – vile, vile experiments.' The newcomer shook her head, frowning. 'The less intellectually gifted too, the simple souls. The Nazis saw them as subhuman, there to be used by the so-called "master race".'

'Nothing masterly about it.' Faye shuddered.

'It could've happened here.' A nurse with a heavy Scottish accent joined them in the staff room. 'Remember Mosley and his British Union of Fascists. It could happen anywhere. Cook said you were through here.'

'Beryl, Beryl MacBride, meet Ellie Peveril,' Faye introduced them. After pleasantries had been exchanged, she went on, 'Beryl has a spare room for rent, which I thought might interest you.'

'Aye, in Westbury Court, the building opposite the hospital, above Clapham South station. It's a new block.'

'Oh, it does interest me, it does, but...' The newcomer's cheeks

15

flushed pink. 'As I explained, I don't have any ready money with me right now. Today. Once the banks open tomorrow I can get some, but I can't pay you anything in advance.'

Faye had warned Beryl what to expect, but left it up to her to decide whether or not to trust the newcomer. As far as Faye was concerned, the jury was out.

'That's alright; I reckon you're good for a night's rent. How'd you find yourself without any cash?'

Trust Beryl to get to the nub of the matter, no nonsense.

'I… are you sure you want to hear, it's a long story?'

Beryl pulled up a chair.

'I've only recently returned to England,' Ellie began. 'I'd arranged to rent a room in a lodging house on the North Side, owned by a widow, Mrs Packham. She seemed respectable and the house was big, full of space and light. I put down a deposit on the room at the front, overlooking the common and sent my things over.'

'How much money d'you give her?' Beryl asked.

'A guinea.'

Faye's glance met Beryl's. A guinea was a lot of money to pay to reserve a room in a lodging house.

Ellie flushed, looking between them, she had noticed their silent exchange. Her chin rose.

'Anyway… when I got there this morning, my things were in a pokey little room at the back. It was dark, with one tiny window on to a delivery yard full of crates and packing cases. Not the room I'd paid for, but she said it was the only one available. And she demanded a month's rent in advance, or I couldn't even have that!' She paused, her mouth pinched and jaw jutting.

Beryl sucked her teeth. Faye could guess what the Scot was thinking. The landlady had seen Ellie Peveril coming.

'She claimed someone else had paid her a month in advance for *my* room, at the front. She made me feel as if it was all my fault, which was ridiculous! We had an agreement, but she didn't stick to it.'

'Don't tell me, she wouldn't give you your guinea back?' Faye said.

'Exactly. I asked her for it; she'd gone back on what we'd agreed, but she denied that she'd agreed to anything and then...' she hesitated.

'What?' Beryl asked.

'She said, if I didn't want the little room at the back, she was going to keep my things in lieu of rent.'

'What! She can't,' Faye said. 'That's theft.'

'I know. The effrontery of the woman. How dare she! I didn't want the pokey room, would never have sent my things there... it's absurd and... wrong.'

'What did you do?' Beryl asked.

'Said I'd see her in court, that I was a legal clerk, that I would get the police... anything I could think of really. It was so unjust! I accused her of stealing.'

Ah-ha. So that was why Ellie had reacted so dramatically to the accusation of stealing earlier, it was exactly what she'd accused the landlady of.

'Attagirl,' Beryl said.

'Weren't you tempted to accept the room? You needed some-where to stay, after all?' Faye asked.

'Of course I was. Except... it was wrong.' Ellie paused. 'If I'd given in to her swindle, we might as well have given in to those monsters in Germany, or to…. For crying out loud! There is such a thing as right and wrong.' Her jaw set. 'And this wasn't fair.'

Life wasn't fair, Faye thought, but said nothing. It wasn't a reason to accept injustice and Ellie's reaction spoke well for her character, even if she had been naïve in handing over the money in the first place.

If the story was true.

'I reckon she's pushing her luck,' Beryl said. 'Sounds like some-thing for your John, Faye.'

'Maybe.' Faye explained, 'My brother's a police constable, based at the Cavendish Road station.'

'That's where I was going when I got sidetracked here!'

'Sidetracked?'

Ellie shrugged and smiled.

'I was cold and hungry and I had no money. Then suddenly I was surrounded by a crowd of young women, laughing and chattering like a flock of magpies, the nurses' capes flapping like wings, full of joie de vivre, happy and... normal.' Ellie sounded wistful. 'So different to how I felt. I... I just followed them, I suppose. I felt so low and their lightness of heart was so appealing. My mother worked in a hospital in Worcester, so I'm used to nurses.'

Maybe that was all true, but Faye was sure it wasn't the whole story. Yet a thought had been forming in her mind; perhaps Ellie Peverill's unfortunate situation could be turned to everyone's advantage?

'Well, you're here now,' Faye said. 'Am I right in thinking you'll be looking for work? Something in the legal line, perhaps?'

'That's right.'

'Until you find something, how about working here, in the canteen? It pays three pounds thirteen shillings a week, for six days a week, one shift on, one shift off, though that's flexible. One of our staff left us recently to have a baby so we're short-handed. I was going to advertise the vacancy, but you know hospital life, you've worked hard and it seems you've fallen into our laps. I wouldn't expect you to stay, you'll have bigger fish to fry, but it might help you – and us – in the meantime.'

'I...' Ellie faltered. 'I don't know what to say.'

The woman flushed, she seemed disconcerted, embarrassed.

Reluctant to do more of this sort of work, perhaps? Thinks it beneath her? It certainly wouldn't be what she'd been brought up to do, one look at her told anyone that.

Or doesn't she want to work for the likes of me? Faye wondered.

The war had changed things, broken down the boundaries of the old class structures, as officers died and rankers were promoted. The return to civilian life didn't necessarily mean a return to the old hierarchies. Certainly not if Faye had anything to say about it.

'Wouldn't I have to report it to the Ministry of Labour?'

It was a fair question; she'd need permission to change jobs. The war-time restrictions on the movement of workers still applied.

'No. It's only a temporary job. The shifts are flexible, so you'll have free time to go into the centre of town, to Lincoln's Inn or the Temple, to find yourself a permanent position. But the pay's fair and the SLH is a good place to work.'

And beggars can't be choosers, she might have added.

Whatever the reason for Ellie Peveril being in Clapham... and, whatever it was, it must've been important to her, would it be enough to make her take the job, defying her inherent expectations?

Ellie took a deep breath and smiled. 'Sounds good to me,' she said. 'What have I got to lose?'

It seemed so.

'Alright, I'll fill in the paperwork and you can start tomorrow as a temporary member of staff.'

They shook on it.

'Welcome to the South London Hospital for Women and Children.'

3

ELEANOR PEVERIL

'It's in here.'

Beryl opened the door.

The room was tiny. Even smaller than the one at Mrs Packham's. Horizontal panes in a small, metal-framed window filled the whole of the opposite wall. The dark expanse outside four floors below was Clapham Common.

There was a single bed, a narrow wall shelf and a thin cupboard with a long mirror tacked to its door. That was all. The carpet was threadbare and the heavy black-out curtains mottled with grey spots of mould. It was cold and unwelcoming.

The room was a horrid end to a horrible day. To have to sleep here... Ellie felt her self-control slipping again but with an effort, she fixed a smile to her face.

'It's small and it isn't warm, but nowhere is this winter.' The shorter woman shrugged and sniffed. She seemed to have sensed the other's disappointment.

Don't be pathetic, Ellie told herself. It's better than a hostel, it's better than walking the streets all night in the freezing cold. You've got no money. What choice do you have?

'Thank you, it'll be hunky-dory. I'll huddle under the blankets.'

Ellie eyed the unmade bed and hoped there'd be some. 'Super. This is so kind of you. Thank you.'

'Well, I wouldn't see someone out on the street and you can pay me when you've got the readies.'

The Scot left her to settle.

Ellie began to remove her greatcoat and then thought better of it. She shook out the contents of her rucksack onto the mattress – a dress and some underwear from yesterday, cosmetics and a comb. Her possessions looked as sad as the room. She wanted to cry.

Beryl returned to place sheets and blankets on the small bed and drew the heavy curtains closed. On top of the pile of bed linen was a folded nightgown, which she brandished with a flourish. It was bright yellow and of a very old-fashioned, voluminous design, buttoned up to a high collar.

'I dare say you don't have any nightclothes,' she said. 'You can wear this if you like. My ma insisted I take it, but I prefer pyjamas and it's... well... a bit big for me.'

The nightgown was made of thick, brushed cotton; it looked clean and as if it would be warm. Her nightclothes were in a suit-case in the lodging house on the North Side, so Ellie took it with thanks.

She held the garment against her body and posed in the mirror. It reached to below her knees and was wide enough for two of her, including the greatcoat. Beryl would have been swamped by it. Ellie caught her eye and they both grinned.

'It wasn't your mother's, I take it?'

'No, nor any of my sisters' neither. We're all... less... ample.'

'Ample is putting it mildly.' Ellie refolded the nightgown. 'How many sisters do you have?'

'Three. Come on, I'll show you the rest of the place.'

Ellie followed her new landlady through into the living area of the flat.

A sofa sat against one wall and there was a well-used armchair beneath a wide window. A small, gate-legged table, flanked by two chairs, stood opposite the sofa against the open partition which separated the living room from the kitchen area.

'My room's through there.' The Scot indicated a door. 'And here's the bathroom.'

Beryl opened a door onto a cupboard-sized windowless cubicle which appeared to be full of drying washing. She quickly closed it again. 'Sorry, it's a bit of a mess. I wasn't expecting visitors and I didn't have chance to clean it.'

'No, no...' Ellie smiled politely, ignoring the smell of damp clothing and, possibly, something worse, wafting into the sitting room.

'Cuppa?' Beryl marched over to the kitchenette where she began to fill the kettle.

'Oooh, yes, please.' A cup of tea might cheer her up. 'Tell me, do lots of the nurses live in these flats?'

'Not many, no. Most of them live in the nurses' home in the grounds of the hospital. It's cheaper.' Beryl spoke through the open shelves of the partition.

'But not you.'

'No, that's not for me.' Beryl poured boiling water into a teapot. 'Matron setting curfew times, lots of young lasses chatting about fashion and lads. I left school a long time ago.'

By Ellie's estimation, she and Beryl were around the same age as many of the nurses, but the frothy, gossipy conversations overheard in the canteen didn't seem the sort of chat which would appeal to the dour, more serious Scot.

'So, what do you like talking about?'

Beryl shrugged. 'Nursing – the job – what's happening in the world, politics.'

Ellie's eyebrows rose.

'I want to change things; the way things are run. I come from Glasgow and, if you could see where I grew up, you'd understand why. There are places in London's East End, crumbling, rat-infested tenements like my old home. The landlords don't care and their bully boys make sure you pay, one way or another. Most of the men are brutal, drunk or both and there are plenty would pay for a night with my little sisters. Coppers walk around in threes, and no one will employ you when they learn where you come from. I can't help where I was born, but the system works against people like me, so I want to change it.' She poured boiling water on to the tea leaves in the pot. 'Politics.'

'You voted for Mr Attlee's government? So did lots of people.'

'There wasn't anything better on offer. Attlee's too milk and water for me. At home, Willie Gallagher's the MP.' When she received no reaction Beryl continued. 'Founding member of the Communist Party of Great Britain. He stands for real change.'

Ellie said nothing. The woman was a communist, a bona fide radical. What on earth had she let herself in for?

'How does that go down in the SLH?' she asked, filling the lengthening silence.

'Oh, I keep my views to myself and it's fine with the SLH...' She hesitated then added. 'I'm... different. I don't fit in and I know it. But the SLH is a better place than most for the likes of me.'

What could she mean? Ellie began to regret her decision to accept the job there. After all, what did she know about the place? What kind of a place was it?

'Why?'

'Because it's a hospital for women run by women. And only women. The South London Hospital for Women and Children. Until war broke out, then we took in casualties, regardless.' Beryl put the teapot, mugs and a small jug of reconstituted milk onto the table.

'You mean there are no men at all?' Ellie asked, astonished. 'I say.' She looked at Beryl in amazement. 'I'd wondered where they were, this afternoon; I thought... maybe it was a hangover from wartime.' She paused, struggling to see how such a thing could work, what it would mean. 'So those women porters weren't filling in for men, they were doing their own jobs.'

'The war's been over for more than a year now.'

JULIE ANDERSON

'But… are the consultants and clinicians women too? I'd assumed the consultants had their own dining room.'

'The SLH doctors are all female and they eat in the canteen like everyone else. Fewer egos than with men. Here.' Beryl poured the tea into the mugs and pushed one towards Ellie. 'The hospital was set up by two women surgeons. Tough ladies. Suffragists and feminists. They raised the money by public subscription and the SLH opened in 1913. Women like being treated by women. It's better for them. And it's my kind of place. Milk?'

Ellie nodded a yes.

'The hospital takes male patients, though, doesn't it?' she asked.

'In wartime, yeah, but not otherwise. Women and children, boys up to the age of seven.'

'Crikey. So, basically, no adult males at all.'

'That's about it.'

Ellie held her mug in both hands to warm them and blew on the surface of the liquid. It gave her some time to consider. The whole hospital was female, including the people running it.

No men assuming automatic superiority, no being looked down upon (or being speculated about); no having to seek male approval, no having to be on show, conforming to men's ideas about women. Being able to be oneself. Feeling safe.

But no flirting, no fun, no protective father figures. And no leaders.

Except, from what she had seen earlier, Matron seemed to be doing well as a leader, she had plenty of authority. Then there was Faye Smith, lower down in the hierarchy, maybe, but a woman in a position of power.

'Who does Faye Smith work for?'

'Miss Barnett, the Hospital Administrator. Faye's local, a south London girl,' Beryl explained. 'She's done very well for herself, though she's worked hard for it. As shrewd a woman as I've ever met, very perspicacious. Nobody messes with Faye.'

The Scot sounded admiring. Something, Ellie suspected, which didn't happen often. The SLH seemed to attract strong, independent-minded and intelligent women, Faye Smith being one of them. Beryl too, for all her politics.

'It's better this way,' Beryl said, as if reading her thoughts. 'There'll be a woman prime minister one day.'

Ellie doubted it very much, but that wasn't to say she thought women shouldn't have opportunities and the SLH seemed to provide them. The hospital began to intrigue her. A place where women looked after women. Yet hadn't women been looking after the whole country for the last six years and doing pretty well at it too?

'I'll go to the bank tomorrow, Beryl, and pay you for a fortnight in advance.'

'I trust you, though the money will be useful. You're one of Faye's strays; you're SLH now.'

Ellie sipped the tea and smiled. It certainly seemed so.

4

ELEANOR PEVERIL

H er greatcoat on top of the blankets made the narrow bed warm and cosy, but the temperature in the small room was icy. She'd had little sleep the night before and a very eventful day, so Ellie expected to fall asleep immediately, but every time she began to snooze images crowded to the front of her mind, visual snippets of remembered reality from the last twenty-four hours.

The shadow of the singer cast by the spotlight onto the glittering curtain. Moira's blonde curls bobbing in the soft half-light as she sashayed through the crowd of shimmying dancers.

Sounds. The clink of their cocktail glasses as they toasted their return to England. A loud guffaw of laughter with something familiar about it.

The group of army officers, empty champagne bottles lying amid debris on their table. Girls with bleached hair and too much decolletage, one shrieking with laughter at the man on whose lap she wriggled. Patrick. A lascivious smile on his handsome face, his arm wrapped around the girl.

The shattering of the cocktail glass as Ellie banged it down on to the table.

People looking.

The instant Patrick saw and recognised her, the smile dropping from his face. The girl sliding to the floor.

Ellie tossed and turned, her fury at Pat jostled with anxiety.

She'd be better off without him, she told herself, over and over, no matter what her situation. In some ways, catching him out simplified matters. It made her choices easier. She'd burnt her bridges and there was no going back. Her life had changed, irrevocably.

Drowsing again.

Mrs Packham's sly face as she stood, arms folded, to block the way into the nasty, little room. The contempt in her voice as biting as the wind, before Ellie stormed away, not knowing where she was going.

Her solid form, watching, seen through the net curtains.

The skeletons of trees against a low, grey sky, pregnant with snow. Branches clattering in the wind blowing around the half-dismantled barracks on the common. People muffled up, out on a freezing Sunday to attend church, to walk the dog, spooning young couples escaping from crowded homes.

The honking of geese overhead, late-stayers flying south for the winter, transmuting into the caped nurses, flushed and wind-blown, but laughing, as they crossed towards the hospital.

Faye Smith's face across the canteen table, sharp cheekbones, pointed chin. The cold, hard look in her eyes.

'You don't need to steal.'

To steal.

She sat up, sharply.

All was dark. Where was she?

Her breathing calmed as she remembered. Westbury Court and Beryl's spare room.

Why had she awoken?

A sound. There had been a sound. From outside.

She shivered as she turned back the covers. Pulling down the long sleeves of the thick nightgown over her hands, she padded over to the window. Behind the heavy black-out curtains the air was even colder, with ice forming on the inside edges of the window glass. She rubbed her eyes and peered out.

Moonlight.

From the fourth floor she gazed down onto the vastness of the common, grass glistening, dusted with frost. To her right was the wide and well-lit South Side with the massive building of the hospital, lights dimmed, but still at work. Directly opposite, a ragged line of poplars ran along the side of the lane below and further away, near the South Side, a thicket of smaller trees clustered around a squat round structure.

A lone vehicle, a van, drove along the South Side and turned into the road next to the hospital.

It was too cold a night to be out. Everyone was huddled up indoors. So what had awoken her?

There! Movement amidst the trees. Ellie shook the sleep from her head and peered out, screwing up her eyes.

Two figures. A man and a woman. A couple. There had been plenty of young couples out on the common the day before, wearing their Sunday finery, but it was very late for a romantic tryst. Were they from the hospital? They must be very determined lovers to be out in these temperatures.

She leaned forward, her nose less than an inch from the glass. It *was* a couple, in a clinch. Ellie yawned.

Why'd they have to make so much noise?

She was about to go back to bed when the woman broke away and began to hurry across the grass towards the lane. She was wearing a nurse's uniform. Her lover followed, calling after her.

A lovers' tiff. Bloody annoying.

Ellie lost sight of her; the glass had misted up with her own breath. She grabbed a handful of blackout curtain and made a porthole through which to see. But the couple had gone. Probably to the underground station. She let the curtain drop and turned back towards her bed.

What was that?

A scream. Cut short.

Now Ellie was alert and back at the window, craning to see.

What was going on out there?

She rubbed the glass clear again and looked right and left but couldn't see anyone.

Who had cried out? The woman? Was she alright?

She listened, concentrating in the stillness, straining for any sound. But there was nothing. No sound other than her own breathing.

Could the couple have been larking around?

It hadn't sounded like it. It had sounded like a cry for help.

Had they gone or were they still outside her building? The only way she would find out was to look directly down on to the lane and to do that she'd have to open the window. It was cold enough in her little room already.

Anyway, it was probably only a lovers' squabble, nothing serious. If it was there'd be even more of a racket, she reasoned. She shouldn't push her nose in where it wouldn't be wanted.

But the woman had screamed; she might need help. It could be serious.

They'd probably gone by now; she wouldn't be able to help anyway.

Ellie dropped the damp curtain and scurried back to the warmth of her bed.

MONDAY

5

FAYE

Faye copied the details from Eleanor Peveril's ration book onto the form for hiring temporary staff.

The Deanery, Cathedral Close, Worcester – that sounded like a nice, genteel address. If Ellie was someone's kept woman, as Faye had speculated, she had fallen a long way. She seemed, for all intents and purposes, to be a respectable, middle-class young woman, someone whom Faye's mother would call a 'young lady' and not in the disparaging way she used the term to her own daughters.

The label in that heavy greatcoat said Harris Tweed and her shoes looked like expensive handmade leather. Not the haversack though, that had seen better days. The story about how she'd found herself hungry and homeless in south London could even be true, but, Faye was convinced, there was something she was holding back.

If Ellie did take things further and report the matter to the police, Faye would speak with John about it, but not before. For the moment, Ellie Peveril was an employee of the SLH and entitled to the respect that deserved. Any further judgement would be reserved. Faye hoped she hadn't made a mistake by taking her on, but, for now, she refused to let it mar her good mood.

It was seven thirty on Monday morning and Faye sat in an

armchair in the nurses' common room, doing canteen paperwork before going down for breakfast service. One of the privileges of her position was being entitled to use the comfortable room, where a fire burned hot in the grate.

She glanced over at the checkerboard of wooden pigeonholes on the wall. Hers contained a pale cream envelope; she had opened it earlier. In it was an invitation to apply for the post of deputy hospital administrator, overseeing the office and its staff as well as her current responsibilities. Miss Barnett, her boss, had been increasingly weighed down by her growing workload, especially now the hospital would be part of the new NHS, but Faye hadn't expected this.

She couldn't stop smiling.

Faye had started out as a fifteen-year-old washer-upper in the SLH kitchens in 1934, her fourth job since leaving school. She'd tried waitressing and cleaning, but she hadn't fitted in anywhere and her father had drawn the line at pub work. 'Too clever by half' her mother had called her. Then she took the job at the SLH and hadn't looked back since.

Miss Barnett had encouraged Faye to study for the certificates she'd not taken at school and to take on more responsibility. Under her tutelage, Faye's confidence had grown. Now she oversaw the canteen and kitchen, its purchasing and administration, as well as production of the emergency meals supplied to the community. Soon she would be second in command.

The new job would mean a pay rise, something her parents would be grateful for. Money was important in the Smith household; it was why she'd left school so early. Faye was the second oldest in a family of six children, three of whom still lived at home. Her father, Reg, was a railwayman at Nine Elms Locomotive Works, her brother John, a policeman. Esme, her mother, was a housewife and her younger sister, Phoebe, suffered from tuberculosis and was too frail and ill to contribute much at all.

Yet her parents would dislike the idea of the new post. It would look too much like a career to them, something to distract her from a future husband and family, a future rapidly diminishing in probability. Now that peace had finally arrived, she could see her mother planning how best to see her eldest daughter married and a grandchild on the way before she was too old and on the shelf. To return to the life they had all known before the war and the future they had expected.

A future that Faye no longer wanted.

Faye loved her parents, including her father, with whom she frequently disagreed, but the world was changing, it *had* changed, and they couldn't see what she saw. They were wedded to the old world. She trusted her own judgement in this. Exactly how she was going to persuade her parents of it was something she'd put off tackling, but she'd have to face up to doing it now. The new job would help. It was handsome of Miss Barnett to give her the chance to apply before the post was advertised, though the invitation stipulated that she should keep the offer to herself. Surely that wouldn't apply to her family. She would have to tell them.

The hospital administrator would expect her answer soon, she didn't like to be kept waiting. Faye determined to respond as soon as she could but, for the moment, however reluctantly, she set that aside and considered the week ahead.

Eleanor Peveril's genteel upbringing could be put to good use. Tomorrow there was to be an important formal luncheon in the board room for a group of local councillors and some of the hospital's financial supporters. If they were suitably impressed, more funding might be forthcoming. The hospital was always fundraising. Even though many patients paid in full and others contributed towards the cost of their care, there was never enough to cover the costs of treating those who couldn't pay at all.

Several of the governors would be at the lunch, two of whom were bishops. As well as organising the table and the waiting team, Ellie could chat to the clergymen, they might know her family and, even if they didn't, Eleanor Peveril of The Deanery, Cathedral Close, Worcester would know how to make conversation with them. Faye would tell her how important it was. It would mean they'd be short-staffed in the canteen, but she could help with the lunchtime service herself.

She would draft her letter of application for the new post as soon as the luncheon was out of the way.

Faye signed the staffing form. She'd drop it off at the office later, along with October's accounts and the stock take for the canteen and kitchens. Everything was going well; it would be a good week.

She had five minutes to spare so she sat back in the chair, enjoying the rare free time. The periodical on the table next to her was the *British Medical Journal*. Someone had marked an article about the Medical Women's International Association and one about the Health Service Bill in Parliament, but Faye's eye was caught by a short piece on streptomycin, a new drug for tuberculosis from the United States. The drug was to be tested in Britain on patients between fifteen and twenty-five years old. Phoebe was twenty.

Faye marked the page; she'd have to find out more about the trial. Was it happening in London? Perhaps one of the clinicians knew about it; she could ask. She would have to be quick about it; medical trials were always over-subscribed. There were plenty of TB sufferers and the new drug could lead to a cure, or at least a stay of execution, because the disease was fatal. Something else to do as soon as she could.

Faye glanced at the wall clock.

Later. Now it was time to go down and check in the day shift.

6

FAYE

High tea was a popular recent introduction at the SLH and the canteen was very busy.

'You must know everyone in the entire hospital,' Ellie remarked, as Faye greeted yet another diner by name.

'Not really,' Faye replied. 'There are always new people arriving, but I know most of them. I've been here twelve years.'

'Twelve years?' Ellie's eyebrows rose. 'Forgive me, I thought you were about the same age as me.'

'I am,' Faye replied. She pressed her lips together to conceal a smile. Eleanor Peveril probably wouldn't know anyone who'd left school at fourteen. The deanery cleaner, perhaps, or her mother's maid…

There was a small silence.

'Would you mind telling me who's who?'

The smooth switch to another subject didn't escape Faye's notice. Ellie had all the social graces.

'There are so many nurses; you won't remember all of them,' she said, 'so let's start with the doctors at the round table by the window. There's Miss Underwood, our new pharmacist, she only arrived a fortnight ago and Dr Horn, another newcomer, one of our pathologists. She's not as tall as the others. Dr Boyd, with the spectacles, is an anaesthetist.'

Faye paused to greet some new arrivals.

'Our men all arrived with the war, except for Mr Fortescue.' She indicated a bald, bespectacled man wearing a pin-striped suit, sitting by the window. 'He comes in to certify the hospital accounts, you won't see him in here often.' She indicated a lanky, sandy-haired man wearing brown overalls who was queuing at the counter. 'That's Les Allen, the head porter. And we have a couple of foreign doctors. There's Dr Zeitel.' She pointed to a very slight, dark man who was part of a group of people.

'A German?'

'A Jewish Austrian. There's a French doctor too, Dr Girard, the one all the nurses moon over, but he's not here now. Neither is Charlie Redmond, our mortuary assistant, he rarely comes in here. That's about it for men.'

The doors swung open to admit a gust of cold air and another crowd of nurses. Beryl was one of them. She waved to Faye and Ellie as they found a table.

'Beryl, you know already. The others are on the same shift, working in the maternity wards.'

'Maternity, that's SLH's specialism?'

Faye's original suspicions resurfaced.

'We're a hospital for women, so, of course that plays a large part in what we do, as do obstetrics and paediatrics. But we have all the usual general hospital departments, including radiology, pathology and so on. We usually have one maternity ward, but, right now, there's an overspill so we have two.'

'Overspill?'

'VE Day was nearly eighteen months ago,' Faye said. 'Enough time for the men to come home and reacquaint themselves with their wives and girlfriends shall we say. We're seeing the start of a post-war population explosion. A baby boom.'

Ellie's expression was one of polite interest, but she said noth-

THE MIDNIGHT MAN

ing, even when Faye left a silence to be filled. Maybe she was just curious.

'The SLH has a nursing and midwifery school,' Faye continued. 'So we're well placed to deal with it. Here's Matron.'

'It's terrific that everyone eats here, together,' Ellie said. 'There isn't the snobbery I've seen elsewhere.'

'That's the SLH...'

A crowd of diners vacated the largest table, leaving their rubbish behind. Already other tray-bearing folk were eyeing it.

'Excuse me.' Ellie hurried away to clear it.

Beryl sauntered over.

'How's she doing?' she asked.

'Well, so far. She's certainly cheered up.' Faye had allowed her to use the telephone in the kitchen staffroom that morning and since then the newcomer's spirits had seemed lighter. 'She works hard. I think she'll do.'

'Good. Are you coming to the WEA meeting tonight?'

'I plan to, though I'm going home first. I'll be off soon, I've an early finish this afternoon. Are you going?'

'Yes. I thought I might bring Ellie along.'

'Good idea, if she'll come. I don't imagine it's what she's used to.'

'Maybe not but I think she's more open-minded than that cut-glass accent suggests, even if I sometimes think she's walked out of an Angela Brazil story. Besides, it'll be warmer than at the flat.'

'I must sort this out.' Faye could see there was a problem at the till. 'See you later.'

As she helped unspool the till roll and reset it, Faye considered what Beryl had said. Perhaps she was making too many assumptions, maybe she should give the newcomer the benefit of the doubt instead of trying to find fault. But she was certain Ellie was hiding something.

'Hello, Faye. Have you seen Jane Cooper? Was she in earlier?' a nurse asked.

'I don't think I've seen her all day,' Faye replied. 'But I could have missed her.'

Till now operating normally, Faye watched Ellie clearing tables, stacking dirty crockery and cutlery on to a small trolley. That was a good idea, she thought, better than a tray. She seemed to have left yesterday's bad beginning behind her and was at ease, chatting with the diners as she cleared around them. She might be in a new place, doing a job she'd never have expected to do but there was no awkwardness. She had the innate self-confidence of the comfortable, well brought up young woman that she was. There was no faking that.

It was time to go. Faye slipped behind the counter into the kitchen. Cook was already overseeing the prep of vegetables for the evening's dinner service and barely gave Faye a glance as she walked through to the kitchen staffroom. That suited her fine.

One wall was lined with lockers for the personal effects of those working in the canteen and kitchen. Faye kept most of her belongings in her locker in the nurses' common room, where she went when she wanted privacy or to get away from the canteen for a while, but she used her locker next to the kitchen for certain things. She turned the key in its lock and withdrew a heavy canvas rucksack.

On the other side of the staffroom was the cold store, where fresh food for the kitchens was kept. Food was a precious commodity and hunger a cruel mistress, so everything was put out of the way of temptation and the door to the store was always locked. Faye and Cook each had a key.

Faye checked that the corridor outside the room was empty and closed the door before unlocking the store.

Racks of metal shelving held cardboard boxes of daily fresh supplies, wooden pallets of less perishable items sat on the floor. There were crocks and dishes of butter and fats and prized sugar and spices kept in sealed jars. Meat was stored in the sealed meat cupboard.

This was what Faye had come for. She took out a thin slab of beef. Brisket, about half a pound of it, she thought, weighing it in her hand. She wrapped the meat in several pieces of greaseproof paper and placed it in her rucksack.

From the boxes she took a bunch of bananas, skins mottled black and a small net of oranges, which were covered with flecks of grey fuzz. Scrape the mildew off and what was left would be edible, full of vitamins and sugars. The fruits followed the meat into the rucksack. Faye buckled it closed and left the cold store, locking it behind her.

She could hear Cook berating someone in the kitchen as she placed the bag on the floor, took her coat from its hook and put it on. Dragging the gloves and scarf from its pockets, she poked her head around the door to the kitchen.

'I'm off now,' she called. 'See you tomorrow.'

She was rewarded with a wave as Cook interrupted her tirade and Faye picked up the rucksack and hoisted it onto her back.

'What've you got there then, eh?' a male voice spoke.

Faye whirled round.

Les Allen, the head porter, was leaning against the other door-frame, his arms folded, a pleasant smile on his face.

How long had he been there, snooping around?

'If I didn't know better, I'd think that our stickler-for-the-rules canteen manager was taking hospital food home,' he said, his gaze flicking towards the rucksack.

'I take the rations I'm due,' Faye snapped. 'Which we are all entitled to do, if we don't use them. It is all recorded properly and is none of your business.'

'No, you're right. Not my business at all,' he said. 'It's just... there are rules, aren't there?' He raised one eyebrow. 'I swear I can smell bananas. You don't get bananas on the ordinary ration, do you? Perhaps Cook's making a banana pudding for tonight.'

'I believe she is, as it happens.'

Faye wrapped her scarf around her neck, tucking it into the upturned collar of her coat. She looked up at him, something she was unused to doing. Faye was tall, but Les was even taller. His face showed a disinterested curiosity, then it broke into a sly smile.

'I'm not a tell-tale, Faye,' he said. 'I just like to know what's what. You wouldn't be black marketeering, would you?'

'Too right I'm not.'

'Especially not with a rozzer for a brother. Now that *would* be embarrassing.'

There was amusement in his eyes, but with a sharp edge. Les Allen was enjoying himself, she realised, tweaking her tail. But Faye wasn't having it. She wouldn't play his game. Saying nothing more, she raised her chin and held his gaze, determined to face him down.

Her stare didn't waver, but neither did his.

The seconds passed and she sensed a shift. He was focusing now, it was a real battle of wills, not a game. He wanted the upper hand. All the more reason not to give way.

'Faye!'

Faye tore her gaze away as Cook bustled in from the kitchen, waving a piece of paper.

'Caught you! Good! Can you do a spice run tomorrow? Here's a list of what I need.'

'I'll pop into Marsh's and pick them up on my way in,' she said, taking the list. Spices were in short supply and very expensive.

'Thanks.' Cook returned to the kitchen.

Les Allen pushed himself away from the doorframe and came into the room. His lazy smile was back, but his eyes were cold and hard. He wouldn't forget this little spat, Faye realised, but she wasn't going to try and placate him, that would be to give him an influence and an authority which he didn't possess.

'You've not let the grass grow under your feet in getting a replacement for Margaret, I see,' he remarked.

Faye said nothing.

'And a good looking one too. Out of the ordinary for round here, more at home in the Old Town maybe? Who is she? You know I like to keep up to date with all the news.'

'I'm not a tell-tale either, Les,' Faye answered. 'If you want to find out, you'll have to ask her.'

Feeling pleased with herself, and ignoring her own pangs of conscience, she pulled on her gloves and left for home.

7

FAYE

Clouds of warm breath flowed behind her in the cold night air. Les Allen was bloody annoying. He was always poking his nose in, worse than any woman for gossip and he liked the power that knowledge brought him.

She stumbled as she crossed the narrow road, catching her heel on a pothole. Damn it!

But it didn't look good, the manager of the canteen taking food home. And it wasn't, not really. It was true, what she'd told him, she was entitled to take it, but only items that were on the ration. Trust Les to know the rules. If Miss Barnett found out, Faye would get a severe dressing down. Management had to set an example; she could hear the lecture now. She'd have to stop taking food home, at least for a while, until she got the deputy job.

She'd also have to keep an eye on Les Allen. He was so sharp he could cut himself.

Faye usually enjoyed the solitude of her walk to and from work, but the darkness seemed ominous tonight. The street lamps on the avenue across the common were few and far between. So she began to stride out, which had the added advantage of warming her up. Either this winter was colder than the last, or her coat was wearing thin. She didn't have enough clothing coupons to get another and certainly not for thick Harris Tweed like Ellie Peveril's.

Ellie had settled in well, though she wouldn't stay long. Cleaning work at the bottom of the heap was not what Eleanor Peveril of The Deanery had been brought up to do. As soon as she got something better, Ellie would be off. And she *would* get something better; she was too well connected not to. That was how these things worked. If she didn't, she'd be heading back for Cathedral Close, Worcester, not staying in a rented room in Westbury Court.

Either way Faye reckoned that she'd be hiring again soon. Ellie Peveril would move on, which was just as well, because Faye had every intention of taking Beryl's spare room herself.

As her mother never tired of telling her, Faye was approaching thirty and it was about time she moved out of the parental home, though what her mother meant by that differed from Faye's own ideas. Beryl's spare room would be the first step on the road to her getting a flat of her own, especially when she had the new job, which would mean working longer hours, so living closer to the hospital would be handy.

Nurses and hospital workers were favoured when it came to getting council flats, but not if they were living at the family home. If Faye was Beryl's lodger, her application for a flat of her own was more likely to succeed. There might be gossip, Beryl being as she was, but she could put up with that. No, that wasn't the problem.

The problem was how she was going to break the news to her mother and father.

The Smith family home was in Sugden Road, off the North Side of the common, in a row of identical terraced houses; red brick with stone and plaster facings around the sash windows and front porches. Number nineteen had a wooden fence above its low front wall, the sinewy boughs of clematis and honeysuckle bare of leaves as Faye pushed the front gate open.

She fished the door key from her pocket and, stamping any dirt from her shoes, entered the hall.

'I'm home!'

'Hello, love,' her mother called.

Esme Smith was peeling potatoes at the large sink in the kitchen at the rear of the house, her greying fair hair pulled up into a top knot, long fingers chapped and red. Phoebe sat in front of the fire, edge-stitching a blanket.

'You'll damage your eyes doing that in this light,' Faye said to her sister as she handed the rucksack to her mother. 'I've brought fruit, some bananas and oranges from last week – you'll need to scrape them – and there's a bit of beef brisket in there too.'

'You shouldn't take food from the hospital,' Phoebe said, voice tremulous. Constant pain and illness had not improved her temper. 'It's practically robbing the patients.'

'No, it isn't!' Faye shot back, sharply. Phoebe's comment was too like Les Allen's for comfort. 'These are canteen stores, not food for the wards. They're old ones too. I'm entitled to my rations from the hospital; I've given up my food stamps. If I don't eat there, I'm allowed to bring food home.'

One side of Phoebe's face was flushed red by the glow from the fire, but it emphasised her general pallor as she plucked at the stitches, bending over the cloth. A tremor shook her shoulders; she was holding back a cough.

'Put those away, Faye. I'll be through in a jiffy.' Esme Smith gave her older daughter a knowing glance and inclined her head towards the door to the scullery.

Faye had just begun placing the fruit and meat in separate boxes in the cold store when her mother joined her.

'What is it?'

'She's been worse today. She was coughing up blood earlier, though she thinks she hid it from me. Isn't there anyone at that hospital of yours who can treat her?'

'It's difficult, Ma,' Faye said. 'There isn't a cure, you know that. Surgery can be fatal. What drugs there are often don't work. Either way the fatality rate is high.'

'How high? If she doesn't get treated soon, she won't be long for this world anyway.' Her mother's face was grey with anxiety.

'She'd be put away, Ma. She has an infectious disease. It's the law. It'd be a public sanatorium for Phoebe and some of those places are horrible, more like prisons.'

And with a death rate of almost fifty per cent.

'Unless we could pay.'

Esme began to shake her head; tears were not far away. 'You know we can't. Your father's already asked the union and they've given what they can. Your brothers have families of their own to support. You and John give enough as it is; you can't afford more.'

'There's the isolation ward at the hospital; it's better than the public sanatorium. It's not cheap either, though I might be able to wrangle a discount, but I don't know how we would pay for it indefinitely.' Faye hesitated. 'There may be another way...'

'What?'

She described the drug trial.

'That's it, that's what we need. You've got to get our Phoebe on this,' Esme said.

'I'm going to try, Ma, but I don't know where it's happening. It might not be at the SLH. You mustn't mention it to Pheebs until I know more.'

'And we'd still have to pay, wouldn't we, for her care?' Esme stared out of the scullery window into the dark garden. She was, Faye realised, considering what they could sell.

'I... there could be a way I could help.'

A spasm of hope flitting across Esme's face and, feeling guilty, Faye quickly looked away. Her own plans would be so much easier to achieve if she had her mother's support, if Esme would raise Faye's new job with her father.

'My boss wants me to apply for a more senior position; deputy hospital administrator,' she said. 'The pay's a lot better; I could contribute more.'

'Will it mean longer hours?'

'Probably. Almost certainly.'

'Those women, the medical ones who work at the hospital, they give up their lives for their work, don't they?'

'They're very dedicated,' Faye said. 'They've had to be, it isn't easy for a woman to become a doctor or a nurse, let alone a surgeon.'

'You can say that again. Though think what they give up.'

'Some of them marry, have children and carry on working afterwards.'

'And some don't.'

'Many don't,' Faye conceded.

Esme leaned back against the bricks of the cold store. 'If you're working all hours at that hospital, where are you going to meet a chap, Faye? We had such hopes of you and Paul, your father and me. Your father...'

'Yeah, well, I had some hopes of my own, Ma.'

'I'm sorry, love, I know you did.' She patted her daughter's arm. 'I'll speak with your father.'

There was a clatter from the kitchen and a low mutter followed by a bout of coughing.

'Phoebe, Pheebs, love, what is it?' Esme hurried to help her youngest daughter. 'What've you dropped?'

Faye sighed and followed her. She'd find out which institution was responsible for the trial and see if the SLH was taking part in it. If it was, she would try her damnedest to get her sister on it. It could be the answer to their prayers.

Esme knelt to join Phoebe in picking up the pieces of a broken cup.

'I'm so sorry, Ma.' Phoebe was frowning, her mouth drawn back, distressed at her clumsiness.

'Don't worry, love. Accidents will happen and it's only an old cup.'

Her mother's topknot had unwound and Esme straightened, still kneeling, to bind the hanks of hair falling around her face back into place. In the unforgiving overhead light, the worry lines scored across her mother's brow seemed deeper, the frown creases etched between her eyebrows and the crow's feet at the corners of her eyes more defined. Her skin looked wrinkled and worn.

Faye gulped down an involuntary whimper. Her mother was fifty-two, the same age as some of the professional women at the hospital, the same age as Miss Barnett; yet, for all their struggles against established tradition and their devotion to their work, all the responsibility which they held, her mother looked older and far more careworn.

'Let me do that, Ma,' Faye said, bending down to retrieve the final pieces as Esme used the table to help hoick herself to her feet.

She collected the shards of broken china, avoiding meeting her mother's eyes.

'I'll be going out tonight, Ma,' she said. 'Don't make any supper for me.'

Too clever by half, Faye thought. That's what I am.

8

FAYE

The applause ended and the audience began to chatter. People stood, lit cigarettes and ambled towards the end of the draughty school hall, where leaflets and books were laid out on trestle tables beneath a Workers' Educational Association banner. A queue formed at the tea urn.

'He was a good speaker,' Faye said. She'd been glad of the distraction. They all watched the man in question climb down a ladder at the front of the stage, someone having neglected to obtain the key to the backstage area.

'Just as well he's fit,' Beryl added, as he reached floor level.

'Hmm, was in the navy I'd heard, though maybe I think that because of the beard,' the nurse beside her said.

'Bit of a dreamboat too.' Her companion said, giggling. 'The big brown eyes.'

'What did you think about it, Ellie?' the Scot asked, turning to Faye and Ellie.

'He spoke well, I think.'

'And about this new institution?' Faye asked. 'The National Health Service.'

'If it means ill or injured people receive the treatment they need, rather than the treatment they can pay for, I think it's a very good thing,' Ellie replied.

'People often *don't* get the treatment they need now,' Faye said. 'Didn't you say that your mother worked in a hospital? She must have seen that.'

'My mother volunteered during the war and still does. She wanted to be a hospital administrator, I think, but that wasn't an avenue open to her. Still, a clergyman's wife gets to help a lot of people.'

'Your dad's clergy?' Beryl sniffed.

Faye hid a smile. Beryl could make a sniff sound like the ultimate in condemnation.

'Yes.'

'And what about a clergyman's daughter? Do you get involved in the charity work?' Faye asked.

'He doesn't think of it as "charity work" and neither do I. It's just helping people.' Ellie's cheeks turned pink. 'I'm fortunate, I know. I come from a world where there's never been any material want, but at least I try to help. What about you, what do you think about this NHS?'

Faye considered before answering. 'I'm a Labour Party supporter, I voted for Mr Attlee because I believe that our future doesn't have to be like our past, it can be better. There is a "brave new world" available for us if we want to build it. And that includes a national health service.'

'I was in Nuremberg when the election took place,' Ellie said. 'So I didn't vote. But, if I had, I would've voted for Mr Churchill because of all he did in the war. That doesn't mean I think change is a bad thing.'

'Glad to hear it,' Beryl said.

They had moved with the flow of the audience and found themselves at the tables. 'I'll get the teas,' Ellie said, adding, 'now that I'm in funds.'

Faye and Beryl wandered over to the books. Faye glanced back at Ellie, who was speaking with a couple of SLH nurses standing in the tea queue, then turned to her companion and raised an eyebrow.

'Her godfather wired her some money,' Beryl explained. 'She rang him this morning and went to pick it up from the post office this afternoon. She's already paid me for a fortnight's lodgings.'

'Ahh.' That explained the telephone call.

'Ladies.' They were joined by the lecturer, a tall, slim, broad-shouldered man in his thirties, though his brown hair already had flecks of grey at the temples. The nurse's friend was right, Faye thought, he cut an attractive figure, a closely shaved beard softening a strong jawline. She was sure she had seen him before. 'Thinking of buying my book?'

Faye glanced down. One of the books on the table bore his photograph on its cover. Its author was Dr Nicholas Yorke. He spoke in the clipped accent of the officer class.

'Are you a medical doctor then?' Beryl asked.

'No, that's a PhD. From the London School of Economics.'

'You're an academic?' Faye asked.

'Is this a guessing game?' he said, smiling at her. 'I teach at Morley College and here, at Henry Thornton School.'

His tweed jacket had been expensive once, but it was patched at the elbows and his leather brogues looked like they needed resoling. Officer class or not, teaching couldn't pay that well, she thought.

'And you write books,' Faye said. 'About society.'

'I'm a sociologist,' he said. 'It's a relatively new discipline. I study social change. And I believe what I said up there,' he indicated the stage with a wave of his hand. 'This is the dawn of a new era. Society really will change. The working man, and woman, deserves a proper living wage, healthcare and education and a safety net when things go wrong. No one should starve in this country, one of the world's richest...' He flushed. 'I'm sorry, I'm preaching at you.'

'You most certainly are,' said Ellie, carefully carrying three paper cups brimming with tea. Beryl and Faye reached out to help her. 'Hello.' She smiled at him.

'Nick Yorke.' He introduced himself.

'Beryl MacBride,' Beryl responded. 'Ellie Peveril and Faye Smith.'

'I've seen you here before, Miss Smith,' he said. 'Overseeing the deliveries of food for the British Restaurant kitchen.'

'Yes, I'm here occasionally,' Faye said, wondering if the school was where she'd seen him. 'It makes sense for the restaurant to be supplied by the SLH; it cuts costs.'

'Yes,' he said. His gaze, fixed on her face, didn't waver. His eyes were a warm, chestnut brown.

She sensed her companions watching with amusement and realised that Dr Nicholas Yorke sensed it too, but he didn't desist. So... he wasn't easily embarrassed or intimidated.

Faye had met plenty of her brothers' colleagues – her mother had dragooned her sons into parading them before her daughter – and so many of them had been little more than huge boys, barely adults even if they were her own age. Not like Dr Nicholas Yorke. And he wasn't wearing a wedding ring.

'We're all from the SLH,' she said, unwilling to let the silence linger. Yet she didn't look away.

'Yes, I know.' The corner of his mouth twitched into a smile.

Good heavens. Was Dr Nicholas Yorke flirting? With her?

'Well, Dr Yorke, thank you for a very interesting talk.' Beryl broke the spell.

'It's Nick, please.' He grinned. 'Glad you enjoyed it.'

'How do you think the medical professions will take to the reforms?' Ellie asked. 'The BMC hasn't exactly welcomed the proposals with open arms. What about freedom to choose?'

'You only get a choice if you've got money,' Beryl stated.

'Many medical people have been seeking reform for years,' Yorke replied. 'They understand that change must come and it has to be for the wider good. Haven't you read *The Citadel*?'

'Introducing a national health service is a huge undertaking,' Faye said.

'Yes, but consider what we achieved during the war. How can a country that covered the south coast of England in Nissen huts to launch the largest invasion the world has ever seen, turn round to its citizens and say it can't organise a national health service? Besides, many people got better health treatment during the war than in peacetime and they were healthier because resources were more evenly spread. It's completely possible.'

'But what about the doctors?' Ellie persisted. 'They'll have to work in this new service. They won't have a choice. Isn't that what the Royal Colleges and the British Medical Association think?'

'They're coming round. Anyway, is that such a bad thing? There will be consistency and a raising of quality, generally. Everyone will get the same level of treatment. And the doctors, and nurses, will be well rewarded.'

'The British Medical Association didn't support the SLH when it was first founded, but they changed their minds,' Faye said. 'And the Royal Colleges wouldn't countenance women physicians and surgeons, but they're admitted now. Change takes time to gain acceptance.'

'Exactly. Once people become used to it, everyone will embrace it,' Yorke said. 'In fact, I've just started some research into how attitudes towards medicine are changing. The SLH is one of the hospitals in my study.' He smiled at Faye. 'I'll be there regularly. I might even visit the canteen.'

'Where you'd be welcome,' Faye replied, her eyes meeting his and prompting another twitch of his lips.

He certainly seemed interested in her. She began to look forward to seeing him at the canteen.

'And we could continue our discussion,' Ellie added, bestowing a wide and generous smile.

'Indeed.' Yorke flushed slightly as he reached for a copy of his book. 'Maybe you'd like a copy. Gratis, no charge. See what you think of it.'

'Thank you,' Ellie said, taking the book. 'That's very kind of you. I'll look forward to reading it. Perhaps we could talk about it when you visit?'

Oh well... Faye deflated slightly, it had been a nice idea, but Ellie clearly liked him too. Faye knew she couldn't win against that kind of competition.

'See if it's any good,' Beryl muttered, *sotto voce*.

There was an awkward silence.

'Oh, by the way,' Ellie said. 'I'm going to make a formal complaint to the police about Mrs Packham, the landlady I told you about. I spoke with my godfather this morning, he said I should.'

'What's he do, your godfather?' Beryl asked.

'He's a policeman. I'll be going to Cavendish Road police station tomorrow.'

'I'll mention it to John later,' Faye said. 'Is your godfather stationed in London? Maybe John knows him.'

'He's at Scotland Yard. Chief Superintendent Phillip Morgan.'

Faye blinked. Of course. He would be.

'I was hoping to do it first thing,' Ellie continued. 'I'll go before shift starts. I'll try not to be late.'

Her comment was almost drowned out as the doors to the hall swung open and a group of nurses came in, all talking at once.

'Brass monkeys out there,' said one.

'Beryl! Did you hear?' said another.

'What?'

'They've found Jane Cooper. She's dead. Murdered.'

'Strangled.'

'Shot, I heard.'

'Do you know any facts at all or is this just whuzzle?' Beryl replied.

The nurse was indignant. 'Eric, who works for Mr Philpott, told Milly Williams that the corpse of a nurse with long, red hair had been found today, when Mr Philpott went to check the shelters,' she said. 'That must be Jane.'

'She didn't come into work this morning,' said another of the group.

'We thought it was odd.'

'Where? Where did they find her?' Ellie asked urgently.

'Don't know.'

'Was it on the common?'

'I think so.'

'Ellie, are you alright?' Faye asked.

Ellie had turned deathly pale; her gaze fixed on the middle distance. She looked as if her legs wouldn't support her. Faye took her gently by the shoulders.

'Ellie.' Faye's voice was soft, but urgent. 'What is it, Ellie?'

'Last night...' Ellie's voice was barely above a whisper as she stared at Faye. 'I was in bed and I think, I think I heard her.' Her voice grew stronger. 'I heard someone, a woman, scream or shout out.'

'Come on, hold up, old girl,' Beryl said.

'When?' Faye asked.

'I'm not sure. I wasn't wearing my watch.'

'Were the street lights on?'

'Yes.'

'So before one o'clock then, or, possibly, after six in the morning,' Faye said.

Beryl nodded. 'Was there any traffic?'

'No, only an SLH van,' Ellie replied. Her voice steadied and she stood up straighter as Faye let go.

'There'd be more than that in the morning and buses too,' the Scot said. 'So probably before one o'clock.'

'Around midnight,' Faye replied, pursing her lips. 'Just as well you planned to go to Cavendish Road station tomorrow, Ellie. You must tell the police about this. It might help them find out what happened to Jane.'

'Yes,' Ellie replied. 'Yes, of course I'll have to.'

'Tomorrow morning, then,' Faye said. 'Cavendish Road station. And I'm coming with you.'

TUESDAY

9

ELEANOR

'You gave Mrs Packham a guinea?' the sergeant asked.

'That's correct,' Ellie said.

She, Faye, Faye's brother John and the sergeant were sitting around a table in a room at the police station. John, a tall, clean-shaven man, with a wide, high forehead and something of the angular look of Faye about him, made notes as she spoke.

'Did you get a receipt?' the sergeant asked.

'No,' Ellie said, mortified. 'Though I realise now that I should have done.'

'It might have been advisable. Some indication of what the payment was for.'

'I'm sorry, I've made a real pig's ear of it, haven't I?'

'I have to say,' he gave her a pained smile, 'it's not likely that you'll see your money again.'

'It's my word against hers, isn't it?'

The sergeant sighed.

'Surely, she has no right to keep Ellie's things?' Faye asked.

'If I have no proof that I paid a deposit, then she has no proof that I'd promised her rent in advance,' Ellie said. 'And she has no right to prevent me taking my own possessions.'

'Sequestering your belongings is clearer cut,' the sergeant

replied. 'She can't take what isn't hers unless she has actual proof that you agreed to the terms. Can you prove that the luggage is yours?'

'Yes. It contains personal items, photographs, diaries and some of my clothes have name tags in.'

'Then I'll get one of our constables to go with you to collect your belongings,' he said. 'This afternoon?'

'Excellent, though...' Ellie looked at Faye.

'Yes, after lunch is fine,' Faye responded.

'I'll come here at about three thirty then,' Ellie said. 'If that suits?'

The sergeant nodded. He placed his palms on the table as a prelude to rising, then saw that no one else had moved and sat back again.

'There's something else?'

'It's regarding the nurse whose body was found,' Faye began. 'Jane Cooper.'

'We haven't released any details about the case and I can't...'

'Jane failed to show up for work yesterday morning,' Faye continued, unabashed. 'Her colleagues were worried by her non-appearance. Ellie, Miss Peveril, may have heard Jane in distress during the early hours of Monday morning.'

Ellie was glad that Faye had broached the subject; she seemed to say exactly the right thing at the right time.

The sergeant shot a look at John Smith, who nodded.

'Well, miss?' he asked.

She began to repeat what she had told Faye and the others the night before.

'Stop there, Miss Peveril,' the sergeant interrupted her. 'I'm going to go and get two of my colleagues. They're from Scotland Yard and they'll want to hear this.' Standing, he motioned to Faye's brother to accompany him.

Ellie exchanged a glance with Faye. Scotland Yard was already on the case.

The sergeant returned, though John did not. The two men who

entered with him were in plain clothes, the younger man walking with the aid of a stick. They sat at the table.

'I'm Sergeant Purley,' said the younger man, 'and this is Inspector Irving.'

Irving nodded a greeting from beneath a thatch of white hair.

A reservist. Many retired police officers had been pressed into service to cover for their absent colleagues during the war and some had stayed on while new police were recruited after it. Much to his chagrin Ellie's own godfather had been prevented from joining up, required instead to stay at home and help organise what was left of the police force.

'We understand that you think you may have overheard something pertinent to the recent death of Nurse Jane Cooper,' the inspector said. His sergeant opened a notebook and produced a ballpoint pen.

'Can you tell me your name and address, please?'

Ellie did so.

'Place of employment?'

'The South London Hospital for Women and Children.'

'Are you a nurse?'

'No, I'm… I work—'

'For me,' Faye interjected. 'I'm in charge of all kitchen, canteen and community purchasing and catering. The sergeant here knows our details. My brother's on the force.'

'Can you tell them what you started to tell me, please, miss,' the uniformed sergeant asked. 'In your own words, please.'

Ellie went through her story yet again.

'And did you recognise either of the people who spoke, either by sight or by the sound of their voices?' the inspector asked, while Purley wrote.

'No, but I could see that the woman was a nurse. She was wearing a nurse's cape and uniform.'

'What makes you think that she was Nurse Cooper? Did you know Nurse Cooper?'

'No, I've only just arrived at the SLH…'

'So why do you think it was her?'

Ellie's mouth felt dry. She felt guilty, as if she had done something wrong.

'It would be a strange coincidence if there wasn't a connection between the nurse Ellie heard shouting for help on a freezing Sunday night and the nurse found dead nearby, on Monday morning,' Faye answered.

'Let Miss Peveril tell her own story, please,' the inspector said.

'Did you consult your watch, or a clock, when you were awoken?' Sergeant Purley took up the questioning.

'No, but the street lights were still on, and I'm told that they're turned off at one o'clock. There was almost no traffic, only an SLH van, so it had to be very late. Around midnight.'

'Hmm. Someone from the hospital was out and about then. Does that have anything...?'

'The hospital works twenty-four hours a day,' Faye said.

'The van was nowhere near the couple I saw.' Ellie frowned. 'It wasn't anything to do with them.'

'Alright,' the inspector replied. 'Now. Are you sure you're not mistaken about what you saw?'

'Completely sure.'

There was a brief silence.

'I think the woman was calling out for help,' she continued. 'I couldn't see her at that point because the couple had crossed the lane to be right beside my building. I would've had to open the window to see out.'

'Why didn't you?' he asked. 'If, as you say, it sounded like the woman was in distress.'

'Because it was late, I was still sleepy, because I couldn't be sure...' Ellie hesitated then said, in a rush, 'Because my bedroom was already freezing and opening the window would have made it worse.'

'I see. Well, this incident may, or may not, relate to Nurse Cooper's death.'

Ellie looked at Faye, who was frowning. Neither said anything more.

'But we'll need you to make and sign a statement, Miss Peveril, setting out what you heard and saw that night.'

'I understand.'

'The sergeant here will help you with that.' The inspector indicated the uniformed sergeant, who gave her an encouraging smile.

'You're not from around here, are you?' Sergeant Purley asked.

'No, I've only recently arrived back from Nuremberg, where I was working on the trials.'

'Any reason why you came to Clapham in particular?'

'It seemed like a good place and wasn't expensive,' Ellie answered, bemused. Why were they asking questions about her and not what she saw?

'Bit of a change, going from legal work to the hospital?'

'It's temporary... And I don't see what that has to do with things!' She was annoyed by the turn the questions were taking.

'Do you have any idea who killed the nurse?' Faye asked.

'Our investigations have only just begun,' the inspector answered. 'It's too early to tell. Thank you, Miss Peveril.' He rose. 'We'll be in touch if there are any developments. We may need you to help identify any suspect whom we apprehend, either in an identity parade or by listening to his voice. We can contact you at the hospital or at your lodgings, I assume.'

'Yes.'

'Thank you.' Sergeant Purley snapped his notebook closed.

'Are you going to try and find who was with Ja... the woman Ellie saw on the common?' Faye asked.

'We're following a number of leads,' Sergeant Purely answered. 'There was a suspicious character seen late on the common on Sunday night, who ran away when he was challenged by a passer-by. From the description he's possibly an itinerant workman, a tinker or peddler, someone passing through. There are a lot of people moving around right now – returning home, seeking work, settling in new places.'

'But I think the couple I saw knew each other,' Ellie said. 'The way they behaved…'

'We can't even be sure that the woman you saw was Nurse Cooper,' the inspector said, halfway to the door. 'And we have few resources, but we'll be using the ones we have to track down the suspicious man seen on the common at about the right time. What you saw may or may not be pertinent.'

'But if…'

'Thank you, Miss Peveril, you've been very helpful. The sergeant will show you out.'

10

ELEANOR

Ellie's strides lengthened as her sense of dissatisfaction grew. The police had been polite but didn't seem interested in what she'd told them about the woman and her nighttime assignation; instead, they seemed to be suspicious of her, had made her feel guilty. Why?

Of course, she couldn't be sure that her woman had been Jane, but, as Faye pointed out, it was a strange coincidence if two nurses had been in the same place on the common on one of the coldest nights of the year, when everyone was indoors. They had to try and find the other man, the one who had run away, but that shouldn't prevent them from investigating what she'd told them. It was likely that Jane had been on the common around midnight and with someone she knew, not an itinerant.

'Ellie?' Faye was speaking to her. 'Ellie?'

'Sorry. Miles away.' She shook herself and paid attention, slowing down. It had been very kind of Faye to accompany her and she was grateful, especially given Scotland Yard's attitude.

'At least now you can go and get your things back.'

For a moment Ellie wondered what Faye meant, but, of course, it was her belongings at Mrs Packham's she was referring to.

'Yes, I'm pleased about that, at least. I was such an utter nincompoop to trust Mrs Packham with that money. I don't understand how I could've been so stupid. It's humiliating.'

'She was probably convincing and you had no reason to distrust her.'

'Perhaps, but that doesn't make me feel any better about it.'

'You mustn't blame yourself; it's she who's in the wrong. Put it down to experience.'

'I know, but… that's not the only thing I've made a mess of, is it? On Sunday night I could have helped someone who needed it, but all I considered was my own comfort. That's what the sergeant thought, I could see it on his face.'

'Ellie, don't be so hard on yourself. You were in a strange room, in a part of London new to you. And no one wants to push their nose into other people's business.'

'But if it was Jane and she needed help…'

'You couldn't have known what was going to happen.'

'She called out in distress, that should have been enough! I could have shouted or called to her. At least she would have known that someone had heard and that she wasn't alone. And maybe her attacker would have been scared off.'

A bus trundled past as they walked in silence. Ellie sensed her companion's gaze upon her and looked over.

'Ellie, none of this is your fault, you know, and you seem to be taking it to heart,' Faye said. 'Is there something else bothering you?'

'It's complicated,' Ellie replied. Some of it she didn't really understand herself.

Faye said nothing, raising the palms of her hands outward in a gesture of submission.

'It's just…' Ellie stopped, unsure of how to continue.

She glanced at her companion, who was now staring straight ahead towards the green of the common at the end of the road. Maybe it would help to confide in someone? Someone who was sensible, who always did and said the right thing. Someone who seemed exactly the sort of intelligent level-headed woman who could keep things to herself.

'Everything seems to be going wrong, that's all,' Ellie said. 'I... I'd decided that I didn't want to go home to Worcester straight away. That I wanted to be independent for a while, away from the family, to work out what I want to do with my life. And I seem to be botching it.'

She puckered her lips and frowned.

'Then there's Pat – Patrick Haverstock, my fiancé. My ex-fiancé, I should say.'

A vision of Patrick's laughing, suntanned face flashed into her mind, his white shirt against muscular forearms pulling the oars of the boat on the river. His dry, leathery scent mixed with the perfume of the campion which grew in the lanes where they walked in the evenings.

Her father's smile, her mother cooing with pleasure. 'Mrs Patrick Haverstock, that's what you'll be.' The glint of the diamond in the engagement ring.

'Your ex-fiancé?' Faye voice interrupted her reverie.

'I broke it off.'

'You broke off your engagement! You certainly seem to be going the whole hog.'

'It wasn't that difficult a decision really. I found him out.' When Faye raised an eyebrow, she began to explain. 'After the war Pat stayed in London, supposedly working for his regiment, while I waited in Worcester for him and for my future. Then I went to Nuremberg.'

The telephone call from Moira Shawcross had made her heart lift. It had been a real lifeline. Instead of doors closing, she got that call and a fresh breeze had blown through her life.

'When we returned to London, my friend Moira and I went out in town,' Ellie continued. 'I came across Pat in a club with his cronies, drinking, dancing, with a girl in his arms.'

'Oh.' Faye's eyes widened.

Ellie pressed her lips together. In her mind's eye the tall, uniformed figure was striding across the dance floor.

'What the hell are you doing here?' he'd demanded.

She'd placed her chair between them and gripped its back like a shield.

'I could ask you the same.'

Pat raised his chin, a forbidding look in his eyes.

'I don't expect my fiancée to be out at this time of night and this isn't a suitable place for you. You're engaged to be married!'

'So are you!'

She remembered the pain in her jaw, it was clenched so tight. Her aching arms, muscles tense as she clutched the chair back, trying not to shake.

'You can forget it, Pat. I'm not coming back to Worcester and I'm certainly not coming back to you. Go back to your cronies. I don't require your company any longer.'

His frown of puzzlement. Her fateful words in as cold a voice as she could muster.

'Our engagement is over.'

Ellie glanced over at Faye, who was walking silently by her side.

'I told him that I never wanted to see him again.'

'And don't you?'

'I don't,' Ellie replied, quickly. 'The Pat I saw on Saturday wasn't the Pat I thought I knew.'

Yet she remembered his gentleness in the London hotel room on the afternoon of her first visit, after the terror of Dunkirk, but before the Worcesters were leaving for Libya in forty-one. The sweet pain and afterwards, the tender triumph and gratitude on his face as he held her close.

Ellie shook away the memories.

'I don't think it was the first time he'd been at that club either. I think he'd been living it up for the past few months, thinking I'd be none the wiser, waiting, patiently, for him at home. I can't marry someone who's capable of that, who thinks so little of me.'

'Hmmm, the war changed people,' Faye said. 'It certainly changed me. I was looking forward to marriage and children, home and hearth, but now I want a different sort of life. Hasn't it changed you?'

'Yes, most definitely. I was desperate for the war to end, like everyone else. Yet, when it did, I felt so... disappointed.'

She thought about Worcester. Then about Nuremberg and the American lawyer she had met there. About her own desires and dreams of independence.

'What happened with you?' she asked Faye, suddenly curious.

'My fiancé was killed at Dunkirk.'

'Oh, I'm so sorry.'

Faye shrugged. 'It was six years ago, though, in some ways, it seems longer. In others, it's like yesterday. The war has done strange things to time too.'

'You must have been heartbroken.'

'I was at the time. And the future I had planned for myself was destroyed, but life carried on and I adapted. By and large, I like my life now.'

'Yes. I can see why. You've carved out your own place at the SLH. You're respected and admired.'

That's what I want, Ellie thought, a place like that. Even if I have to be alone to get it.

She glanced at her companion, who was staring straight ahead again, towards the common. Faye must have sensed her scrutiny because she turned to her.

'It isn't perfect, you know,' Faye said, smiling. 'But what does your family think? About your new life.'

'I... I haven't told them yet,' Ellie admitted. 'And I'm feeling guilty about that too. I wanted to get settled first, to find some work, a place to rent. But...'

'You have a job and a room.'

'As of two days ago.'

How exactly was she going to explain to her parents that she was cleaning tables to make ends meet and living in a tiny, rented room in south London? The pressure to return home would be over-whelming, how long would she be able to resist it?

'Even if it isn't what you or your family might have expected,' Faye continued. 'It's something.'

'I know and it's not that I'm ungrateful, believe me.' Ellie meant what she said. 'Meeting you and Beryl, the room in Westbury Court and the job at the SLH saved my life. If I hadn't met you, I'd have ended up slinking back to Worcester with my tail between my legs. A humiliated failure.'

'So it was pride, then, that forced you on, kept you going?'

'Pride, yes, but anger too, fear of failure, worry that I was missing the opportunity to have the sort of life I wanted to have,' Ellie agreed. 'It was all of those things. I was in a desperate state really.'

Faye looked across at her and grinned. 'We've got more in common than you'd think,' she said.

11

ELEANOR

The VIP lunch was a great success.

'The local councillors were impressed,' Faye said. 'And your background helped.'

The clergymen had been charmed, particularly when they learned that Ellie's father was dean of Worcester Cathedral. The talk was of diocesan matters, clergy appointments and local fetes, but she'd spoken about fund-raising in general and then funds for the hospital.

'Bishop Jenkins has promised us more funds from the charitable trust. Miss Barnett, my boss, was very pleased, she asked me to pass on her thanks to you,' Faye continued. 'You made a real difference.'

Ellie's cheeks flushed with pleasure. She and Faye sat in the staffroom, Ellie with her coat ready, about to leave for the police station.

'Just doing my job,' Ellie replied, but she grinned.

'It was a triumph.' Faye grinned back. 'The consultants told me so too. And we could certainly do with some good news right now.'

The news of Jane's murder had reverberated around the hospital, disturbing and distressing everyone. The atmosphere at meal times in the canteen was subdued and anxious. Once the drama of the discovery had died down, a creeping sense of fear replaced it.

'I'm glad it went so well,' Ellie said.

And she was. She felt, for the first time, as if she was repaying the kindness shown to her by Faye and the others, that she was pulling her weight at the SLH. She had drilled her little team of local girls in etiquette and they'd set the long table with the best silver and crystal the hospital could beg or borrow, polished until it gleamed and glinted. All that and Cook's excellent food too, so the diners were predisposed to agree to further funding, which Ellie steered them towards.

She'd enjoyed doing it. It was so much better than cleaning and clearing up after people. This was what she was good at, where she could be of most use. It was too bad that tomorrow she'd be back to mopping floors. Still, it had reminded her of what she was capable of and restored her confidence in herself.

She would need that confidence soon. Mrs Packham wouldn't give way easily, that was certain, even when faced by the police. It would be an unpleasant confrontation and Ellie wasn't looking forward to it, but she was determined to go through with it.

Whenever she thought of how the woman had tricked her, she seethed with anger. How could she think that she'd get away with it? That was what was so belittling; to know that Mrs Packham considered her easily fooled and that she would meekly accept the situation.

'Is it your brother coming with me this afternoon?' she asked Faye. She hoped it was, she needed an ally against the hatchet-faced harridan.

'I don't know, but I don't think so. It'll be someone more experienced, but I'm sure they'll be helpful. Let's hope you get your things back, at least.'

'I hope I'll be able to bring them back with me.'

'How are you going to transport them?'

'I... I hadn't thought about that.'

She'd been so taken up with preparations for the luncheon and then steeling herself to face Mrs Packham, that she hadn't given any thought to how she was going to get her belongings back to West-bury Court.

'You might borrow an SLH van,' Faye suggested.

'But I don't know how to drive.'

'Ask one of the porters to help you.'

'Where do they congregate?'

'In a little room in the basement just past the stores, there's usually one or two of them back there. Or speak to Les Allen, he's often around the canteen, he has a locker here.' She waved towards the row of metal lockers.

Ellie sensed something awry in Faye's tone when she mentioned the head porter. Her manner had changed.

'He's the very tall fellow... you pointed him out yesterday?'

'Yep, that's him.'

'How did a man come to be in charge of the porters?'

'Les was born with talipes, or clubfoot, so was exempt from the call up. He made the best of it, became a scout leader and generally got on with things. When we needed stretcher bearers during the Blitz, he and his Ranger Scouts volunteered. Les organised it all, was quite the hero. When the war ended, he stayed on. Not indefinitely, but for now.'

'I see.'

'The porters like him,' Faye went on. 'They say he's good to work for and defend him fiercely if anyone has a go at him, especially about not fighting, which is fair enough. But in my opinion, he pokes his nose where it isn't wanted, is too much of a gossip, though I'm in the minority. There's something I don't like about him... Anyway, he's a popular chap. Rowed for the Thames Tradesmen.'

'Well, let's give him something to gossip about.' Ellie stood and reached for her coat. 'I'll go and find the porters. I'll be back in time for the evening shift.'

'Good, we'll be busy tonight. It's Guy Fawkes and I hear there's a bonfire on the common, regardless of... There'll be plenty of minor injuries, always are.'

'See you later.'

Ellie headed in the direction of the hospital stores. As she approached the porters' room, she could hear women talking.

'Who could have killed her?'

The same question was being asked in corridors and consulting rooms.

'Some say it was a tramp, a vagrant, wandering on the common.'

'I've heard it was a serviceman,' said another voice. 'There are still some at the old gunnery emplacements. They're dismantling the whole site.'

'Or it could've been a building worker. They're repairing property all over Clapham, if they can get the materials.'

'It could have been anyone, that's what's so frightening,' said another, her voice falling away to a whisper.

'You girls had best be careful,' a male voice said. 'I'm serious. Don't wander about after dark alone, even in the afternoons. If you have to go out, go in pairs.'

There was a moment's silence.

'Are you going to protect us personally, then, Les?' one quipped. 'Now you're fancy free again.'

The awkwardness was lost in ribald laughter.

Ellie stood in the doorway.

'Hello, sorry to disturb you,' she said. 'I wonder if you could help me?'

The women were sitting or lounging in a small room overlooking the vegetable plots in the SLH grounds. A low coffee table stood at its centre on which sat a large brown teapot and mugs. As Les rose and came towards her, Ellie noticed a slight hesitation in his walk; he dragged his left foot.

'Always ready to help, me,' he said, chuckling.

The women porters laughed. 'Leave it out! She's out of your league, Les,' said one. 'Friends with Faye Smith.'

'And Beryl MacBride,' said another with a sly smile.

'Take no notice of this lot,' Les said and grinned. 'How can I help?'

'I've got to collect my things, a trunk and a case,' Ellie explained. 'From a lodging house on the North Side.'

'Is that from Norah Packham's place?'

'Mrs Packham, yes.'

'I'd make sure that there's nothing missing once you've got them,' said one porter, sourly. 'I hear George Packham's home again.'

'Now, now, ladies, what has George Packham ever done to you? No, I don't want suggestions,' Les said.

'You want the van?' asked the woman who seemed to know of the lodging house. 'Or is it the van and someone to drive it?'

'Van and driver, please.'

'Alright, I'll help you out. When?' the same woman said.

Ellie agreed that the van would arrive outside Mrs Packham's in about an hour.

'Thank you very much,' she said.

'We aim to please,' Les retorted. 'But you're not walking across the common on your own, are you? It'll be dark soon.'

'No, I'm going to Cavendish Road police station first,' she explained. 'I'll be accompanied.'

'Good.'

'See you later.' Ellie nodded to the porter who'd volunteered. 'And thank you.' To Les she said, 'I owe you a favour.'

He winked at her.

12

ELEANOR

The small back room at the lodging house felt very crowded with three people in it; Mrs Packham, Ellie and a police constable whom she had met only half an hour before. In the light from the single overhead bulb, the policeman, fresh-faced and clean-shaven, looked little older than Faye's brother.

'These items belong to me,' Ellie said, indicating the wicker trunk and the suitcase. 'I'd like to arrange for them to be collected. Mrs Packham has no legal right to prevent me doing so.'

'You owe me money. I'm keeping hold of these until I get it.'

'Exactly what money does Miss Peveril owe you, Mrs Packham?' the constable asked. 'And how much?'

'She owes me a week's rent.'

Ellie pressed her lips together, holding her tongue. On the way over, the constable had insisted that she let him do the talking. She stared out of the little window into the empty yard.

'Have you ever lodged here, Miss Pev—'

'Rent is payable in advance.'

Ellie shook her head, frowning.

'And how much would that be?'

'Twenty shillings a week.'

'What? But—' that was what the larger room would have cost.

The constable cut across Ellie's protestations before she really began.

'Do you have a copy of the lodging agreement, Mrs Packham?'

'I don't use lodging agreements, Constable. These days people want more flexibility.'

'Rent in advance isn't flexible.'

'I don't want to lose money on an unoccupied room,' Mrs Packham answered sharply. 'People might want to be flexible, but I still have my costs to cover.'

'But you are asking me to pay for something I don't want and never did,' Ellie couldn't stop herself from saying.

'Something you agreed to.'

'No, I did not. I paid a deposit to reserve the room at the front of the house. When I arrived here you told me that someone else had taken the front room and paid a month in advance.'

'How much was the deposit, Miss Peveril?' the constable asked, though he already knew.

'A guinea,' Ellie answered.

'So, in fact, more than a week's rent in advance.'

'She didn't give me anything. I didn't have to keep any room for her,' Mrs Packham said. 'I didn't agree to that at all, there was no such agreement.'

'If there's no agreement, I don't owe you any money!' Ellie retorted. 'So you can't keep my things in lieu of it.'

'The front room has been let, you say?' the constable asked.

'Yes. Why?' Mrs Packham was wary.

'I'd like to speak with the person renting it.' He turned to leave the room.

'He's not here right now,' Mrs Packham said, eyes sliding towards the corridor. 'He's at work.'

Ellie sensed the woman's discomfort. Why this reaction? Did the constable know something she didn't?

'And the name of the tenant?' The constable got out his pocket-book and pencil.

'George,' the landlady responded. 'George Packham.'

'That would be your son, would it?'

'Yes.'

'And he paid you a month's rent in advance, did he?' the constable went on. 'At twenty shillings a week, or would the front room cost more, after all, it's bigger?'

'No... yes,' said Mrs Packham.

'What time does he usually come home?'

'Six thirty, seven.' The woman ground the words out from between gritted teeth.

'And where's he working now?'

'Not sure.'

'Right, I'll be back round here to talk with him about all this.'

'This is nothing to do with him. You never leave him alone, you lot. You're always picking on him.'

'He's germane to the point in question,' the PC said. 'In the meantime, Miss Peveril can have her things back.'

'I want—'

'Without a legal agreement you have no right to prevent her taking them,' the constable overrode her.

'I'd like to take them now, please,' Ellie said, quickly. 'I've got a van waiting. If you would help me carry them out?'

The constable put away his notebook and walked past Mrs Packham to grasp one of the handles of the wicker chest. The landlady hovered, scowling, but didn't stand in their way.

As Ellie hurried to grip the other handle, she shot Mrs Packham a look of triumph, making her scowl all the more. Together she and the constable carried the chest downstairs, out of the front door and onto the pavement, the policeman returning to collect the suitcase.

Ellie waved to a van parked opposite in a pool of light from a street-lamp and two hospital porters climbed out and collected the trunk, manoeuvring it into the back of the van. One of them took the suitcase from the constable and stowed it away.

'Do you want a lift?' she asked.

'No, though thanks for the offer,' Ellie replied. 'The walk'll be good for me.'

She had her own reasons for wanting to accompany the constable on the walk back across the common. She wanted to find out where Jane's body had been found. If the woman she heard on Sunday night was Jane Cooper, then she couldn't help but feel, in part, responsible for what had befallen her afterwards.

'See you back at the SLH,' said the driver as she sat behind the wheel. 'I'll drop these at Westbury Court.'

13

ELEANOR

'Thank you very much for your help, Constable Dawkins.'

Ellie and the policeman passed from one pool of lamp light into another as they walked one of the paths crossing the Common. Ellie was glad he was there; she wouldn't have walked that way alone.

'It's my job, Miss.'

'I know, but you did it well.' Ellie smiled at him. It was true, it wasn't just flattery, though flattery, accompanied by a smile, usually worked. 'How did you know it was Mrs Packham's son who had taken the front room?'

'I didn't, not at first,' the constable replied, enjoying his moment. 'I thought I recognised a scarf hanging up in the hall, see. I went to school with George Packham, at Grosvenor Secondary, that was the school scarf. Then, it occurred to me, if it belonged to George, could he have returned home? And if he had, was it him that had taken the front room, the one you thought was yours?'

'I see. How observant of you. Was he in the forces?'

'Army, though he was demobbed last year. I saw him at VJ Day. George has been back over a year.'

'Would he have paid his mother something for the room?'

'Not if I know George Packham. And he won't be pleased when

he learns I might be coming round to speak to him. He'll make sure he's somewhere else.'

'So... he's "known to the police", as they say?'

'Certainly is. One of the best-known fences in south London is George – a receiver of stolen goods. Did time for grievous bodily harm before the war; two years.'

Ellie wondered about the crates and boxes she'd seen from the little bedroom window on the first occasion she'd been there. What was in them and where had they gone?

'Evening.' The constable returned the greetings of an elderly couple. 'My mentioning George was enough to put the wind up his mother, but I don't think Mrs P will be giving you your deposit back any time soon and, as long as she sticks to her story, I can't make her.'

'I understand. I was foolish not to get a receipt. It's my word against hers. Maybe I'll follow it up, maybe I won't.' She couldn't afford to lose a guinea, her savings wouldn't keep her going forever.

'Crown Court's your best bet,' the constable said. 'You're in the legal line, aren't you?'

'Legal clerk.'

'You'd know all about it then.'

Ellie smiled but didn't respond. Running a country solicitors office didn't include taking cases to court. She couldn't afford to pay for a solicitor, so she'd have to find out for herself how to go about pursuing it.

'Major.' The constable touched his helmet as an elderly, well-padded gentleman with a West Highland terrier nodded to him.

'What's going on with this blasted bonfire?' the man asked, stopping. 'Wood should be used for building materials, not for burning.'

'As far as I understand it, sir, the bonfire's mostly wood scavenged from the common, bits of brushwood, that sort of thing,' the PC responded.

'Hmm, see that it is,' he said, gruffly, resuming his path. 'Crowds out on the common, all sorts. Who knows what could happen. We've already had one tragic death.'

JULIE ANDERSON

'Yes, sir.' The constable watched the old gentleman walk away.

'You're very patient.' Ellie glanced at him. 'Could I ask you about something else?'

'Fire away.'

'Jane Cooper, the nurse who was killed...'

'I can't discuss that I'm afraid.'

'It's just that I think I heard her during Sunday night. I think she was calling out for help and, well, I didn't help her. I wouldn't even open my window for fear of letting the cold in. When she may have been in fear of her life.'

'I'm sorry.' The policeman shrugged. 'I can't say. But you shouldn't blame yourself.'

'So I'm told, but I do. I made a statement at the station and spoke with the Scotland Yard detectives, told them all about it. Can you tell me where she was found? If it was on the common, I'll never forgive myself.'

'I can put your mind at rest there, anyway,' the constable said. 'She wasn't found out on the common.'

'Really?' Ellie gazed at the constable, wide-eyed. 'Then where...?'

'I shouldn't, but...' he gave a little shrug, 'you've already spoken with Scotland Yard, so... She was found inside the entrance of one of the shafts to the deep shelters.' He pointed towards the low circular structure visible in the distance between the trees.

'Why was she there? Was she sheltering from the cold?'

'Well... she was inside. Inside the door. The doors are kept locked.'

'She was behind a locked door?'

'Yes. Those shelters aren't used any longer, though Mr Philpott checks them on a regular basis.'

'Who's Mr Philpott?' Ellie remembered a nurse had mentioned him at the WEA meeting.

'He's in charge of the deep shelters all over London. There are more of them south of the river, so he's based here in Clapham. He was a commie, it's said, fought in Spain, but knows Herbert

Morrison personally; is on speaking terms with the Leader of the House of Commons, no less.'

'Was it Mr Philpott who found her?'

'Yes, he was checking the shelters on Monday morning.'

'So she was killed sometime during Sunday night.'

She'd been right. It *was* Jane she'd heard.

'Maybe. We haven't had the pathologist's report yet.'

'So you don't know how she died?'

'No. And I couldn't tell you even if I did. That's confidential information relating to the case.' The constable lifted his chin and squared his shoulders. 'If you ask me, she shouldn't have been wandering around at that time of night. Asking for trouble she was. God rest her,' he added.

'But she was a nurse... she worked shifts... at night.'

'At the South London. An odd place, that hospital. No men. All women. Isn't natural.'

'It may have escaped your notice, Constable, but women have been managing pretty well without men for the last six years.'

'But the men are back now, aren't they, to take their rightful places. Only not at that hospital. It's a strange place, needs a man to take charge, someone to stop all the nonsense.'

'What nonsense? And there are people in charge, haven't you met Matron?' Ellie asked, incredulously. 'Fancy standing up to her, do you?'

The constable had the grace to look uncomfortable.

Ellie fumed inside. He'd seemed so nice, practical and observant and he was local and knew the hospital and the good work that it did. How could he spout such utter balderdash when he knew the reality?

'Besides, it was a *man* I saw Jane Cooper with, that night on the common. A *man* who committed the crime.'

They had reached the busy, well-lit junction of Cavendish Road and the South Side.

'I'll be going back to the station,' the constable said, indicating the turning. 'Time to clock off. I'm taking my young cousin to the bonfire tonight. Are you going?' He seemed hopeful of seeing her again.

'No, I'm working.'

At the hospital which you seem to dislike so much, she wanted to add, but saved her breath.

'Ah well, good luck with getting your money back.'

'Thank you,' she said with a sweet smile. 'And thank you for putting my mind at rest.'

With a wave she continued towards the underground and Westbury Court, the smile sliding from her face. She circled around the squat, round building she'd seen from her bedroom window.

It was enclosed by a wooden picket fence, some of which had collapsed into the nettles and brambles that seemed to be reclaiming the ground for the common. Single storey and flat roofed, it was made of concrete and circular in construction, a pillbox, but with a square side addition, which wound part way around the central core. A metal door at the end of the brick extension seemed to be the only way in. Ellie walked around it again, coming to a halt by the door.

So this was where Jane Cooper's body had been found on Monday morning, just inside this door. How she had got there was a puzzle. Ellie shuddered and not just with the cold. Like it or not, she was involved in this mystery, she had some responsibility. She had to find out more about what happened to Jane Cooper.

ELEANOR

E llie stood in the doorway, surveying the tiny room she now called home.

The wickerwork trunk sat beneath the window, a folded blanket on its lid acting as a cushion. It had strong claims to be the coldest window seat in London. She knew. She'd sat on it. Her clothes were now hung in the thin wall cupboard and her shoes and boots lined up beneath the bed. Her leather writing case sat on the narrow wall shelf, which also held a framed photograph of her parents and sister, standing outside the Cathedral, her father in the robes of his office.

What would they say if they could see her now, living here, working in the SLH canteen? And when was she going to tell them that she wasn't returning to Worcester? Her conversation with Faye had crystallised her intentions, made her consider what she really wanted. Staying in London wasn't the short, temporary arrangement she'd originally thought it would be. Her return to Worcester could be postponed indefinitely.

The framed photograph of Pat which usually accompanied the family snapshot was still in her suitcase and that's where it would stay. Her decision in The Black Cat Club had changed the trajectory of his life as well as hers and she had a sneaking suspicion that he wouldn't take it lying down. It was a worry, but what could he do? Sue her for breach of promise? Maybe, but that would mean the public humiliation of being rejected and Pat wouldn't want that at all. At least he didn't know where she was.

She'd have to tell her parents about breaking off her engagement. She would have to tell them about not returning home too, something she had promised her godfather that she would do as soon as she had sorted out lodgings and a job. She'd have to do it soon; the guilt wouldn't go away. And she also had to telephone Moira in Edinburgh, to get the legal contacts she'd promised.

Her gaze travelled along the shelf to her hairbrushes, combs and curlers at its end, within easy reach when looking in the mirror on the cupboard door. Her small and treasured supply of shampoo (provided from the American army stores in Nuremberg) she had put in the flat's small and sparkling clean bathroom. She would share it with Beryl, a small enough thank you for taking her in.

Her legal books were stacked in a corner and the few other books she possessed sat on the floor next to the bed, making a low bedside table. Dr Nicholas Yorke's face peered out from beneath the base of her reading lamp.

She thought about the sunlit, comfortable room in Worcester where she'd slept since she was a child. Her large bed and walnut dressing table, the thick rugs on the polished wooden floor, the heavy frilled curtains at the large windows and the familiar view to the cathedral. How could she compare this with that? Comfort, warmth and childhood or utility, spareness and adulthood. Independence. Self-determination. Cold and clear, as chilly as the wind on the common, but her own to make of it what she would. She knew what she preferred.

Beryl came to stand by her side. She was wearing her overcoat.

'You got your stuff back, then?'

'Yes, the police constable was very helpful,' Ellie answered. 'Though he thinks I won't see my guinea again.'

'And you think otherwise?'

'I could pursue the matter through the courts, though I'd have to do it myself. I couldn't afford a solicitor.'

'If you've the time and leisure...' Beryl harrumphed. 'I'm going back to the SLH to have some supper before shift. I just popped over to get my textbook.' Beryl was studying for her staff nurse exams. 'You coming?'

'Yes. I'm working tonight too, but I'll finish here first. See you in a short while.'

As the apartment door slammed shut, Ellie went to the window and pulled open the heavy curtains. Poking her head out of the window she watched Beryl emerge from the door on the ground floor into the white-yellow light of the street lamps. The nurse walked beside the building, past Clapham South underground station and crossed the South Side to the massive red brick building of the SLH.

Ellie felt a spurt of affection for the place. It was her haven; her fortunes had changed after she had taken refuge there. She felt safe there, that was one of the reasons she liked it. Jane Cooper would have felt safe there too. Yet Jane had been out late with a man, her lover, perhaps, on the common and hadn't been safe at all.

If she had looked out on Sunday night, what would she have seen?

She craned her neck to look to the left.

Her window faced directly onto the lane before the façade of Westbury Court bent away from it to create the space of Westbury Gardens. A street lamp illuminated the edge of one of the rose beds and a bench seat. Beyond this was a lawn bordered by a low wall, its truncated metal railings clearly visible. She couldn't see the building to which the lawn belonged.

Directly across the lane and to the right, about fifty yards away, was the pillbox-shaped building of the deep shelter entrance, beneath the bare tree branches.

Ellie drew back and closed the window and curtains.

She was acutely aware that she should've opened the window and shouted, so Jane knew that someone had heard her, that help wasn't far away. If she had opened that window and called out, Jane Cooper might be alive now.

A prickling between her shoulder blades meant she felt her father's gaze staring out from the photograph on the shelf. What would he say to her now? She had failed to help a woman in distress. Had she become a different person since she left Worcester? Someone so self-centred that she wouldn't open a window to aid another human being because she was cold. So much for moral fibre and backbone.

She knew she had to atone for her lapse and she could do so by finding out what had happened to Jane Cooper; how she had met her end. But she would need help.

Ellie reached for her heavy coat. As she'd told Beryl, she was working that evening and it was time to go across to the hospital. And it was time to discuss all of this with Faye.

15

ELEANOR

A toddler screeched, the ear-scalding note rising higher than the general hubbub in the corridor. A harassed-looking mother tried to quieten two children, one of whom was already snivelling and the other about to start. People, mostly families, queued outside the overflowing waiting room for the outpatients department. The SLH didn't have an accident department, but that didn't stop the locals coming in to have their burns and cuts soothed and bandaged.

Ellie opened the canteen doors to bustle and noise. Very different to earlier in the day.

The first person she saw was a tall man with a close-cut beard, Dr Nicholas Yorke. The academic wore the same tweed jacket but had an overcoat over one arm. He was accompanied by a youth wearing a bandage over his left eye and he was speaking with Beryl. They were laughing.

Ellie tucked a stray lock of hair back behind her ear. Just as well she hadn't already changed into her canteen uniform, it wasn't the most flattering.

'Good evening,' Yorke called over to her.

'Hello.' She returned his smile with one of her best.

'Young Brian, here, managed to get some sparks in his eye, so I brought him in. As I was passing...' he said, then indicated the canteen. 'You're busy tonight.'

'Always are,' Beryl said. 'Especially on Bonfire Night.'

'Don't suppose you've begun reading the book?' Yorke asked Ellie.

'Book? Oh no.' Ellie flushed, then smiled. 'Too much else to do, I'm afraid.'

'No matter. Is your friend around by any chance? Miss Smith?' There was a hopeful glint in his eye.

Ellie blinked, discomfited. It was clear who Nicholas Yorke was hoping to see and it wasn't her. *Vanity, vanity, all is vanity.*

'Yes, she's here, I believe, but she's probably busy,' Ellie answered. 'What do you want to talk to her about? Maybe I can help?'

'Oh, nothing.' Yorke shrugged and smiled, but the glint had gone. 'We'll be off then, I...' His voice trailed away and then the smile returned, he'd caught sight of Faye entering from the kitchens.

'Here she is!' Beryl's jolly tone was so foreign to her usual manner that Ellie had to turn her laugh into a cough.

'What's this, an unofficial splinter group meeting of the Clapham WEA?' Faye asked as she joined them.

'I've brought Brian in,' Yorke repeated.

'He got some sparks in his eye,' Beryl said.

'Erm, yes. He did, actually.' Yorke looked slightly disconcerted.

'Come on then, Brian,' Faye said. 'Let's get you a restorative cup of tea.' The youth gave Yorke a baleful glare. 'And we'll see if we can find a piece of cake.'

Grinning now, Brian trotted after Faye as she went over to the canteen counter and Yorke followed.

'Do you think...?' Ellie began.

'Yep. Already ahead of you,' Beryl answered.

'He seems a good sort.'

'Yes, good luck to him. But Faye's not been interested since her fiancé died,' Beryl explained. 'At Dunkirk.'

'Yes, she told me. Well, maybe it's time?'

'Mebbe.' She shrugged. 'I'll be off then. See you tomorrow.'

Ellie hung up her overcoat in the staffroom and, resigned, pulled on her uniform. When she returned to the canteen Yorke, Brian and Faye were sitting at a table, so she wandered over and sat next to Faye.

Yorke was speaking while he stirred his tea, a half-smile on his face. Faye was paying attention, but with a flicker of amusement in her eyes. It seemed she was aware of the academic's partiality, but whether she welcomed it or not Ellie couldn't tell. By Yorke's side, Brian concentrated on eating his oversized portion of pudding as quickly as was humanly possible.

'Have you begun your research yet?' Ellie asked Yorke. 'Here at the SLH?'

'I've visited a couple of times, conducted a few interviews, with medical staff mainly. I spoke with Nurse Cooper, the nurse who died.'

'Really?' Faye's head swivelled round. 'Not on...?'

'Sunday. No, last week. I thought I recognised the name when it was mentioned last night; she was one of a dozen people on my list. A redhead, vivacious and pretty. More articulate than I thought she'd be too. I was impressed by her.'

'What did you ask her about?' Faye quizzed him; her chin raised.

'The same as I ask all the interviewees. What are their views on the introduction of a national health service? How they think health services can be improved. How they think their job and the SLH will change.'

Faye was staring at him.

'It's only fact finding,' the academic said, sensitive to her reaction. 'That's all. I'm doing the same with several south London hospitals—'

'I see,' Ellie said, interrupting. 'Shall I take that, young man?' She reached for the now empty bowl, which Brian pulled towards him, wrapping his forearms around it. He looked pleadingly at Faye.

'That's all you're getting,' she said. 'One dish of medicinal pudding per patient only.'

Ellie whipped the dish away.

'We should be going, anyway,' Yorke said. 'I must get Brian back to his mother. Thanks for the tea and the dessert.' He prodded the youth beside him.

'Thank you for the pudding,' Brian said to Faye, who acknowledged his thanks.

'Perhaps we'll coincide again sometime,' Yorke said to her as they rose.

'Perhaps,' Faye answered, which seemed to disappoint him.

Yorke and the boy made their way from the canteen.

'You've made a conquest,' Ellie remarked.

'Hmm, maybe. I'd like to find out exactly what he's been asking his 'interviewees' about. And when he spoke with Jane. He seemed to like her. I wonder who else is on his list?'

'Actually, I've been thinking about what happened to Jane,' Ellie said, glancing around the busy canteen. 'Could we talk somewhere?'

Ellie followed Faye through the kitchens into the empty staffroom.

'I want to find out what happened, Faye. I'm sure that it was Jane I heard on Sunday night and she was in distress. I should have helped her then, so I feel I ought to try and help her now. Rightly or wrongly, I feel involved in this.'

Faye sighed, then gave a silent laugh.

'She was SLH, one of our own. I think quite a lot of us would like to know what happened to her.'

'Did you know her?'

'Yes, she was often in the canteen, laughing and joking. Though I didn't know her well.'

'Her body was found inside the deep shelter entrance on the common on Monday morning by someone called Mr Philpott.'

'Owen?' Faye's eyebrows shot up. 'How do you know? Did your godfather tell you?'

'No, I asked the PC who accompanied me to Mrs Packham's, that's all,' Ellie answered.

'Well done on tackling Mrs Packham, by the way. Beryl told me about it.'

'Yeah, but I didn't get my guinea. Anyway... the PC wasn't supposed to say anything, but...'

'You managed to persuade him. Ellie, I'm seriously impressed by your powers of persuasion.'

'It's not so hard,' Ellie said. 'But... Constable Dawkins surprised me. He said Jane was asking for trouble being out late at night, even though she's a nurse working shifts. He didn't seem to like the SLH either, or at least disliked the way it was set up. Yet he's a local, he must know how much good the hospital does.'

'The SLH isn't universally loved, you know,' Faye said. Seeing Ellie's look of incredulity, she continued. 'Much of Clapham treasures us, lots of people benefit from the care they receive here. Plenty have reason to be grateful for our services, sometimes paid for, sometimes free. And we raise a lot of funds within our little part of south London, often from those who can least afford it. But the SLH is different, and difference sometimes engenders dislike, even hatred.'

'How could anyone dislike, let alone hate, a hospital?'

'A hospital run by and for women.'

'But still... I don't understand it.'

'As I said, most people value us. For some, however, this place is an inversion of how things ought to be,' Faye continued. 'They think that women shouldn't be running things, making their own decisions.'

'Women have been running things at home in practice for the last six years. I told the constable!'

'Yes, but now things are returning to how they used to be, so the SLH's difference stands out even more. The hospital's only thirty-four years old, it's still young and vulnerable, especially now, when it's about to lose control over its own destiny.'

'The NHS? I thought you were a supporter.'

'I am, but it makes me fearful for the hospital. The new NHS managers will want to control us. The founders had to work so hard to set this place up, getting the money, then fighting the narrow-mindedness and preconceptions of the professional bodies. There's still a lot of mindless prejudice around, your constable is an example of it. The same people who tried to ridicule it being created will be out to criticise it and Jane's sad death will give them ammunition.'

'I see.'

'Then there's this research that Nicholas Yorke's doing. I wonder what that's all about and how it might be used.' She pursed her lips.

'Well, that's easy to resolve, you only have to ask him,' Ellie replied, grinning at her. 'I'm sure he'd be happy to explain, would willingly spend quite a lot of time in your company doing so, in fact.'

'Hmm.' Faye tried not to smile but her mouth turned up at the corners. 'He probably would. If I let him.'

'I don't think Nicholas Yorke's a problem,' Ellie said. 'Whatever he asks in his interviews, he's an educated type with modern views. But the constable...'

'Harry Dawkins is just old-fashioned. People generally tend to accept the status quo, they make assumptions, think in the traditional way. Even those who know the SLH and benefit from it,' Faye said. 'Jane's murder will bring all their doubts to the surface again. The longer the murder is unresolved, the worse it will be for the SLH. And for all of us. Everyone's jittery, there could be a killer in our midst. This evening's just a temporary respite. No one feels safe.'

'Though it seems the police are totally focused on the vagrant theory. I suppose it could be true. Jane could simply have been in the wrong place at the wrong time. An itinerant or a drunken serviceman about to ship out back home, or a workman?'

'You saw her on the common with someone she seemed to know, so I think it more likely that she knew her killer.'

'So?'

'I'd like to talk with the man who found Jane's body,' Faye said.

'Owen Philpott spoke at the WEA, he's an interesting man, I think he might remember me.'

'Sounds like Nicholas Yorke's got competition.'

'I don't think so. Let's "bump into" him tomorrow morning when he does his rounds to check the shelters. I'll see you at seven thirty outside the florists on Nightingale Lane.'

'See you then.'

WEDNESDAY

16

FAYE

Faye's foot slipped on the icy pavement and she shifted her weight to avoid a fall. Ahead of her, dawn glowed behind the SLH, its bulk obscuring the rising sun and keeping the lane in shadow. On the busy South Side the street lamps were switching off as a new working day began.

She was late and fretting. She'd quarrelled that morning with John, who had maintained that it was Scotland Yard's business to pursue Jane's killer, not hers. Now she was irritable and uneasy. She and John usually saw eye to eye; he was her favourite brother and she disliked disagreeing with him. She also had a sneaking suspicion that he was right. Yet it seemed that Scotland Yard weren't, or couldn't, do their job and it was a job that had to be done.

Up ahead, outside the florists, Ellie stood like a rock amidst the stream of commuters flowing around her towards the underground station. Faye smiled and waved as Ellie spotted her.

'Sorry, I'm late.' She drew back her sleeve to check her watch. 'Owen should be about to start his rounds about now. Let's go and find him.'

The women walked onto Westbury Parade. Faye pointed out a moustachioed man muffled in a greatcoat and wearing a tweed cap, walking towards them, purposefully.

'Mr Philpott,' she called. 'Owen, over here.'

He slowed as he saw them.

'Faye Smith,' he said, smiling. 'To what do I owe this pleasure?'

'I'm after some information.'

'No pleasantries with you are there? No "How are you, Owen?" or "Nice to see you, Owen."' He chuckled. 'Much more straight forward.'

'It's the nurse, Jane Cooper. She was one of us. We want to find out what happened to her, how she met her death. The police aren't telling us anything.' They all stepped to one side, out of the flow of people.

'You've spoken with the police?'

'Yes. May I introduce my colleague, Miss Ellie Peveril.'

'Pleased to meet you, Miss Ellie Peveril,' he said, taking the hand offered with an open smile, his gaze slightly out of focus, as if surprised. It was an expression that Faye was coming to recognise whenever an adult male encountered Ellie for the first time. Even sensible men like Owen Philpott weren't immune.

She sighed and pressed on. 'Ellie heard her, the nurse, Jane, on Sunday night. That's one of the reasons we're trying to find out more.'

'Ah, I see.'

Ellie repeated her tale.

'Hmm, I understand, but now that you've reported it, this is police business. It'll be up to them.'

'But they don't seem too eager to follow up what we've told them.'

'They're stretched thin,' Philpott said. 'They don't have enough men. Do they have any theories?'

'They think that Jane was attacked by someone passing through, a transient or itinerant.' It sounded lame, even as Faye said it. 'Apparently a witness saw a stranger on the common behaving suspiciously.'

'The man I saw with Jane that night wasn't a tramp or a peddler,' Ellie said. 'It was someone she knew.'

'But the itinerant theory is convenient for the police,' Faye added. 'Even if they don't apprehend anyone, they'll say there's no reason for anyone to feel afraid because the killer's moved on. Then no one around here will feel safe.'

'You don't know that, Faye,' Philpott said. 'They'll investigate, I'm sure. You shouldn't interfere.'

'We're not interfering, Owen,' Faye countered. 'It's just that we feel we have an obligation to find out where and how she died, at least.'

'I heard and saw her,' Ellie said. 'And I didn't help her.'

Philpott wore a pained expression on his face. Was he wavering?

'Are you checking on the shaft head entrance now, anyway?' Faye asked. 'We could just walk alongside you, couldn't we, and maybe ask a question or two?'

'I can't stop you walking alongside me, I suppose,' he conceded with a sad smile.

'Thanks, Owen,' Faye said.

They crossed Nightingale Lane to the little compound, wading through the nettles.

'It's getting dilapidated,' he grumbled. 'Nature's taking it back. I don't have the time or the money to maintain it, but what I can do is keep it safe. All the entrances to the shelters are kept locked. There's over a mile of tunnel beneath us at this one and it would be easy for someone to get lost down there.'

The door was up two steps in the square adjunct to the circular building.

'I do my rounds at about this time every weekday morning, to make sure the doors are locked and there's nothing trapped inside; sometimes birds or squirrels get in through the ventilation ducts. As it happened, I was late on Monday, it was about eleven when I arrived here that morning.'

'Was the door locked then?' Faye asked.

'It was.' Philpott produced a key. It was flat, with a groove containing small spurs running down its middle as well as having an incised edge. 'It's a security key,' he said, noticing Faye peering at it. 'Unique. Each door has one, different to the others. And they can't be copied.'

He stood to one side, so that Faye and Ellie could see him turn the key in the lock.

'The door opens inwards. On Monday morning, however, there was an obstruction and I had to push it hard.'

Ellie put her hand to her mouth.

'Yes, it was the body of the nurse. Jane, did you say her name was?'

'Jane Cooper.'

'Do you know how she died?' Faye asked.

'No.' He shook his head and pushed the door further ajar. 'She was here.' He indicated the space behind the door. 'I'm not going in and you mustn't either. But the body was just here, behind the door. Whoever dumped it there must have propped it against the wall and it fell towards the inside of the door when the door was closed.'

The weak November sunlight didn't penetrate very far into the darkness of the concrete passageway beyond the door. There was nothing much to see, but both women peered into the corridor, which wound away to the left. Eye-level signs indicated that this was the way to the lift and the shelters, followed by a list of names: Anson, Jellicoe, Pellew.

'The shelters were divided into sections which were named after British Admirals,' Philpott explained when he saw Ellie reading the signs. 'They're in alphabetical order. People were allocated a bunk in a specific place, so they had to be able to find it.'

'Do the shelters still have power and water?' Ellie asked.

'Yes, I can switch the power on in the office, at the top of Balham Hill, but it's usually switched off. Each shaft head has a power switch too, but that's for the lifts and emergency lighting only.'

'Who has the key to this door?' Faye asked. 'Someone must have unlocked it.'

'Only I can do that. I have keys to all the deep shelters; a spare set is kept in the safe in the office and only I know the combination.'

'So, you must be suspect number one then, Owen?' Faye said.

'Don't joke about it.' Philpott looked chagrined. 'It was as well for me that I had an alibi for all of Sunday night. I was out at Guildford, staying with my sister. She's ill. That's why I was late starting on Monday morning.'

'But how did Jane get inside?' Ellie asked.

'I don't know. It's a complete mystery. She was on the wrong side of a locked door.' He pulled the door closed and Faye and Ellie went down the steps as he locked it behind him.

'We know so little. We don't even know the cause of death,' Faye said, her lips pressed closed in frustration.

Philpott gave her a sharp glance. 'Really? But the police took the body to the SLH. With it being so close by, they didn't wait for the police pathologist.'

'I didn't know that... thanks, Owen.' Faye smiled at him.

'I still say this isn't any business of yours,' he said. 'Not that you'll take any notice of me. Now I'd best get on. Take care.'

Philpott walked back towards his office, leaving the two women standing on the South Side opposite the SLH.

'Your Owen Philpott seems a kind man,' Ellie said. 'And unusual.'

'He is, but how do you mean exactly?'

'He showed us the shaft head entrance and told us about Jane's body being taken to the SLH, even though he thought we were meddling,' Ellie said. 'A lot of people would have told us to mind our own business and walked off.' She smiled mischievously. 'He certainly seems to like you.'

'At one point, after Paul died, I did wonder... though he's a bit old for me,' Faye said. 'Anyway, I didn't notice many admiring glances coming my way this morning. Rather more in your direction, I thought. He's an interesting man. He was a communist, fought in the Spanish Civil war, alongside female soldiers. He thinks women are just as competent, intelligent and capable as men are. It's a refreshing attitude.'

She liked him for it. It was a shame that she wasn't attracted to him.

'Men don't have to be communist to appreciate that women are all those things,' Ellie said. 'But I suppose society doesn't encourage it, that's what your Dr Yorke might say.'

'Be careful, Beryl's politics will be rubbing off on you.'

'I don't think there's any danger of my becoming a communist any time soon.'

'And he's no more *my* Dr Yorke than Owen is *my* Owen Philpott. Anyway, you seem to be able to get your way when it comes to persuading men to do your bidding.'

Ellie's full lips twisted into a wry grin. 'My friend Moira, the one who's training to be a lawyer, always says flattery works and, if it doesn't, to appeal to men's sense of chivalry, to be helpless. But then Moira's absolutely gorgeous and that helps.'

Faye contemplated her friend, with her big, violet-blue eyes, her flawless complexion and tumbling dark hair.

'It *is* a puzzle, an impossible one,' Ellie continued. 'How could Jane Cooper's body be placed behind a locked door when only Owen Philpott has a key? Unless he put her there?'

'Hmm, the police will have checked his alibi, I'm sure, but I'll ask John.'

'You've spoken with John about this?'

'I mentioned it to him.' Faye said no more, she wasn't keen to share John's views on amateur sleuthing with Ellie.

A group of porters waved and shouted a greeting; they were moving new beds up the ramp into the front door. Ellie waved in response.

'A couple of the porters helped me get my things yesterday, with the van,' she said. 'Les Allen was really helpful and very kind.'

'Good.'

'He takes good care of the porters, doesn't he. And takes all the joking and ribaldry in good part.'

'I don't think he has much choice.'

'They're fond of him, I think.'

The two women entered the hospital through the ground floor door.

'Do we have time to visit the path lab before we're needed in the canteen?'

Faye consulted her watch.

'I think so. If we can persuade someone to let us in.' She led Ellie into the older part of the hospital. 'Dr Horn, the pathologist, is new here, so she's an unknown quantity. I pointed her out to you on Monday. But the technician is a local man, Charlie Redmond. He joined us when he was invalided out of the army. He's an awkward so-and-so, hasn't been the same since he was sent back from the Battle of the Bulge. I think it might test even your powers of persuasion to get us inside.'

'I can but try.'

17

FAYE

In all her years at the SLH Faye had never visited the Pathology Laboratory. It sat next to the mortuary and chapel in the Victorian part of the hospital. She was curious about it and was also intrigued to see if Ellie's charm would work on Charlie Redmond.

Redmond was a thin-faced thirty-year-old with deep-set eyes, a sallow skin and a permanent scowl. The left sleeve of his overalls was pinned together above the elbow. Undaunted, Ellie launched into her tale about hearing the scream in the middle of the night and feeling involved in what happened. Faye watched closely as Redmond's initial hostility softened and his scowl was replaced by a look of interest and even a smile. He was captivated.

How did she do it? The slight tilt of the head, the lips curved into a half-smile. Those big blue eyes were opened wide, luminous and sparkling, fixed on the object of their attention. She was physically beautiful, but there was something else too, a power, an aura which men didn't seem able to resist. There was something inherently glossy and sleek about Ellie, curvaceous, rounded and yielding. Above all, there was a sense of fun bubbling not far beneath her surface.

Not like me, Faye reflected, ruefully. All angles and arguments.

'So we'd like to pay our respects,' Ellie drew to a conclusion.

'I'm not supposed to let people in,' said Redmond, but he was already leading them towards the double doors to the mortuary, where, they'd learned, Jane's body was being kept. 'But I'll make an exception for you, Ellie – and Faye of course.'

Faye had to stop herself from glaring at him. Cheeky sod, it was Miss Smith and Miss Peveril to him, as well he knew.

The room beyond the doors was windowless and dark, it echoed as one of the doors hit the wall when Redmond pushed them open. He pressed a series of switches and a large space was illuminated by harsh, fluorescent ceiling lights. Brick walls painted a clotted cream carried heavy water pipes at waist level to feed sinks and sluices. Faye shivered. Whatever the temperature was outside, in here it was always winter.

In the centre of the room three metal tables were bolted to the floor above a narrow channel running from one side of the room to the other. For carrying the blood from the corpses, she realised. Two of the tables held forms draped with white sheets.

Redmond pointed to the second. 'That's Jane Cooper,' he said.

'Thank you.' Faye dismissed him. She didn't want him staring at a naked Jane while they examined her body.

For a second it seemed as if he wasn't going to go, but he must have thought better of trying to stay. His footsteps echoed on the flagstones on the floor.

She waited until she'd heard the doors close before folding back the sheet to reveal the dead woman's head and shoulders. Jane's red hair was dark against her skin, even paler now than normal.

'Like Millais' *Ophelia*,' Ellie said. 'Except she didn't drown.'

It was immediately apparent that Jane had been strangled, her neck was black and purple and her shoulders too were bruised.

'It's like someone gripped her by her shoulders and upper arms,' Faye said.

'And someone's struck her.' Ellie said. 'Very hard.'

The skin across Jane's left cheekbone was split. Such violence, when there had already been so much. Faye had thought any appetite for brutality had been exhausted, but, in this room of death, it seemed otherwise.

Screwing up her face in distaste Faye raised Jane's right wrist. The skin was cold and clammy to the touch, the fingernails were broken and the flesh on the fingertips red and raw.

'She was scratching, clawing at something.'

'Her other hand's the same,' Ellie said, lifting the sheet. 'Her attacker must bear scratch marks. Something the police will be on the lookout for. Did she try to fight them off?'

There was a clang as the doors to the mortuary flew open.

'What's going on here?' Dr Horn, the pathologist, strode into the room. 'No one should be in here without my knowledge or agreement.'

She was considerably shorter than both Faye and Ellie, but indignation at finding her domain intruded upon added at least a foot to her height.

'I'm sorry, Dr Horn,' Faye began to explain. 'My colleague and I—'

'Out, now!' The pathologist pointed to the door.

'She didn't get these bruises in the quarrel I saw,' Ellie said.

'What? Did you see her, arguing with someone?' Dr Horn stared at Ellie. 'Have you told the police?'

'My friend here saw a disagreement between a man and a woman from the window of her flat overlooking Clapham Common late Sunday night or early Monday morning,' Faye said. 'We went to Cavendish Road station yesterday; Scotland Yard was already there.'

The pathologist raised an eyebrow, but she no longer urged them to leave.

'We saw an Inspector Irving.'

'Irving!' Dr Horn shook her head.

Did the pathologist know him, Faye wondered. Otherwise, why react like that? She had a hunch...

'Dr Horn,' Faye asked. 'Were you a police pathologist during the war?'

'That's a very good guess, Miss Smith, or did you happen to know?'

'It was a guess.' Faye answered.

As a pathologist Dr Horn would be used to violent death, but, as a police pathologist, she would be used to investigations too. If they told her what they knew, she might be able to help.

'When I saw Jane – the woman – I didn't see the man strike or slap her,' Ellie said.

'I'd say she was punched, not slapped,' the pathologist said in a matter-of-fact voice.

'That wasn't what I saw.'

'Jane's body was discovered inside the locked door to the shaft head of the deep level shelters on the common. Near where Ellie saw the argument take place. So we think it *was* Jane who Ellie saw. We didn't know cause of death.'

'Strangulation.' The pathologist walked to the table. 'After a violent fight, but what did you see?'

'It wasn't a physical fight.' Ellie shook her head. 'There were shouts and I heard a scream, but they were out of my sight when I heard that.'

'The beating must have happened afterwards,' Faye said.

'Though it appears that, at some point that night, Miss Cooper had sexual intercourse with someone. There is semen.'

'Oh.'

Faye hadn't expected that, but then she wasn't party to Jane's private life.

'Was she raped?' Ellie asked.

'I don't know, it's possible. Or she had intense sex with a lover who then beat and killed her. Or a third possibility is that she left him after coitus and was then unlucky enough to cross the path of the person who killed her. Unlikely, perhaps, but not impossible.'

'And the physical evidence... of the sexual activity?' Faye asked.

'Isn't definitive.'

Not a lot of help then, but an added complication.

The doors to the mortuary opened again. This time Matron

walked in, attended by an anxious Charlie Redmond, who was scowling once more.

'You may go now, Mr Redmond,' Matron said, without turning, and waited for him to leave. She acknowledged Faye and Ellie 'Miss Smith, Miss...'

'Peveril.'

She walked over to the mortuary table and looked down at Jane's body.

'This shouldn't have happened,' she said, sighing. 'And it certainly shouldn't have happened so close to the hospital. None of us will feel safe until her killer is apprehended.' She turned her gaze to Faye. 'Why are you here?'

'My colleague saw and heard Jane, outside Westbury Court, on the night she died,' Faye ventured. 'We told Scotland Yard, but they didn't take much notice of us. They think Jane may have been killed by an itinerant.'

'It wasn't a vagrant I saw her with,' Ellie said. 'She was with a man she knew.'

Matron looked at Dr Horn, who sighed.

'Inspector Irving is in charge of the case,' she said. 'He should have retired, but the war... He's overwhelmed with work and has few support officers.'

'A witness saw someone on the common, who they thought was a vagrant, behaving suspiciously,' Faye said. 'And I can see that that needs checking, but what Ellie saw needs to be followed up too and Inspector Irving doesn't seem interested.'

'He'll probably want to close this down as soon as he can,' Dr Horn said. 'If there's any evidence to support the theory that the killer has moved on, he'll grab it with both hands.'

And there would be no justice for Jane, Faye thought.

'Hmmm, leaving the real culprit free to kill again. I am responsible for the safety and welfare of the staff here, so identifying Jane's killer must be of paramount importance. If this case isn't resolved soon there may be worse to come,' Matron said. 'I'm also mindful of damage to the reputation of the SLH. So any details will remain strictly *entre nous*, no talking to the press.'

Matron was right, it could be worse, especially given what they had just learned from Dr Horn. If the newspapers got hold of that information, it would be open season on Jane's personal life. A nurse 'no better than she should be' had been beaten, possibly raped and killed. The proximity of Jane's death to her place of employment, a women-only institution, led by women – some of the papers could have a field day with that one. Retired colonels would be writing to the letters page to denounce such an aberration.

'The whole case makes me decidedly uncomfortable.' Matron turned to Ellie. 'Could we offer the inspector some more help? Is there anything that you saw or heard which seems important now that you know more?'

'I… I don't know. I'd have to think about it,' Ellie responded.

'We can do that later today,' Faye jumped in, quickly.

'Good. But keep me informed and, whatever you do, take care to keep on the right side of the police. I don't want the commissioner getting involved.'

'Yes, ma'am.'

18

FAYE

'Let's go through the events of Sunday night again,' Faye began. 'First of all, tell me exactly what you heard. See if it will jog your memory. There may be something you've forgotten, something which might help the police, or point them in the right direction.'

It was relatively quiet in the canteen. The two women sat at one of the tables, Faye with a pen and notepad.

'I don't know exactly what woke me,' Ellie said.

'Did Beryl hear anything?'

'No. But I could ask the other residents, I suppose.'

'You're new; they don't know you. I suggest you persuade the caretaker to ask them for you.'

'Good point. I will. Once I looked out of the window…'

'Concentrate on what you heard first, separate the sounds from the sights.'

Ellie closed her eyes. 'I heard the growl of the engine of a van driving along the South Side. Its note changed as it slowed and turned into the road just before you get to the hospital.'

'There was no other sound, no voices?'

'Actually, yes, now you mention it, I could hear something. There were two voices. I think the couple were talking, though I could hardly hear them at first.'

'Who was clearer, the man or the woman?'

'The woman. Her voice became louder; she was talking quickly and quite urgently. Then the man, but his voice was lower, more indistinct, until he shouted.'

'Hmm, now, try and recall exactly what you saw, like you did with the sounds. Picture them. Where did you say they were?'

'At first they were beneath the trees by the deep shelter building. They were embracing.'

Faye sat forward on her seat. 'Embracing? Not struggling?'

'I… I think embracing, not struggling. In a clinch, I thought at the time.'

'Good. Now, what did they look like?'

'I couldn't see them clearly. The branches of the trees were in the way, moving in the wind. They were just two figures.'

'That's quite a long way from Westbury Court and you're on the fourth floor, but you heard their voices?'

'Yes, though I couldn't tell what they were saying.'

'Alright, but they couldn't have been whispering. What happened next?'

'I didn't see exactly, but the woman began to hurry through the trees, towards my building,' Ellie continued. 'She must have been moving quite quickly because her cape flapped, that's how I know she was a nurse.'

'Was she still talking?'

'No.'

'And…'

'The man started after her. He was hurrying, but not running. He… he was striding out; I think he had long legs and I heard him shouting. I tried to see the woman again, but I'd lost sight of her. And then I lost sight of him too.'

'Right. So, the police should be looking for a tall, or tallish, man,' Faye said. 'That's something new we can tell them.'

'If they'll even listen to me. They didn't really take what I told them seriously last time, were more interested in who I was and why I was here than what I saw. They're looking for a tramp and I've told them that the man I saw wasn't a tramp.'

Faye sighed. 'Alright, but let's see if you can remember anything else. The more information we have, the more likely it is that we'll get their attention. Now, think. Was the man wearing a coat? A hat?'

'A coat, but not a hat. I'd have noticed a hat.' Ellie frowned.

'And you thought they were lovers quarrelling?'

'It seemed so. I was tired and it was cold. I'd had a long day and not much sleep the night before, so I wasn't exactly concerned about them. I just wanted my bed. But then I heard the scream, the cry, whatever it was. That's when I should have opened the window and seen where they went.'

'What was it exactly? How did it sound?'

Ellie was thinking, concentrating, with her eyes closed again.

'It was a scream,' she said. 'And it came from near the base of Westbury Court. I'm pretty sure about that.'

'Could the couple have come into your building?'

'I... I don't know. I don't think so, but I can check with the caretaker. I assumed that they were heading for the underground.'

'Except it would have been closed at that time of night.'

'Yes, but I didn't think about that at the time.'

'So, Jane screamed. What does this tell us?'

'That she was frightened? That her lover threatened her, or struck her?'

'Maybe. If the midnight man was her lover.' Faye frowned in frustration. 'We don't have enough information. But the police should be looking for him, he's a witness to Jane's whereabouts that night, even if he isn't her killer.'

'I'm sorry, I'm not a lot of help.'

'But you are. Now, let's think about this,' Faye said. 'Consider the police theory – could the man with Jane have been the itinerant or workman seen earlier on the common, who ran away when challenged?'

'The man I saw didn't look like a tramp. He was a tidy figure, wearing a heavy overcoat, not a peddler's clothes, either. Besides, why would Jane be canoodling with a tramp?'

Good question, thought Faye, though it mightn't be impossible – an old friend down on his luck, perhaps.

'That man could be anywhere by now,' Ellie said. 'They'll never find him.'

'Maybe, but on Sunday night he was here,' Faye said. 'It was freezing at midnight on Sunday. Wouldn't a tramp have found himself as warm a hidey hole as possible and stayed there? There are still bomb sites that would provide some shelter. He wouldn't have gone wandering around the common at that hour. And a workman wouldn't be out at that time, either, he would be in his digs.'

'Unless he worked somewhere that was open round the clock.'

'Like the SLH.' Faye paused. 'But you can count the number of men who work here on one hand. Could it have been a serviceman? Was he wearing a uniform?'

'No. At least, I don't think so.'

'Hmm. Whoever it was, they managed to put Jane's body into that building, through a locked door, the only key to which is in the possession of Owen Philpott?'

'It's a complete mystery. The door was locked.'

'Though, ask yourself, why hide the body there at all? There are better places to hide a corpse. Why didn't the killer hide it out on the common, under some branches and dead leaves away from the roads? It might take longer to be found. It's just not logical.'

'Perhaps the killer didn't know about Owen Philpott doing his regular rounds?' Ellie suggested, then her face fell. 'But then how would he know about the shaft head? And how would he get through a locked door? You're right, it doesn't make any sense.'

Faye struck the table in frustration. There was something missing, something at the back of her mind. A piece of information, she knew was there, but it wouldn't come to her.

The canteen door swung open. It was Miss Barnett, the hospital administrator, Faye's boss. She ran the non-medical side of the hospital with precise efficiency and was a formidable presence in twinset and pearls.

Both younger women stood.

'I'll go and replenish the stores,' Ellie said quickly, and started to leave.

'Well done with yesterday's luncheon, Miss Peveril,' Miss Barnett said, as Ellie passed her. 'That was excellent work.'

'Thank you.'

'She's a real asset,' the older woman said, once the door had closed behind Ellie. 'Your instincts were correct. Well done.'

'Thank you. She's used to hospitals,' Faye replied. 'Her mother worked in Worcester Infirmary during the war. But Ellie won't stay long. She's got bigger fish to fry.'

'Speaking of bigger fish, Faye, I'm still expecting your response to my letter.' Miss Barnett sounded tetchy, her voice querulous. 'This is an important step I'm offering you.'

'I know and I'm going to take you up on it,' she said quickly, her mind whirring. Now the VIP lunch was over she could answer Miss Barnett's letter as planned. 'There's just one thing – I was hoping to discuss it with my family. I wanted to check that was alright with you, given that you emphasised the need for secrecy. I live at home, as you know and the new job would probably mean longer hours, which would disrupt their lives too.'

'It's not exactly secret, merely requiring the usual discretion about such professional matters,' Miss Barnett replied. 'You're in Sugden Road, aren't you?'

Faye nodded, relieved that Miss Barnett seemed to have accepted her explanation.

'It's quite close by, but we would offer you overnight accommodation if you needed it. After... recent events... Matron and I are anxious that none of our staff are put in harm's way. As things are, the nurses who live off-site shouldn't go to and from their lodgings unaccompanied.'

'That might be difficult for some,' Faye said.

'I know, but we'll do what we can to help. I'm having a back gate opened up from the hospital grounds into Hazelbourne Road. The nurses who lodge there can have a key. It's closing the stable door after the horse has bolted, but at least we can try to ensure that it doesn't happen again.'

Keys, keys, this mystery is all to do with keys, Faye thought.

'I'll speak with my family tonight.'

'Very well,' Miss Barnett said. 'Your family is important, but remember, so is the SLH. We like to think of ourselves as a family too, so, if you're one of us you owe loyalty to the hospital and the people who run it.'

Faye bridled at the homily, though she didn't let it show. She'd always been loyal to the SLH, she didn't need reminding. She had also been loyal to Miss Barnett personally, eschewing the giggling speculation indulged in by some of the younger staff about the prim and proper administrator. She always had the interests of the hospital at heart, that was why she was doing what she was doing.

Miss Barnett's voice grated as she turned to leave. 'Leave it too late and someone more suitable might come along in the meanwhile.'

'Thank you,' Faye said. 'I won't. I promise.'

19

FAYE

The frosty pavement glittered in the light from the street lamps.

Faye thrust her gloved hands deeper into the pockets of her overcoat, as, beside her, Ellie drew the collar of her greatcoat up higher around her neck. It was bitterly cold, yet winter had only just begun. Their breath formed clouds as they walked over to the squat pillbox structure, invisibly drawn to the place where Jane's body had been found. Commuters were hurrying past, anxious to get home and uninterested in the two women loitering on the pavement.

'Jane was strangled somewhere near here, after she'd had intercourse with a man, who may or may not have been her killer.' Faye thought aloud as she gazed at the shaft head building.

'Could that have been the motive for killing her – a sexual encounter that went wrong?' Ellie speculated. She glanced up at her own dark window in Westbury Court. 'Perhaps she didn't want to. Maybe that was the reason for their argument and he pursued and forced her, then had to kill her to cover up what he'd done.'

'That's one possibility,' Faye replied. 'But only one. The problem is we don't know much about Jane herself. I often saw her, but what do I really know about her?'

'She was with a man; was that her boyfriend?' Ellie asked.

'Did she have a boyfriend? How did she spend her free time? Who were her closest friends? I know she came from up north somewhere and didn't have family in Clapham.'

'The nurses would know more,' Ellie suggested. 'I'll ask Beryl.'

As they turned away from the shaft head building Faye recalled the bruises and the split skin of Jane's face; the bloodied, broken fingernails. There had been so much violent death. But not now, now the war was over, this shouldn't be happening now.

Outside the door to Westbury Court, they stopped.

'I think I'll walk home along the Lane tonight, even though it's the long way around,' Faye said. 'I don't fancy being on a badly lit road on the common tonight.'

'Faye, before you go.' Ellie reached out a gloved hand. 'Something's been irritating me all day. It's trivial, I know, but...'

'Ye–es?'

'It's about the names of the shelters. Inside the entrance this morning there was a sign on the wall, remember, pointing to shelters named after British admirals. Now, this might seem like a silly question, but, what about Admiral Nelson? He's probably the most famous British admiral of all time, but his name wasn't on that list. Didn't they name a shelter for him?'

Faye stared at her friend until Ellie began to look troubled by it.

'They did, Ellie!' she cried, clapping her hand to her forehead. 'They did! Stupid me! I must be losing my marbles!'

She began to pace back and forth, her brain kicking into top gear.

'Jane's body was found at the top of the shaft on Clapham Common, but there's another shaft near here. On Balham Hill. Owen mentioned his office on Balham Hill this morning, that's where the second shaft head is, it's within the compound there. That's where the Nelson shelter is, it's one of the shelters entered from *that* shaft head.'

How could she have forgotten?

'There are two big deep shelters, not just one and there are two ways in as well. One leads to a shelter running beneath the north-bound Northern Line tunnel and the other leads to a shelter running beneath the southbound Northern Line tunnel.'

'But...?'

'And – this is the important thing – during the rocket raids the SLH had space in those shelters for patients. We used the Balham Hill entrance; it was less exposed than the one on the common. And, Ellie... we had our own key! Our own key!'

Faye reached out her gloved hands to Ellie, who stared at her, mouth open.

'Don't you see? I knew there was something I was missing! The SLH key! Owen has the only key to the entrance where Jane was found, but he's not the only one who can get into the deep shelters. The SLH key will open the other entrance!'

She began to pace once again.

'Where is that key now? We must find it and find out who could have used it. That must be the answer!'

'Unless it's been returned to Owen Philpott?'

'We must ask him. Tomorrow – he won't be there now.' Faye halted. 'Ellie, what if Jane's body hadn't been placed behind that door at all? Everyone has been assuming that her killer put it there, to hide it, even though it was impossible and didn't really make sense, but what if that wasn't the case?'

'Then how'd the body get there?'

'Maybe we've been thinking about this the wrong way? Jane could have got there herself, as alive as you or me. What if she'd been down in the shelters and was trying to find her way *out*? To the top of the stairs and out through that door.'

Ellie looked thoughtful, but Faye continued.

'If I recall... there's a link between the two major tunnels. You can go into the deep shelter system at the Balham Hill entrance and, if you know the way, you can find your way out at the common entrance.'

Ellie blinked. 'Are you saying that she was killed just there, inside that building?' She glanced back at the pillbox shaft head, her face paler.

'Exactly. Maybe Jane's body wasn't hidden there, maybe it wasn't placed there at all. Perhaps Jane had come *from inside* the deep shelters and was killed as she tried, desperately, to escape?'

20

FAYE

F aye strode along Sugden Road. There was mist in the night air, but in her mind the fog was clearing.

They'd been thinking about this all wrong. Jane could have been deep beneath the ground not just in the building at the surface. But why? Was it a clandestine romantic tryst? But then who did Ellie see her arguing with on the common and how did she get from there to the shelters?

She felt for her keys as she walked to the door of number nineteen. Keys were at the crux of the mystery. Who else had access to the SLH key to the deep level shelters? This could be bad news for the SLH so they needed to find out.

And they needed to find out more about Jane herself.

'I'm home!'

As she hung her coat on the hook, Faye noticed her father's overcoat and the coat of John's police uniform. Everyone would be at supper tonight. Just when she needed time to think! Just when she was getting somewhere.

In the kitchen, her mother was at the stove while John laid the table. Her father was sitting in the chair in the corner reading the *Evening Standard* and Phoebe sat next to the fire, coals glinting behind the fireguard.

Where had they come from? The depot?

Faye frowned but could hardly criticise. She also realised that she hadn't done anything more to find out about the streptomycin trial.

'Just in time,' Reg Smith said, truculently. 'Your mother's been holding off serving up, waiting for you.'

'You shouldn't have waited, Ma.'

'I didn't wait long, don't you mind your father,' Esme Smith replied, sharply through tightly compressed lips. 'Come and sit down now.'

Her parents had been arguing, Faye recognised the signs.

Esme brought the cooking pot over to the table and began to ladle out a thick stew.

'That looks good,' Faye said.

'Best scrag end, courtesy of Mari Evans' Welsh uncle,' Esme replied. 'She got back from Wales last weekend and brought some with her.'

'Black market, Ma?' John commented, sourly.

'Nonsense, she's just bringing what belongs to her family.'

'Does smell good though.' John drew up his chair and everyone sat at the table. For a while there was silence as the family ate.

'What's this new job then, Faye?' her brother asked, covertly glancing from their father to their mother as he brought his spoon up to his mouth.

So that was why they'd been at odds.

'It's the offer of a job,' she replied. 'Deputy hospital administrator. Now the war's over things are going back to normal and someone needs to oversee the office. I already do the records for the canteen and kitchens, so it makes sense to Miss Barnett that I take on the office as well. It's more responsibility, but more pay too.'

She ate a spoonful of stew and waited.

'It means longer hours, your mother said.' Reg glowered at her across the table.

'It's likely to.'

Faye knew, from experience, that her father would say what he'd got to say, regardless of any arguing on her part. It was best to just let him say it.

'So if you take it, we'll see even less of you than we do now.'

'Probably.'

'And what about more coming and going? If you live here, you eat here, with us, as a family.'

'Now, Dad...' Esme tried to interject.

'I probably won't be able to do that as much as I do now. Miss Barnett has said that I can have accommodation at the SLH when I can't get back here at night. Especially after what's happened.'

'That's another thing.' Reg was warming to the argument. 'What was that nurse doing that got her killed?'

'Reg!'

'She wasn't doing anything she didn't have a perfect right to do!'

'Dad, the girl was murdered,' John interjected.

Reg said nothing, knowing that he'd overstepped the mark, but Faye saw the anger still simmering behind his eyes. The others' condemnation made him worse. He had to be right all the time.

'This is a home, not a hotel,' Reg eventually said.

'John stays at the station house when he has to.'

'That's different and you know why.'

'Why? He's working, just like me.'

'John's a man. He can look after himself.'

It always came down to that. Different expectations of women, double standards.

'Dad, I'm twenty-seven years old, I'll be twenty-eight in April. I can vote, I have a responsible and well-paid job...'

'And still unmarried!'

That was at the heart of it; marriage, children, grandchildren.

'And, if I choose to, I might just stay that way! After all, it's up to me!'

'That's where working at that hospital gets you. A spinster, like all those women. You don't need to take this job; you need to think about having a family.'

'Reg!' Esme snapped. 'It's not her fault she's unmarried. And there's plenty of others in the same boat.'

Faye watched her father as he concentrated on eating. She believed that, at some level, he knew that she was going. That he could sense it. She was going beyond his reach and there was nothing he could do about it. A wave of tenderness for him washed over her.

'I'm going to take the job, Dad.'

'Not if you want to live in my house, you're not.'

'Then I'll live somewhere else. I don't want any pudding, thank you, Ma.'

'Then you go to your room, love,' Esme replied.

'I didn't say she could leave the table.'

'John'll bring you up a cup of tea in a minute.'

Faye rose. She caught John's eye. Phoebe stared into her empty bowl.

In the tiny room at the top of the house, she flung herself into the chair. In years gone by she'd have been crying into her pillow, tears of frustration and anger, but she was long past that. Now that the war was over she had her escape route planned.

There was a knock on her door and John entered, carrying two mugs of tea.

'He'll come round. He always does,' he said, squatting on the small footstool.

'I know. He's not a bad man and he loves me. But I'm going, John.'

'I know. So does he, he just doesn't want it to happen.'

'It's only a question of when.'

'At least wait until the fuss around this murder has died down. How's your new friend, by the way? I heard she got her stuff back.'

'Ellie? She's fine. Lodging in Beryl MacBride's spare bedroom.'

John looked over the top of his mug at his sister. 'Does she know?'

'What? That Beryl doesn't like men, in a physical way, prefers

125

women? No, I don't think so. Not that it should make any difference.'

'Well, no, but...'

'Stop sniggering!'

'I'm not!'

'Anyway, half the men in Clapham seem ready to fling themselves at Ellie's feet if she gives them so much as a glance.'

'She's a looker alright. Jealous, sis?'

Am I? she wondered.

'A bit. She's good company though.'

Tentatively, Faye began to tell him about what they had discovered about Jane Cooper's death.

'Sis, I told you—' he stood, shaking his head and turned to leave.

'Wait, listen, John. Has anyone thought that Jane might have been trying to get *out* of the shelters when she was killed?'

'Eh?'

Faye explained her theory, because that, she realised, was what it was, about the SLH key to the Balham Hill entrance.

'I don't know if it's still around,' she concluded. 'Whether or not we still have it or it's been returned to Owen Philpott, but there *is* another key. And if there's another key, Jane, or someone with her could have used it to get into the deep shelters.'

'Hmm, I knew that she was strangled and where her body was found,' John said, when she'd finished. 'But I never thought she might have been trying to get *out* of the place. Nobody did.'

'It's just a theory. We're going to speak with Owen tomorrow to see who had, or has, the additional key.'

'And when are you going to speak to the police about this? It's our job, sis. You shouldn't be doing it.'

'Scotland Yard's job. Trouble is, they're *not* doing it, or not doing it properly at any rate. This can't drag on, it's too upsetting and everyone's scared.'

'You need to tell them.'

'They took no notice of Ellie before, why would they listen to us now?' Faye argued. 'Besides, I'm afraid that at some point someone is going to start blaming the hospital.'

'That might be unavoidable.' John grimaced sympathetically. 'But you should tell them anyway.'

Faye stared into her mug of tea. 'I know,' she conceded reluctantly. 'I will.'

Then John laughed. 'The truth is you just can't resist a puzzle, can you?'

He was right. Faye acknowledged that, despite Matron's warning and John's disapproval she had begun to obsess over the case. She couldn't help it; she had that sort of brain; drawn to puzzles and mysteries. Yet it was none of her business; she really shouldn't get involved.

'I—'

'It's true. But be careful, sis, whoever killed Jane Cooper might still be around. You don't want to be drawing attention to yourself, or your friend. This is police work. It could be dangerous.'

'Hmm, even Owen said the police wouldn't have the resources to tackle it.'

'Owen is it now?' John raised an eyebrow.

'Tsch, don't be an idiot.'

'You could do worse.'

'Not you as well!'

John grinned. 'I'm serious, though. If the killer is still around, he won't be welcoming any amateur sleuthing. Be careful!'

'Don't worry, if we come across anything useful, we'll pass it on to Scotland Yard. Ellie's godfather is a chief superintendent there.'

'Ooooh.' John pulled a face, pretending to be overawed, but Faye could tell that, underneath, he was impressed.

'Shame they don't have lady detectives,' she said.

'You'd be good at that, right enough. Ah, well.' John slapped his hands on his knees and rose, taking Faye's empty cup from her hands. 'You staying up here?'

'Yep.'

'Right. 'Night then,' he said.

21

ELEANOR

'What do you know about Jane Cooper, Beryl?' Ellie asked as she placed the mugs on the draining board and emptied the sink.

'Nothing much.' Beryl was wiping up. 'I didn't have much to do with her, nor her friend. They weren't really my sort.'

'How do you mean?'

'They were lairy lasses, the head tossing type, you know what I mean. Lots of drama, sultry glances across a crowded room. All fur coat and no knickers, as my old ma would say.'

Ellie laughed. 'I've never heard that saying before.'

'Aye, well.' Beryl half-smiled. 'It beats saying 'outwardly respectable', though I don't think there was really any harm in them. It's probably just me being censorious – it's my Calvinist upbringing.'

'Calvinist...' Ellie's mouth snapped shut when she saw Beryl's sardonic expression. She was becoming familiar with the Scot's dry sense of humour, but sometimes it still caught her by surprise. 'Jane wasn't local, was she? From up north?'

'Yes.'

'She was in digs?'

'In Hazelbourne Road. Like her friend, until she took off.'

'Took off?'

'Aye. Polly Brooks, that was her name. Worked in the office. She knocked around with Jane for a while, they were inseparable. Did everything together. They lived in the same lodging house.'

'You didn't like her?'

'She was a flighty piece, not my cup of tea at all. Had long blonde hair, but not in the way that nature intended and didn't have any problem getting the peroxide, even in wartime. She was very aware of herself, fancied she looked like a film star.'

Ellie snorted. 'Which one?'

'Lana Turner, the blonde, but Polly was too brassy. Jane was more likeable and was genuinely striking, with her red hair. Anyhow, Polly came into some money I heard and went off without a by your leave. So much for friendship then. She wasn't from around here either.'

'Did either of them have a boyfriend?'

'Don't think so, not usually, they were too full of themselves. Although recently Polly started walking out with Les Allen, the head porter. Les was devastated when she left, apparently.'

'And Jane, did she have a regular beau?'

'Not as I know of.' Beryl put the last item in the cupboard. 'But then, why would I know? That was their business, not mine. Right, I'd better be off soon. I'm on the night shift. Are you coming over to celebrate?'

'Celebrate?'

'Parliament passed the NHS Act today. Free healthcare for all, paid for by people's taxes. Something to celebrate. There's booze in the nurses' home, top floor.'

'Does Matron know?'

'I wouldna think so, would you? Though sometimes I think she knows more than she lets on.'

'Yes, I'll come over. Why not?'

'See you later, then.'

Ellie followed Beryl through to the tiny hallway. 'Actually, on your way there's one more thing you could help me with, if you would?'

'Of course, if I can. What is it?'

Five minutes later Ellie was leaning out of her bedroom window looking down at Beryl who was standing on the other side of Nightingale Lane, beyond the poplars.

'Can you hear me?' Beryl called.

'Yes, go further away.'

'What's going on here then?' Ron, the Westbury Court caretaker, came out of the building to stand in the light from the street lamps, glancing from Beryl to Ellie.

'We're doing an experiment, recreating the conditions from Sunday night,' Ellie shouted down.

'Eh?'

'You can help – you can be the man. Go with Beryl and stand under those trees, then start talking to each other.'

'Come on, Ron,' Beryl called, beckoning him.

Ellie watched as they walked towards the deep level shelter shaft head building, then stopped. In the light from the South Side, she could see from their gestures that they were speaking, but she couldn't hear them at all. There was some traffic, but not sufficient to cause constant noise.

'I can't hear anything!' she yelled at them.

'How 'bout now?'

'That's better, I can hear you if you shout, Beryl. What about you, Ron?'

She heard a lower voice speaking, but not what it said. That was it. Just like on Sunday night.

'Super. Now come towards the end of Westbury Court and keep talking.'

Beryl and Ron did as she asked and their voices became more distinct, but she couldn't make out the words unless they shouted. That sounded about right.

'Right, now scream, Beryl.'

'Bloody hell! Not right in my ear!'

Beryl snorted with laughter.

'"*What light from yonder window breaks?*"' It was a male voice from the lane below.

Ellie stretched further out of the window and saw the speaker standing in the lamplight, a man with wavy black hair, muffled in a great coat and gloves. He was gesturing up at her.

'"*It is the east and Juliet is the sun...*"'

Beryl and Ron had stopped to watch. Beryl started to laugh again.

'Antoine, what are you playing at?'

'I'm being Romeo,' the man replied. 'If the fair lady would deign to notice me? "*Arise fair sun and kill the envious moon.*" A poor suitor reciting beneath her balcony, or, in this case, window.'

'We're in south London, not Verona!' Beryl said, laughing.

'Introduce us,' the new arrival demanded of her.

'Miss Ellie Peveril, Dr Antoine Girard.' She pronounced it 'Gerard'.

'Pleased to meet you, Dr Girard,' Ellie said in her best French accent.

'Ah, a British woman who doesn't murder my name. I'm smitten already.' He placed both hands on his breast and assumed a tender expression. 'Are you coming to our party?'

'It's a party now, is it?' Beryl commented.

'Party?' Ron asked. 'What party?'

'Not here, Ron, you don't have to worry,' Beryl said. 'Over at the SLH.'

'What time's that start, then?'

'Any time soon. Ellie, have you finished? I'll have to go if I'm going to say hello to everyone before my shift starts.'

'Yes, thanks, Beryl. And thanks, Ron. I'll be down in a minute.'

'*Adieu*, lovely lady,' the Frenchman made a mock bow. 'Come to the party. Let me toast you in champagne.'

'Vinegary beer, more like. Come on.' Beryl grabbed his arm and pulled him towards the SLH. 'And stop being an idiot.'

Laughing, Ellie closed the window and watched them leave. As she went to draw her curtains, she noticed a man standing outside the tube station, hand in pockets, his collar pulled up against the cold and a hat pulled down low on his head. Probably waiting for his date. She smiled, wondering how long he'd been there and if he thought they'd gone doolally.

At least now she knew that the unknown couple from the other night had certainly gone towards the other end of Westbury Court, away from the tube station and the South Side. She would talk it through with Faye at work tomorrow. Maybe they should go back to the police; this was new information. The police ought to know about it, and Faye's idea of how Jane had got into the deep shelters in the first place. Perhaps this time they would listen.

22

ELEANOR

Ellie glanced at her reflection in the long mirror and straightened her blouse and skirt, then reached in the cupboard for a long-sleeved blue dress, holding it against herself. The colour matched her eyes.

Why not? she thought. It's a party.

She removed her outer clothing and turned sideways to the mirror, feeling her tummy, probing the flesh. It was flat, like it usually was. She could feel nothing unusual. Her breasts were full and round, but then, that had always been the case, even on the ration. As for food cravings – she was as hungry as everyone else.

The sixth day without bleeding, but no other signs. Would there be?

Yet again she calculated the timeframe. She and Moira had joined the British delegation in Nuremberg in January and she'd met her American in spring. It was only in late September, after six-months of growing ever closer, that they had become lovers. She was fond of him, but, she'd realised quite quickly, not in love. She'd known he was married, that there would be no strings, but that had suited her. Now he was back in Connecticut with his wife and son and she was six days late.

There was one way to know for certain. She was working at a

hospital, after all. All she had to do was ask a doctor for help. It would end the anxiety, but... it might ruin everything. She'd have to decide what to do.

Could she go back to Worcester if she was pregnant?

The dean's unmarried daughter – there would be such a scandal. Perhaps she could go for a visit soon, before she showed, then return to London to have the baby quietly and give it up for adoption; her parents, and her father's congregation, need never know. There were private clinics, expensive ones, that could help a woman who found herself in a situation like hers. She didn't have many savings, but she could borrow some, maybe.

She shook her head – she didn't want to find out. She didn't want to have to face it.

Ellie pulled on the dress and smoothed it down. It was closely fitted and lay tight on her hips, flaring out to accentuate her figure. She knew it suited her. Reaching into her small jewellery box she drew out a beaded necklace. Lapis lazuli, a present from Pat.

If she was pregnant a husband would be very useful. Had ending their relationship been a mistake? No, she wasn't about to marry a man she didn't love to save her reputation. And there was no point in moping. Either she was pregnant or she wasn't. She'd find out soon enough.

Sufficient unto the day is the evil thereof.

Tonight, she would enjoy herself. She clipped on the matching earrings, brushed her hair, pinched her cheeks and smiled at herself in the mirror. She didn't look too bad.

As she ran the nub of lipstick over her lips, she considered who would be at the party. Lots of nurses, Jane's colleagues. She would ask about Jane Cooper and her friend Polly Brooks; plenty of people would have known them both. Better than Beryl had, perhaps. And there was the charming Frenchman to meet.

Ellie slipped on her greatcoat and swept up her keys as she left the flat. She wouldn't stay late, she had a couple of meetings in the Temple tomorrow, friends of Moira's. But it had been a long time since she'd been to a party.

When she stepped from the lift into the small, polished marble lobby of Westbury Court Ron was hovering. He had a tartan scarf wrapped around his neck and an oversized bottle of beer in his hand.

'Thought I might come along,' he said, hopefully. 'There's nobody'll want me for an hour or so.'

She could hardly say no. 'Alright.'

They walked out on to Nightingale Lane.

'Just a minute, please, Ron,' she said as he made to turn to the right. 'I want to check something.'

Ellie walked alongside the building in the opposite direction, to the lawned area she had seen from her window. The lawn belonged to a flat-fronted, three-storey, rambling Victorian pile with a classical portico. It was in decent repair, but had a dishevelled air about it, a building that wasn't loved, even if it was reasonably well maintained. An institution of some kind. Ron joined her as she looked at it.

'That's the station house,' he said.

'A police station house?'

'Yes, somewhere for the coppers who aren't from around here to live. There's been a shortage of coppers 'cause of the war. The Met tries to recruit from among local people, but sometimes they can't get the numbers, so they take on folk from outside. Then they have to provide housing for them. It's a bit like your nurses' home, but for coppers.'

That would explain why Matron rules the nurses' home with a rod of iron, she thought. Lots of young men and young women in close proximity and far from home.

But... could Jane have been going to the station house? To the police?

'Do you know, is there a reception? Somewhere for people to call in?'

Ron shrugged. 'Don't think so. The proper police station's down Cavendish Road.'

Could someone at the station house have heard what had

happened out on the common late on Sunday? Faye could ask her brother to inquire.

'We going to this party, then?' Ron was getting impatient.

'Yes, alright.'

Ellie and Ron walked back along the pavement to the South Side. The man who'd been waiting outside the tube station had gone, perhaps his date had turned up, either that or he'd given up and gone home. He wouldn't be hanging around in the cold.

'What was all that about before then? The screaming and such,' Ron asked.

Once again, Ellie explained what she had seen and heard on Sunday night or Monday morning.

'And it was that nurse you saw, the one who was murdered?'

'I think so. Tonight was an experiment,' she said. 'To try and recreate what I heard. Did you notice anything going on in the early hours of Monday?'

'Me, no. But I often has a kip in the early hours. Can't keep awake twenty-four hours a day. I'd have seen 'em if they'd have come into Westbury Court though.'

'Would you ask the other residents, just in case anyone heard the same or something similar to me?' She bestowed a smile on him. 'It would be really helpful.'

'Yeah, course I'll do that,' he answered, cheering up.

As they crossed the South Side Ellie spotted Charlie Redmond up ahead, just beyond the ramp to the front entrance. He was speaking with another man and seemed to be giving him some money. As Ellie and Ron approached, he glanced across at them and slipped out of sight behind the ramp.

'What's old Charlie after now?' Ron speculated. 'Talking to George Packham. He's a rogue if ever there was one.'

So that was the elusive George Packham. A solid chap, trilby pulled low and shadowing his eyes. Ellie saw a long nose and a small mouth beneath a moustache. His hands moved quickly as he pocketed the notes given him by Redmond.

'The war did for Charlie as surely as if he'd copped it,' Ron was continuing. 'Left him without an arm but buggered up his mind as well. Poor sod.'

'What do you mean? Shell shock? Combat stress?'

'I don't know what it's called, but he won't be right again. Like plenty of others.'

Too many, Ellie thought.

'What was your regiment, Ron?'

'I was a Surrey, Queen Mary's Own, North Africa, then Italy. Wasn't pretty.' Ron's thin face grew sombre. 'Wasn't pretty at all. Though there was some who managed to keep themselves out of things altogether.'

He was looking up the ramp and Ellie followed his gaze. Les Allen was directing the two delivery boys and a porter with a large, wheeled casket into the hospital entrance. As she watched, Les glanced down at Charlie and George Packham with a look of severe disapproval on his face.

What did Ron mean by that?

'Now, where's this party? he asked.

23

ELEANOR

'Drink, Ellie?' A nurse standing at the kitchen table swept her hand above an array of bottles.

'Yes, please.'

'Hey!' The nurse remonstrated at someone jogging her elbow as she handed Ellie a paper cup of brownish coloured liquid.

The little kitchen was full, mostly with nurses, though there were a surprising number of young men for a women-only hospital. Ellie suspected that many of them were off duty policemen from the station house. Perhaps one or two romances might begin tonight. Youth would have its way.

She and Ron had walked through the hospital grounds to the nurses' home at the rear. The party was being held in the top floor dormitory, as far from Matron's ground floor apartment as it was possible to get. Beds were pushed against the walls and couples danced to music from a wireless. A banner made from a bedsheet, bearing the letters 'NHS' had been slung from the ceiling.

Ellie scanned the room, but there was no sign of Beryl, who'd probably already left to begin her shift. Ron had been swallowed up by the crowd. She noticed a couple of nurses chatting by the sink who she recognised. They might have known Jane Cooper.

'Hello. This seems like a good party,' she said as she joined them.

'Not bad,' said the first in a lilting Welsh accent.

'Though it seems strange to be celebrating after what's happened. Were you friends of Jane Cooper?'

'I suppose you could say so,' said the second.

'Not really,' the other added. 'She was close to Polly Brooks. They went about together all the time.'

'Til Polly took up with Les.' The second nurse raised her beer bottle to indicate the tall head porter, who was gradually making his way through the crowd to the drinks, greeting everyone on his way.

'Popular chap,' Ellie said.

'Oh yes. Les is popular, alright. Though Polly put Jane's nose out of joint a bit when she started walking out with him.'

'She left suddenly, didn't she? Polly, I mean.' Ellie prompted.

'Yes. Didn't say anything to any of us. Not that we knew her well. She worked in the office.'

'D'you know why she left?'

'She'd come into some money,' the Welsh nurse said. 'Couldn't wait to spend it, if you ask me, was splashing the cash all over.'

'Les was pretty cut up about it, I think, when she went. Quite a glamorous catch for him. And no one likes being dumped. It won't be easy for him to find another girl now that the boys are back again.' She gave a sympathetic frown.

'So why'd she leave?'

'Dunno. Not our business. What was odd, though,' the Welsh nurse added, 'was that Jane was convinced that something had happened to Polly, that some sort of evil had befallen her.'

'Only because Polly didn't tell Jane she was leaving,' the other said. 'Jane never could bear to be the last to know something. She was such a gossip. She was just trying to save face.'

'God rest her.'

In the lull in conversation which followed Ellie could hear big band music from the dormitory.

'Well, well, who do we have here then?' Les Allen's low and pleasant voice cut across the awkward atmosphere. 'You got your stuff back alright, I hear.' He was clutching a bottle of pale ale.

The two nurses moved away and Ellie slid into the space they'd vacated, as did Les. He was broad-shouldered and well-muscled; he was a rower she recalled. He looked fit, but his movement was a little awkward. Somehow, he seemed older than many of the young men at the party, though he was only in his late twenties or early thirties.

She recalled the comment from Ron, the building caretaker and it occurred to Ellie that the end of the war hadn't only meant a huge change for the women who stayed at home, but for the men who stayed at home too. Through no fault of their own, men like Les Allen would be resented and suspected, as men who didn't fight. It would take years to eradicate the difference between those who fought and those who stayed at home; if it ever happened.

'Yes, thanks for the help. And yes, before you ask, my things were all there.'

'Good. Glad to be of service. You're up from the country, aren't you? Deepest Worcestershire?'

'Yes, but how do you know that? Who's been talking?' Ellie smiled but wondered if she really was the subject of gossip. It was only natural, she supposed, given her recent arrival, but it made her uncomfortable given her circumstances. She remembered Faye saying that Les was a gossip.

'Not much goes on here without I get to hear about it,' Les answered with a twinkle in his pale grey eyes. Then he confessed. 'Actually, your home address was on a luggage sticker on your trunk.'

'Ah.' She half-laughed.

'There was one for an address in Belgravia as well and for a hotel address in Germany, in Nuremberg. Did you go to the trials?'

'I was a legal clerk with the British delegation.'

'So how'd you end up working in the canteen at the SLH then?'

'Long story. What about you? How'd you end up working in a women-only hospital?'

'Just as long a story, only far less intriguing than yours, I'll bet.'

He waited for her to reply and, when she didn't, went on. 'But I suppose it's none of my business. I shouldn't be so nosy.'

Mind your own affairs. Thessalonians, chapter four, verse eleven. It was one of her father's favourite admonitions.

'I'll forgive you,' she said, pushing herself away from the sink. 'But I'd like to go and watch the dancing. You coming?'

'I don't dance, myself.' His face grew serious. 'So I don't watch.'

Of course, he probably couldn't!

Ellie cursed herself for being inconsiderate and insensitive. She gave him what she hoped was a sympathetic smile. What else could she say? She began to edge her way through the crowd and out of the kitchen.

In the dormitory people were watching the dancers. Ellie joined them. She took a sip of her drink and grimaced; Beryl had been right, it tasted like vinegar.

'Ah, my Juliet.' The Frenchman from earlier that evening came to stand at her side. He wore the uniform of one of the Free French battalions, but the red cross badge marked him out as a medic. 'Are you enjoying yourself?'

'Yes, thank you, are you?'

'I am now. But why don't you dance?' he took the paper cup from her hand and placed it on a windowsill. 'Please, may I have the pleasure?' He bowed.

Ellie smiled. He was a charmer, with a mass of dark curls, worn longer than the fashion and brown eyes. His heavily accented English sounded romantic and alluring. The evening was looking up.

Even better, as they stepped on to the floor the music changed to a slow tune. Ellie was relieved, she wasn't sure she could do the new dances. And besides, a small voice at the back of her mind said they might be too energetic for someone potentially in her condition.

'Good, this way I get to talk with you,' the Frenchman said as he held her in a formal pose. 'You're a friend of Beryl MacBride?'

'I lodge in her spare room,' Ellie answered, studying him. He had a high-bridged nose and wide mobile lips with a suggestion of five o'clock shadow. 'I found myself unexpectedly homeless and Beryl was kind enough to offer me the room.'

'I see.' He grinned. 'I like Beryl.'

'So do I.'

'But not in *that* way,' he clarified.

'No, of course.' She wondered why he made sure that she was clear about that.

Around them young couples smooched.

'You have a lovely smile, my Juliet.'

'Ellie, my name's Eleanor. Like the Queen.'

'Ah yes, Eleanor of Aquitaine, a compatriot of mine, but Queen of England. Did it have any special significance for your parents?'

'They liked French names. I have a sister named Marguerite. I think the Peverils came from France originally, it isn't a very English sort of surname.'

'Charming.'

'And your name is Antoine, I understand.' He nodded. 'Why are you here and not in France, Antoine?'

'Like many others, I escaped to London when France was occupied. I was billeted in Clapham and I came to the SLH to help with casualties when the air raids began. It was hard in 1940.'

'I can only imagine.' Ellie grew sombre. 'I lived out in the country then. My town took in evacuees, children mostly, but we didn't suffer the nightly bombing raids like London and other cities. We had our own tragedies, like everywhere – the local regiment was at Dunkirk and then Tobruk, so... – but there were places much worse off than Worcester.'

'Worcester...' he echoed.

'But the war's been over a while now,' she continued. 'Have you decided to stay?'

'Perhaps.' He smiled a crooked smile. 'If there's something to keep me here. We shall see.'

The song came to an end and a big band swing number began. Ellie and Antoine retired to the side of the room.

'Which part of France are you from?' she asked him.

'A small village near Poitiers, where Queen Eleanor was born.'

'*La France Profond.*'

'Exactly.' He raised his eyebrows in surprise. 'But tell me, how do you know France?'

'I don't. I've never been there. I've never been anywhere really, apart from a recent trip.' She found she didn't want to tell him about Nuremberg, it was too grim and would channel the conversation in a particular direction. 'I'm from a rural town in the middle of England, where we grow fruit and hops, corn and cows. As far away from the borders as you can get unless you count the one with Wales. But when I was a child I was fascinated by maps, especially of Europe, so I learned as much as I could in the hope that one day I would visit.'

'Ah, well, who knows, perhaps you will.'

'I hope so, though, for the moment, the SLH is exotic enough for me. It's all so new to me, the big city,' she said. 'Do you like it?'

'It's bloody cold!' Antoine answered, laughing. 'Though the common is lovely in springtime. Ah!'

'What?'

'Another slow tune,' he responded to Ellie's questioning look. 'You're going to dance with me again. I don't intend to share you with anyone else.'

As they walked out on to the impromptu dance floor, it didn't escape Ellie's notice that they attracted admiring glances. Antoine clearly had his admirers, but then, so did she. They made a handsome couple.

'Very well,' she said as he held her again. 'But this must be my last dance. I have an important meeting tomorrow morning, so I can't stay out late. Besides, I turn into a pumpkin at midnight.'

Antoine frowned, puzzled, then laughed. '*Cendrillon*! Of course. Cinderella. Though I'm sure that's not... anyway I must make the most of your company now, before you become a garden vegetable.'

THURSDAY

24

ELEANOR

Ellie got off the underground at Clapham Common, one stop early. She wanted to be alone to think and she did that best while walking. Ignoring the bitterly cold wind, she set off to make a half-circumference of the common, ending at Westbury Court.

She had risen early and gone into town, to Essex Street and the Temple, to meet two legal contacts. The first had been kind but couldn't help. He'd suggested that she try the courts, where her Nuremberg experience might count for something, but he hadn't held out much hope. Alternatively, he said, her uncle might find an opening for her if he knew any London solicitors. But her uncle didn't know that she was looking. The second contact had, she suspected, only agreed to see her because of the Shawcross name and any help he was willing to provide would come at a price she wasn't willing to pay. Her hopes of getting legal clerking work had been thoroughly dashed.

It would be the same in many lines of work that women had been doing for the last six years. The men had returned home and taken their jobs back; it was to be expected, they were the bread-winners. Women had to return to – what? Home and hearth, family and what jobs they could get? She'd had a taste of something different and that wasn't for her.

But what was she good for? What could she do?

Her eyes watered in the wind. She frowned and pressed her lips tightly together.

She had no qualifications or training. In the future previously mapped out for her she hadn't needed any. She'd had a sheltered and comfortable life. Growing up in Cathedral Close, then a girl's school and working at her uncle's solicitors practice until, she'd assumed, marriage and children. A whole life lived in the town where she was born.

Some of the professions admitted women, but not many. And one needed to study to even stand a chance – to be lawyers, like Moira, or nurses, like Beryl, or doctors like the clinicians at the SLH. It would take years... and she was already nearing thirty. Without qualifications, what kind of work could she find? And how could she be independent if she couldn't find work? It was hopeless.

She could do office work – she could organise and be efficient. There was shop work; she could, as Faye had pointed out, be very persuasive, but she couldn't see herself as a saleswoman. She was too old to be waiting on tables and didn't want to work in a public house. She liked working at the hospital, though not her job as it was repetitive and dull – she knew that after only three days – it didn't pay well and it didn't use her brain. She could do so much more, but right now, wherever she went she'd be starting at the bottom.

Her mouth turned down at the corners. She started to stride out, putting her head down to battle against the wind as she fought to keep control of the inner turmoil.

Perhaps she could find something else at the SLH? It was a good place to work, where everyone had a shared sense of purpose. It might not be a professional career, but it would certainly be more than just a job. That's what she wanted, a sense of purpose: to be useful.

If she could.

She didn't relish the idea of the Labour Exchange. The thought of queuing up outside some soulless office with all the other unemployed, giving her details and her few accomplishments, filled her with foreboding. But there was no use being finicky about it. It's what she would have to do. It's what people did when they had to find work. She'd ask Beryl where the nearest one was.

The bell of Holy Trinity began to toll midday as she passed the Georgian church and saw the door of Mrs Packham's house open and a man emerge. It was George Packham, of dubious reputation, whom she had seen with Charlie Redmond the evening before. Today he wore a heavy winter coat with the collar up, the trilby on his head was pulled down low on his brow. He was headed in her direction.

Ellie dropped her gaze as he approached, avoiding eye contact. She assumed he would walk straight by, but he stopped in the middle of the pavement.

'Would you have a light, Miss?' he asked, holding a cigarette to his mouth.

'No.' Ellie shook her head. 'I don't smoke.'

She started to walk forwards, but Packham blocked her path.

'You're Miss Peveril, the one who upset my ma?' he said. 'And brought the old bill to my home?'

'I don't know what you mean,' Ellie replied. 'If your mother is Mrs Packham, she still owes me a guinea.'

'Jumped up and posh, she said you was. Film star looks.' His eyes travelled up and down her body, making Ellie feel despoiled, even though she wore her greatcoat. 'What're you doing round here again?'

Her chin rose. Always stand up to a bully.

'I live here. I have every right to walk here. It's a free country.'

'For some it is,' he said and Ellie remembered that he'd been imprisoned. For assault. He was capable of violence.

'I think I'll have to find out where you live.' Packham took the cigarette from his lips and placed it back into a cigarette case. 'Pay you a visit, maybe. Make a social call.'

Ellie set her jaw and barged past him, lengthening her stride. She heard his laughter behind her.

How dare he!

She strode along the North Side, past bare mounds of earth, gun emplacements without their guns. The temporary barracks were empty and half-dismantled, their occupants having returned home. Displaced people going home to resume their lives.

She wouldn't do that. She wouldn't.

She was shaking. On top of everything else that morning, George Packham was the final straw.

Feeling vulnerable and cold, Ellie decided to go directly back to Westbury Court walking across the common. On the path ahead of her a man looked in her direction and she recognised him. It was Antoine Girard.

Immediately her mood lightened. She'd feel safer walking with him. George Packham wouldn't menace her with Antoine at her side. She waved, surreptitiously wiping the tears from her cheeks. He waited for her.

'*Bonjour*, Mademoiselle Ellie,' he called. 'Will you walk with me?'

'*D'accord*. Gladly.'

'You are taking a constitutional?' he asked as they strolled side by side.

'I'm on my way back from town,' she replied. 'I wanted to walk the last part of the way. To think. What about you?'

'I'm going to work,' he said. 'My lodgings are back there in Cedars Mews.'

'So you walk across the common to work every day?'

'Yes. I used to cycle, it was quicker, but my bicycle is broken and I must have it repaired.'

'I used to cycle in Worcester all the time. How about in your little town near Poitiers?'

'It's called Ligugé and, yes, I used to enjoy cycling around the lanes there.'

'Tell me, is Ligugé on a river?'

'The river Clain. It has an abbey too, very historic.'

'Like Worcester,' she said.

'Worcester is much bigger, I think. The Severn is a much larger river than the Clain.'

'D'you know it then? Have you been there?'

'*Non.*' Antoine lowered his eyes, then raised them, smiling. 'I have a confession to make. After last night's party I checked an atlas, to see where it was. You are far from home.'

'Not as far as you,' Ellie said, laughing. 'At least I'm in the same country.'

Although sometimes it seemed that London might as well be a foreign country, it was so very different to Worcester. At least neither had been occupied.

'Was Ligugé Vichy or occupied by the Germans?'

'Occupied. From 1940.'

Ellie couldn't imagine what that must have been like, the constant worry about family and friends, living in fear for their lives. To wonder what would remain of your hometown when, or if, you ever returned. Her own troubles paled into insignificance by comparison.

'I'm so sorry.'

'Don't be. It's not your fault,' Antoine urged, apparently touched by her sympathy. 'And I don't like to see you sad. Let's go to Mount Pond to see the ducks.'

There were more people on this part of the common and, as they walked around the pond, Ellie noticed a police constable striding in their direction, accompanied by a sour-looking, uniformed man wearing the distinctive red beret and flash of the military policeman.

'Good morning,' the PC said.

'We meet again, Constable,' Ellie said, for it was the man who had accompanied her to Mrs Packham's. 'Are you looking for me?'

'No, Miss, it's this gentleman we're after.' He indicated Antoine. 'You are Commandant Dr Girard?'

'I am. What is this about, may I ask?'

'Of the 2nd Armoured Division of the First Army of France, under General Leclerc?' The military policeman barked out his question.

'That is correct.'

'Then I must arrest you as being absent without leave,' he said, producing a set of handcuffs. 'You will be taken—'

'This is nonsense!' Antoine protested, stepping away from them. 'I have been serving as a doctor at the South London Hospital for over a year, after my return from France. I fought to liberate Paris. My presence here has the approval of my general.'

'He's well known and respected at the hospital,' Ellie exclaimed. 'This must be a mistake.'

'I'm afraid you're going to have to come with us, sir,' the PC said. 'Put them away, mate.' This to the military policeman.

'This is a military matter,' the MP insisted. 'He's my prisoner.'

'But you're on my manor.'

The redcap scowled but did as he was bid and pocketed the handcuffs.

'I am not a deserter, I'm not absent without leave,' the Frenchman began to entreat the PC. 'This is all a nonsense.'

Ellie sensed panic beneath his calm surface. She didn't know much about military prisons but suspected they were not pleasant places.

'There may have been a mix-up, but we've received an army report and we have to follow it up,' the PC stated, firmly.

'Where are you going? Cavendish Road?' Ellie asked.

'Yes, Miss, but no need for you to come along.'

'I won't.' She turned to the Frenchman. 'I'll go straight to the hospital, find Matron and Miss Barnett and a governor or two if necessary, then we'll come to make sure you're released.'

'*Merci beaucoup, mon* Ellie.'

'It's the least I can do,' she replied, glaring at the two policemen. 'When you are in my country to help us.'

'Come along now,' the PC said.

'*Au revoir,*' Antoine said, looking back at Ellie.

'We'll be there soon,' she called after him as her protector was led away.

25

ELEANOR

'And he's been taken to Cavendish Road police station.' Ellie was breathless from running. 'I don't know how long he'll stay there, the redcap was insisting it was a military matter. He wanted to take Antoine away with him immediately.'

'The MPs have power of arrest,' Matron said. 'Though the local police can be difficult if they want to be.'

Grouped around the office desk, Matron, Miss Barnett and Dr Boyd, a senior consultant, had listened with attention, Faye hovering at Ellie's right hand.

'Antoine Girard has served with distinction and is here official-ly,' Miss Barnett said. 'Do we know how this 'report' arose?'

'No and I don't think Dr Girard did either.'

'It could be malicious or it could just be a mistake,' Dr Boyd suggested.

'Either way, we need to go and prove the good doctor's bona fides. Quickly. It'll be much more difficult to help him if he's hauled away to the glasshouse. Do you have his letter assigning duty here, Felicity?' Matron asked.

Miss Barnett was already at the filing cabinet drawer.

'Here it is.' She handed the letter to Matron. 'I've got his passport and other documents too, if we need them. Dr Girard prefers that they are kept here, it's more secure than his lodgings and he can always come and get them if he needs them.'

'Bishop Jenkins is visiting today,' Faye said. 'I saw him in the canteen earlier.'

'Good thinking, a governor would be useful and, dare I say it, a man.' Matron stood.

'He'll probably be with the Lady Almoner,' Dr Boyd said.

'I'll go and find him,' Faye said, moving towards the door.

'Bring him to the main entrance, Faye. Thank you, Miss Peveril, for acting so quickly.'

'Happy to do so,' Ellie replied and she hurried after Faye.

'Why on earth would someone make a malicious claim against Antoine?' she said as they strode along the corridor.

'Antoine is it now?' Faye said. 'Yet another man falling at your feet.'

'Hardly, though I do find him… interesting.'

'And charming and attractive. He's quite a heartbreaker, apparently. Woos, beds and moves on, that's what the nurses say. Here.' Faye pressed the button and the lift door opened. 'And you're riding to his rescue.'

'This is serious!'

'I know. Military prison is very unpleasant. Especially when you're an outsider.'

The lift delivered them to the second floor. Faye pulled the grille aside.

Within minutes Ellie and Faye had explained the urgency and extracted Bishop Jenkins, delivering him to the main entrance as promised. Matron was waiting there with Miss Barnett.

'May I accompany you?' Ellie asked. 'I don't start shift until one thirty,' she added with a glance at Faye.

'Yes, of course,' Matron replied. 'If we're all ready?'

The hospital deputation set out for the police station, Matron and the Bishop striding out in the lead, with Ellie and Miss Barnett following.

'And you were coming back from town, when you happened to

meet Dr Girard, crossing the common,' the hospital administrator remarked.

'Yes, I'd been to the Temple.'

'Ah, looking for a position. Faye tells me that you're a legal clerk.'

'That's right. I used to run a solicitors practice in Worcester.'

'It's a shame we can't keep you at the SLH.'

'Yes.' Ellie hesitated before she answered. 'I like the SLH very much, but I'm used to doing a different type of work.'

'I don't doubt it.' Miss Barnett affirmed but said no more.

They walked up the path, past the familiar blue lamp and into the police station on the corner of Klea Avenue. The desk sergeant was the same man who was on duty on Tuesday.

'To what do I owe the pleasure?' he said to the group. 'Didn't think I'd see you again so soon, miss.'

'I understand that you have one of our medical staff in custody here,' the Bishop said, his tone urgent and businesslike. 'Dr Antoine Girard.'

'Yes, sir, he was brought in just now. We received an absent without leave report.'

'From his battalion?'

'No, actually, from one of ours.'

'We have his letter of posting to the SLH,' Miss Barnett said, handing over the paper. 'It's self-explanatory.'

The sergeant read it. 'It is.'

'He is still here, isn't he?' Ellie asked.

'He is, miss.'

Ellie sighed in relief and the others relaxed. They had got to him in time.

The sergeant handed back the piece of paper and, raising the flap of the desk, came out from behind it. 'I thought it was a bit strange from the off,' he said. 'Most of us have seen him around here for months, working at the hospital. If you'll take a seat, I'll go and get him.'

'You've not locked him up?'

'Yes, miss, that is what happens when people are arrested.'

JULIE ANDERSON

They sat on the hard chairs that lined two sides of the room. Matron, Miss Barnett and the Bishop began discussing a recent meeting and Ellie's attention wandered. She began reading the notices on the board opposite. 'Air Raid Danger, Conceal Your Lights', 'Metropolitan Police, Traffic Regulations' and 'Metropolitan Police, Recruits Wanted, five pounds and ten shillings per week'. The advertisement carried a drawing of a PC in his uniform.

There *were* jobs available, she thought. Just not for women.

'Here you are.' The sergeant and Antoine returned. 'Commandant Dr Girard, I apologise for detaining you, but we have to follow up on all reports received.'

'Of course, Sergeant.' Antoine's manner was gracious, but his face was very pale.

Ellie sensed his discomposure. It must have been disturbing for him to be detained, suspected, even though he'd done nothing wrong. Military prison would have been hard.

'Glad to see you, Antoine,' Matron said. 'Thank you, Sergeant, we'll be getting back now.'

Matron and the Bishop flanked the Frenchman as they made their way back to the SLH. Both were solicitous and apologetic, with Miss Barnett indignant that the police hadn't checked with her first. Ellie said nothing; she was thinking.

Antoine was exposed in a way that she was not, because he was foreign. He was treated as an ally, certainly, and a respected member of the SLH staff and the community, but he *was* different. She remembered Faye's comment about the SLH being different and, therefore, being vulnerable. It was the same. People were tribal by nature and didn't like change.

Matron, Miss Barnett and the bishop walked up the ramp to the formal entrance, but Antoine hung back.

'*Merci*, Ellie' he said. 'You are my angel of mercy as well as my Juliet.'

Ellie smiled. 'It was the least I could do.'

'To be honest, I was worried that I'd be suspected of worse than being AWOL.'

156

'Oh, you mean... Jane,' Ellie answered, surprised. 'Surely not.'

But she could see why he was afraid, he was 'a stranger in a strange land'. An easy target. Perhaps that's why the tramp seen on the common had run away.

'Either way, I am now in your debt and must repay you,' he said with a determined glint in his eye. 'With dinner if you would permit?'

'That would be lovely, thank you.'

'Good. I will check my shift times and propose a date.'

'You know where to find me.'

26

FAYE

Faye spotted Ellie hurrying into the canteen and caught up with her in the locker room, where Ellie was pulling on her uniform.

'Well?'

'They hadn't taken him away, so we got him out,' Ellie replied. 'I don't think the policeman really believed that Antoine was AWOL, but he had to follow procedures and the redcap insisted. They received a report, so...'

'Who from, I wonder?'

'The sergeant said it came from a British battalion. Probably an administrative error. Got the wrong name. Who would make a false report anyway?'

'You'd be surprised. Like I said, the SLH isn't universally loved,' Faye replied. 'And Dr Girard, Antoine, he's no worse for the experience?'

'Shaken up a bit,' Ellie replied. 'It must be difficult sometimes, being a foreigner here. There's a sadness in him. I suppose he knows that his world can be turned upside down at the drop of a hat. His hometown was occupied, you know, that must leave a mark. Though he's been in Clapham for years, he lodges in Cedars Mews.'

'So he crosses the common to come to work?'

'Yes.'

'At all hours of the day and night, I'll be bound. Could he be the man you saw with Jane on Sunday? I wonder if he was working late? Is he tall enough?'

'I suppose so, yes, but... the cadence of his speech is different from that of a native English speaker. I think I might have noticed that.'

'Would you?' Faye asked. 'I thought you said that you couldn't hear the man's voice clearly.'

'I... I couldn't, though I really can't remember. I'm sorry.'

'I wonder if the police have considered Antoine as a suspect for Jane's murder?'

'That's what he said he was afraid of.'

'Did he now! It's natural, I suppose, for a foreigner, as you said. Though I wonder...?' Faye narrowed her eyes, but then noticed the shocked expression on Ellie's face. 'Well, we can't dismiss anyone. I'm not saying it was him, but he must be a candidate to be the mystery man.'

'His face wasn't scratched,' Ellie said, smartly. 'And Jane scratched at her attacker.'

'Hmm. I've been thinking about that... Anyway, I hope Antoine appreciated your efforts on his behalf.'

'He did.' Ellie flushed pink.

'I see! Are you and he...?'

'Dinner,' Ellie said. 'At a date and time to be agreed.'

'Don't make it sound like a business meeting.' Faye laughed. 'Talking of which, did you have any luck at the Temple?'

'No.' Ellie's smile disappeared. 'Nothing. "You can't type, you don't take shorthand, so what can you do?"'

'But you didn't want a secretarial position.'

'I know, but that's all they think of. One suggested that I canvas local solicitors firms.'

'Good idea.'

'Yes, but if they have vacancies, they'll want references and my last employer was my uncle. He'd mention it to my family if I used his name.'

Faye smiled in sympathy. 'You're going to have to tell them, you know.'

'I know, but it'll be difficult. I've been putting it off until...'

'You can get something better than cleaning tables.'

'Well, yes. They might accept my remaining in London more readily if they think I'm pursuing a legal career. Does that seem snobbish to you?'

'It does a bit. But you know your parents.'

Faye contemplated her companion with affectionate irritation. Ellie didn't look down on people doing menial jobs, she treated everyone the same. Yet she didn't see herself doing one for anything more than as a stopgap. It wasn't good enough; her expectations were different. It was how she'd been brought up.

Yet some people would be glad to have that job and want to hold on to it. Maybe it'd been wrong to offer the job to Ellie, who really wanted something better and would move on. Even in her cleaning uniform she was glamorous and sleek, completely incongruous.

But then, wasn't the SLH incongruous too? Perhaps that meant it was the right place for Ellie.

'I never thought I was a snob,' Ellie said. 'But, thinking about the job, perhaps I am, really.'

Time to change the subject, Faye thought. Too much intro-spection.

There was enough worrying going on at present, with nurses frightened and speculation rife about what happened to Jane Cooper.

'Last night, did you ask around about Jane Cooper? Did you speak with Les?'

'I chatted with him, but it wasn't that sort of conversation,' Ellie replied. 'The nurses told me he'd been hurt by her friend, Polly, when she left without warning. They said he'd really fallen for her. It didn't seem appropriate somehow.'

Faye raised an eyebrow.

'Jane Cooper and Polly Brooks were great friends, did everything together. Then there seems to have been a rift between them and Polly started walking out with Les. Sometime later she simply left.'

'About a month ago, I think,' Faye said. 'I'll check with the office when I get the chance.'

'It seems that she'd come into some money; she'd been seen with plenty of extra cash.'

'Are we talking about a legacy?'

'I think so, though no one seems to know for certain. The nurses I spoke to said Jane believed that some misfortune had befallen Polly, suggested that maybe she hadn't left of her own volition. They were also sure that Jane was making excuses because she didn't seem to know what her erstwhile bosom buddy was up to anymore.'

Faye noticed the Head Porter enter the canteen. 'Perfect timing,' she said. 'Let's ask Les.'

'D'you think he'll come over?'

'Smile at him.'

Sure enough, Les Allen brought his mug of tea over to their table.

'Afternoon, ladies. You were enjoying yourself last night,' he quipped to Ellie.

He seemed relaxed and jovial, apparently having forgotten the unpleasant encounter in the staff room. Strange. Faye decided to play along and smiled. She'd let Ellie do the talking.

'Of course! It was a party,' Ellie replied, laughing. 'It's good to get to know more people. I see lots of folk in here, but I don't often have the chance to chat. Can I ask you about Polly Brooks?'

The Head Porter shrugged and took a seat.

'You and she were... close?' Ellie asked.

'Not as close as I'd have liked.' His quip fell flat and he looked down into his mug of tea. He took a sip. 'Polly thought she could do better than me,' he said, his lips crinkling into a humourless smile. 'Can't blame her.'

Faye tutted in sympathy.

'And when she came into some money, well, maybe she could,' he added, in a jaundiced tone. 'Or maybe she was never going to stick around anyway.'

'Came into money? How?' Ellie asked.

'I don't know for sure. I'd assumed there was a bequest or something.'

'Where was she from?'

'Somewhere in Kent. Grays, I think. She didn't talk about her family; I got the impression that she didn't get on with them. But then she wouldn't necessarily confide in me about them anyway. I asked her about them, of course, but she wasn't saying.'

'Who would she talk to? Jane Cooper, perhaps?'

'Hmm, maybe, but I think they'd had some sort of falling out. Anyway, if she did Jane can't tell us now.'

'No.'

'Did Jane ask you about where her friend had gone?' Ellie asked.

'Yes, it was... difficult.'

'Why?'

'I wasn't exactly Jane Cooper's favourite person,' he continued. 'I think Jane blamed me for her falling out with Polly, though I didn't know anything about it – it was nothing to do with me. And Poll had her own ideas.' He made as if to rise. 'I'd best be off.'

'Thanks, Les. Sorry to rake all that up,' Ellie said.

'S'alright,' he said as he stood. 'It's all water under the bridge now.'

'Plenty more fish in the sea,' Ellie added.

Faye watched the porter head towards the door. There had been no trace of the animosity that Les had showed in the staffroom. Perhaps Ellie's magic had done the trick?

'I'd like to find out more about Jane Cooper and Polly Brooks,' she said. 'I'll try and look at their staff files, see where they worked before, and I'll check the home address given by Polly. I wonder if anyone's told her that her former best friend is dead?'

'One other thing,' Ellie said. She described the experiment the

162

evening before. 'The couple I saw definitely went to the foot of Westbury Court, to Westbury Gardens or beyond them.'

'Interesting. Could Jane have been going to the police station house? I'll ask John to find out if she got there, or if anyone inside heard anything. I suspect that if they had they would have come forward by now.'

'I thought so too,' Ellie said.

'Now, I'd best get back to my place,' Faye said, indicating the lectern.

'And I'll get to work, though, when I'm off later I'll go and ask Owen Philpott if the SLH key to the deep shelters was ever returned. I'll try out your theory on him while I'm at it,' Ellie volunteered. 'That Jane was trying to get *out* of the shelters.'

'Good. I'll go and check the personnel records later. We can compare notes tomorrow morning.'

'Right. Toodle-pip.'

Faye nodded and sat, watching Ellie collect her trolley and speak with several diners.

Then what would they do – tell the police what they'd learned? Ellie had seen the murdered woman having a row with a man, hours, perhaps only minutes, before her death. Yet the police hadn't thought that of any importance. Would they be receptive to anything else she or Ellie had to say? She doubted it, but they had to tell someone in authority.

Except there was one major problem.

Faye's suspicions were growing that the hospital was connected to the murder. Jane had been a nurse here and the SLH operated around the clock close to the scene of the crime. If the SLH key to the deep shelters still existed, it must be linked to the case. Perhaps the police's lack of interest wasn't such a bad thing if the hospital was implicated in some way.

It would all have to come out in the end, though, and the sooner the better, but she wanted to know what was going on first.

27

FAYE

'Jane Cooper, you say?' The secretary stood. 'I'll just get the key.'

Miss Barnett kept all the hospital keys in the top right-hand drawer of her desk in the adjoining room. That drawer was always kept locked. Faye had recently been given a key to it, anticipating her new position, but this was all unofficial and she didn't like to advertise the fact, so she'd asked Jean.

'Yes, please, Jean.'

The secretary returned, opened the filing cabinet next to the window and rifled through the files. Jean had been at the SLH for as long as Faye could remember. First as filing clerk then as secretary to Miss Barnett.

'And Polly Brooks' file too, please.' She glanced back at the door to the office. 'Was that Dr Girard I saw just outside in the corridor?'

'Antoine, yes.'

Jean's cheeks turned pink. There was something in the way she said the name. Faye adopted a neutral expression.

'He popped in to give us his documents back. There was a kerfuffle yesterday.'

'So I heard,' Faye said. 'Does he pop in often?'

'When he needs his papers,' Jean looked coy. 'Here's Polly's file.' She handed Faye a manila folder. 'She took her last pay packet four weeks ago. Though she didn't formally hand in her notice. That would have cost her if she'd ever asked for a reference or a recommendation for a new employer. Here's Jane's file too.'

'Thanks.'

Faye opened Polly's file first.

The home address Polly had given was in Grays, Kent, as Les Allen had told them. Faye noted it down. Her personnel file showed she was an efficient office clerk, though not considered a candidate for promotion until two weeks before she left. Then she had been formally reprimanded by Miss Barnett.

'What's this, Jean? Polly attracted the ire of Miss B?'

'Oh yes, I remember. When I came back from collecting the post Polly was at the cabinet.' She tapped the open drawer. 'Going through the medical files. Patient medical information is completely confidential and she'd have no reason to look through them anyway. They're strictly off limits.'

'What was she looking for? Did she say?'

'No. And she was rude too, told me to mind my own business when I asked her. Then Miss Barnett walked in and, well...'

Was that why she left? Faye wondered. But then why wait a fortnight before doing so?

'A mystery then.'

'Yes. And not the only one. Polly had been poking her nose into various places she had no business in.'

'How do you mean?'

'She was checking the purchasing ledgers for the last few months. Not yours, the canteen and kitchens, but for the stores and the dispensary. And I happen to know that she had pulled some of the old ledgers from the basement file store too. Looking at the equivalent ledgers for 1938, from before the war.'

'Why would she do that? She hadn't been asked to, had she?'

'No. Miss Barnett hadn't asked her to and there's no one else – except you of course.'

'Well, I didn't. Can you show me the ledgers Polly looked at?'

'Course, give me a few minutes, I'll have to go and get the old one.'

Faye sat at the desk opposite Jean's. Nominally it belonged to Miss Barnett, although she preferred to use the one in the office next door as it was more private. She ran her hands over the polished wooden desktop. This would be hers, she supposed, when she took up post.

Except she still hadn't replied formally to the job offer. She must get round to that and do it!

Faye opened Jane Cooper's personnel file. Jane was a Manchester girl who had qualified as a nurse five years ago. Her reports were fair to middling, but she hadn't been disciplined like her friend. She lodged in Hazelbourne Road, next to the hospital, at the same lodging house as Polly Brooks. The words on the piece of paper gave no indication of the vibrant, gossipy, laughter-loving person who Jane had been. But there was nothing remarkable in her record.

Jean returned carrying a large ledger bound in thick cardboard.

'Here's what Polly was looking at from 1938,' she said, placing it on the desk. 'And this...' she went across to the shelf of ledger files in the office, 'is the current version. She went through that too.'

Faye studied the recent ledger, which recorded all medical stores and dispensary purchases with a corresponding payment reference when the bills were paid. The SLH had an account with several medical supply companies and made payment monthly, although supplies were delivered almost daily. It was similar to the purchasing ledger for the canteen and kitchens and the system operated in the same way.

Near the bottom of the list there was a recent purchase, of a consignment of streptomycin.

So the SLH must be included in the drug trial. Perfect! Faye's mood lightened. This meant there was hope for Phoebe. She'd ask Miss Barnett which clinician was in charge and then try to speak with them.

She made herself concentrate on the ledgers. The earlier of them showed the same sort of purchases but for 1938.

'Do you know why Polly wanted these?'

'Nope. The orders used to come through Miss Lowell the pharmacist. You remember her? Such a shame – to have survived the war only to be run down by a lorry. Now Miss Underwood's joined us she might have her own ideas.'

'How do you allocate the drugs to each clinician?'

'We don't. The drugs are taken to the dispensary and the doctors ask the pharmacist for what they've ordered. Nurses stock the wards. The medical staff are the ones who know what they need.'

'What happens if they've under-estimated?'

'They don't tend to, especially now that things are more regular. Of course, during the war, when we started getting bomb casualties, it was more difficult to judge, so we did regular stocktakes and, if we came close to running out, Miss B would authorise an emergency order.'

'But it's settled down again now?' Faye asked.

'By and large, after the Emergency department closed. Now we're back to in-patients and out-patients estimating is easier.'

'Do we collate the purchase information and compare it with what's used, do a cross-check to keep tabs on the ordering?'

'Not anymore. We used to, but we've been short-handed for so long now...' Jean let her sentence tail off. 'We could start again if you think we should. If you're going to be my new boss, you could reintroduce that?'

'We'll see.' It might be a good idea. 'If I get the job,' Faye said. 'You know how all this works, Jean. Can you see what Polly was looking for? Anything odd?'

'I'd say she was comparing these two particular ledgers, otherwise, why fetch one from the basement?'

Faye leafed through the old ledger. Purchases of drugs and medical supplies seemed consistent, month on month, in 1938. The current ledger showed more variation.

Why should that be? There might be perfectly good reasons, but there was something strange about Polly Brooks checking these records as they were nothing to do with her. And she'd left shortly afterwards. Faye needed to find out what was going on.

'Jean—'

The office door opened and Miss Barnett walked in.

28

FAYE

'Good morning, Faye. Getting your feet under the table, I see.'

'No, not at all,' Faye answered with a nervous smile. 'Just checking on something.'

'I require a formal answer to my letter before you take on any new duties.' Miss Barnett's voice had an edge to it. 'And I haven't had one yet. This is an excellent opportunity that I'm offering you, one you might not be offered elsewhere. When I asked you yesterday you said you would be replying once you'd spoken to your family. Have you now done so?'

'Yes.'

'And?'

'I would like to take the position.'

'Then you had better reply, hadn't you? In writing.'

'Yes, Miss Barnett.'

Faye tried her best to seem contrite, but a part of her rebelled. Miss Barnett was treating her like a recalcitrant child, not a fellow professional. Faye wondered if she had offended her in some way, she couldn't understand why she was being so peremptory and formal. But she *must* reply.

Never mind that now.

'Could I just ask…'

'What?'

'The SLH key to the deep shelters? Do we still have it?'

'Yes. Why?'

'Are we certain – we haven't had reason to use it since last year?'

'I am entirely certain.' Miss Barnett gave her a steely glance, but Faye didn't look away. 'Very well, let's check anyway, shall we?'

The hospital administrator marched through to the office next door and looked in the open desk drawer. She rifled among its contents and drew out a flat, grooved key, very like the one Owen Philpott had used to open the shaft head on the common. This was the SLH's key to the Balham Hill deep shelters. It was kept in the key drawer, along with all the others.

Faye felt a small surge of triumph, she'd been certain they had one and it felt good to be right, but she kept her eyes lowered.

'Satisfied?' Miss Barnett held it up.

'Yes, thank you, Miss Barnett.'

'Why did you want to know?'

'It's just – ever since Jane Cooper's body was found inside the shaft head building on the common, I've been thinking about how she might have got there.'

'Rather than replying to the job offer, obviously.' Miss Barnett was waspish. 'No one can use this key, if that's what you're thinking. This drawer is kept locked.'

But not all the time, thought Faye, though she wasn't going to point that out. She changed the subject.

'Polly Brooks was looking at patients' records before she left,' she said.

'And was reprimanded for it.' There was a severe expression on Miss Barnett's face. 'Patient records are confidential. If I had more time – or a deputy – there would be more oversight. As it was…'

'I hope I'll be able to help with that,' Faye offered, then continued, tentatively, 'We'll have to review all our systems and procedures.'

Miss Barnett sniffed but seemed to relax a little.

'I don't suppose,' Faye added, 'Polly said *why* she was looking at patient records?'

'She did not.'

'Because she was also looking at our purchase records.'

'Was she? Jean?'

'That's right, Miss Barnett.'

'What for?'

'That's what I was asking myself,' Faye said. 'She seems to have been doing a comparison with pre-war purchases.'

'Why?'

'My question exactly. It seems a bit – fishy.'

The suggestion of a frown crossed the hospital administrator's brow. 'Hm, well, we can't ask her now. When there is someone in place who can properly manage our office processes and procedures, we can work to improve things,' Miss Barnett said. 'Until then, which, *one way or another*, will be soon, we'll carry on as we are.'

'I'm not suggesting that we don't,' Faye tried to conciliate. 'It's just that it seems an unusual thing for Polly to do.'

'Brooks has gone. And good riddance.' Miss Barnett glared at Faye. 'I don't know why she saw fit to breach our rules of confidentiality, but that's not your concern. You haven't applied for the position offered and you certainly haven't taken up post. Yet you're here checking our systems and questioning our security, putting the cart before the horse.' Miss Barnett's mouth was a thin line, her voice icy. 'It's my job to ensure this hospital runs efficiently, which I do to the best of my ability and under considerable pressure. I expect my staff to support me in doing so, not make extra work or chase after irrelevancies.'

'I didn't mean to suggest—'

'I'm disappointed in you, Faye, you don't seem to understand how a hospital like this is run. It takes a great deal of organisation and dedication, a strong focus on the job. Many SLH people give their lives to this institution, often making great personal sacrifices along the way. Our ethos and our identity is a very strong one. I likened the SLH to a family the other day and that's what we are, we all depend on each other, we do *not* try to find fault with each other.'

'But I—'

'What can I say, perhaps I made a mistake in thinking you'd be a good candidate for the post? The SLH has always provided opportunities for local women, women who might not have had the sort of education available to others and you've done very well up until now, even if you don't seem to recognise the help you've been given. But maybe this is a step too far and I was wrong to offer you the post.'

'No, Miss Barnett—'

'That's all I have to say on the matter. There'll be no more asking about Polly Brooks. Now I think you'd better get back to your post. Concentrate on doing your existing job.'

'Bu—'

'And you can stop playing detective. It hasn't escaped my notice that you visited the path lab yesterday. Dr Horn happened to mention it. Then today I find you checking the records of the dead woman.' She pointed at the personnel files on the desk. 'Hole-in-the-corner conferences and asking questions around the place. And you don't need to co-opt your newest canteen employee into helping you either. We'll have no more of it – not if you want to keep working for me! Concentrate on what you should be doing!'

Miss Barnett strode through the office into the adjacent room and closed the door behind her. Jean looked at Faye, her mouth agape.

'I—'

Faye couldn't form words. All she could think about was getting out of the office.

The corridor outside was empty. In a horrified daze Faye put one foot in front of the other, without seeing what was in front of her. Around her the business of the hospital continued as normal; patients went to outpatients, nurses walked from radiology into the hospital's main corridor, porters bustled along with their trollies.

What had she done?

Had she blown her chances of getting the new job? Miss Barnett as good as said that she wouldn't give her the job now. All her plans – the independent life she wanted, her own little flat, the chance to make her own choices without pressure to conform to out-dated ideas. All of it lost.

Stupid, stupid.

Why hadn't she responded to Miss Barnett's letter? She'd planned to do it after the VIP luncheon, but then Jane's murder had distracted her. She'd made things worse by asking questions about it; the chat with the pathologist, her 'playing detective'. Was that what she'd been doing?

She cursed herself.

Too clever by half, the words rang around the inside of her skull. Why couldn't she button her lip, keep her mouth shut and do as she was told?

Without thinking, she turned into the stairwell and her feet took her down towards the canteen.

But there *was* something strange going on at the SLH.

The SLH key to the deep shelters, the only way into the tunnel system other than Owen Philpott himself, linked the SLH to Jane's death. That must be how she got into the shelters in the first place. But now it was in the drawer where it was kept, so it must have been returned.

Who had returned it? Whoever had done so must know what had happened. Whoever had done so could have killed Jane.

Then there was Polly Brooks' odd behaviour. What had been going on in that office and was it, too, linked to Jane's death?

Faye came to an abrupt halt.

Stop it, she admonished herself. Stop this speculating now!

Miss Barnett had instructed her not to pursue it further and Miss Barnett was her boss. If she wanted any kind of career at the SLH, if she wanted to keep the job she had, she must stop. She loved the SLH.

Faye started down the stairs again.

But how could she turn a blind eye to murder? Jane deserved

justice, not to be conveniently forgotten, shunted into the 'unsolved case' pile. How could she stop? What's more, her killer could still be out there. And the SLH was involved somehow, she was sure.

Befuddled and profoundly dismayed, Faye pushed open the doors to the canteen.

29

ELEANOR

Ellie crossed the South Side to the top of Balham Hill where a walled compound surrounded the familiar pill-box shape of a deep shelter entrance. The pavements were busy with housewives in hats and headscarves shopping on the parade. There were people waiting at the bus stop, two young women wearing smart coats and hats, who looked like they were on their way up west, a man in a grey overcoat, smoking and a uniformed delivery boy.

The high metal gates to the compound were wide open and Ellie walked through a yard stacked head-high with pallets towards the single-storey office building.

'Mr Philpott! Hello. I say! Are you there?'

Owen Philpott appeared in the office doorway.

'Why, it's Faye's friend, Miss Peveril, isn't it?' He smiled.

'Yes, do call me Ellie, please.' She returned his smile, hoping that he would be less reluctant to help this time. 'Do you mind if I ask you a couple of questions? And there's a theory Faye and I have given some thought to, which I'd like to ask you about.'

'I might have known Faye Smith would have a theory. You know that I think this is police business,' he said.

'I know,' Ellie said. 'We're going to speak with the police again, not investigate on our own account.'

'Hmm, that doesn't sound like the Faye Smith I know. But... ask away.'

'The key to the door of the deep level shelter on Clapham Common is kept in the safe here?'

'Yes.'

'And no one can open the safe but yourself?'

'That's correct.'

'Faye remembered that the SLH had access to the deep level shelters too, at one time, to take patients to safety when the rocket raids began in 1944,' Ellie said. 'Didn't the SLH also have a key?'

'That's right, there is another key. It's held by Miss Barnett, the hospital administrator. But it's not to the entrance on Clapham Common, where the body was found. It's to this entrance here.' He pointed to the pillbox building to one side of the yard.

'Does Miss Barnett still have it?'

'I suppose so. It hasn't been returned to me. Perhaps it should be.'

'So there *is* another key out there, which someone might have got hold of and used to let themselves into this entrance?'

'I'm sure that Felicity Barnett would have kept the key secure.' Mr Philpott shook his head. 'As I said the other day, there's miles of tunnel down there, anyone could get lost. We can't have people just wandering in. She understands that.'

Faye will be able to check where it's kept, Ellie thought. Probably in the office.

'I'm sure she does. Tell me, is it possible to go from the tunnels entered from this entrance to those which lie beneath the shaft head on the common and vice versa?'

'Yes, the tunnels are connected, though most of the links are closed off now. Ah – so you think that poor girl may have arrived where she did via the tunnel system?'

'Exactly. If someone has a key to this entrance they could have gone in here and crossed through the tunnels to the other shelter and climbed the steps to go out.'

'Yes, it's possible that the nurse could have walked all the way through and ended up inside the door on Clapham Common.' Mr Philpott stroked his chin. 'But you still have the problem of the key.'

'I know. I'll check how and where the key is kept at the SLH. Are there any other keys, or copies?'

'These are security keys; they're unique and, as I've said before, they can't be copied. There are no others.'

Ellie gave him a searching look.

'I'm certain. I didn't think about the SLH key the other day because it's to this entrance here, not the one where the body was found.'

'I see. Well, thanks for your help, Mr Philpott.'

'Call me Owen.'

'Thanks, Owen. I'll be going now.'

Ellie waved as she retraced her steps across the yard. She decided to head back to the SLH to tell Faye that she had been right about the key.

'Hey, Ellie!'

A gaggle of off-duty nurses was crossing the road. Dressed in trousers and overcoats, wrapped up against the wind, Ellie almost didn't recognise them, until they stopped to talk to her.

'We're going to the pictures on Saturday,' said one, pointing to the Odeon further along the parade. 'It's the royal premiere film, special showing, London cinemas only. I read about it, *A Matter of Life and Death*. It's supposed to be really good. D'you want to come? Cheap tickets for SLH staff. It'll be sold out.'

Why not? She had nothing better to do. 'Thanks, I'd like that. What time are you going?'

'Seven o'clock.'

'See you then. At the SLH main entrance.'

The nurses continued onward.

The housewives were still on the parade, but the bus must have arrived because the people at the stop had gone, including the man in a grey overcoat, who had been smoking. A thought struck her. Hadn't she seen him, or someone like him, hanging around by the underground station last evening?

177

Yes. Outside Westbury Court when she, Beryl and Ron had been experimenting. He'd been wearing a hat then, that was why he looked different, but it was the same man. Was he a local? But he never seemed to be doing anything or going anywhere, he was always loitering, smoking. And watching.

The hairs on the back of her neck prickled.

Ellie crossed the road and the shop bell rang as she ducked into a cobbler's. The shopkeeper was working at his last and chatting with a customer, so she pretended to be interested in some of the footwear on a stand next to the window. This gave her a good view of both sides of the road.

Grey Overcoat hadn't caught a bus, he was standing on the same side of the road as the cobbler's shop, next to a lamppost, looking up and down the street as if he'd lost someone.

As she watched he dropped his cigarette and ground it out beneath his foot, before hastening along the road towards the SLH. The bell rang again as Ellie left to follow him, keeping close to the shop fronts in case he might turn around and see her, but he seemed oblivious to her presence.

Grey Overcoat pushed open the corner door of a small café. Pale checked curtains hung in the windows of the café to halfway height. The only way that Ellie could see inside was to walk right up to the window and peer over the top of them.

Then he might see her. But did it matter if he did? The South Side was busy, he could hardly rush out and attack her.

When she looked in, Grey Overcoat was sitting at a table facing the windows with another man who had his back to her. Grey Overcoat caught sight of Ellie the moment she saw him and must have said something to the other man, who turned to look in her direction.

Her heart seemed to stop.

It was Patrick Haverstock.

30

ELEANOR

The café door swung back with a crash.

'What the hell are you doing here?' Ellie demanded, marching up to the two men.

Patrick rose, turning towards her. 'Ellie, calm down—'

'Calm down! Is he watching me? Are you paying him to do that? What gives you the right?' Her hands became fists.

'You're my fiancée! I've every right.' His face was thrust forward into hers.

'Didn't you hear me the other night? We're finished, Pat. I'm no fiancée of yours and, even if I was, what you're doing is wrong.'

'Erm, perhaps this isn't the place—' Grey Overcoat ventured.

'Shut up!'

'Be quiet!

The only other occupants of the café, a wide-eyed woman with a young child, made their way hastily out of the door.

'Does your family know what you're doing, following me around, setting someone to snoop?'

'No, but then I don't think yours knows you're even here. When I spoke to your mother yesterday, she told me you were staying with the Shawcross family.'

What! He'd spoken to her mother?

'You needn't worry, I didn't tell her,' Pat snarled, a sulky look on his face. 'But I might, if you don't come to your senses.'

'Come to my senses! I've never been surer of anything in my life!' Ellie took a deep breath. 'I'm not going to marry you, Pat. That's all there is to it.'

She turned on her heel and left but hadn't gone ten yards before her arm was grabbed from behind.

'Ow! That hurt.'

Pat let her go. 'Well, don't walk out on me!'

'Pat, you don't seem to understand. I make my own decisions. I can do whatever I choose to and that includes walking out on you.'

'No. You owe me an explanation! We've been engaged for six years, Ellie. If it hadn't been for the war, we'd have been married for four. For God's sake, we could have had children by now!'

'But we aren't, and we didn't. After what I saw last Saturday night, I'm glad we're not and never will be. I don't owe you anything.'

'A mistake! One mistake and you dump me. We were going to spend our lives together, Ellie.' He reached out.

Ignoring him, Ellie began to walk back to the SLH but Pat strode beside her.

'How'd you find me, anyway?' she asked.

'The man cleaning tables at the club overheard you saying that you had a room in Clapham, near the common.'

'Clapham's a big place.'

'One I happened to know,' he said. 'I tried the Ministry of Labour first, then telephoned around the local police stations, saying I had found an item belonging to you. I used Phillip's name. The desk sergeant at the station—'

'You pretended to be my godfather! You realise that's impersonating a police officer and a criminal offence?'

'I didn't, I just mentioned that you were the goddaughter of a Scotland Yard superintendent. That's how I learned about you losing your baggage and money and that you were working here.' He pointed to the hospital. 'Ratcliffe found out the rest.'

'How do you know Clapham, Pat?'

'Some of my friends, fellow officers, keep... rooms here.'

Hmm...

'I'm not coming back to Worcester, Pat.'

'You don't have to if you don't want to,' he said. 'We could live in London if you want. There's the Eaton Square house mews. We could do it out, have it as our own, if you wanted to spend time here.'

'So you can enjoy your London life?'

'I don't need that, I'll have you.' He tried to catch her around the waist and swing her towards him, but she slipped free and carried on walking.

'Patrick, you're going to inherit a three-hundred-acre farm. *That*'s going to be your home.'

'I could let Johnny run it, he's the one who's always liked farming. If you don't want that life. I thought you liked it all, the Cathedral, the countryside, the County Show...'

'I... I thought I did.' Ellie stopped. 'I've changed, Pat. The war changed me. Nuremberg changed me. I couldn't be content with that now.'

Maybe the war had changed him too. They would have had to get to know each other all over again. So many couples would have to do that. But not anymore. Now it was all over.

Had she ever really loved him? If she had to ask herself the question, then she thought she knew what the answer was. And now? The arrogant and crude Patrick she had seen in the Black Cat Club – someone so different from the gentle Patrick who had wooed her in Worcester – that Patrick she didn't even like.

'Are you sure you haven't changed in other ways?' he demanded.

'What do you mean?'

'Ratcliffe told me all about your flat-mate.'

'Beryl? I rent my room from her. What of it?'

'A Glaswegian communist dyke.'

Ellie swallowed her surprise. 'Beryl's a decent sort, whatever her – preferences and politics.'

Pat raised an eyebrow. 'You didn't know, did you?' he said. 'Ye gods, you're not fit to be allowed out on your own! First that lodging house woman swindles you out of what money you have and now you're going to be taken advantage of by a lesbian.'

'Don't be ridiculous. Even if Beryl is that way inclined…'

But Ellie heard her own hesitation. She had been stupid about the guinea deposit and had almost lost her things. Then she remembered how Beryl had described herself as 'different' – was that what she had been trying to tell her?

She also remembered how kind Beryl had been to her and how she was liked by so many people at the SLH, including Faye.

'I'm comfortable in this place, Pat,' she said. 'Whether you like it or not.'

'Are you sure they didn't see you coming? I can imagine the jokes, the comments behind your back.'

She remembered the porter's sly remark about her being a friend of Beryl and Antoine's insistence that Beryl was not an object of desire.

So it was clear to her now. They all knew.

Perhaps Patrick was right? Maybe they thought her an unsophisticated country bumpkin, a know-nothing. Even Les Allen made a point about where she came from, about her being 'up from the country'. They all knew about Beryl. And they knew she didn't know.

Faye knew. And she hadn't told her.

'What can I do, Ellie? How can I persuade you to stick with me, to have the future we always planned?' Pat stopped, he opened his arms, as if to welcome her.

'That's it, Pat.' She turned around to look at him. 'I don't think I want the future we always planned. I'm not sure I ever did.'

'You won't get a better offer.' His tone became harder. 'It's not as if everyone is as broad-minded as me about their future wife. And now you're gallivanting around, in Clapham of all places.'

'Gallivanting! And what do you mean – broad-minded? Because I gave myself to you, my fiancé, before you went off to war.'

'Yes, well. It wouldn't take much to tarnish your reputation, would it?'

'Tarnish my...' Ellie was aghast. 'Let me be sure I understand. You are threatening to tell people that I am a woman of light virtue because I slept with you, when you were my husband-to-be, about to leave for battle?'

'Men don't like used goods.'

'Rest assured, I would never want any man who regarded a woman as "goods". I am not going to marry you, Pat.'

'Let's meet to discuss things. I don't think you've thought through what this might mean for you.'

'If you decide to blacken my name, you mean!'

'That's not what I said.'

'I'll meet you to discuss how we manage things, if you want, but I'm not changing my mind.'

'Soon. We need to talk about the future,' Pat said.

'Very well, but you pay Ratcliffe off. He stops following me. Immediately.'

'I will. When shall we meet? Tomorrow night, we could go for dinner?'

'No. Sunday afternoon. We can go for a walk on the common.'

'Ellie, be sensible. It's freezing.'

'Alright. Meet here, outside the SLH, at three o'clock on Sunday afternoon. We can go to that café, if you want.'

'I'll find somewhere better. Local, in public. Alright?'

'Alright.'

'I'm not going to give you up, Ellie. Not without a fight. And believe me, I fight dirty.'

What's that supposed to mean? she thought.

His jaw was set and the expression on his face was hard. Shaking her head, she walked away.

FRIDAY

31

FAYE

'Faye!'

She heard her name and turned to see Ellie hurrying up the stairs towards her.

'I was looking for you earlier, you weren't in the canteen,' Ellie said. 'I spoke with Owen Philpott. He confirmed that there's a connection between the two deep shelters and that the SLH still has a key to the entrance of the Balham Hill shelter. He told me that Miss Barnett holds it. Your theory could work.'

'I know,' Faye said. 'I asked Miss Barnett about the key yesterday. She... she wasn't best pleased. She keeps all her keys locked in her desk drawer in the office.'

'Who has a key to that?'

'Miss Barnett, Jean and... me.'

'The key to the shelters is important,' Ellie said.

'I know it is,' Faye replied. 'It means that someone with access to it, probably a man, is involved in Jane's death. Someone here. Someone we know.'

The two women gazed at each other, absorbing the fact.

'The midnight man?'

'Maybe. I think so.'

Ellie broke the silence. 'Did you take a look at the personnel records?'

'Yes.' Faye sighed. It had almost certainly cost her the new job. 'Jane was from Manchester. Her records didn't contain anything unusual or remarkable.'

'What about Polly?'

'The home address she gave is in Grays. I've written it down.'

'So Les was right.'

'Yes, but... '

Miss Barnett had been crystal clear. If she carried on asking questions, she could lose the job she had, let alone any chance of advancement. Faye had agonised all night about whether to continue investigating, but, in truth, she knew she couldn't stop.

She would have to be more careful about it, that was all.

'Polly was looking at patient records, she got a reprimand for doing so,' she said. 'And she was examining our purchase ledgers, comparing our current ledger with a ledger from before the war.'

'What for?'

'I don't know.' Faye shook her head. 'Ellie, listen. I've been instructed to stop asking questions about Jane's murder.'

'Who by?'

'Miss Barnett.'

'Oh.' Ellie's eyebrows rose. 'Couldn't you have explained?'

'She wasn't in any mood to listen. She won't take kindly to my continuing.'

'But... what about Jane?'

'I know, but there are circumstances... I can't mention.'

Faye was very tempted to tell Ellie all about the new post, but she had promised not to mention it.

'Then... I suppose that you'll have to stop.'

'Even though murder has been done.'

'So how can you stop?'

'I can't.' She took a deep breath. 'I think identifying the midnight man is even more important now, in light of what we've discovered.

Important for Jane and important for the SLH.' If it came to it, this was more important than her future there.

'The man who I saw.'

'Yes, he must be a witness if not the killer.'

'I was thinking... could it have been Owen Philpott?' Ellie asked. 'He was quick to point out his alibi and it was convenient that he happened to be away that particular night.'

Owen was a tallish man, Faye thought. Could it have been him? No.

'I don't think Owen killed Jane,' she answered. 'Not because I know and like him, or because of his alibi. But, if he'd killed Jane, he wouldn't have 'found' her body. He has access to plenty of places in those shelters where he could put a corpse and no one would find it until long after it could be identified. So, no, I don't think it was him.'

'So, who could it be?'

'Let's go through the possible candidates. It must be a man who could have used the SLH key, who is closely associated with the hospital – there aren't that many of them. I take it from your description that the midnight man isn't Dr Zeitel nor Mr Fortescue?'

'The first's too small and the second's too... rotund.'

'What about Charlie Redmond?'

'The midnight man had two arms, I'm sure of it.'

'That leaves Antoine Girard, who crosses the common on foot at all hours and has a reputation as a ladies' man.' Faye paused. 'Then there's Les Allen, Polly's former boyfriend and someone who also works non-standard hours, though his foot might rule him out. What about him?'

'He's easily tall enough, but I don't know if he'd have been able to move quickly enough.'

'I'll bet Les can move fast enough when he wants to,' Faye replied. 'When you saw the man with Jane was there any sign of him limping?'

'No. But then, would I have noticed?'

'Maybe not.' Faye swallowed hard. 'Then there's Nicholas Yorke, the inquisitive sociologist, who interviewed Jane days before she was killed, here at the SLH.'

'Do you really think it could be him?'

'I... I don't know, but he's tall, he's often at the hospital and Jane seems to have made an impression on him. You've spoken with him and the others, do any of their voices ring a bell?'

'No, but I would probably only recognise the man's voice if he was shouting, I didn't really hear much else.'

'Aside from picking a fight, I don't see how we can test that.' Faye smiled, grimly, at her own logic.

'Also, none of them have scratches on their faces,' Ellie said. 'And Jane's nails were broken.'

'But she could have broken her nails trying to open the shelter door.'

'Hello, Faye!' A nurse ran down the stairs into view, calling after them. 'We've been looking for you. Thank heavens I've found you.'

'What is it?'

'It's your sister. She's been admitted. She's in the isolation ward, your mother's with her. We've all been trying to find you.'

It took a moment for Faye to take in the news. Then a shock ran through her whole body. She spun round and began to run up the stairs two at a time. The isolation ward was at the very top of the hospital, looking out over the roof.

'What happened?' Faye asked.

'She had a violent choking fit, apparently, and coughed up a lot of blood,' the nurse explained as she followed. 'It looks, I'm sorry, Faye, it looks like tuberculosis.'

Hardly a surprise.

Faye grimaced. She still didn't know who was running the drug trial.

'The thing is, Sister has admitted her to Isolation, being as she's your family, but...'

They'd have to pay if Phoebe was to remain there.

'I'll speak with the Lady Almoner,' Faye said.

The Lady Almoners were notoriously tough, requiring any who could to pay for treatment, or at least to contribute towards its costs. Only the very poor or destitute got treatment for free.

'What happens if she can't stay here?' Ellie asked, gasping for breath as they rounded another corner and started on the next flight of stairs.

'The public sanatorium,' the nurse said.

'But they're—'

'I won't let her go there, I won't.' Faye forced the words out.

Yet how could she prevent it?

32

FAYE

A t the far end of the white ward a woman sat, bent over, by a bedside.

'Ma!'

She glanced up and Faye almost ran to her, the breeze of her passing causing the curtains drawn around other beds to quiver. A cold wind gusted in through windows opened to reduce the risk of contagion.

'Faye!' Esme, her face crumpled, stood to embrace her older daughter.

'Ma, Ma, what happened? How is she?'

Phoebe lay, made fast beneath tucked sheets and blankets, her face pale on the white pillow. Dark streaks of hair were stretched across her forehead. A cylinder of oxygen stood like a sentinel beside the bed. Phoebe's eyelids, blue-veined and seeming tissue-thin, fluttered open.

'Sis!' she mouthed, wordlessly.

'Don't speak,' Faye said to her. 'Just lie still.' She looked at her mother.

'She was coughing fit to burst,' Esme said in a low voice. 'Blood was coming up, great gouts of it and she couldn't stop. I got Phyllis's girl from next door to run to the phone box and call for an ambulance.'

'Oh, Ma. I'm sorry I wasn't there.'

With tired, red-rimmed eyes Esme looked up at Faye, who felt her heart lurch.

'S'not your fault, love and, besides, when they saw it was your sister, they brought her here rather than out to Claverly. For which I'm grateful.'

Claverly was the closest public sanatorium. Its buildings were old and decaying, its staff tried hard, but couldn't compensate for the lack of money. It was a sad and desperate place of last resort, for those who couldn't afford anything better, or who had no one to look out for them.

Faye glanced at the figure in the bed. Phoebe wouldn't last a week in Claverly.

'Faye...' Esme pointed and Faye turned to see a staff nurse approaching them.

'Mrs Smith,' she greeted Esme. 'Faye, if I could have a word.'

'Of course.'

Faye followed the nurse to the medical station at the side of the ward.

'The consultant will be doing her rounds in half an hour,' the staff nurse began. 'She'll want to know your sister's details. Fill in this admittance form for her, please.'

Faye took the piece of paper offered. It was part completed by the staff nurse and Phoebe's condition was described as *'acute progressive bilateral pulmonary tuberculosis'*.

'Doctor can usually spot a long-term sufferer when she sees one,' the staff nurse intruded on Faye's thoughts. She gave her a meaningful look. 'Though we often get new patients who are only recently diagnosed.'

Phoebe was clearly a longstanding sufferer with a disease designated as contagious. The staff nurse was allowing Faye to report Phoebe's symptoms as recent and undiagnosed. The Smiths weren't alone in failing to report a sufferer, many families did the same, for fear that their loved one would be incarcerated and die. Cases like

JULIE ANDERSON

hers had to be reported to the authorities by law and there were fines for non-reporting.

They'd have difficulty paying for Phoebe's care, the meagre insurance they paid weekly wouldn't cover the costs of hospitalisation and a fine would be the final straw. Faye glanced back at her mother beside Phoebe's bed. To be fined would destroy her mother. And it would mean the end of Phoebe.

'Thanks. Do you have a pen?'

Minutes later Faye looked up from completing the form to see her father hovering outside the ward on the landing with Ellie.

'May he come in?' she asked and she gestured for him to enter when the nurse agreed.

Reg Smith was a big man, but he seemed diminished, a black smudge walking through the white of the isolation ward. Faye joined him as he passed the nurses' station.

'How is she?'

'Not good. Doctor hasn't seen her yet.' Faye kept her voice soft. 'I've said it's a recent thing on the form.'

Her father nodded. 'But…'

'Doctor'll understand.'

They walked to the end of the ward.

'How are we going to pay for this, Dad?'

'I don't know love.' He took his wife in his arms as they arrived at the bedside. 'Esme, mother.'

Phoebe's eyes opened when she heard his voice. 'Daddy,' she whispered.

'Phoebe, love.' He reached out a hand.

'Don't touch the patient, please, sir.' It was the staff nurse. 'Tuberculosis is a contagious disease.' She tucked the covers on the bed even more tightly. 'I'm sorry, but there should be no contact. Keep at least six feet between you and them. It's better that way.'

Reg held his wife even closer, a rasping, strangled sound escaping from his chest.

'Is she going to…?'

'She's stable for the moment, sir,' the nurse said. 'We'll know more when the doctor has seen her.' She returned to her station.

'Did you speak to the union again?' Esme asked.

'Yes.' Reg shook his head. 'They'll pay for a few days, but that's all. Other members have families with medical problems, problems that can be cured. Our Phoebe needs constant nursing and there's no end of it in sight.'

'Faye, Faye, you've got to get her on that trial, that experiment.'

'I'll try, Ma. I'll try my hardest, I promise. But we'll still have to find the money for her to stay here. I'll talk with the Lady Almoner, see if we can get some of the fees waived, or have time to pay, but I can't promise.'

'It must mean something, love, that you work here.'

Faye crossed her fingers. 'I'm sure it will,' she said. 'I'll go and speak with the Lady Almoner now.'

'Yes, go,' her father said. 'Anything, Faye.'

It was hard to leave them there, but she wanted to be doing something.

'Have this, Reg,' she heard her mother say as she turned to leave. 'It's worth something. If I can get it off.' Esme handed Reg her wedding ring.

Faye walked the length of the ward through a mist of tears.

33

ELEANOR

'Faye, how is she?'

Her friend looked shell-shocked. Ellie had seen that look on faces in Nuremberg. People who came to try to find out what had happened to their families and loved ones.

'We don't know yet. Doctor hasn't seen her.'

'She'll pull through, won't she?'

'I hope so.'

That empty look, where emotions should be, but which can't be acknowledged for fear of complete collapse.

'Faye.' A male voice.

A large man, Faye's father, Ellie assumed, came out on to the landing. His shoulders stooped forward, as if a massive weight was bearing down on him and the deep lines in his face seemed to draw him downwards.

'Tell John what's happened, telephone him at the station and get him to tell your brothers. You concentrate on – what we said. I'll stay with your mother for the time being, then I'll persuade her to come home.'

'Alright, Dad.'

The man returned to the Isolation Ward and Ellie followed Faye down the stairs.

'Ellie, I've got things I must do. Can you handle the canteen for lunch service?'

'Of course.'

'I don't know how long I'll be, but I should be back by the early afternoon. I've got to speak with the Lady Almoner about some help to pay for this and then I've got to find out about a drug trial. If we can get Phoebe put on the trial it might help her. Otherwise...' Faye's face was chalky white. 'The public sanatoriums are places people like Phoebe never come out of.'

Ellie desperately wanted to help. Perhaps... She had her savings, her safety net, scraped together over many months in case of emergencies.

What was this if it wasn't an emergency?

'Faye, listen, I've got money, not much, but it'll be something. At least it'll ensure she isn't thrown out of here.'

'What?'

'Savings. When I came back from Nuremberg, I was going to use them to tide me over until I got a legal job, but now I've got my wages from SLH and the room at Beryl's. Thanks to you. If you can use the money, it's yours.'

'Oh, Ellie, that's so kind of you, but I...'

'I was in a desperate state and you helped me.'

When Ellie had been at her lowest Faye had offered kindness, friendship and practical help. To return the favour was the least she could do, even if it meant cleaning tables for a while longer.

'I did what anyone would do...'

'Faye, if you can't raise money any other way, take my money as a loan. It could cover Phoebe's immediate care. I don't imagine the isolation ward is cheap. You can pay me back as and when it's possible.'

'Thank you, Ellie.' Faye reached out and gripped her hand, eyes brimming. 'But I... I hope I don't have to.'

'So do I.'

She squeezed Faye's hand, prompting a determined smile.

'I'll go down to the canteen, make sure everything's in place for

197

the lunch service, see that everything runs smoothly,' she said. 'At least you won't have to worry about that.'

'Thank you.'

They had reached the upper-ground floor.

'Chin up,' she said, as she watched Faye walk away, deeper into the hospital, along the wide corridor to the Lady Almoner's office.

34

ELEANOR

Lunch service was nearly over and the canteen was almost empty. To Ellie's immense relief, it had all gone well – Faye had enough to worry about without problems in the canteen. Cook had overseen the counter as well as the kitchen, while Ellie managed the dining area, stamping the diners' ration books and helping at the till.

Still Faye hadn't returned.

Ellie poured herself a cup of tea and sat at a table near the windows, wondering how her friend was getting on. Would Phoebe be allowed to remain in the SLH? The family would rally round, she was sure, but she wanted to help if she could. To repay Faye for all her kindness.

Outside the sky was grey and dense, the clouds heavy-bellied with rain or snow. The weather forecast on the wireless said that there was to be no let-up in the cold weather and worse was on the way. It would be bitterly cold on Sunday when she had agreed to meet with Pat.

Faye's news had pushed their encounter of the previous evening to the back of her mind, but memory of it bubbled up now. It was obvious that he wanted to control her and was, apparently, ready to abandon any principles to do so. That he had set a man to watch her felt like an invasion. His anger and viciousness had surprised her, this wasn't a side of Patrick she had ever seen before. Though his offer to live in London, if she chose to, was unexpected, it made no difference; she was not going to spend her life with the man Pat had become.

Yet it was becoming increasingly likely that she might need a husband. That or to do the unthinkable.

Then there was George Packham. His threat was probably empty, he wanted to scare her, that was all, but she would report him, he was trying to intimidate her. Besides, there were the packing cases and crates she had seen at Mrs Packham's; someone there was dealing in something. Maybe not legally? Would the police be interested? Without evidence… probably not. But she'd report him anyway. Never give in to bullies.

Ellie forced herself to focus on doing something more constructive. The midnight man. Miss Barnett may have forbidden Faye to continue to investigate, but that didn't prevent her from following up what they had already learned.

Seeing the nurses in their trousers on Balham Hill, then hearing about Beryl from Pat had made her reconsider what she had seen on Sunday night. Had she made certain assumptions about the couple she'd seen that night on the common? Could the man she thought she saw with Jane actually have been a trouser-clad woman?

Ellie tried to conjure the picture in her mind of the two figures in the trees. They had been indistinct at that distance, though when the second figure hurried after the first she had thought it was a man. The voice was certainly a deeper one and they were taller than Jane. She frowned. Could it have been a woman?

The canteen doors swung open and Miss Barnett entered.

The hospital administrator caught sight of her and came over to her table. It occurred to Ellie that, given she had told Faye to stop investigating, she might have an ulterior motive? Could she be protecting someone, perhaps?

'No, please, don't get up,' the woman said. 'May I join you?'

'Yes, of course.'

'How's it gone? The lunch service, I mean.'

'It's been alright. Busy, but without hiccups. We all know what our responsibilities are, how we're meant to operate. Miss Smith makes sure of that. And she keeps an eye on us.'

Miss Barnett smiled. 'Very laudable, Miss Peveril, your loyalty to your colleague, but I happen to know that Faye Smith has been in the Lady Almoner's Office for the past two hours.'

'Ah.' Ellie felt her cheeks flush. 'I'm sure she'll be along as soon as she's free.'

'I suspect that she has enough on her plate at the moment. Though, in fact, it was you who I wanted to speak with.'

Ellie was curious. Why did Miss Barnett want to speak with her?

'I understand that your mother was a hospital volunteer?'

'Yes, she helped run the admin at our local Infirmary. Nothing like the size of the SLH, of course. It was a country hospital.'

'But you chose to go into a different line of work?'

'I was – am – a legal clerk.'

Or would be, if any work was available, she thought.

'You wouldn't consider a more permanent role here, then? I don't mean clearing up in the canteen. Something more suitable for a young woman with your education and background.'

'What do you mean?'

'I have a vacancy in the hospital office, overseeing the administrative processes, enabling the hospital to run smoothly and giving the medical staff as much help as possible.'

A glow of happiness began deep in Ellie's insides and started to spread through her whole body. This would be perfect, a hospital administrator job. What would her mother say?

'You handled the VIP luncheon very well. You have a gift for enabling people to help you, you charm them, I'm sure you would be a great asset when it comes to fund-raising.'

'It's—'

'Don't answer hastily, hear me out. I accept that you might see your longer-term future elsewhere, but it's a good job and a challenging role. The SLH is a good employer. If it would suit you, I can offer you a short-term contract, renewable every six months. The pay is significantly higher than your current post and, as a permanent member of hospital staff you would qualify for benefits like housing.'

Ellie knew she could do such a job and do it well. And the SLH was a good place to work. This was just what she needed, just what she'd been hoping for!

'You would work directly to me, in the same way that Faye does. You'll find that I'm a fair boss, though I expect my staff to work hard, operate in a proper manner and be prompt.'

'Thank you for the offer, Miss Barnett. I'll certainly think about it.'

'Good, but don't take too long. I don't like to be kept waiting.'

Miss Barnett put her palms on the tabletop and stood. 'I'll be advertising the vacancy if I don't get an answer by the start of next week.'

'I understand, Miss Barnett.'

'Good.' The woman walked away.

Ellie sat, smiling from ear to ear and marvelling at her good fortune. A hospital administration job was perfect. Her parents could hardly object and it meant more money and a stronger connection to the SLH. She couldn't wait to share the good news with Faye.

But now it was time to close the canteen and prepare for the tea service. The last few lunchtime stragglers were finishing, but they would be on their way soon. Cook and the kitchen staff knew what they had to make for tea and then dinner, all she had to do was close the doors and clean.

As she mopped, Ellie grinned and a small laugh escaped her. Things were finally beginning to go her way.

35

ELEANOR

Teatime and the canteen was filling. Ellie stood at the lectern, stamping ration books and checking off names. Beryl waved a greeting as she and a group of nurses arrived.

There was a small commotion as Faye entered, pale-faced and red-eyed. News of her sister's admission had got round the hospital and people stopped and spoke to her as she passed. She thanked them, was polite, but to Ellie's eyes, she didn't seem herself. Her essence seemed to be somewhere else.

'Make her sit down, I'll get her some tea.' Beryl was at Ellie's elbow, as one of the servers came to take Ellie's place.

'Sit down.' She ushered her friend towards an empty table. 'Sit.'

'I've been sitting down all day,' Faye responded, but took a seat.

'Tea.' Beryl put a mug down on the table. 'Well? How's Phoebe?'

'Quiet now, thank you for asking. They've given her some sort of sedative, she'll sleep. My Mum and Dad have gone home.'

'Phoebe's staying here?' Ellie asked. 'In the Isolation Ward. Can you...?'

'My dad's union is paying for the immediate costs.'

Beryl grimaced. 'And then?'

'The Lady Almoner says that the SLH won't charge the full fees, but we still have to raise some money.'

Ellie and Beryl exchanged a look. Neither said anything.

'It's not easy, I know,' the Scot said, as she stood. 'I've got to go, I'm on shift now. If you need anywhere to kip, Faye, so that you're close to the hospital, there's always the sofa at my place. Ellie's got the only other bed, but the settee isn't too uncomfortable. You can stay with us if you want to.'

'Thanks, Beryl. That's kind of you.' Faye smiled. 'I might take you up on that, though, right now I need to be with my parents and the rest of the family.'

'Aye, well... the offer's there. Oh, and one more thing... your Nicholas Yorke.'

'What about him?'

'You mentioned his interviews – there's a schedule of them pinned to the nurses' noticeboard, you can see who he's talking to. Quite a few people, it seems. He's using Barnett's office; Jean mentioned it to me.'

'Really?'

'Yep. Thought you might like to bump into him, perhaps, when he's here? Cheer you up.'

'Maybe. Though not right now.'

'Just a thought.'

'She's very kind,' Faye said, her gaze following Beryl as she left.

'She is.'

Ellie glanced at her friend, she looked exhausted. Faye would have been worrying all day, about her sister, about raising money... Maybe a distraction was what she needed, something to take her out of herself.

'I've been thinking about our case,' Ellie said.

'The midnight man.'

'Well, I've been wondering about that,' Ellie said. 'Do you think the person I thought was a man could actually have been a woman?'

'But I thought you said the couple were... oh, I see.' Faye contemplated her friend. 'Two women. It might explain the lateness of the hour, they mightn't want to be seen. But didn't you hear Jane's companion?'

'Yes.'

'Could that have been a woman speaking?'

'I didn't think so at the time, but I suppose it could have been. A woman with a deeper voice than usual.'

'I understand that you're questioning your own preconceptions, but you probably saw exactly what you thought you saw. A man with Jane. She had intercourse, remember, there was evidence.'

'Of course, I'd forgotten about that.' Ellie banged the table with her hand, she was annoyed at herself.

Faye sighed. 'I'm not a lot of help, I'm afraid. I'm sorry, I'm not at my best at the moment.'

'Don't apologise, it's natural, you're worried and tired. My offer still stands, Faye, as regards the money,' Ellie said.

'Thanks, though we might not need it.' Faye gave her an affectionate look. 'My brothers are going to come in tomorrow. They can't afford much, but they'll help.'

'That's something. Oh, I must tell you, before I forget. I've had a surprising offer!'

This could cheer her friend, some good news.

Faye raised an eyebrow.

'Of a job, here, at the SLH,' Ellie enthused. 'Running the administrator's office... Faye, what is it?'

Her friend's face had lost what little colour it had.

'Running the...' Faye seemed unable to form words.

'Office. A temporary contract, for six months, but I'd enjoy doing that type of work.'

'Running the office...'

'Yes. I... I don't want to seem ungrateful to you, for all the help you've given me, but it's a good offer. It's a better job than working in the canteen.'

Her friend was staring at her. 'And are you going to accept it?' she asked.

'Yes, why not? It's going to be difficult to find myself any legal work and I like it here at the SLH. And we'll be working together.'

'I see.' Faye's voice was barely above a whisper.

'Is something the matter? Aren't you pleased for me, Faye? I thought...'

Faye stood. Her hands were trembling.

'Faye, are you alright?'

'Yes, yes, I'm tickety-boo.'

Something was wrong, something was severely wrong, but Ellie had no idea what or why. Was this to do with Phoebe? What else could it be?

She stared, mouth agape, as Faye strode, head down, out of the canteen.

36

FAYE

No! No! No!

Another set of doors hit the walls with a loud bang as Faye thrust them open. She stormed along the corridor, legs stretching, arms swinging.

How could she have thought there might be any chance of getting the job after receiving that dressing down? She had hoped against hope that she could mend matters with Miss Barnett, that she would come round. But Miss B hadn't wasted any time; there'd be no deputy administrator job if there was an office manager post instead.

Tears of rage pricked her eyelids. Her brows were drawn together, and she stared in front of her, seeing nothing. People leapt out of her way.

And now! Especially now.

She'd counted on that extra money. With it they might manage to pay for Phoebe's care. Without it there was even less chance of keeping her in the SLH. She had been deluding herself. All the agonising about what to do; it was all pointless.

Everything was conspiring against her.

And Ellie.

Did she know?

Had Eleanor Peveril played her for a fool? With her supposed naivety, her friendliness and her charm. Was this what she'd been planning all along – to insinuate herself into the SLH, impress Miss Barnett, get herself a job. Get herself a job at Faye's expense. She could hardly credit it.

This is what happens, when you take a chance, do someone a kindness!

'Hello, Faye. What are you doing here?'

Startled, Faye looked round.

'Taken up tobacco, have you?'

She had walked the entire length of the hospital wing and out of the back of the building into the darkness of the SLH gardens. A clutch of caped nurses was sheltering from the wind as best they could in an open glass porch, smoking cigarettes in the light from the corridor.

'Er, no.' Faye shook her head as she began to shiver.

'You missed a good do on Wednesday,' a nurse said. 'A real cele-bration.'

'How's your sister? She's in isolation, isn't she?' another asked.

'She's... as well as can be expected. Thanks for asking.'

'I'll bet you're glad she's here.'

'Yes. Yes I am.'

'Come on, let's go home.'

'I want the warmth. It's too flippin' cold out here.'

They hurried off between rose beds, towards the monolithic building of the nurses' home. It *would* be much warmer there, warmer than Sugden Road too, Faye thought. A decent place to live once more, now it had been repaired.

For a moment she saw it as she had on the morning after one of the worst air raids, the eyeless black holes of windows shattered, a corner of the roof missing, its metal beams sticking out like broken bone. Bewildered nurses emerging from the air raid bunker beneath the building, having spent the night there following the siren's call. Faces blank and shocked to find their home so violently changed.

She refocused on the present, the sky grey and heavy, its low cloud underlit by ambient light, no longer blackness riven by searchlights. The nurses' home looked solid and reassuring. The light had returned, people were no longer dying in bombing raids.

Get a grip, she told herself, stop feeling sorry for yourself.

Forget Ellie. Do something useful.

Streptomycin was shown in the purchase ledger. Some had been delivered to the SLH, so the hospital must be taking part in the trial. Get Phoebe on it.

Faye re-entered the building and began to retrace her steps.

She had to find out who was in charge of the trial, so as to persuade them to put Phoebe on it and soon. The trial places would be filling up fast, this was a heaven-sent opportunity, but she wasn't moving quickly enough. It was probably someone senior, a surgeon. Dr Falconer was the senior chest physician, so it was likely to be her, but Faye couldn't be sure.

After yesterday she couldn't ask Miss Barnett and, anyway, she'd gone to a conference about the new NHS regional health boards. She could ask one of the clinicians, but probably not until tomorrow and she needed the information now if she was to prepare what to say. There was one quick way of getting it. To look in the personnel files.

She'd already been chastised for scrutinising Polly Brooks' record; after yesterday's contretemps Miss Barnett wouldn't countenance her looking at records relating to a consultant. But there was no point in dithering. It had to be done.

It was a Friday, Jean usually knocked off early on Fridays, the secretary would have gone home by now. She wouldn't be disturbed.

Do it now.

37

FAYE

Bright bars of yellow light from the street lamps on the South Side formed steppingstones across the floor of Miss Barnett's dark office. Muted traffic noise competed with the ever-present sounds of the hospital, the distant echo of voices. The office was cold, the embers in the grate had last given out their heat several hours ago.

Faye unlocked and rummaged around in the key drawer of Miss Barnett's desk, feeling for the set of small keys to the filing cabinets which were usually near the front. She pulled them out and went through to the office next door where the personnel records were kept in the top drawer of the filing cabinet.

Her gaze fell on the two purchase ledgers, still sitting on the desk from yesterday.

Ever since she had spoken with Jean about Polly Brooks, Faye had wanted to take a more detailed look at them. She wanted to see exactly what Polly had seen. Faye sat at the desk, opening the heavy ledgers side by side. She could read them easily in the light from the street lamps.

What was it in these files that was being compared? It could be any kind of purchase, but the food and stores all went through her own purchasing ledgers, not these, which showed repeat orders of equipment and medical stores and, by far the most frequent entries, drugs. All the drugs purchased at the SLH appeared in the ledgers. Polly could have been looking at anything, but if she'd been looking at drugs purchasing this was where the trail would be found.

Faye turned the pages of one ledger, then the other.

The office was buying more drugs than before. There was a rise during wartime, but that was to be expected, when the hospital took in casualties. Now the SLH was back to pre-wartime levels of occupancy and sickness, so shouldn't the level of purchasing be reducing too? She looked at the left-hand column. The hospital was ordering a huge variety of drugs, but one caught Faye's eye; neurocaine or cocaine hydrochloride. This appeared frequently, with repeat purchases, large and small, in the current ledger, but didn't feature at all in the earlier one.

Maybe the drug was new, or had only recently been licensed? Perhaps there were equivalents in the earlier ledger, but she didn't recognise them. She didn't know enough to be able to take a view. What she did know was that cocaine was highly addictive and that it was used for pleasure. It would also command a high price on the black market.

Faye closed the ledgers. She needed to find out more about drug purchasing and to do that she would have to speak with Miss Underwood, the pharmacist.

Now for the consultant's record.

The drawer rumbled on its rollers as she opened the filing cabinet. A, B, E, F – Falconer. She angled the file towards the window to read its contents.

Penelope Falconer, FRCP. At the bottom of the record was a newly typed note 'Medical Research Council randomised trial of streptomycin, London 1946. SLH component'. Trial patients to be included were to have 'acute progressive bilateral pulmonary tuberculosis of recent origin, bacteriologically proved and unsuitable for collapse therapy'. The trial was to run for fifteen months.

Fifteen months! Her family could barely afford to pay for one.

She placed the record back into the cabinet. In the yellow light she saw that the next was for Antoine Girard.

May as well be hung for a sheep as for a lamb.

The file was mostly in French, and Faye's French was non-existent, but even she understood *'espose'*. He was married.

Ellie seemed to have formed an attachment to him. How would she break the news to her? On the other hand, why should she tell Ellie anything at all? Maybe they were well suited to each other, both incomers, both chancers.

But... there were things women should always tell other women. Her heart sank, she realised that she had to warn her erstwhile friend. She slipped the file back into the drawer and was about to slide it closed when a tell-tale bar of light appeared under the door to Miss Barnett's room.

Could her boss have returned, late, to her office?

Faye stared at the pale strip in the gap between the foot of the door and the floor, her pulse quickening. If she was discovered in a dark office, covertly looking through the personnel records of the surgeons, it would mean more than a reprimand. She'd be out. She heard the beating of her blood in her ears and realised that she was holding her breath, so she forced herself to breathe evenly, quietly.

Yet she couldn't close the filing cabinet without alerting whoever was in the next office to her presence. She listened attentively, waiting for any sound indicating that they were going to open the communicating door. There was nothing.

Of course, it might not be Miss Barnett. It could be a cleaner. Faye checked her watch in the lurid yellow light. Half past six.

The chances were that it *was* a cleaner.

She might be able to bluff her way out. A cleaner wouldn't think it odd that she was here.

Faye made a decision. She quickly crossed to the door to the corridor, picking up a pile of files that lay on Jean's desk. She flicked on the light switch and walked, as if she had just entered, into the office. The communicating door opened and a head peered around it. It belonged to a man.

'Les, what are you doing here?'

'Oh. Faye. What are you doing here?' He looked down at his feet. She waited.

When he looked up his eyes were wary and cold. His jovial manner in the canteen seemed to be forgotten. They were back to their encounter in the staffroom on Monday.

'Oh, alright,' he admitted, lips twisting. 'I was hoping to get Polly's home address.'

'How?'

'I thought I'd sweet-talk the secretary into giving it to me.'

'At half-past six? You know perfectly well when Jean goes home. You knew she wouldn't be here.'

'So, what if I did?' he snapped. 'I was going to try and sneak a look at the staff records, see if I could find them. They must be kept here somewhere. After everything that's happened recently, I wanted to contact Polly. Make sure she's alright. She should be told about her friend, at least.'

Faye wasn't in the mood for any nonsense. She didn't particularly like, or even trust, Les Allen, but he was a fool if he was clinging on to a one-sided relationship.

'I can't give you that information, Les, it's personal. Personnel records are locked away.'

'But—'

'If Polly's still in contact with anyone here, she'll hear about Jane. If she's not, well, that may be because she doesn't want to be. That's her decision.'

Faye walked across to the filing cabinet and closed it, turning its key in the lock.

Les gave her a level stare.

'Are you sure I can't persuade you?' he said. 'It's not like I'm doing anything dreadful, I only want to contact Poll. I'm not breaking the law, only a piffling little hospital rule.'

'No, Les, I—'

'It's not like I'm stealing or taking things I shouldn't be. Like bananas, for example.'

So he'd been waiting for the best time to play that card, she thought. He must want Polly's address very much. Tread carefully, he could probably get her dismissed, especially now that her relations with Miss Barnett were so strained.

'I have every right to take home any of my rations I don't use. And what you're doing is blackmail, Les, I don't give into that. You say anything more and I'll have to report *you*.'

He had a speculative look in his eyes as he considered her. 'Miss Barnett—'

'Would want to know exactly what *you* were doing in her office at this time of night.'

Faye could bluff too. She would out face him.

He pursed his lips and tilted his head on to one side but said no more.

'Forget it, Les. You'll get no change out of me.'

He clamped his mouth shut, narrowing his eyes. She had won.

'Now, I'll lock things up behind us.'

She ushered him towards the door into the corridor and turned the key with a click when he was gone.

He had some nerve. Not just coming in here to try and find Polly's address, but then attempting to blackmail her. Well, he wouldn't try that again. She'd have to keep a close eye on him in future, she wasn't exactly fireproof and Les had a talent for showing up at the most inopportune moments.

Moving into Miss Barnett's office she replaced the filing cabinet keys in the open desk drawer. The SLH key to the Balham Hill shelters entrance lay there. Somehow there was a link between that key and Jane's murder and, once Phoebe was on the drug trial, she would work out what it was.

She pushed the drawer closed, locked it and marched out of the office.

38

FAYE

There was no moon. The sky was dark and dense as Faye trudged through maelstroms of brown and yellow leaves. Her hands were thrust deep into her coat pockets and her scarf wrapped tight around her head and neck. Tree trunks creaked and heaved, branches thrashing in the wind as if they would uproot and march across the common, a sea of leaves and twigs. Traffic was light and Faye was the only pedestrian.

Would Dr Falconer be in the hospital tomorrow? She could be on the rota, the board in the entrance hall would tell Faye for certain and she could ask in the Nurses' Common Room. Then she could pick the best time to go to her room and speak with her. This evening she would think through what to say – it was important that she got things right.

Penelope Falconer was committed to finding a treatment for TB, which was why she was conducting the trial. She'd be looking for the most suitable patients and Phoebe met all the criteria. The lady almoner had already agreed payment and the Smith family was arranging to pay what she'd stipulated. She could tell Dr Falconer all of that, which would count in Phoebe's favour. That Faye was an SLH employee, her family was from Clapham and her extended family were south London born and bred would help. Plus, Phoebe was already there, in the hospital, in the Isolation Ward, ready and waiting. That would help too.

Faye staggered, knocked sideways by a particularly powerful gust of wind. She stepped back onto the pavement through a whirl of dust and detritus.

A car drove by, meandering around potholes, headlights illuminating a broad band of the common. It was the only sign of life for some time. Faye looked longingly at the comforting light seeping around the curtains in the windows of the houses on the Westside. The high four-storey villas were far beyond the tennis courts and bowling green.

For a moment the wind died.

It was then that she heard it. Someone else was walking through the dead leaves.

She could see no one up ahead, so she turned, but the road behind her was empty. Outside of the circles of lamp light everywhere was dark. The wind rose and Faye stretched her legs, battling against the blast. As she passed through the dark between two pools of brightness, she spun round.

There *was* someone. She'd swear it. A figure had shrunk away, out of a pool of light. Someone was following her and didn't want to be seen. Faye continued onward, increasing her pace.

There was a cold sensation in the pit of her stomach. The common, so familiar during daylight, had become a wild and mysterious place in the darkness.

It could be Jane's killer.

Unable to see, she couldn't leave the road; to run across the grass would be too dangerous. Could she get close to the houses and shout for help, but would anyone hear her in this wind? And, even if they did... she thought of Ellie hearing Jane's cry and doing nothing.

The wind was roaring in her ears. She dragged wayward strands of hair from out of her eyes.

She had reached Mount Pond. The tips of its wavelets were

catching the lamplight and the reeds around its edge whispering and shirring in the wind. Then the street lamp flickered.

Off. On. Off. On.

Dark. Light. Dark.

Dark.

Faye ran. Ignoring the uneven pavement and cracked paving stones; she had to get to the next pool of light. Her breath came in short gasps and the sound of the gusting wind was drowned out by the loud pounding of her heart. She glanced behind her again.

No one. But whoever it was might be anywhere, moving out of sight in the darkness.

Faye's feet were growing heavy. She slowed and ran her tongue over her dry lips, looked over her shoulder.

There was a light in the darkness, a pinpoint of white and it was coming towards her. Could it be the light from a torch? Had her follower abandoned any attempt at concealment? Faye redoubled her efforts, fear-fuelled adrenaline surging through her.

Panting, she reached the next circle of lamp light. The disk of light was approaching very quickly, outrunning it would be impossible. The wind obscured most sounds, but she heard a stuttering, whining rumble. She laughed and bent double, hands on her knees to catch her breath. Above the gusting and buffeting she could hear the growl of a motorbike.

She began to wave, stepping into the road to flag it down.

As the bike drew level, she recognised its rider. Beneath a leather cap and goggles was her brother Matthew.

'Sis? What's up with you then? Why are you flapping your arms like a madwoman?'

'Matty, am I glad to see you,' she gasped.

'Are you alright? What's the matter?'

'I'll tell you later. Just give me a lift home now, will you?'

'Hop on.'

As he stood, sliding forwards, she clambered onto the saddle of the bike behind him. She wrapped her arms around her brother's waist when he sat back down, placing her head against his back. She felt weak with relief.

'Hold tight,' he said.

The motorbike roared away.

39

FAYE

F aye pulled the blanket more tightly around her legs.

She sat, wearing her overcoat, in the kitchen at number nineteen. The hearth was cold and a chill draught blew down the chimney to meet its cousin coming in under the door to the side return. Yet it wasn't only the temperature that made her tremble. When Matthew had asked her why she'd flagged him down she laughed it off, but the episode had left its mark. Faye didn't often feel real fear, but, alone on the common that night, she had been very frightened. Someone had been following her, she was certain.

Now she pressed her lips together and forced herself to be still.

On the settle John curled his legs beneath him and held a blanket around his shoulders. Reg Smith was the only family member not snuggled into a coat or a blanket, mainly because he was awaiting the return of his wife to her place by his side, before pulling a thick bedspread around them both. She had been sitting in the crook of his arm.

'This place is like a funeral house and twice as cold,' Matthew said, rubbing his hands together.

'Pipe down.' John whacked his younger brother with his hot water bottle.

'Let's get started,' Reg said, as Esme took her place. 'We'll fill

Vince and Ray in later. Now. You know that your sister's in the South London. Faye, tell us what's happening.'

Faye took a deep breath and began.

'Phoebe had a very bloody coughing fit and was admitted to the SLH earlier today. She's in the Isolation Ward and has been diagnosed with tuberculosis. We all knew that was likely. It's a contagious disease, so she has to stay in isolation until she's non-contagious.'

'Which will be when?' John asked.

'We don't know.' Faye paused. 'Maybe never. Often the 'cure' can be fatal – fifty per cent of sufferers undergoing surgery die – and sulphonamides, the drugs used against the disease, often don't work. The standard advice is for the patient to rest.'

'Are you saying there's nothing to be done?' Matthew asked.

'Give her a chance,' John said.

'There is one possibility,' Faye continued. 'A new drug, called streptomycin. It's from America and it's still at the trial stage here. The SLH is taking part in the trial, which is being run out of the Brompton Hospital. Our chest physician, Dr Falconer, is in charge.'

'We've got to get her on this trial.' John slapped his hands together, then caught his blanket as it fell.

'Hang on a minute,' Reg said. 'Go on, Faye.'

'From what I've been able to find out, Phoebe is in the right age range and she is at the right stage of the disease. She's also recently diagnosed, which is one of the requirements and what it says on her admittance record, though I suspect any medic would be able to tell that she'd had the disease for a while.'

'Will that make any difference, love?' asked Esme.

'I hope not.'

Faye exchanged a look with John, he knew that they might get fined for not reporting it.

'I'm going to try my hardest to get her on the trial,' she said. 'But our problems don't end there.'

'Money.' This was Matthew.

'Exactly. I spent a long time speaking with one of our Lady

Almoners today. The SLH won't charge its full fees for Phoebe's care, but free care is only for the most desperate.'

'We are desperate!' Matthew said.

'No, we're not,' Reg countered. 'Six of us have jobs.'

'And expenses.' John pointed out.

'I know, son, but it's not like we've got nothing and there are plenty like that.'

'We've been doing the sums,' Faye said. 'Dad's union has contributed enough to keep Phoebe in the SLH until the end of the month. After that, it's up to us.'

'Three weeks?'

'Is that all?'

'How long does this trial take, Faye?' John asked.

'From what I've been able to discover – fifteen months.'

There was a stunned silence.

'There, there, mother.' Reg kissed his wife's forehead. She was weeping, silently. He nodded to Faye to continue.

'Mum and Dad think they'll be able to raise some money by selling off things and I have a little put by, together that's probably enough to get us through until the end of February.'

'I can contribute,' John said. 'Between now and then, week by week, that should build up. Vince said he'll have to talk with Agnes, but he thinks that they could contribute some. From their wedding money, if need be.'

'Oh, I hope not, Vince and Agnes have saved so hard,' Esme said. 'Faye's new job might help.'

'Ah, well, I'm not so sure that's available anymore.'

John caught his sister's eye but said nothing.

'But I'm sure I'll be able to make a contribution and I can help in other ways.'

She could bring food home, though she'd have to be even more careful now. If Les had noticed, others might too. And, since they had crossed swords again, Les would be on the lookout for any way of catching her out.

'What's the alternative to keeping Pheebs in the South London?' Matthew asked.

'I don't think there is one. She must be in a hospital that is part of the trial,' Faye answered. 'There are other hospitals taking part, it's a national trial, but the SLH is our best bet for help with the cost. We're a local family and I work there.'

'I'm not having her go to a public sanatorium.' Esme was adamant. 'I'd have her back here rather than that.'

'You can't – it's a contagious disease, Ma. Now she's in hospital she won't be allowed to come home.'

'This new National Health Service...' John began.

'Won't be up and running until next year, or even later,' Faye said. 'It isn't in place yet. But you're right, John, the free treatment might begin before the end of the fifteen months. We don't know. On the other hand, it might come too late.'

'The point is, we can't bank on it,' her father said. 'We've got to assume that we have to pay.'

'A shame she had to have that coughing fit right now,' Matthew said.

'It's been coming for weeks! Months!' Esme Smith was indignant. 'The girl's been suffering for so long.'

'Alright, calm down.' Reg stroked his wife and glared at Matthew. 'He didn't mean anything by it.'

'I didn't. Sorry, Ma.'

'Faye's going to try and get Phoebe on to the trial; your mother and I will be raising money by selling some off some things; and, starting from now, we try and live even more frugally,' Reg said.

'Can't you still get coal from the depot?' Matthew asked, blowing on his hands.

'Maybe I can, but we're not going to be using it.'

'You're talking about selling it?' John exclaimed. 'That's black-marketeering, Dad. It's a criminal offence. Black-marketeers go to jail!'

'I didn't say I was going to do any such thing.'

'Plus, it's stealing!'

222

'We know, John,' Faye said, breaking into the stunned silence. 'The point is, we'll have to tighten our belts.'

'You mean tighten them even further.'

'We do alright, Mattie. Better than many,' John said. 'Perhaps we should think about this place.' He waved his hand to signify the room, the house. 'I could live at the station house and Faye... you could lodge at the hospital, couldn't you?'

'I—'

'No, no, this is a home,' Esme protested. 'You must all have a home to come back to if you need it one day. Our Phoebe will come back to it.'

Faye caught her elder brother's eye. Matthew looked at his boots.

'The rent agreement runs until the end of March,' Reg said. 'We have to pay the rent until then anyway, we can't make any savings out of this place.'

By then they should know Phoebe's fate.

40

FAYE

The wind whistled around the roof of number nineteen. In her tiny room under its eaves, Faye lay awake, curled up beneath the blankets and her coat, staring at the slanting ceiling.

John was right about the house, she thought. Just not in the way he'd meant. Her parents might be able to sub-let her room and John's too. He could stay at the station house and, as canteen manager, she was entitled to a bed on site at the SLH. She would speak with her brother and mother in the morning. Yet it seemed like a desertion, to leave her mother at Sugden Road in such bad times.

As deputy hospital administrator she would've been entitled to her own room. There seemed no chance of that now.

If only... If only she'd written that application. Such a simple thing to do. So why hadn't she applied?

A mix of reasons, she suspected. Her boss's high-handedness hadn't helped – sometimes Miss Barnett reminded her of her father, with all his talk about rules, family and an assumed superiority. Miss Barnett hadn't listened, just like he didn't listen. Plus, she acknowledged, she'd allowed herself to be distracted. Like John said, she could never resist a puzzle.

If she'd written that letter, she would have been deputy adminis-trator by now, with all that entailed.

If wishes were horses, then beggars would ride.

Ellie hadn't vacillated. She decided to stay in London and had ended her engagement. She didn't consult her parents, she didn't even tell them, she just did it!

Now it was Ellie who'd be in the office, working more closely with Miss Barnett, probably speaking with the governors and raising funds. Ellie would be good at that, she charmed people, people wanted to help her. She would thrive. She was the right class and had the right background and education, like the lady almoners. Miss Barnett liked her. She would fit in.

Everything was going wrong. And it had all begun when Ellie Peveril arrived, with her beauty and glamour, her social confidence and her county-town, middle-class family. The way every man for miles fell at her feet and she didn't even have to try. A woman who could afford to turn down an offer of marriage from a wealthy landowner from her own world and class. Who could decide to strike out on her own, regardless.

But...

Ellie couldn't help her looks and her background. She was fun and clever and intrepid. She'd taken on the Packham woman when it would have been easier to give up. It wasn't her fault that Faye had messed things up with Miss B. She was becoming a good friend. Was...

Faye felt very sad.

Then she smiled to herself. Dr Nicholas Yorke wasn't impressed by Ellie's glamour. It was clear who *he* preferred.

Then Faye reminded herself that Nicholas Yorke was a candidate for being the midnight man. His interviews were being conducted in Miss Barnett's office. What if the top drawer hadn't been locked, or he had taken an impression of its key? He would have had access to the key to the deep shelters. Could he have killed Jane?

Asking questions about Jane's death had brought her nothing but trouble, she might even lose her job over it. Yet the key linked the SLH office with the murder of Jane Cooper. And the office clerk, Polly Brooks, had been searching through hospital records, comparing current and pre-war purchases and checking patient records. Were these two elements connected?

Getting to the bottom of it was urgent. Scotland Yard weren't interested – they wanted an open and shut case, Jane Cooper killed by a vagrant, someone passing through. Her death would soon be old news and other crimes would demand their attention. Meanwhile the killer went free and no one would feel safe, everyone would be jumpy and nervous because no one would believe the vagrant theory. There would be a killer on the loose in Clapham.

Nonetheless, her priorities were clear.

First and most important, get Phoebe on to the drug trial. Once she was, it wouldn't matter what happened to her own prospects, she'd find a job somewhere, maybe a better job than the one she had, even if it meant leaving the SLH. At the first opportunity after breakfast service tomorrow, she would go and see Dr Falconer.

Then she would draft a letter of application for the deputy administrator's job and submit it. She would take some of her free hours, she had a lot of them built up, and go and sit in the Nurses' Common Room to write it. She'd said that she'd do it, so she would, even though she wouldn't get it now. She didn't know if she could work for Miss Barnett even if it was offered. She'd done some thinking since the confrontation in the office and decided she wanted to be treated with respect as a fellow professional who was good at her job, not some sort of promising apprentice.

Afterwards she'd continue the investigation. It was the right thing to do, whatever Miss Barnett said. To get some form of justice for Jane, to find out just how the SLH was involved before the police found out, so as to protect everyone.

Having made a plan of action, Faye turned over and soon fell asleep.

SATURDAY

41

ELEANOR

The canteen was warm with the smells of breakfast – bread toasting, eggs frying.

Ellie exchanged greetings with diners as she wheeled her trolley between the tables. She'd got to know so many of them in such a short time, it was easy to forget that she'd only been working at the SLH for a week. Now it seemed she might be staying for a lot longer.

She glanced towards the lectern. Faye was at her usual post, checking identification when needed. The two women had exchanged few words that morning and Ellie had ascribed Faye's strange behaviour the day before to her desperate situation. Now Faye was concentrating on her job and there were dark shadows beneath her eyes. Her movements were slow and heavy; she looked as if she hadn't had any sleep at all.

Ellie watched her stamp ration books, smile and speak to people, as she did every working day, despite her worries. How strong and indomitable she was. Faye had survived the war, its privations and sadness, adapting and emerging stronger. She had made a place for herself, only to be knocked sideways by misfortune. And want of money.

Ellie had seen poverty – accompanying her mother to cottages built from mudbrick and without water – circumstances so far removed from her own that she thanked her lucky stars for what she had. The Smiths weren't poor either, they were solid and respectable, with jobs and good lives. Then Faye's sister had the ill luck to contract a serious disease and the medical costs hit them.

She heard Beryl's voice in her head, telling her it wasn't ill luck when families were sick from living in damp and decrepit proper-ties, because their owners wouldn't repair them. Or when men were injured because they were desperate enough to do dangerous work. She heard Moira's voice too, telling her to be careful or she'd end up a socialist.

When she looked towards the lectern again, Faye was gone.

A group of nurses arrived, coming off nightshift, including Beryl. All hungry for some breakfast before getting some sleep.

'Morning, Ellie.' The Scot had a full tray, which she unloaded on to a table. 'Is Faye around?'

'She was. Gone to see her sister, I expect.'

'Worry by the bucketload.' Beryl poured watery milk into her tea. 'Back to powdered again, I see. At least the hens are laying, it's a pity the SLH doesn't keep cows.'

'May I join you?' Ellie asked.

'Course.'

'There was something I wanted to ask Faye about, but it seemed she wanted to keep herself to herself today. Can't say I blame her. She's got enough to cope with. I wondered if I could ask you?'

'Fire away.' Beryl attacked her egg on toast with gusto as Ellie sat.

'You know Miss Barnett, the hospital administrator?'

Beryl nodded, chewing.

'She approached me yesterday, after lunch service, wanting to talk about a position, a vacancy, here at the SLH. Running the hospital office, she said. Fair pay and some benefits. D'you know anything about it?'

'Aye, something. A deputy post, someone to take on some of her duties.'

'Oh no, I don't think it was such a big role. Just running the office. She said I'd be working to her in the same way that Faye works to her now.'

'Oh.'

Beryl had stopped eating, her fork suspended between the plate and her mouth.

'What, Beryl? What is it?'

'You didn't say you'd take it?'

'I said I'd think about it. Why?'

Beryl put her knife and fork down. 'I happen to know that Miss Barnett offered a post to Faye, a new post of deputy hospital administrator. It involved her taking on responsibility for the office as well as what she does now.'

'That's a step up.'

'It is.'

'How does that fit with me running the office?'

'It doesn't. You'd be doing the work that would have been part of the job she offered to Faye.'

'What? But... I mentioned this to Faye yesterday,' Ellie said, aghast. 'She seemed... upset. No wonder. She thinks I'm stealing her job!'

And that would explain why Faye had hardly spoken to her since. It wasn't a preoccupation with Phoebe or money, it was because Faye thought she was a snake in the grass.

'Maybe old Barnett's changed her mind,' Beryl said. 'But the job, and the money that goes with it, would be even more important to Faye now, with medical bills to pay.'

Bloody hell! Ellie sprang to her feet.

'I didn't know. Beryl, I didn't know. Oh heavens, I've got to find her. To tell her I won't take it. I wouldn't do that to her.'

'Alright, alright, I believe you, calm down,' Beryl said. 'She's probably gone to see her sister. Remember, you can't go into the isolation ward.'

'Yes, I know, but I could find out if she's there. Thanks, Beryl, see you later.'

In her haste to propel her trolley to its space by the counter, Ellie crashed it into the wall.

'Perhaps it's just as well that you don't drive a car.' It was Les Allen. 'Fancy a cuppa after your shift?' he asked, indicating the pot of tea on his tray and the two teacups and jug.

'Oh, Les, no. To the tea that is. Thank you very much for the offer, but I really can't. I—'

'Everything's okeydokey, isn't it? Only you look a bit...' He frowned.

'Yep, yes, everything's alright. I just need to... be somewhere else.'

'Anything I can help with?'

'No, thank you, Les. I must find Faye. You haven't seen her, have you?'

'No, but she'll be around somewhere. Shift's not ending for a while yet. Do you want me to ask my girls to keep an eye out for her?'

'That's kind of you, Les, but there's no need, I'm sure I'll find her.'

She smiled at him and hurried out of the canteen.

42

FAYE

Faye straightened her blouse and tucked an escaping lock of hair back into her chignon as she tapped on the wooden door.

'Come in.'

'Dr Falconer, do you have two minutes?'

'No, but then I never do. Come in, Miss Smith, what can I do for you?'

Penelope Falconer was a tall, imposing woman with a strong face. She sat behind a large wooden desk that held a telephone and a tall pile of manila folders in an office she shared with another consultant. A similar pile sat on her colleague's desk together with a large brown glass bottle half full of liquid.

'Sit down, please.'

'I've come to ask about the streptomycin trial.' Faye perched on the edge of the chair that Dr Falconer had indicated.

'Ah, yes, I understand that your sister was admitted to isolation yesterday.'

'Yes. She's twenty years old and has "acute progressive bilateral pulmonary tuberculosis".'

Dr Falconer's eyebrows rose.

'That's what it said on her notes. She's also very weak.' Faye focused hard on keeping her hands still in her lap and her voice even.

Don't sound desperate, she repeated to herself, over and over.

'I've spoken with the Lady Almoner and we've agreed a schedule of payment for Phoebe to remain and be treated in the SLH,' she went on.

'Can your family afford that?'

'We're not paying the full amount,' Faye answered. 'And it will be a struggle, but we'll have to. My father's union has contributed and there are my brothers and me. We can all chip in.'

'I see.'

'So, I was hoping that she would be a good candidate for your trial.'

Faye waited.

'As it happens,' Dr Falconer said. 'I'd already thought about Phoebe as a potential trial subject. She fits the criteria and, as you hesitated to point out, surgery wouldn't be possible in her case. The one concern I have is that the disease is too far advanced. Her admittance form shows her newly diagnosed, but—'

'We couldn't afford to pay for a sanatarium.'

'So your family didn't report the disease. I thought that might be the case.'

'We couldn't be sure what she was suffering from.'

The consultant tilted her head to one side, a sceptical look on her face.

'She wouldn't go to a doctor,' Faye said, quickly. 'She was afraid of being sent away.'

'You say that your family couldn't afford a private sanatorium, but you can afford to pay for treatment in the SLH now?'

'The lady almoner—'

'Has agreed a level of payment with you, I understand. But this trial is scheduled to run for fifteen months. Can you continue to pay for all that time?'

'We'll have to.'

Dr Falconer smiled. 'Actually, you might *not* have to. If Phoebe makes significant progress in the first twelve months she may be allowed to go home after that.'

Some good news, at least. They had enough to pay the fees until March; there might only be eight more monthly payments to find after that.

'I have to do some medical checks,' the consultant went on. 'So I can't promise, but, as you've already realised, Phoebe is a good candidate for the trial. If the checks come back negative, as I anticipate they will, I'll sign her up.'

Faye took a great gulp of air. 'Thank you, Dr Falconer. Thank you.'

'You know that streptomycin has proved effective in trials in the United States?'

'Yes, I've read about it in the BMJ.'

'You've certainly done your research. Now—'

Faye rose. 'May I ask, Dr Falconer? Is that the streptomycin?' She nodded towards the brown bottle on the second desk as she made her way to the door.

'That? Heavens, no. We keep the streptomycin under lock and key, it's very new and very expensive. That's just cocaine solution, a local anaesthetic in general use. My colleague's an ENT surgeon, they use it all the time. It should be in the cupboard, it's light sensitive.' She stood and went to put the bottle away.

'Is that what's called Neurocaine?'

'In a suspension, yes.'

'Well, thanks again.'

Faye closed the door behind her.

Yes! Phoebe was on the trial! She felt as if a great weight had lifted from her shoulders.

She bent double, hands clenched into fists, eyes closed tight, a grimace of triumph on her face. Then she breathed again, glancing along the corridor both ways, just to make sure no one had seen.

It wasn't completely certain yet, she reminded herself, but almost. Now she must telephone John at the station, then he could contact the others, but first she had to tell her sister.

In the chilly isolation ward a caped staff nurse stood at the nurses' station. Faye nodded a greeting as she strode towards Phoebe's bed at the end of the ward, wishing that she'd brought her coat.

'Hello, Pheebs.'

The only visible part of Phoebe was her head, the blankets were tucked tightly in beneath her chin and a heavy coverlet lay over the bed to keep her warm. She opened her eyes.

'Faye.' Phoebe's voice was almost a whisper.

'It's going to be alright, Pheebs,' she said, sitting on the chair placed at the foot of the bed. 'I think it's all going to be alright.'

Tears traced silvery lines down her sister's cheeks.

'The drug trial, Mum told you about it?'

'Yes.' A slight nod of the head.

'Well, it looks like you're going to be on it.'

'But how will you pay? How, Faye?' Phoebe paused, battling for breath. 'What will you all lose because of me? Vince's wedding? Mattie's motorbike?'

'No, no. Breathe gently now. It's not as bad as we thought, Pheebs. The SLH is helping. We don't have to pay for as long, either.'

'You're already… and Dad, I know him, he'll do anything…'

'He doesn't need to Pheebs, we've worked everything out.'

'…always to look after poor Phoebe.' Her breath was coming in gulps now. 'The drain on the family, the sick sister.'

'Calm down, quiet, or I'll be told off for upsetting a patient.'

Phoebe sniffed and Faye reached out to wipe her sister's nose with her own handkerchief.

'Miss Smith!' The staff nurse shouted. 'Maintain a distance, please.'

Faye sat back, raising her palms in the nurse's direction. Ducking her head she said 'They'll be throwing me out next.'

Phoebe half-smiled, one corner of her lips curling upward.

'This drug, Pheebs, they've used it in America and people have been cured, not temporarily, but cured. You could be well again, living a normal life, sis.'

'That'd be good.' Her sister blinked back more tears. 'When's it going to start?'

'Dr Falconer's already done some tests, she's waiting for the results and then – hey presto!'

She raised both hands, her fingers crossed.

'You got me on this, didn't you?'

'Dr Falconer said she'd thought about you anyway,' Faye replied. 'You're a suitable candidate, the right age and you fit the other criteria.'

'Hmm.' Phoebe smiled at her sister, then fought to stifle a yawn.

'Right, I'll be off now, let you get some rest.' Faye stood. 'Mum and Dad'll be here tomorrow and the boys, if nurse will let them in. I wouldn't put it past them to stand in the corridor and make funny faces at you if she doesn't. I've got to go and tell them all the good news.'

'Thanks, Faye.'

A grin on her face, Faye hurried down the stairs. Pheobe had a chance, she had more than a chance, she might get well again!

On the ground floor Faye skipped as she hurried to telephone John and pass on the news. One brief conversation later, she propped herself against a wall, weak with relief.

Now for the pharmacy.

43

FAYE

The general dispensary was a long, thin room with three arched windows high up on one side opposite the hatch to the outpatients department on the other. All the remaining wall space was taken up by cabinets and shelves covered in jars, bottles and boxes. A door at the far end marked 'Stockroom' was closed. The pharmacist, a bespectacled woman with a wayward halo of chestnut hair scraped back into a ponytail, was weighing a fine powder on a set of scales on one of the central laboratory benches. She didn't look up.

'Just a moment,' she said, as she carefully poured the powder into a pre-folded piece of paper and deftly formed a tiny paper package. Then she turned to her visitor. 'Hello, Miss Smith, Faye, how can I help you?'

'Miss Underwood. I've been looking at some of our purchase ledgers and, I wonder, could you answer some questions I have about our drug purchasing and dispensing?' she asked. 'It's not really part of my current responsibilities, but it would help me to know.'

Miss Underwood's answering smile was a knowing one. 'Of course. Felicity Barnett's been talking about getting a deputy, this wouldn't have anything to do with that would it?'

'Umm, I'd rather not say. If you could just keep this between us...?'

'Alright, mum's the word. What do you want to know?'

'The office purchases drugs on a weekly, where necessary a daily, basis. We pay monthly. How does the hospital know what to order? What's the process?'

'We keep a small stock of drugs which are used regularly, antibiotics, painkillers and so on, in the stockrooms on each ward and I have the main stock here. It's the responsibility of the staff nurse on each ward to ensure that stock is maintained, so I or my staff are told what is needed on a weekly basis. I collate those orders and put them into the office. More unusual drugs, those which are prescribed for specific patients, will be requisitioned by the doctors and consultants, through me.'

Faye nodded her understanding.

'Most of the drugs will be stored here and I'll fill the prescriptions in the normal way. Some consultants do keep some drugs in their offices, local anaesthetics for example, or to help with examinations.'

'Like cocaine solution?'

'Yes, the ENT surgeons all use that. It limits blood loss as well as acting as a local. I make that up myself and, when they've run out, they ask for more.'

'And how do we know the drugs get to the relevant patients? That there isn't any confusion?'

'A porter takes the drugs for the ward stocks to the wards where the nurse in charge signs for them. If, for any reason, they run out of a particular drug and need it urgently, a nurse comes down and asks for more, which I and my staff provide. We keep our own records.' She waved her hand towards a shelf containing a row of box files.

'Does anyone ever cross-check those records with the office purchase ledgers?'

'No, but perhaps we should.' Miss Underwood gave her a speculative look. 'Why? Do you think someone's been stealing drugs?'

'It's just that we're purchasing more drugs now than ever before, yet we've returned to the same patient numbers as before the war and we don't have an emergency department anymore.'

'There are more drugs available now,' the pharmacist responded. 'Often new drugs to treat old illnesses.'

'Like streptomycin.'

'Exactly. By the way, how is your sister? Dr Horn told me that the test results were sent to Penelope Falconer this afternoon. All clear. I assume she was testing your sister for the trial.'

'Yes. Thank you for telling me!'

It was good to hear.

'The streptomycin and its use will be closely monitored. It's part of a central trial and, anyway, it's a very expensive drug. We'll keep it here.'

'But other new drugs...?'

'We buy a range. Some drugs will suit some patients better than others, the doctors might try more than one as part of the treatment. That means we buy more than before, I suppose.'

The office ledgers showed all drug purchasing by the hospital, but the office staff wouldn't really understand what was normal and what was out of the ordinary. Only a doctor or the pharmacist could do that.

'Tell me, if an individual did want to purloin drugs, how would she do it?'

'It wouldn't be easy. Quantities are checked when they enter my stockroom and the ward stock cupboards. We keep the prescriptions for a while.' The pharmacist paused; her expression thoughtful. 'I could do it. I know how the system works and I'd have more opportunity than most.'

'I'm sure you're not...'

But Miss Underwood was in mid-thought. 'The cocaine solution, for example. I could claim to have dropped a consignment on its way to the consultants, but then steal the cocaine that I'd supposedly mixed. That would be a way of doing it. But I couldn't do that very often, lots of people would notice.'

'So, what does a prescription look like and how does that translate into what the nurse gives the patient?'

'Look.' Miss Underwood reached for a handful of paper chits skewered on a spike. 'These are prescriptions which I've filled. You can see the name of the drug, the name of the patient and the dosage and regularity, signed by the consultant. This,' she handed a labelled box to Faye, 'is what would be taken to the ward.'

The label carried the same information as the prescription, but with reference to other elements of that patient's regime.

'One must consider other medications that specific patient may be taking, or other forms of treatment being undertaken. Anyway, lots of people are involved and dosage is strictly controlled, the drug is administered to the patients by the nurse, according to the prescription. So if any individual was trying to steal drugs, they would soon be found out. That's the point I'm making, really.'

'Thank you, Miss Underwood. That's very helpful,' Faye said. 'But how can we be sure that all the drugs we're ordering, especially those that have other uses, like cocaine, are actually used here? Cocaine, or neurocaine, would be worth a lot of money on the black market.'

'It certainly would! With cocaine it's relatively easy. It's a controlled substance,' Miss Underwood explained. 'All controlled or restricted drugs must be recorded and tracked in our Register of Drugs.' She crossed to a shelf and withdrew a large ledger. 'Pharmacies that hold such drugs must keep one of these registers and it can be inspected by the General Pharmaceutical Council at any time. The GPC checks that correct records are being kept and that quantities in and out balance.'

She placed it on a bench and opened it. 'Look.'

Faye saw recent entries in Miss Underwood's rounded handwriting and, flicking back several weeks, the elongated script of Miss Lowell, the previous pharmacist. The ledger noted drugs in from suppliers and drugs out via prescriptions to patients. She riffled through the book's pages, seeing entries going back until

1944. The inward and outward columns were added up and balanced at the bottom of each page.

'We keep all the ledgers here.' Miss Underwood indicated a row of ledgers from which she had taken the latest.

'May I borrow this?'

'I don't know... that would be highly irregular.'

'I just want to track items through and match them with our office information, to see how we could improve our admin controls.'

'Very well, but for half an hour, no more. Take good care of it and bring it back straight away. It's in use daily and I don't want to fall behind.'

'Thank you.'

'Will you be reporting back to Felicity?'

'I've got to investigate some other processes first, but I will, eventually,' Faye replied. 'Thanks again. I'll bring this straight back.'

Grasping the ledger Faye headed off towards the office.

In the office corridor she ran into Jean, who was wearing her overcoat and on her way home. She was accompanied by Les Allen.

''Night, Jean.'

'See you Monday.'

The secretary carried on to the main entrance hall, but the porter stopped.

'Are you still after Polly Brooks' address?' Faye asked. 'Trying to persuade Jean, eh?'

He shrugged, looking sheepish.

'Forget her. She's gone.'

'It's not so easy,' he said with a wry smile. 'D'you think your friend might give me a glance?'

'Ellie? Join the queue.' Faye unlocked the office door. 'Oh, you don't happen to have seen her around today, have you?'

'No. I'm certain I'd remember if I had.' He waved and left.

Faye switched on the light in Miss Barnett's room and unlocked the key drawer. She rummaged among the disorderly tangle of all the keys belonging to the hospital, including the security key to the deep shelters and eventually found the keys to the filing cabinet.

One thing had been puzzling Faye about what Polly Brooks had done. She believed she understood why Polly was comparing the entries in the two purchasing ledgers, but she didn't know why the clerk had been looking at patients' medical records. That was what had got her a reprimand, as she knew it would, if she was caught, so why was it so important to her? Why did she do it?

The patients' files were specific records; every patient in the SLH had a file. Using the Register Faye planned to do a cross check. She chose cocaine to do it and looked for the patient record relating to the most recent cocaine entry in the Register. The patient's record showed her receiving the medication.

Was this what Polly Brooks had been doing? Or something like it?

Faye flicked back three pages in the Register. The entry at the top was for Myfanwy James, receiving medication including cocaine. There was no patient file for her. Odd. She was a local woman; her file should have been there. The next entry in the Register had a corresponding file in the drawer, but thereafter there were a series of Register entries which didn't link with patient records. Two more pages back and, again, there were details relating to patients who, it seemed, didn't have records.

Frowning, Faye relocked the cabinet.

Why didn't some of entries in the Register relate to corresponding patient records? Maybe one or two of these patients had moved on to another hospital or clinic and their records transferred, but not all of them, surely. It was a puzzle.

One that a few words with Jean might've been able to solve, but the secretary had gone home.

Faye checked her watch. It was time for dinner service and she ought to take the Register back to Miss Underwood. Then she would go down to the canteen; it would be getting busy.

She replaced the cabinet key, shoved the drawer closed and locked it. She crossed to switch off the office light but hesitated.

There was something niggling her at the back of her mind. Something she'd seen or heard. Something significant.

Keys. The thought jangled in her head. It's all to do with keys.

Shaking her head, Faye switched off the light and locked the door behind her.

44

FAYE

In the canteen, the dinner queue was snaking around the room. Tables were filling. There was no sign of Ellie.

Faye was immediately surrounded by a group of well-wishing nurses, all intent on commiserating with her about Phoebe. When they moved on Faye was left staring straight at Dr Nicholas Yorke. He was standing, holding a shopping bag and looking directly at her.

'Miss Smith, I heard about your sister,' he said as he approached. 'Miss MacBride mentioned it to me. I'm so very sorry.'

'Thank you. It wasn't unexpected.'

'No, I don't imagine it was. Will she be staying here, do you know?' The faint suggestion of an anxious frown on his forehead showed that he knew the alternative and the costs involved.

'Yes, I believe so.'

Yorke looked relieved.

'The other good news is that there's a new drug, from America,' she said. 'It's being tested here and Phoebe's on the trial, thank heavens.' Faye stopped herself from saying more, it was nothing to do with him and there was no reason why he'd be interested. She reminded herself that he was also a suspect for Jane's murder.

'That is good news... really excellent.' His eyes were full of sympathy and care. It seemed he *was* interested. 'I'm very pleased to hear that.'

There was a small silence.

'I hope you won't think it presumptuous of me,' he pressed on, 'but I've brought these for the invalid.' He proffered the bag, which, Faye could now see, contained books. 'They're from my own collection. Novels mostly, she might like them. Classics, you know... Ivanhoe... Dumas, that sort of thing.'

'That is so kind of you.' Faye took the bag, peering inside. The books were well-thumbed favourites by the look of them. They must be his own copies.

Faye glanced up at him. He knew they wouldn't be returned, the isolation ward wouldn't allow it. This was a precious gift indeed. It *was* very kind of him.

He gave a wry smile, as if he could read her thoughts. 'Sometimes, especially when you're feeling low, a good adventure story helps take you out of yourself. That's what I find, anyway.'

'Yes.'

'You'll pass them on, give them to her.'

'Yes, of course. I'm sure she'll enjoy reading them.'

He waited, then turned to leave.

No. Don't go yet!

Faye was flustered. She had to thank him properly.

'Thank you, Dr Yorke. Thank you so very much.' Faye found her voice. She looked at him with heartfelt gratitude and he smiled in response, turning back towards her. 'These will be so much appreciated; it is such a thoughtful gift.'

'Not really, I thought... what do you want when you're stuck in hospital? Oh, and it's Nicholas – Nick.'

'Exactly. Nick. Do call me Faye.'

'Faye.'

Somehow her name sounded magical on his lips, ethereal. Not, she chided herself, like her at all.

'I wonder, would you like to meet some time, for tea, say? You could let me know how she's doing. Talk about things in general.'

He waited and she understood that this invitation was more than just to chat and have tea.

'I'd like that,' she said. And she meant it. 'I think I'd like that very much.'

His smile broadened and his stance relaxed.

''Scuse me.' He was jostled by a canteen customer who pushed past.

'Sorry, sorry.' Yorke smiled at Faye again. 'Good. How about next week some time? Or maybe it'd be better if I call round when you're not so busy and we can fix something up?'

'Do that,' Faye said. 'I'll look forward to it.'

She watched him as he walked towards the doors, a tall figure skirting groups of nurses and staff, smiling all the while.

'Now there's a man who looks like someone's made him happy,' said a Scottish voice at her elbow.

'Beryl.' Faye tore her gaze from the retreating man. 'He was kind enough to bring some reading matter for Phoebe. It really was very thoughtful.'

'He's a thoughtful man, I'm sure,' said the nurse. 'Very thoughtful.'

'Tsch.' Faye felt her cheeks flush with embarrassment. She was a grown woman, why was she behaving like a schoolgirl?

'Have you seen this?' Beryl thrust a copy of the *Daily Mail* into her hand. 'The vultures are circling.'

On the front page was a photograph of the hospital taken from the common beneath the headline 'Nurse Murdered after Assignation in Clapham'. The report that followed was full of innuendo, placing as much blame on the victim as on her killer and snidely suggesting that such regrettable crimes were only to be expected in close proximity to an institution like the South London Hospital for Women and Children. Tomorrow's letters page would no doubt pick up on the report.

'Vultures is right,' she said.

It had been inevitable. The SLH had too many enemies and at least one of them had connections in Fleet Street. Fortunately, they hadn't got hold of some of the juicier aspects of the pathology report. Again Faye wondered who was paying for Nick Yorke's research work. Maybe she could ask him.

Maybe he was party to it all? No. That was her overly suspicious mind at work.

Then she remembered her search for Ellie.

'Beryl, have you seen Ellie?'

'No, I haven't. But, listen, Faye, there's something I need to tell you. Let's sit down.' Beryl took a seat at the end of a table that was already occupied. She kept her voice low. 'She didn't know, Faye. She'd not a clue.'

'Who didn't know and about what?'

'The job that Barnett offered her, office manager. Ellie had no idea that it was part of the deputy post that you'd been asked to apply for.'

'Bloody hell, Beryl, did everyone know about the deputy post?' Faye was surprised. 'Miss Underwood knew about it too, though she heard from Miss Barnett. I didn't tell a soul.'

'No, but Jean did. She likes you. She's been hoping that you'd take it. She's been asking me why you hadn't applied.'

'Jean?'

'Why didn't you apply?'

'I have, I did. Just now. I always wanted the job, but I wanted to speak with my family before I accepted it,' Faye said. 'I shouldn't have bothered, I knew what my father's reaction would be, I should've just accepted it and saved time and trouble. Then there wouldn't have been a problem.'

'You're twenty-seven, Faye. It's about time you made decisions of your own.'

'I know! But the war got in the way, normal life was set aside for six years.'

'But—'

'I know, I know, you've been independent for a long while, but you always knew what you wanted to do; get qualifications, make sure you could make your way in the world. It was different for me.

I had Paul, we were going to settle down, have a family. Then...'
Faye waved her hand in the air. 'All change.'

Beryl smiled as Faye lowered her voice, aware that others could overhear.

'Now I think I know what I want and I have to go and spoil things. I mess around, getting caught up in this investigation rather than remembering what's good for me.'

Beryl sighed. 'I thought there might be something, otherwise why was old Barnett offering that post to Ellie. D'you know why she changed her mind?'

'She got sniffy when I kept her waiting. And she didn't like it when Ellie and I started asking questions about Jane Cooper's death; said we were 'playing detective'.'

'Weren't you?'

'Well, yes... then I asked her about the SLH key to the deep shelters and she thought I was criticising her. Plus, I was checking the ledgers, which looked like I was questioning her way of doing things, making out that I could do it better.'

'You probably could,' Beryl said. 'But then Barnett's got a whole load of other things she has to spend time doing, she can't concentrate on everything. She and Matron keep this hospital running between them. It's not an easy job and she does it very well.'

'I know. She's rushed off her feet.' Faye raised an eyebrow. 'She needs a deputy.'

'Anyway. Ellie's chewed up with guilt. She thinks you're ignoring her because she betrayed you by taking your job after you helped her. Last I heard she was asking everywhere in the hospital, trying to find you to explain. Les even offered to ask his porters to look for you on her behalf.'

'I've been in the nurses' common room.' Faye looked thoughtful. 'Avoiding people. Ellie might feel awful about it, but it's not her fault. After all, she'd be good at the job. Are you on shift tonight?'

'No, I worked last night. I'm just here to eat, then I'll go home and get some more shut-eye, I'm on tomorrow. Why?'

'I need to find Ellie, urgently. I may be worrying over nothing, but – I just need to find her.'

'Alright. I can ask at the nurses' home. See if anyone has seen her. Then I'm off to my bed.'

'Good, thanks. I'll check the places she may have been looking for me.'

'What's up, Faye? You look worried.'

'It's probably nothing, but I'll just be glad when we find her.'

45

ELEANOR

'Cheer up, Ellie, it might never happen,' a nurse quipped.
'Sorry!' Ellie smiled.

She didn't feel much like smiling. Today wasn't a good day.

Despite searching the hospital from top to bottom she'd failed to find Faye, who seemed to have disappeared off the face of the earth. She was probably lying low and Ellie didn't blame her. Faye had offered friendship and practical help when Ellie needed it most and she'd just had dreadful news about her sister. This was the woman whose trust she, Ellie, had betrayed. She was responsible for Faye's longed-for job no longer being available to her.

She was desperate to explain that it was a mistake, that she wouldn't take the position, that she hadn't known. Had she known she would never have contemplated taking it.

'Take no notice, Ellie,' a second nurse said. 'Hey!' The nurse yelled at a car that had braked at the last minute as they were halfway across the South Side. The others shouted and gesticulated at the driver, who grimaced apologetically and raised his hands from the steering wheel; not a match for a group of SLH nurses.

Their high spirits were contagious, Ellie felt her mood lift a little. She was glad she'd said she'd go to the pictures with them. Besides, it would be warm, the tickets were cheap and the film, by all accounts, was a good one. Maybe she'd forget her troubles for a while.

The driver tooted his horn as he pulled away and drove down Balham Hill and the nurses waved him on his way. They walked past the deep shelter compound, laughing, excited at their evening to come. Ellie began to look forward to it too.

Outside the Odeon, a queue of people wound across the pavement, all stamping their feet in the cold. Ellie's group joined its end.

'So, what's this film about, then?' she asked, determined not to be a dampener on the others' jolly mood.

'It's a love story,' one nurse replied.

'About a pilot,' another said.

'David Niven and Kim Hunter.'

'He dies.'

'No, he doesn't.'

Some shouting came from behind them, audible above the chatter and buzz of the people waiting for the cinema.

'That's the point... he's...'

Ellie's attention was snagged by the voices. She focused on the shouting, there was something about one of them.

She gasped and felt a shock of recognition. That was it! It was the same voice she'd heard shouting on Sunday night on the common.

Where was it coming from?

From inside the deep shelter compound.

Ellie glanced at her wristwatch in the light from the street lamp. It was after seven, she had just under half an hour before the main feature began.

'Excuse me,' she said to the others. 'I'll join you inside. I've just remembered something.'

'Don't be too long!'

'It starts at half past.'

Ellie hurried back to the high metal gates, which were slightly ajar. It was dark inside, the high walls keeping out much of the glare from the street lamps, but dull lamp light emanated from the office window, illuminating a segment of the small yard. The shouting had stopped, the people had gone inside.

Could she be certain the voice was the same? She needed to get closer to be able to tell for sure. She wouldn't stay long, just long enough to be certain. She only needed to listen for a moment. Then, if it was the same, she'd go and call the police. They would have to take her more seriously this time.

Ellie slipped through the gate into the darkest of the shadows and flitted across the yard, skirting piles of pallets and crouching down so that she couldn't be seen from the window. She flattened herself against the wall and peered inside.

On the far wall of the office, she could see the shadows of two men, continuing to argue, though quieter now. One, wearing a hat, was animated, gesticulating and raising his hands; the other was calmer, still except for a shake of his head as he interrupted his companion.

'It was bloody stupid!'

His was the voice she had heard on the common. She was almost sure of it.

She pressed her ear to the edge of the window. It was some sort of dispute; they were arguing about something. Then the conversation turned to logistics, deliveries to a factory of some kind. Why were two men talking about this in a half-lit compound on a Saturday evening in an office that had a different purpose entirely.

Something illegal? She had heard enough. It was time to go.

It had been relatively easy to cross the dark yard towards the light, but it was more difficult going the other way and Ellie crept forward, hesitant. She couldn't see obstacles until her eyes grew accustomed to the darkness.

Then she heard the scraping of chairs on the floor of the office. The discussion, whatever it was about, seemed to have concluded. They were leaving, moving towards the door. Quick! She needed to get out or find somewhere to hide. Maybe this hadn't been a good idea after all?

In her haste she stumbled. Damn!

Two oblongs of bright yellow light appeared on the concrete of the yard. Ellie ducked behind a stack of pallets, keeping her head down.

'I heard something,' one man said. 'Somebody's out here.'

Ellie's heart was thumping so loudly she was sure the men could hear it.

'Who'd be here at this time of night?' the familiar voice replied. 'The gates are closed. It's just a cat.'

Ellie frowned, concentrating. Who was it?

The bright oblongs of light were gone and so was the lamp light. The men were crossing the yard, a single wand of light moved over the piles of equipment – one of them had a torch. She held her breath for fear they could hear her.

'We're agreed then?' said the voice she knew.

'Alright.' The other man sounded begrudging.

'Tell them they're going to have to get another supply. They don't have a choice if they want to continue as we are.'

'Alright, will do, but I'm not going to put it that way. These are dangerous men. I'd be more careful if I was you.'

'They can't get rid of me.' The speaker sounded amused. 'And keep the payments coming. Usual arrangement.'

They had reached the gate; she saw the sliver of street light as it opened.

'I'll check and let you know.'

'Thanks, George.'

The light disappeared. The gate had closed.

Ellie waited.

The low growl of traffic on Balham Hill was muted by the high walls of the compound, but there was no sound or movement within.

Had they really gone?

Nothing stirred. All was still.

They must have gone.

She exhaled and stood upright.

What was it that she had overheard? It had sounded like a business discussion, but very hole-and-corner, definitely not above board. And she had recognised the voice, that *must* be enough for Inspector Irving. The midnight man was still in Clapham, something he couldn't ignore. She had Irving's card; she'd telephone him from the SLH.

One of the men was named George, that might help too. She thought, immediately of Mrs Packham's son, though George was a common name. It sounded like he had accomplices – a gang, perhaps? Maybe Phillip would be interested, that was his specialty, organised crime.

But it was the other man she puzzled over. She knew him. She was certain that she knew him and yet she couldn't place him. She knew his voice, and not only from Sunday night either, although it was his shout she had heard then. No, she'd heard him speaking much more recently than that. In a completely different context.

Ellie threaded her way towards the gates. She ran her hand over them until she found the metal handle and turned it. The gates wouldn't budge. She tugged and the gates moved but remained shut. They had locked the gates behind them when they left.

'Damn,' she muttered and shivered, turning up the collar of her overcoat. It would be below freezing tonight, just as it had been for the past fortnight. Not a night to spend out of doors. Owen Philpott wouldn't arrive until Monday morning. And so much for phoning the police.

Wait a minute.

There was a telephone in the office, she'd seen it when she'd been there on Thursday. With any luck, the door to the office wouldn't be locked and she could phone from there. It would afford her some shelter too, at least until she was rescued. She made her way back across the yard, no longer taking care not to be heard. The men had gone.

The office door opened at her touch. It was darker inside than out, but she couldn't feel a light switch near the door. There had to be a lamp, to have cast the shadows she had seen. She remembered the desk by the far wall, a chair behind it. Ellie shuffled forwards, circumnavigating the room, by feeling her way around its walls until she found the desk. On it sat a kerosene lamp, she felt its glass hood. No matches on the desk next to it though. Perhaps in one of the drawers.

Her fingers found a box in the first drawer she tried.

Ellie struck a match and a small flame flickered into life. She removed the lamp's hood and lit the wick. A warm glow illuminated her and the corner of the room where she stood. The telephone sat on the desk near the lamp and Ellie reached for the handset, trying to remember Phillip's number.

The office door squeaked as it closed.

'Leave that alone.' A voice spoke from the darkness on the other side of the room.

Ellie spun round to see a figure step forward, the light reflecting on the barrel of his gun.

46

ELEANOR

'Yes.'

'Oh dear, you don't look surprised. I must be losing my touch.'

He stepped towards her, into the light.

Ellie's back was against the wall, there was no way past him to the door. Her gaze flicked from the gun to his face.

'I recognised your voice but couldn't place it,' she said. 'Then it came to me, just now, when I was lighting the lamp, where I'd heard it before.'

He raised his chin and smiled in acknowledgement. It wasn't a pleasant smile. Her blood ran cold.

Talk to him, engage him, she told herself.

'Did Jane work it out?' she asked.

'Jane? No. Not clever enough. She just wanted to find out what happened to her friend,' he replied. 'Thought I had something to do with it, wouldn't let it rest.'

'And had you... something to do with Polly's disappearance?'

Ellie slipped the box of matches into her coat pocket.

'You could say so.'

'Jane was clever enough to work that out then. And persistent enough too.'

His mouth turned down at the corners. 'She got what was coming to her. She kept on at me. Pity, she was a good-looking woman. Prettier than Polly.'

She remembered Dr Horn's comments – Jane had had inter-course before she was murdered. Ellie's heart rate increased. Was it Les?

'You get the picture,' he said.

'Faye's looking for me, she's—'

'I know. She asked me if I'd seen you. I told her I hadn't.'

They regarded each other in silence for a moment.

'So...'

'This way.' He stepped aside and gestured towards the door with the gun.

'What if I refuse?'

'You die. I shoot you in the head, then throw your body down the shaft to the shelters. Even if they find you, it's a long way down, your body will be so mangled they might not even realise you'd been shot.' His eyes didn't leave hers. 'Actually, that sounds like a good idea anyway.'

'Except someone might hear the shot,' Ellie retorted. 'And you'd have to carry my corpse, I'm heavy. And there'd be the blood. You wouldn't have a lot of time to clean up, either. In just over an hour and a half's time more than a hundred people are going to be walking past here when the Odeon throws out, it's a full house tonight. A light would be noticed.'

'Maybe, but I'd be long gone by then.' He shrugged.

He had the gun, there was nothing she could do but obey him and wait for an opportunity to get away.

'On the other hand, I'm in no hurry to leave,' he said. 'And it's not so much fun, just killing you. But I can certainly hurt you, so, unless you enjoy pain, you'd better come this way.'

He looked entirely capable of carrying out his threat. Reluc-tantly, Ellie walked in front of him across the yard. He pointed towards the round building. Like the shaft-head on Clapham

Common, the entrance was in a side annex. Allen drew a key from his pocket.

'Ah, the SLH key?'

'Yes.'

'How did you get that?'

'I can get it when I need it.' She saw the flash of his teeth as he grinned.

'What do you mean?'

'I've got a copy of the key to the drawer where all the hospital keys are kept. Including this one.' He opened the door. 'There isn't anywhere in the hospital where I can't go, nothing is hidden from me.' His tone became brash. 'All I need to do is go into the office after hours, open the desk and get whatever key I want.' He stepped back and motioned for her to precede him. 'You'd be surprised what I find out when people think they're alone, or in private. Everyone keeps secrets.'

He waved the gun towards the passageway. 'Inside.'

It wound to the right and, like it's cousin on the common, it carried signs indicating the way to the lift and the shelters, this time shelters Nelson to Parry.

Allen locked the door behind them, sealing them off from the world and rescue. All sound ceased.

'Go on,' he said, flicking a switch. Overhead strip lights sputtered into life.

The passage ended at a circular lift shaft. Concrete stairs with metal handrails painted red ran around the central lift cage and disappeared into the depths. Allen summoned the lift and the chains and pulleys inside the cage began to move, clanking.

Once inside the small lift cage Ellie watched the stairs go by as they descended. The temperature rose. She controlled her breathing, fighting down the panic. Had he brought Jane Cooper down here like this? Was that what he had planned for her?

She told herself not to antagonise Allen unduly. He would have no compunction about killing her down here. He could dump her body in any of the peripheral tunnels and it might not be found for weeks. Owen Philpott checked the shelters regularly, but he didn't walk every mile of them.

The lift stopped and he pulled the grille open.

'Out.'

She would need to keep her wits about her. Notice her surroundings, the details of the tunnels. She had to try to remember their route.

She stepped out into a wide tunnel, its roof and walls made of curving metal panels bolted together. The arched ceiling, with its thick ridged bands and massive screw heads resembled a metal version of a medieval ceiling, bossed and coffered. Every fifteen feet, ceiling lights cast pools of brightness onto the concrete floor – emergency lighting, Owen had spoken of it. She could see a flight of wide steps in the near distance descending further.

On the left was an alcove with a wooden door marked 'Control Room'. Outside it was a diagram showing two circles side by side, marked 'No. 9 Shaft Balham Hill' and 'No. 10 Shaft Clapham Common'. Above each circle in the diagram was a further circle, which Ellie took to represent the tunnels for the underground lines. It was a map, of sorts.

'Come on.' Allen grabbed her arm and pulled her down the stairs.

Almost all traces of his limp had disappeared. Yet he couldn't have fooled the doctors at the SLH, there must have been something wrong with his leg, just not as much as he made out.

At the foot of the stairs an even wider tunnel extended away into the distance. The emergency lights showed black openings in the tunnel sides at regular intervals – unlit side tunnels. Allen took the nearest right-hand opening into a smaller tunnel. Flattened, folded bunks and boxes lay stacked against its sides. A sign on the wall pointed to a canteen in one direction and medical stores in the other.

'I've got somewhere cosy,' he said as they marched along the tunnel. 'Where we can talk.'

Why was he keeping her alive? Perhaps he wanted to find out what she knew? No, she was expendable now, he could deal with her – he wanted to find out what Faye knew. Then she remembered what had happened to Jane before she met her death.

His grip on her upper arm hurt her, it was vice-like as he pulled her along. She stood no chance of overpowering him, he was much bigger and stronger. Though maybe, if it came to it, she could catch him off balance and run. She might be faster, able to outrun him, but then, where could she run to? She couldn't get out and he had the gun. All he would have to do was to follow her and shoot her when he caught her.

Unless she could find somewhere to hide, somewhere he didn't know about.

If she could get away from him and stay alive, she might be able to find her way to the lift shaft and climb all those steps, like Jane must have done. If she could get to one of the doors when Owen was doing his rounds, she could shout for help. Les couldn't guard the tunnel entrances forever; he'd have to return to the SLH eventually and he could only be at one entrance at a time. It might be a fifty–fifty chance, but one she might have to take.

'Here.'

He pulled her into a side-tunnel; its far end lit by a single light bulb hanging from the low ceiling. Metal storage cupboards lined one wall and opposite them was a low camp bed. A table stood against the end wall, with bottles and metal mugs on it, a pack of cigarettes and half a bar of chocolate. Allen pulled out a chair from beneath it.

'You sit there.' He shoved her onto the bed.

Ellie twisted round to face him as he sat, her back as close to the curving wall as she could get it.

'I'm not going to hurt you,' Allen said. 'At least, not yet. Here.' He sloshed some liquid from one of the bottles into two of the mugs and handed one to her. 'Whisky.'

'I'd prefer water,' she said.

Allen raised an eyebrow and pulled a fastidious face. 'I think I can oblige,' he said. He hunted in one of the metal cupboards. Ellie saw cardboard boxes inside it containing metal canisters.

'Here.' He tossed her a canister. 'Apologies, I don't have any ice.'

She unscrewed the metal top and drank the water, greedily. It was warm in the shelters and fear had made her thirsty. He watched her, and she kept her eyes on him.

'I'd take that off if I was you.' He indicated Ellie's heavy overcoat.

She wrapped it more tightly round herself.

'Give me your watch.'

'What?'

'Your watch. Give it to me.' He held out his hand.

Ellie stared at his palm. If she didn't know the time, she couldn't judge when Owen was going to be at the shaft heads.

'Now!'

She fumbled with the strap as she unbuckled the wristwatch and handed it over. He put it in his pocket.

'You are going to die,' he said. 'Understand that. No one is going to find you. No one is going to help you. The only choice you have is how you die; slowly and painfully, or quickly and mercifully.'

She said nothing. There was nothing to be said.

Les Allen stood, looming over her. In the small tunnel his head almost touched the ceiling.

'Now I'm going to leave you to think about that.'

What? Why? Why was he leaving?

'The lift will be held at the surface and the door will be locked. Even if, by some wild piece of luck, you could find your way back to the lift shaft you can't get out. I'll be back later tonight. Then, if you're nice to me and you tell me what I want to know, I might let you live a little longer. Your fate is in your own hands.'

He turned and she made to rise.

'Stay here,' he snapped. 'If I see you following me – and there's nowhere to hide in these tunnels, believe me, I can see you from a long way away – I will shoot you. Don't harbour any illusions. If you cross me, you die.'

Ellie sank back on to the bed.

'That's better. I'll see you later.'

Les turned on his heel and disappeared into the larger tunnel.

47

ELEANOR

As soon as Allen left, Ellie sloughed off her coat and leapt to her feet. She didn't have much time.

He needed the power to use the lift – she couldn't see him climbing all those stairs – but he'd almost certainly switch it off as he left the shaft head building. She would be in darkness unless she could find some sort of light.

She started looking in the open cupboard, pulling out boxes, searching for candles or lanterns. The box of matches that she'd taken from the office she placed on the bed. Metal canisters of water, rolls of bandages and sticking plasters, plastic bottles of rubbing alcohol – these were medical stores. The next cupboard held prosthetics and crutches. Boxes of splints, strapping, gauze and small instruments were in the next. Ellie pulled out a pair of scissors.

She had just begun to open the fourth cupboard when the light went out.

The blackness was complete.

Panic engulfed her. She sank down upon the floor, head in her hands.

What could she do if she couldn't see?

She could think.

She fought down her fear, controlled her breathing and calmed herself. She knew her immediate surroundings, that was good. She reached behind her and found the half-empty metal bottle of water on the bed. She had plenty of water, that was good too. She drained the bottle and screwed the top back on.

Could she retrace her steps to find the diagram, which showed the tunnels and the underground? But without the means to see she would be wandering in the dark and could easily lose her way in the labyrinth of tunnels and without a light she wouldn't be able to see the map anyway. Allen would be back. She didn't know why he'd left, but she suspected whatever it was wouldn't take too long. She didn't have hours.

What could she do? She had matches, but only a few. What could she use as a torch?

She concentrated, trying to summon a picture in her mind of what she had seen immediately before the dark had descended. Rubbing alcohol. Bandages. Metal water bottles.

All the means to make a lamp. Memories of half-forgotten rainy afternoons with the other Guides in the Scout hut resurfaced in Ellie and she thanked her lucky stars that she had attended regularly. She knew how to make an impromptu lamp. The empty bottle, the scissors and the matches were on the bed. She needed alcohol and some bandages from the cupboard. She should be able to lay her hands on those.

Ellie stood, holding her hands in front of her to feel for the cupboards. They were only a couple of feet away. In the first she found glass bottles of liquid, one sniff told her these contained rubbing alcohol; and bandages, which she placed on the floor. Then she stepped back to the bed, a bottle of alcohol in her hand. By feel she unscrewed the cap on the empty metal canister, filled it with alcohol then tightened the cap again. Casting around on the floor, she found the bandages and began to cut a piece into strips. These she plaited tightly into a thick string. She stabbed a hole in the canister screwcap and fed the string, her wick, into it. In theory, it would soak up the alcohol and the wick could then be lit.

A spirit lamp.

She placed it on the floor and felt around her for the precious matches. Her fingers counted five. That was all she had and she had to make each of them count. She took one of them out, holding it at the tip of the wood. She had to hold it for as long as she could, so that the wick of bandage had a chance to catch light.

She struck the match on the sandpaper surface of the box and a small orange-yellow flame glowed in the blackness. She held it close to the cotton.

The bandage took the flame!

The small tunnel was illuminated, shadows forming in the ridged metal walls. The impenetrable darkness at its end seemed darker still.

Ellie stood, poured away the whisky from Allen's metal mug and placed the canister lamp in the empty mug. Now she had a portable lamp which, if she carried some spare bottles of alcohol with her, she could refill as need be. It was a victory!

The flame went out, leaving a brief, burnt gold after image.

She flopped back down upon the camp bed. She was sure she had done everything right. Why had it failed? The cotton had caught light and the principle was sound. Perhaps the bandage wasn't absorbing sufficient alcohol.

Taking great care, Ellie dismantled her lantern in the dark. She soused the whole of the cotton wick in alcohol. Then she put the contraption back together. That might do.

She felt inside the matchbox. Four matches left.

The cotton caught light when she struck another match, but this time the flame grew. It had taken. She checked the matchbox again, though she knew there were only three matches left. Better find some more and maybe make a couple more lamps, so she could light one from another as it burned low.

In the eerie light from the little lamp, she worked. Now she knew what she was doing, it didn't take her long.

On the floor beneath the table was a battered wicker shopping basket that seemed usable. With it she could carry spare lamps, bottles of alcohol, bandages and some full canisters of water. The scissors she put in her skirt pocket. As a weapon they were almost useless, but it made her feel better to have them ready.

She hung the basket on her arm, took a slug of whisky from the bottle, shuddering at its heat, then started out to find her way back to the lift shaft and the map.

48

FAYE

Faye looked up from her newspaper as the clock struck ten, her anxiety about Ellie mounting. She'd scoured the hospital and her friend was nowhere to be found. The canteen night shift would contact her if Ellie turned up there.

She was curled up in an easy chair in the nurses' common room trying to do a crossword. She couldn't face returning to the cold house in Sugden Road and would stay at the SLH tonight. John was visiting colleagues at the station house so her parents, she suspected, would already be in bed; it would be the warmest place. This would probably be the first of many such nights, the newspaper warned that the cold snap was about to get even colder.

The black and white squares danced before Faye's eyes, but a more important puzzle was occupying her mind, just as it had since Jane's body had been discovered. Who killed her and why?

Jane's death was linked to the SLH in two ways: the hospital's key to the deep level shelter and whatever was going on with Polly Brooks in the office, though, she acknowledged to herself, she didn't fully understand that.

First, the key. If Owen Philpott was ruled out as a suspect, and Faye had never really suspected him, the most likely way into the deep shelters was using the SLH key. The key couldn't be copied. It was locked in a drawer in Miss Barnett's desk which only she, Miss Barnett and Jean could open.

Who else could get into that drawer? And what man, specifically, had the opportunity to take the key?

Antoine Girard could've persuaded Jean to open the drawer for him or have taken an impression of its key. He had charmed the secretary and, as Jean had said, he often visited the office. Then there was Nicholas Yorke. Miss Barnett allowed him to use the office for his interviews, so he could have done the same. And who was paying for his research and those interviews? Then there was Les Allen, he'd been hanging around the office too, supposedly lovelorn and looking for Polly's address. There was no other reason for him being there unless he was up to no good.

But none of them bore the marks of a struggle. And what possible motive could any of these men have for killing Jane?

Was it sexual, as Ellie surmised? Antoine Girard was a practiced philanderer, used to deceiving and getting his way with women, he mightn't take kindly to being rebuffed. Ellie had told her that he was worried about being apprehended for the crime. But then, he might have reason to be worried, someone had already wrongly reported him AWOL and he had his secrets, as she had discovered.

Nicholas Yorke – Faye doubted her objectivity when it came to Yorke – but he had interviewed Jane and seemed to have taken a liking to her. He'd remarked on how pretty she was and he was a man of the world. Had he done more than interview Jane? Arranged a meeting, an assignation, perhaps? But could it really be him?

Yes, it could, came the unwelcome answer.

Les Allen was Jane's best friend's beau. Had he turned to Jane when Polly left him? He claimed that Jane didn't like him and, it seemed, gossip bore out his story. Faye disliked Les, he was a busybody who would use what he knew to his own advantage, she had experienced that firsthand, but was he a killer?

Les Allen was a known quantity, had a long history in Clapham, whereas Girard and Yorke were relative newcomers, their backgrounds less understood. What did she – what did anyone – know about Antoine Girard and Nicholas Yorke?

Perhaps the motive for killing Jane was different entirely? In her search for Polly, had Jane happened across something else, something illegal, perhaps? Was she going to the police about it? This was where the second link with the hospital might come into play; whatever Polly Brooks was doing.

The SLH was ordering a lot of cocaine. Yet the pharmacist had explained how difficult it would be to steal any. Faye went through it again, step by step. How did the process work?

The pharmacist and the doctors asked for specific drugs to be purchased and the office ordered them. Upon arrival the drugs were locked away in the dispensary. The nurses then stocked the individual ward medicine cabinets with those drugs frequently in use on the wards. Doctors prescribed specific drugs for their patients and the pharmacist prepared the dosages according to the prescriptions. They were then taken to the wards and administered by the nurses.

There were prescription charts for every patient. Faye had seen them. There was one at the foot of Phoebe's bed. A clipboard with a grid showing drugs prescribed, dosage quantity and regularity. A nurse signed it each time the patient was given their medication. So either the pharmacist, at the start of the process, or a nurse, at the end, would spot any anomaly.

And all the restricted drugs were accounted for in the Register, showing amounts in and amounts out. Faye sighed. There was nothing wrong with the process. She was grasping at straws.

Maybe Polly had just returned to Grays, as she'd said she was going to, and Jane was killed by someone passing through, like the police thought. But that didn't feel right. She knew that there was something wrong, even as it was eluding her. And there were the links with the hospital, which were too much of a coincidence.

What was going on in the office? Polly Brooks had been caught looking at patients' medical files. Why was she doing that? Jean said Polly had been rude when she'd challenged her and wouldn't explain. Could Polly have come to a similar conclusion as Faye – that there was something fishy going on? What had she found?

Nurses said that Polly suddenly seemed to have a lot of cash, supposedly from a legacy, before she left. Where did the cash really come from and why did she leave? Her departure was unexpected. Could Polly have been scared off or bribed to go?

Or... the hairs on the back of her neck rose. Something was very wrong here. Polly had disappeared and when Jane tried to investigate her friend's disappearance she had been strangled.

Then there were the missing patient records. Faye recalled the entries in the Register and the lack of corresponding patient files. But what if those missing records weren't 'missing'? What if they'd never existed?

Faye sat up, suddenly rigid and tense. What if those patients listed in the Register weren't real? What if they were 'ghosts'? The drugs prescribed for them would never be taken to the wards and could be stolen.

Who completed the Register? Currently, it was Miss Underwood, who had been so helpful. But until four weeks ago it had been Miss Lowell, who had died so tragically. Could the pharmacist herself have been in on the theft?

That could be it!

Polly Brooks had come across this and, like Faye, had crosschecked in the office. And Polly Brooks was Les Allen's girlfriend. What was Les Allen really doing in Miss Barnett's office yesterday evening?

When she thought about it, the story about him trying to find Polly's address didn't add up; staff records were locked away. He must have known they weren't available to anyone who asked. Jean had gone home so Les Allen couldn't have got to them. Unless he had a key.

The SLH security key had been in the drawer when she locked it earlier. She'd seen it. So he couldn't have been after that. Yet she couldn't remember seeing that key when she had first opened the drawer. Was that because it wasn't there? Perhaps Les wasn't in the office to take the key, but to return it. Did Les Allen have a key to Miss Barnett's desk?

Les Allen, the Scout leader, the stretcher bearer, the popular chap, had he fooled everyone? He had a hard side – his attempt to put pressure on her testified to that – but stealing drugs and murder? That was a different level entirely.

He didn't appear to be an addict. So what was he doing with the cocaine? Was he selling it? Was that what this was about – a trade in illegal drugs? If it was, he must have underworld contacts.

Underworld and underground. The deep shelters would make an excellent place to store any stolen drugs; they would make an excellent base of operations for illegal activity generally. Had she and Ellie stumbled upon something bigger than theft of drugs from the SLH? Maybe Jane had found out about it too and had determined to go to the police?

Was it Les whose shouts Ellie had heard on Sunday night with Jane? He could have lured Jane to the common, before forcing her to go to the southern shaft head and down to the deep shelters. There wouldn't be anyone around to see them at midnight on Sunday on one of the coldest nights of the year. What happened down in the shelters, Faye didn't know, but it seemed that somehow, Jane had escaped him and made her way to the northern shaft head, where he caught up with her and killed her.

And Polly Brooks? Had she met the same fate?

And where was Ellie? She wasn't afraid of asking direct questions. Had she asked one too many?

Faye sprang from her chair.

She had to find Ellie. Now.

49

FAYE

'It's me, Faye.'

She spoke into the intercom in the foyer of Westbury Court.

'Come up,' Beryl answered, her voice thick with sleep. 'Can you remember, turn right when you leave the lift.'

A tousle-haired and bleary-eyed Beryl was waiting for her, door ajar, when she reached the flat.

'What is it? What's the matter?'

'I can't find Ellie anywhere. Has she come home?'

'No.'

'Look, Beryl, I'm worried. I think Ellie might have been asking too many questions.'

'Eh? What are you talking about?' The nurse blinked sleep from her eyes. 'Come in. Let's check her room.'

The small bedroom was neat and clean. If Ellie had been back there while Beryl slept there was no sign of it.

'The building caretaker said he hadn't seen her.'

'When I was looking for her earlier,' Beryl said. 'I was told that she was going to go to the pictures with some of the nurses this evening.'

'What time was that showing? Wouldn't it have finished an hour ago?'

Beryl checked her watch. 'Yes.'

'But she's not come back here and she's not at the SLH—'

'I also heard that she had a stand-up row with a man in the street two days ago. A man she clearly knew.'

'That's likely to be her former fiancé.'

'She could have gone off with him?'

'She could have done,' Faye murmured. 'But, from what she told me, I think that's very unlikely. I think – this might sound bizarre – but I think she might be in danger.'

'You're right, it does sound bizarre. Are you sure you're feeling alright?'

'It's not me having a fit of the vapours,' Faye said. 'It's just...' She took a deep breath. 'You know that Ellie and I have been trying to find out more about how Jane met her death, digging around, investigating. Well, the trail led to Polly Brooks.'

'Aye, Ellie was asking me about Jane and Polly.'

'Polly was nosing around in the patient records before she disappeared...'

'Left. She went home.'

'Ellie and I questioned whether Polly had gone home, or even left at all. It wasn't only patient records she'd been looking at. She'd been looking at purchase ledgers too. I examined the ones she'd been checking and noticed that we've been ordering more drugs than before the war, yet our intake of patients is the same.'

'That doesn't mean anything, Faye. There are more drugs around now and we might be treating different illnesses. If someone was stealing drugs it would be noticed.'

'I'm not so sure.'

'A nurse signs off every time a dose is given to a patient following the doctor's prescription. The drugs are held in the cabinets in the wards. Someone would notice if drugs were going missing.' Beryl was certain.

'What if the drugs never got to the ward?'

'Then the pharmacist would notice her stores being pilfered.'

'What if the pharmacist is in on it? Say she was. Could it happen?'

The Scot frowned, thinking. 'Aye. But a pharmacist wouldn't do something like that.'

'That's what I thought,' said Faye. 'And I'm sure Miss Underwood wouldn't, but what about her predecessor?'

At first Beryl said nothing, but she stared at Faye intently. Then she asked, 'The drugs we're ordering more of, what are they?'

'Cocaine.'

'The pharmacist has to keep a Register—'

'I know. I tried to track through some of the dosages in there and found that the patients prescribed for didn't have records. I think that they were phantoms; they didn't exist.'

Beryl gave a low whistle. 'If she was doing this and was exposed, it would mean the end of her career, prison, the works.'

'Too late now. She's dead.'

'Alright, but how does this link to Ellie being in danger?'

'I think Miss Lowell was rumbled, by Polly, or, if Polly told him, by Les Allen. Then I think he decided to get in on the act.'

'Les!' Beryl looked astounded. 'But...'

'I know. I haven't pieced it all together yet.'

'And you're saying what?'

'I'm not certain, but my theory is that Miss Lowell somehow came into the power of Polly and Les. Then they made her order more drugs.' This part sounded lame to Faye's ears.

'Drugs that they then stole, which never got to the patient.'

'Exactly.'

'So what happened to Polly?'

'I don't know. Maybe she ran off with some of the spoils, maybe Jane was right and she didn't get the chance. Look, can you get dressed and come over to the SLH and help, there are things still to check? Can you find those nurses who went to the pictures with Ellie? Make sure she went with them and what she did afterwards.'

'What are you going to do?'

'Track down Les Allen.'

50

FAYE

As she hurried down to the basement the only thing Faye could think about was Jane Cooper's strangled and beaten body lying on the mortuary slab. She hoped against hope that the same wouldn't happen to Ellie.

The porters' room was snug and warm, its heavy curtains closed. There was only one porter there, having a cup of tea, the rest of the night shift were out and about in the hospital. Faye knocked on the half-open door.

'Evening,' she said. 'I'm looking for Les. Is he around?'

'Yeah, I saw him half an hour ago.'

'Eh?' Faye was non-plussed. Was Les Allen here, in the hospital? 'You sure?'

'Course I'm sure. How many men are there in the SLH?'

'Where was he?'

'Here. He always clocks the night shift on at nine and the morning shifts at six and eight. He makes sure everyone's here. He's been taking even more care to do it since the killing. He doesn't want any of us to go the same way as Jane. Good old Les.'

Suddenly her logic seemed faulty. What if she was wrong?

Her theory was just a stupid theory and Les Allen was 'good old

Les' who was such a decent sort and looked after the women in his team.

If Les Allen was in the SLH, he couldn't be in the deep shelters with Ellie. The alternative – that he had done the deed already and that Ellie was lying strangled somewhere, chilled Faye to the bone.

'You don't know where he is now, do you?'

The porter shrugged and shook her head.

'Thanks.'

Faye strode off towards the stairs and the office.

Could she be wrong...? No. She wasn't wrong, she was sure.

She let herself in and flicked on the light. It took Faye only a few seconds to unlock the top right-hand drawer of Miss Barnett's desk. She rummaged inside it but couldn't see the key for the shelter. It was big, flat and heavily incised, it couldn't be confused with any of the others.

Up-ending the drawer's contents out on to the desk, she spread out the sets of keys. There was no key for the shelters.

But it had been here before, when she'd been checking out the patient records only a few hours ago – she had seen it. Someone must have taken it since.

She was right! Les must have it!

That meant he could be in the deep shelters right now. With Ellie.

She closed the drawer and locked it. From her pocket she drew a piece of paper. She'd been carrying it around all evening. On it was written 'Phillip Morgan, Chief Superintendent of Police, Specialist Crime Directorate 7, Scotland Yard' and a telephone number.

Now she had to be really convincing. Faye reached for the telephone.

51

FAYE

'I sincerely hope you've got a very good reason for calling on me at this hour.' Matron's voice was almost as icy as the temperature outside.

Faye stood, shivering, before her as the senior nurse sat in front of the fire in the living room of her flat in the nurses' home. Even wearing slippers and a dressing gown, with her hair in papers, Matron still had an air of authority.

Faye took a deep breath.

'It's Ellie Peveril,' she began. 'I'm very worried that she may be in danger.'

'Why?'

'She and I have been trying to find out what happened to Jane Cooper. Well, perhaps we should have been more circumspect, but I fear that whoever killed Jane has Ellie in his sights. She was supposed to go to the pictures this evening and got as far as the queue, but Beryl – Nurse MacBride – tells me that the nurses accompanying her say she rushed off, promising she'd be back for the film. She was at the top of Balham Hill. No one has seen her since.'

'You've checked everywhere?'

'Yes.'

'Am I to understand that you think you and Ellie may have identified Jane Cooper's killer?'

'Yes. And Matron, I think SLH is involved, through people working here.'

'Who?'

'Les Allen, the Head Porter and Miss Lowell, our late pharmacist.'

'Belinda Lowell? You'd better be sure of your ground, Miss Smith.' Matron frowned. 'It's easy to accuse someone who can't answer back, but Miss Lowell's friends will have something to say about any unsubstantiated allegations. And Les Allen is widely liked and admired and has had enough to contend with in life. Besides, if you're going to accuse anyone, let alone a respected pharmacist, you had better have evidence. Do you have any?'

'Some circumstantial evidence, yes.'

'So why haven't you taken it to the police.'

'I've only just put all the pieces together,' Faye said.

'Sit down and explain.'

Faye perched on a footstool.

'I believe that drugs are being stolen from the SLH. That Les Allen, with Miss Lowell's connivance, was stealing cocaine. I think Jane Cooper believed that something was amiss and was killed because of that. It's all connected. But the police haven't been pursuing the murder with any enthusiasm,' she said. 'They didn't take Ellie's statement about hearing Jane and a man on the common seriously, as you know. Yet she could help them identify who Jane was with that night because she heard him. Now Ellie has disappeared and, given what I've discovered, I don't think we have a choice but to involve the police. We need their help.'

'The inspector from Scotland Yard who's in charge of the Cooper case?'

'No. Ellie's god-father is a chief superintendent at Scotland Yard—'

'And might act more quickly. I understand,' Matron interjected. 'If what you believe is true, he needs to be informed anyway and he may be able to help us.'

'I've already contacted him. He's on his way. My brother John, a policeman, will contact Inspector Irving.'

'Do you have any idea where Miss Peveril could be?'

'Yes. I think she's been taken into the deep level shelters. I think that's where Jane Cooper was taken. She was trying to escape when she was killed.'

'By Les Allen? Are you sure about this?'

'I believe so, yes.'

'Have you looked for Mr Allen?'

'I saw him earlier outside the office – the second time I've seen him there this week. The porters say he clocked the shift on at nine. He hasn't been seen since. The thing is, the first time I saw him in Miss Barnett's office, he was there after hours, in the dark. He's got no business being there.'

'Isn't that where Felicity keeps the key to the deep level shelters?'

'Exactly, she keeps it locked in her desk. I have a key to that desk drawer and I've just checked it. The security key to the deep shelters entrance is missing.'

'I see.' Matron paused, a frown furrowing her brow. 'I sincerely hope you're wrong, Miss Smith, and this is a wild goose chase. If it is, you'll have some explaining to do, to the police as well as to the hospital management board,' she said with a deep sigh.

'I hope I'm wrong too, but I don't think I am, Matron. I fear I've got Ellie into a lot of trouble.'

'Leave the self-blame until later,' Matron said, brisk now. 'Concentrate on doing what's necessary now. I'll contact Owen Philpott and Felicity Barnett.'

'Yes, ma'am.' Faye rose. 'Miss Barnett won't be pleased. She ordered me to stop 'playing detective'.'

'If you're right I'm very glad you've persisted.'

'Chief Superintendent Morgan is on his way and we can get John here even sooner, but – they can't come soon enough for me.'

'Wait for them at the main entrance,' Matron said.

'Yes, ma'am.'

52

ELEANOR

The light from the little spirit lamp seemed puny and insignificant in the blackness of the larger tunnel. Ellie set out, planning to retrace her steps to the wide staircase and the diagram she'd seen earlier. It was at the top of the stairs, by the lift shaft. That's what she wanted to see.

She zigzagged from wall to wall, anxious not to miss any of the signs and directions. One wrong turn could mean she would be wandering through the tunnels for ages. She'd left her coat on the bed, it would have made her much too warm, yet she felt the sweat running down her back, making her blouse stick to her spine.

It was silent, except for a regular rumbling noise, which, she assumed, was a Tube train passing above. Ellie walked carefully, trying to move as silently as she could, listening out for the tell-tale sound of the descending lift.

There! The sign she'd seen earlier on the wall, pointing the way to the Medical Stores and a canteen. She was near the tunnel that led to the stairs. Les had turned right from the main passage so Ellie turned left at the junction and walked on, the circle of light moving with her.

Surely the stairs must be here somewhere. She remembered them as being very close to the mouth of the branch tunnel.

Then, suddenly, she was upon them. The darkness and her own fear had made the distance seem longer. Ellie sighed in relief.

The diagram was at the top of the stairs, it showed the two deep level shelter tunnels in cross section, one circle coloured white and the other red. The white route was the one attaching to the shaft at Balham Hill, the one she was in; the red route was entered through the shaft on the common outside Westbury Court. There were several small linking passages between the two, although all but one of these had been scored through with a pen. Owen Philpott had said that most of the links between the two main tunnels were closed off, maybe they were blocked in some way.

Best of all, the diagram showed that the one link passage that remained open had an exit, leading up to the southbound Northern line tunnel which ran above the deep level shelter.

A way out!

If she could find it. If she could orientate herself in the right direction. There were miles of tunnels. If she went the wrong way, she'd never find it.

Her spirit lamp flickered. Was it already running out of alcohol? That hadn't lasted long. She couldn't afford to lose her light.

She placed it on the ground and took another lamp from her basket. When the dying flame of the old lamp was held to the pristine cotton wick of the new it caught light immediately, and she put it into the metal mug. The old, empty canister she put in the basket, it was too hot to refill now, but she could do so, if needed, when it had cooled.

Ellie set off again, going down to the main tunnel. If she had worked things out correctly, this one ran beneath the northbound Northern Line. She would listen for the sound of the next Tube train and work out which direction it came from. She needed to go north, in the same direction as the train. It wasn't long before a growling rumble began, coming from her right. It passed overhead and followed the tunnel left. That was the way to go.

She hurried now, still moving as silently as she could, listening for any sounds of Les Allen's return. It must be half an hour or more since he'd left, without her watch she couldn't tell. He could be back at any moment, and she wanted to be gone long before then.

Ellie strode down the wide tunnel. Every hundred feet or so there was a crossroads, though the right-hand way was always blocked off, wooden planks hammered across frames at their ends. These were the tunnels shown on the diagram with their entrances scored through.

The left-hand side carried signposts. There was a canteen, lavatories and washhouses, an emergency medical post and offices. There was a whole world down here, deep beneath the surface. What would it have been like when the shelters were full of people, seeking safety from the destruction visited on them from the skies? Crowded. Now, it would be easy to get lost in it.

Her thoughts turned to the world above. Was anyone up there looking for her?

Beryl was doubtless deep asleep after having been on last night's shift. She wouldn't notice if Ellie wasn't in her room. Faye wouldn't notice her absence either, she was too taken up with her own troubles; besides, she would no longer care.

The second spirit lamp was spluttering now. She stopped to repeat the earlier process and the new lamp flickered into life. She still had one lamp left before she would have to refill the first one.

What?

She blinked hard and screwed up her eyes. The tunnel was flooded with light. The emergency power was back on.

Then she heard it. The clanking sound of the lift descending.

53

ELEANOR

No! It's too soon!

Ellie's hands shook as she re-screwed the bottle top and put everything but her little lamp back into the basket.

What should she do? Where could she go?

She had to get as far away from the lift shaft as she could and into a side tunnel. The main tunnels were wide and completely straight. Once he was at the foot of the stairs, he would be able to see any movement she made, even in the distance.

Run!

Clutching her lamp and basket Ellie made a dash for the nearest side tunnel, about fifty yards ahead. She skidded to a halt at its entrance and threw herself into it. Once inside, she bent over, panting for breath. Her heart was thumping so loudly she was sure Allen would be able hear it from the lift shaft.

The weak flame of the spirit lamp seemed stronger in the unlit side tunnel. It showed tables and folding chairs stacked by one wall and a serving counter on the other. This looked like a canteen. As her breathing calmed, she realised that this might be a stroke of luck; there would be matches here. More of those could be useful.

Venturing deeper inside, Ellie saw stores; metal racks holding cardboard boxes piled high, forgotten; dried foodstuffs spilled from corners bitten by rats or mice. Two large chests sat against the right-hand wall and there were more of the metal cupboards she had seen in the other small tunnel. Inside those she found candles and boxes of matches. These must be emergency stores in case the power failed, or the power station was bombed. She stuffed several of each into the basket.

More boxes and piles of paper packages, little sachets, empty or filled with a white powder. Huge jars of sugar or salt. Except it didn't look like either, neither refined nor crystalline enough. What's more, she knew she'd seen something like it before and recently, but not at the hospital. She put a sachet in her pocket.

The groaning of the lift ceased, and she heard the grille sliding back. Sound travelled clearly through the silent, still air. He would be walking down the stairs now.

Once out of the lift and down the stairs Allen would, she assumed, go into the branch tunnel leading to the Medical Stores, where he believed he would find her waiting. That would be her chance, her opportunity to run to the link tunnel with the stairs. It couldn't be much further; she had passed two closed tunnels on the right already.

She peered around the edge of her side tunnel. The main tunnel was illuminated only sporadically by the emergency lighting and, fortunately for her, its mouth was in darkness. She could see as far as the stairs. The main tunnel was completely empty, but perhaps he hadn't started down the stairs yet.

What if he didn't go to the Medical Stores? What if he walked along the main tunnel? Ellie was consumed by the fear that he knew where she was. He would pass the end of her canteen tunnel. She needed somewhere to hide or a way of escape. Becoming frantic, Ellie raised her lamp and looked around the kitchen storeroom.

Nowhere. The tunnel ended at a brick wall, there were no doors or connecting corridors. The counter was open, the cupboards were too shallow and had fixed shelves. The chests. They looked large enough for her to climb inside and lower the lid. The only possible hiding places.

Ellie imagined Allen walking towards her along the main tunnel, right at that moment.

The first chest wouldn't open at all, despite her desperate tugging, so she moved on to the second. When she began to raise its lid, she was assailed by a rush of foul-smelling air. Whatever was in there had gone off quite some time ago. Not a place she would want to hide unless she absolutely had to.

Yet something made her open the lid again. She held the lamp over the chest and looked inside.

Her skin crawled.

Something was lying, crumpled at the bottom of the chest. It seemed to be a body. Its flesh had rotted, the skull visible through what skin remained. The nose cavity looked like a screaming mouth. Stretched lengths of tendon lined half-fleshed femurs, still clad in red cotton. The bones of fingers were clearly visible. And fingernails.

Nails wearing red nail polish.

Ellie saw, but her brain couldn't process the horror.

She forced herself to look again at the head. The skull had stray strands of wavy peroxide blonde hair falling to the corpse's shoulders.

Like Lana Turner's film star hairstyle.

Ellie recoiled, letting out a cry of revulsion and disgust. She had found Polly Brooks.

54

FAYE

'The key, the key is missing,' Faye said, striding rapidly along the hospital corridor. 'That's what clinches it.'

'Which key?' Beryl was struggling to keep up.

'The hospital's key to the deep shelter entrance. We had one because we needed to be able to evacuate patients when the sirens sounded. It was kept in the office, but it's not there now. I think Les has taken it. I think Les has been using it all along.'

'Eh?'

'I think Les has himself a lucrative and deadly side line in cocaine.'

'Slow down!'

Faye moderated her pace but kept going.

'And you think he's got Ellie?'

'I believe so. That's what I've told Chief Superintendent Morgan, Phillip, Ellie's godfather. He says he's on his way.'

'So we're going to wait for him out front?'

The cold hit them like a slap as they emerged from the formal entranceway onto the ramp down to the South Side.

Street lights reflected from the large windows of the SLH building on to an empty thoroughfare. One or two vehicles drove past and a few late stayers emerged from beneath the glowing red-

and-blue London Underground sign of Clapham South station. It might be a Saturday night, but it was a night to be in by the fire, not out on the town, the temperature was well below zero.

'No. We can't wait. It'll take too long. Ellie's in danger. Matron can wait for him.'

'Matron?'

'She knows about it all and she's contacted Owen Philpott and Miss Barnett. Owen will bring his keys to both the shelter entrances.'

'We're waking up half of south London tonight!'

'Yes, but probably not soon enough. The point is, we must get into the deep shelters.'

They strode down the ramp.

'How? We don't have a key.'

'I think there's another way in,' Faye said.

'What, as well as the entrance shafts?'

'Yes. D'you remember, when the Ministry of Works was building those shafts, the workers would go down through the underground station, down to the tunnels which had already been bored through the ground.'

'Aye, I think so.'

'The machinery for the lifts was lowered down the shafts from the surface, but there were workmen down there waiting for it. There must be a way to the deep level shelters through Clapham South underground station.'

Beryl looked at her watch. 'It'll be closing soon.'

'I know, which is why we can't wait for Phillip Morgan and Owen Philpott and whoever he brings with him. We must go down now.'

'How will we be able to see down there?'

Faye produced a heavy torch from her overcoat pocket.

'You've thought of everything,' Beryl said.

'Oh no, I've been very slow on the uptake, believe me.'

They hurried across the South Side to the underground station. The retractable security grille at the entrance was already drawn across. The ticket collector's glass booth was empty, and the ticket hall seemed deserted.

No! Faye grasped the latticework of the grill. She wanted to shake it. Then she caught sight of a movement beyond the glass at the inquiry desk hatch.

'Excuse me! Sir!' She waved, wildly. A middle-aged London Underground guard appeared from the door, pulling on an overcoat over his uniform, ready to leave.

'Yes, what is it?' He looked at his watch, his face sour. 'We're closing.'

Beryl's eyebrows rose. 'About to knock off early,' she said, *sotto voce*, then asked 'is Larry around?'

'Yeah, he's sorting out – why d'you want to know?'

'He knows me, I'm Beryl MacBride, from number 40 upstairs. You'll have seen me around. We're from the SLH. It's urgent.'

The guard muttered in a non-committal way, but he unlocked the padlock and pulled back the grille.

'So?'

'We believe our friend is in trouble,' Faye said. 'She's been taken down to the deep shelters by the man who murdered the nurse the other night.'

'Eh?'

'What's going on?' A younger man in a similar uniform joined them. 'What's up, Beryl?'

'I'm off, this is nothing to do with me,' the first guard said, stepping on to the pavement. 'G'night.'

'Let us in, Larry, please. Our friend is in danger, we must help her. She's in the deep shelters.'

'There's a way in, isn't there?' Faye added. 'From here.'

'Yeah, but that hasn't been opened up since... well, since the V2s.'

'We need you to open it now, Larry,' Beryl insisted. 'It's to do with the murder on Sunday.'

'Stone the crows! Alright, but I'll have to find the key.' Larry started to return to the ticket office.

'I'll go,' Faye said to Beryl. 'You go and get some reinforcements from next door just in case... John's there, at the station house. Tell him, tell them all, where I've gone. Make sure they understand.'

'Are you sure, Faye? It could be—'

'Just do it.'

'Here.' Larry returned and handed her a heavy key. 'The doors are on the southbound platform, at the end. Look, you can't go on your own, I'll come with you.' He made as if to close the grille again.

'Don't, there's help on its way.'

'I can't leave the station open and unguarded,' Larry said. 'Either it's open and I'm here or I close up and come down with you.'

'Then I'll have to go down alone,' Faye said, moving towards the stairs.

'Be careful, Faye,' Beryl called, anxiety in her voice. 'Don't get yourself shot!'

Larry unlocked a wall box marked 'Danger' and flicked a switch. The escalators rumbled into life.

'Tell me, are the rails still live?' she asked as she began to descend.

'Yes, they'll be live until the whole system closes down,' he replied, leaning over the balustrade. 'In about an hour.'

'Thank you, thank you so much.'

His face disappeared from view as Faye hurried down the moving escalator.

She ran through the arch onto the southbound platform. At its far end there was a pair of metal doors, just as the guard had said, each with a ventilation grille.

At the first attempt the key he'd given her wouldn't turn and Faye cursed it. She stopped, calmed her breathing and tried again. The door swung outwards.

There was no sign of a light switch so Faye produced her torch. Its light showed a dusty concrete corridor with stairs going down to the left about three paces in. They were wide and shallow.

This was it.

Somewhere down there was Les Allen, probably armed. Ellie was down there too.

Phillip Morgan and Owen Philpott were on their way but would almost certainly arrive too late. John was closer, but not close enough.

She was here. Now. It was up to her.

It was dangerous, there was no saying she would come out alive, let alone succeed, but she was Ellie's best hope, probably her only hope to survive.

Eleanor Peveril, of Cathedral Close, Worcester, privileged, cosseted, beautiful and intelligent. And about to take the job that Faye had been offered. About to ruin Faye's own hopes for a new life, for an escape from her family home. Her hopes for a career and independence.

She should wait for John. This was ridiculously dangerous. Wait for Owen and the police.

Eleanor Peveril, of Westbury Court, curious and interesting, generous, honest, fearless, questioning her own prejudices, determined to live her own life.

Gripping her torch more tightly and summoning up all her courage, Faye started down the stairs.

55

ELEANOR

E llie clapped both her hands over her mouth. Surely Allen must have heard her?

She closed the lid of the chest on the partially decomposed body of Polly Brooks and, grabbing her basket, scurried to the end of the tunnel. She blew out the flame of the lamp and, muscles tensing, she peered around the corner.

Nothing.

No one.

Alternating pools of light and shadow fell on the floor of the main passage all the way back towards the stairs. There was no sign of Les Allen. But he must have heard. If he'd gone to the medical stores tunnel it would take him some time to return. How long? A few minutes? Less? She didn't have much time.

Ellie took to her heels, heart hammering in her chest. If he entered the main tunnel he would see her, there was nowhere to hide, but she had to get to the linking one and this was the only way.

Where was it?

Up ahead on the right, about twenty yards. The dark mouth of a route that wasn't blocked off.

She stretched her legs, feet pounding on the concrete and

gripped the basket handle so hard the wickerwork cut deep into her fingers. She careered around the corner into the dark tunnel and halted, panting, before swinging round to look back whence she had come. There was no one to be seen.

Eh? He *must* have heard; he must have done. His bad leg might make him slower than she was, but he wasn't that slow. So where the hell was he?

Calm, be calm, she told herself. Wherever he is, it doesn't matter, concentrate on finding the way out.

There was no emergency lighting here, so, hands shaking, Ellie put the basket down and drew out her lamp. Fishing a box of matches from her pocket she lit its wick and a glow of light grew, reflecting on the tunnel wall.

'So that's how you did it.'

Ellie almost dropped the lamp.

The voice came from behind her. She raised it high and turned. Les Allen, a twisted grin on his face, leant, with arms folded against the tunnel wall, on the other side of a dark opening. The stairs to the underground at Clapham South. The way out.

'I still have the gun,' he said, drawing it from his pocket. 'And a torch. Don't try anything.'

Tears of frustration and helplessness welled in her eyes. Anger too – he was so obviously enjoying her plight.

'How did you know?' she demanded; fists clenched. 'Tell me!'

'The spent matches,' he said, smirking. 'On the floor in the side tunnel. I knew you had light of some kind. My money was on a torch, bandages wound around a stick, perhaps, but that little lamp is even better.'

Damn, damn, damn!

She glared at him.

'I thought I'd surprise you.' His smile widened, revealing his teeth. 'The shaft heads were locked, so this had to be where you were headed, but I don't understand how you knew about it. The odds on your coming across this exit by chance must be millions to one. So you knew it was here. How? Your turn to tell.'

'The diagram,' Ellie said, her voice flat. 'Near the control room.'

'Of course!' He sounded genuinely annoyed. 'Stupid of me not to realise.'

After all, he had underestimated her. He'd probably underestimated Jane too. Ellie prayed that he would do so again and that she could exploit it, it was a lifeline to cling to.

'Time to return to our little hidey-hole, I think.'

Ellie knew that, if she did, she would probably never leave it. Her best bet was to stay close to the stairs and hope that someone was looking for her.

Keep him talking.

'Was that where you took Polly? I found her body by the way. Why did you kill her?'

'Polly got greedy,' he said, sharply, then pressed his lips together in a moué of distaste. 'And I was growing tired of her. It was Jane I'd fancied from the start, though Poll spotted me with the keys in the office one time. After that it was best to keep her close. So... we became a couple.'

'You killed her... just like that.'

Allen gave her a level stare, cold amusement in his eyes. Ellie's insides gave a lurch. He had never loved Polly, as he'd claimed. He didn't even make excuses. This man really was a cold-blooded killer.

'And... and Jane?'

He shrugged. He was enjoying her fear. 'She left me no choice. The bint was banging on about Polly – Polly this, Polly that. I'd have shown her a good time, but she didn't believe my story, caught me out.'

'I heard you. You and Jane, on Sunday night, on the common, just after midnight,' Ellie said, determined not to seem frightened. 'You were arguing. You came towards my building, Westbury Court, towards the station house. Was that where she was going?'

'To the police.' His voice was flat and emotionless.

'So? They may not have believed her. And it was only your word against hers.'

'I couldn't risk it. They might have checked with Polly's family, asking about her so-called "legacy". It would only have been a matter of time before they'd be asking questions at the SLH, about her and about me. That's a good billet, very lucrative, I couldn't have Jane spoiling that.'

'So… you're stealing drugs from the hospital and selling them.'

'With a little help from my friends,' he replied with a sneer.

'George, that's what you called him. That wouldn't be George Packham, would it?'

The constable had called George Packham a 'fence', someone who sold stolen goods. He would have a network of accomplices.

'My, my, you *are* putting things together quickly, aren't you.' He pulled the pistol from his waistband. 'I don't think I can let *you* go. Now, this way.'

Ellie shrank back against the tunnel wall.

'You know criminals who sell to drug addicts.'

Perhaps her godfather would know them too. If she got out of there…

'You overheard that, did you?'

'Yes. Addiction is vile and horrible, it destroys people,' Ellie said. She remembered the evidence of Nazi drug use at Nuremberg, testing new drugs on concentration camp internees and their own soldiers and airmen. 'Destroys families, destroys lives.'

'As if I cared. Anyway, a lot of users aren't addicts, just people who know how to enjoy themselves.'

In an instant, Ellie realised where she'd seen paper packets like the one she had in her pocket. In the night club, among the debris on the table where Pat was sitting. Did Pat use cocaine?

Keep him talking!

'How did you manage to steal the drugs? Did you get the hospital to order more than it needed? Is that what you did?'

'So, you've sussed that, have you? What a clever girl.' His eyebrows rose. 'Or was that Faye Smith's doing?' His facial expression grew hard and bitter, violence close to the surface. 'I should have dealt with her when I had the chance. I don't like the way she looks at me. As if she knows what I'm thinking.'

'Maybe she does. She seems to know most things.'

'Not as much as I know,' he said. 'You'd be surprised how much I know. And Faye Smith's got her secrets too, everyone has their secrets. What's yours, I wonder?'

Ellie's skin crawled as his eyes narrowed to slits and he thrust his face forwards, as if he was smelling her. Smelling her secrets.

'How – how did you fix things?' she asked, desperate to distract him.

He smiled, showing that he'd decided to play along for the moment.

'Dear old Miss Lowell, late of this parish. Poll spotted her behaving strangely, she suspected Lowell was snorting the white stuff. Lowell had been ordering extra and filling in that register with names of patients who didn't exist to account for it. Polly checked the files.'

'I see, comparing the purchasing ledgers and then checking the patients' records.'

Allen's expression turned sulky, it seemed he didn't like her knowing things. No, her role was to be submissive and adoring. He wanted to show off to her, even now. Her fingers tightened around the scissors in her pocket.

She had to get him talking again.

'Doesn't matter. I'm so sorry, I interrupted, please go on.'

'Polly thought we could blackmail the doc,' he continued with less enthusiasm, wary. 'I agreed, but not in the way Poll proposed, for cash.'

'Didn't Polly know about your drug side-line then?'

'Oh no. She had no idea.' His lips stretched back into a humourless grin. 'Quite a surprise to little Poll it was, waking up in the Medical Stores tunnel. George had some fun with Poll, creeping up on her in the dark.'

Ellie swallowed hard, trying to keep the horror from her face. 'But you gave her some cash?' she said.

'Yes. I told her I'd got it from Lowell. But she couldn't keep hold of it, was splashing out on all sorts. Fool. People noticed and we had to come up with a story.'

The legacy.

'Anyway, it was far more lucrative for me to blackmail the doc into getting more drugs, which I could then sell on.'

'I see. Was that when you contacted George Packham?'

Allen laughed. 'George and me go way back,' he said. 'He's been helping me shift stuff for years. Went to school together. But I'm getting bored with this conversation.' He raised the pistol. 'I think we're finished here.'

56

FAYE

Faye licked her lips, the air in the stairwell was stale and dry. She ran her hand along the metal rail as she descended, taking care not to make too much noise. There was a landing just below, where the stairs zigzagged back upon themselves. The third; she'd passed two landings already.

As she approached it, she slowed. She could hear voices, attenuated by the echo in the stairwell. People were speaking, a man and a woman.

That sounded like Ellie, but who was she talking with? Les Allen?

Faye switched off her torch. Holding on to the rail she crept down to the landing in the dark. There was a glow of light coming up from below. Faye crouched where the stairs turned the corner and, taking a deep breath, looked around.

She couldn't see anyone, only an opening, the exit from the stairs, but she could hear the man, he must have been standing close to the left side of the exit. A woman's voice came from further away on the right, where the source of the light was. Faye heard the name 'Lowell'.

Ellie was buying time. Asking him questions, flattering him, keeping him talking. Was Allen credulous or vain enough to fall for that?

Surely Beryl had found John by now? What about Owen Philpott and the chief superintendent? Owen only lived in Balham, he didn't have far to come and, when she had spoken with him, Chief Superintendent Phillip Morgan sounded as if he would be breaking all speed limits to get to Clapham as quickly as possible.

But would they get here in time?

Faye crept a few steps lower. She could hear them clearly now. Ellie was apologising. The conversation went on.

Allen laughed. 'George and me go way back,' he said. 'Went to school together. But I'm getting bored with this conversation.' Allen's long legs and lower body came into view. He was holding a pistol! And he was pointing it at Ellie. 'I think we've finished here.'

No! She mustn't go with him.

'But I want to know how it worked.' Ellie hadn't given up. 'Please. Please. It... it doesn't cost you anything to tell me, no one's going to know. No one's going to come to my rescue, you've made sure of that.'

'That's true enough. And don't you think otherwise.'

'I don't, truly. If you want to you could indulge my curiosity.'

'If I wanted to... but then you're going to have to indulge me in return.'

Faye sensed him becoming less nervy, his voice was more confident. Ellie's magic was working.

'Didn't anyone else notice Miss Lowell was buying too much cocaine?'

'No, you don't understand.' His tone grew didactic. 'She wasn't doing a lot of that; it was just on her own account and she was very careful. She *was* an addict, that's what Poll spotted. Then it was only a matter of scaring her into doing what I wanted. I needed a regular supply. So, I got Lowell to buy a lot more, under different brand names and pass it on to me. It meant there were more phantom patients in case someone spotted a discrepancy in that register

Lowell had to complete; in case the authorities came sniffing around.'

In the darkness, Faye nodded.

'Ahh, clever.' Ellie's voice purred.

'I thought so.' He sounded cocky now.

'And you took them to George, your old schoolfriend and contact in the underworld.'

'George knew people, he was prepared to act as middleman, for a cut of the profits. Though the idiot took too many risks – dealing in daylight so close to the hospital!'

'But the overall plan was yours?'

'Yep.' He laughed. 'Don't imagine I don't know what you're doing, stringing me along. You're going to have to be a lot nicer to me than this if you want to stay alive.'

'I understand.' Ellie's voice was low and seductive. 'But what about if it's a real partnership? I could help you better than Polly ever could. Miss Barnett's offered me the job of office manager. I could fix things even more.'

Well done, Ellie, Faye thought. Quick thinking.

'Office manager... everyone knows that job's meant for Faye Smith.'

She was surprised by the venom in his voice when he said her name. He hated her, Faye realised.

'Barnett's offered it to me.'

'Well, well, some friend you turn out to be, a proper little cuckoo-in-the-nest.' He sounded admiring.

'One does what one has to, to get what one wants.'

'One most certainly does.' He was sarcastic, then his voice hardened. 'How? How can you fix things?'

'I could rig the purchasing, then copy the signatures of some of the other consultants on to prescriptions for phantom patients.'

'Nah, order very large amounts and the new pharmacist, Underwood, would ask questions. It'd be spotted straight away.'

There was a short silence.

Come on Ellie. Think!

She had to keep him talking.

'I could fake doctors' signatures? Locums, so there'd be no questions asked.'

'That might work, except the SLH doesn't use locum doctors,' he sneered. 'You don't know how things work here, really, do you? You'd be no use to me, you're just stalling.'

'I could find out. It'd be useful to have me in the office working with you.'

'Nah, I don't trust you. But you have other uses; now you're going to have to be *really* nice to me, I fancy moving up the social scale. Old George'll be pleased when he knows who I've got down here too. He'll want some pay back of his own.'

Faye saw Allen moving across the opening below, the gun in his hand. What could she do? She was weaponless. She began to creep further down the stairs.

'Come here!'

'Les, I'm pregnant.'

Faye's jaw dropped.

'So what? What difference does that make to me? I said, come here!'

Faye realised that she'd have to do something. Ellie would never comply. She straightened up, stepped halfway down the flight of stairs and shouted. 'No, come here, quickly!'

Allen whirled around to face her and began to raise the pistol. Faye shone her torch directly into his eyes.

'Ellie, run! This way!'

A gunshot sounded and she felt a searing pain. Time slowed as she watched the torch tumble over and over down the steps to the tunnel below. Bending double, she clutched at a wound in her side.

There was a loud scream, then Ellie ran up the stairs, something grasped in her hand, shouting at Faye to follow. Across the opening below Les Allen reeled, flapping and beating at the flames that were engulfing his clothes.

Faye swivelled, grasping the handrail with one hand, while trying to staunch the blood flowing from the wound with the other.

The throbbing agony in her side pulsed through her whole body and she shut her eyes against it, focusing on staying conscious and rational, not giving in to the pain.

'Come on!' Ellie called.

She forced herself to lift one foot and began to stumble up the stairs.

57

FAYE

'Faye! Come *on!*'

She heard Ellie shout again, but she was already out of sight, beyond the first landing.

Faye clenched her jaw and climbed, but then slumped against the wall and began to slide floorward. She grabbed at the handrail to steady herself.

'I've been shot,' she called, her voice shaking. 'I won't... be able to... You go on.'

The stairway above was in darkness, though Faye could see steps up to the first landing in the flame light from below. Ellie came hurrying down.

'Not a chance. Do come on, Faye. He'll be after us in a moment.'

She ducked beneath Faye's arm and Faye felt lighter, Ellie was taking her weight. Together they climbed the stairs, one step at a time.

'What did you do?' Faye asked, trying to ignore the fierce, throbbing pain.

'I had a spirit lamp... because he left me... down there in the dark.' Ellie's breathing was ragged, she was struggling to hold Faye upright and climb the stairs. 'When you... surprised us... I threw it at him.'

'Won't stop him for long.' Faye felt her strength leeching out of her. Her right hand was wet.

'Long enough. Come on now, how far is it to the surface?'

'Two more flights, I think.' Faye gasped as Ellie shifted her hold when they reached the first landing. A shard of pain pierced her side. 'Beryl's getting more police.'

'More police?'

'Your godfather... John... and Owen Philpott. They're on their way, will be coming down soon. I must... Ellie... must sit down.'

Faye's eyes felt heavy, her world was spinning.

'Well, you can't. You've got to keep going. Les Allen might not be the quickest mover in the world but as soon as he's doused those flames he'll be after us.'

Faye gritted her teeth and focused on the handrail. She had to take some of her own weight. Ellie couldn't carry her all the way up. She pulled herself forward and, together, they started the next flight of stairs.

'Did you hear?' Ellie asked. 'He confessed to it all.'

'Some... of... it.'

'But why are you here anyway? Not that I'm not grateful.'

'I... worked it out. Had to be him.'

Everything was grey now, there was nothing but pain.

'Come on, not much further.'

Ellie's voice seemed far away, then close at hand, then far away again.

Faye was having difficulty preventing her head from nodding to one side. It was too heavy for her neck. She tried to concentrate on putting one foot in front of the other.

Up the stairs. Climb the stairs.

'Just want to rest—'

No more stairs.

'No. Come on! I can hear him, he's catching us up.'

'Arghhh!' Pain ripped into her side again.

'Sorry, sorry, but I've got to get us out of here.'

Faye's feet were dragging. She seemed to be resting on Ellie's hip, in the way that her mother had carried her when she was a child. But she was slipping.

'Faye, come on, Faye.'

Ow!

Her cheek stung where it had been slapped and Faye opened her eyes, shocked.

'We're nearly there!'

There was light up ahead now. A wide rectangle of light.

Faye forced her feet into motion, thumping first one foot then the other on the ground, staggering.

They fell through doors onto the underground platform.

'Damn!'

'What, what is it, Ellie?'

'There's no one. No one's here.'

She heard the catch in her friend's voice.

'Ellie, you go. Go on. I can't... I can't go any further.'

'Alright, I'm going to put you down.'

She felt a hard bench beneath her and slid down to lie upon it.

'If we can't outrun him, I'll have to think of something else.'

'Ellie, Ellie.' Faye reached out and grasped her friend's hand. 'This time, aim for his head.'

Ellie knelt, rootling in the basket, then feeling in her pocket.

'You fucking bitch!'

Les Allen emerged from the stairwell, the burnt shreds of his jacket hanging from his shoulders, his face and hands black and pink.

'Faye Smith!' He held the pistol in two hands and pointed it at Faye. 'You're dead.'

Faye saw a ball of fire flying through the air and Les Allen screamed as flames exploded on his head. The gun fell to the floor as he lurched, hands beating, desperately, at his face and hair. He staggered across the platform.

'The rail...' Faye struggled to get her words out. 'It's—'

There was a flash of hard, electric white and a guttural cry, followed by a buzzing, sizzling sound. Then she smelled burning, like the smell from a chip pan fire. The smell of burning fat, of burning flesh.

'Hey!'

There was a shout from along the platform.

'It's alright.' Ellie was grasping her hand. 'It's alright, everything's going to be alright.'

Then she saw anxious faces looking down at her. John, pale and worried; Beryl looking close to tears. Nicholas Yorke – what was he doing here?

'Make way, light along, make way.'

Sounded like stretcher bearers. Had there been an air raid?

Faye closed her eyes and drifted away.

SUNDAY

58

ELEANOR

Flashing lights and noise filled the area around the underground station. Insensible to the cold, Ellie walked beside Faye's stretcher, grasping her friend's limp hand. Onlookers formed a corridor through which they walked. Dressed in night clothes under greatcoats, wearing footwear entirely unsuited to a sub-zero November night, many of them were from the SLH. Ellie recognised the faces, some with shocked or anxious expressions, all curious.

Then Matron was there, walking beside her.

'Take her to theatre straight away,' she ordered the stretcher bearers. 'Don't bother with a trolley, we don't have time. You!' She pointed at a nurse. 'Go and warn the duty surgeon that we're on our way. And you! Get Miss Smith's records from the general office – here's the key to the filing cabinet, second drawer down. We'll need her blood type. Then let the duty surgeon know what it is.'

Two nurses sprinted away.

'Ellie, Miss Peveril, how are you?' Matron looked her up and down.

Ellie realised that she was covered in blood.

'The blood's Faye's not mine,' she replied. 'I'm alright. Faye's been shot. In the side.'

When Ellie looked down, her friend's face was almost chalk white. Beryl had bound up the wound in Faye's side as best she could on the underground platform, using pieces of clothing, but the makeshift bandage was blood soaked.

'Ellie!'

A male voice was calling her. She looked round to see the familiar figure of her godfather striding through the crowd, coat flapping.

'Phillip! What—?'

Before she could finish her question, Ellie was wrapped in his arms and he hugged her close. She sighed in relief, her tension relaxing. Phillip would know what to do.

Then he let her go and Ellie swayed. She steadied herself and stood up straight.

'Are you alright? Your friend called me, told me she thought you were in danger. Told me to get myself over here as soon as was humanly possible. I came as quickly as I could.'

Ellie hurried to catch up with the stretcher once more and he kept pace with her, looking down at Faye, grim admiration on his face. 'What happened?'

'It's complicated. Did you find the body?'

'On the track? Yes, whose was it?'

'Les Allen, head of the porters at the SLH. A killer, a rapist, thief and more. He confessed to killing Jane Cooper and Polly Brooks...'

'Slow down. Faye told me about some of your suspicions, but I don't know it all.'

'He was stealing drugs with the connivance of the pharmacist from the hospital and selling them,' Ellie said. 'There was an underworld contact called George Packham and the drugs were packaged up and sold on. It was all being done in the deep shelters.'

'He, Allen, told you all of this?'

'When he was going to kill me. He thought it didn't matter that I knew.' She gulped in the cold night air. 'I was keeping him talking, hoping against hope that someone would come to my rescue. And they did.' She glanced down at Faye. 'She saved my life, Phillip.'

'It seems she knows what she's about.'

'She does,' Ellie said, trying not to give way to tears. 'For which I have reason to be grateful.'

They were at the ramp now and Phillip Morgan fell behind as they hurried up it to the front doors of the hospital.

The small group crossed the marble-floored entrance and started down the corridor to theatre. Nurses, porters and, it seemed, some patients, poked their heads around the doorways, everyone must have heard about the drama.

Ellie spotted John, Faye's brother, in his police uniform, pushing his way through to them. As he drew level, he fell into step on the other side of the stretcher.

'She was shot,' Ellie answered his questioning look. 'In the side. She's lost a lot of blood. We don't know how bad it is. We won't know until she gets to theatre.'

'Is she going to...?'

'Be alright? I hope so.'

'We'll take it from here, thank you.' The theatre staff nurse allowed the stretcher through, but blocked their entrance. 'You can wait if you want, there's a room back there, but I don't know how long it's going to take.'

'Will you let us know when you have an idea?' John asked. 'I'm her brother, I need to tell my – Faye's – parents.'

'I will,' the nurse said over her shoulder, as she followed the stretcher. The doors to the operating theatre closed behind her.

It made Ellie think about her own parents. They might hear about all of this; it would probably be in the newspapers.

'I'm going to find my godfather, the chief superintendent,' she explained to John. 'I shouldn't be long.'

'I think you ought to take a rest,' he said. 'You're bound to feel a reaction.'

'I will, I promise, but there's something I need to do first.'

Ignoring the curious glances, Ellie hurried back along the corridor to the main entrance hall. Chief Superintendent Phillip Morgan was there with his sergeant and Owen Philpott.

'We'll have plenty of sightseers by midday tomorrow,' he was saying. 'The press will be here too, I should think. Scotland Yard will make a general statement, no details.'

'The shelters are locked,' Philpott assured him. 'No one can go down.'

'Good, but we need to secure the access from the underground platform. Can you do that, sergeant? Get whoever is responsible out of bed. I want those doors padlocked before the Tube starts running tomorrow morning and no trains stopping at the station.'

'Yessir.' The sergeant hurried away.

'Phillip.'

'What?' His peremptory tone changed to one of concern. 'Oh, yes, Ellie, what is it?'

'How should we break the news to my parents?'

'You'll have to tell them, Ellie, they'll never forgive you if you don't. Besides, it'll be reported in the newspapers, they're bound to see it.'

'I know. But I'd like to know that Faye is alright before I telephone them. That comes first.'

'Ellie.' Morgan sighed. 'I promised you that I wouldn't tell them, but I can't hold off any longer. You're their daughter, they have a right to know. I'll be telephoning your father this evening. I hope, by then, you'll have spoken with them, so what I have to say won't be news to them. I can just fill them in on some of the details.'

'Fair enough.'

'What are you going to do now?' he asked.

'Wait.'

59

ELEANOR

Upright chairs lined the sides of the small waiting room. When Ellie returned, two more of them had been taken. Faye's father, whom Ellie had seen outside the Isolation Ward, sat with his arm around a fine-boned woman who bore such a strong resemblance to Faye that she had to be her mother. John introduced her to them as Faye's friend.

'Do you need to be seen to, love?' Esme looked with concern at the blood on Ellie's clothes.

'Oh no, it's not... Maybe you're right. I need to get cleaned up.'

'What happened?' Reg asked in a belligerent voice.

'Steady on, it's not Ellie's fault,' Esme said.

Except, Ellie thought, in a way it was.

'It began with the death of the nurse, Jane Cooper. You heard about that,' John began to explain. 'Faye and Ellie tried to find out what happened to her. They realised that her death was linked with the earlier disappearance of another young woman—'

'I heard her, you see,' Ellie interrupted. 'On the common, outside my window, in the night. She was calling for help and I didn't do anything.'

'So how did our Faye get involved then?' Reg Smith demanded.

'Everyone thought Jane had been killed on the common and her body dumped inside the shaft head of the deep shelter, but Faye realised that Jane had been trying to get *out* of the shelter when she was killed. She must have already been inside the deep level shelters before then,' Ellie said.

'Something nobody else thought of,' John said.

'Trust your sister to look at things differently.' Reg clamped his mouth closed.

'We realised that Jane was killed because she was trying to find out what had happened to her friend, Polly, who was mixed up with the man who was stealing drugs from the hospital. He was with a gang that was using the deep shelters as a base,' Ellie said. 'We went to the police, but they didn't believe me, didn't take what I said seriously.' She cast an anxious glance at John. 'A Sergeant Purley and an Inspector Irving.'

'I thought you said that chap's name was Morgan,' Reg remarked to his son. 'Chief Superintendent.'

'It was, Dad, but he's not in charge of the case.'

'So what's he doing here then?'

'He's my god-father,' Ellie said. 'My parents live in Worcester, where I'm from, so he's come to see that I'm alright. Also, he'll talk to Inspector Irving.'

Reg looked mollified, but he wasn't done yet. 'So how come our Faye got shot?'

'She worked out who had killed the nurse,' John said. 'Les Allen, the Head Porter here.'

'The fellow who ran the Venture Scouts stretcher bearers?' Esme asked. 'Got a gammy leg?'

'That's him,' John confirmed.

'I'd heard a man shouting in the night on the common with Jane,' Ellie said. 'And when I heard shouting last evening, I recognised the voice as the one I'd heard that night. The problem was, Allen realised that I'd identified him and he made me go down into the deep level shelters with him. He was going to kill me, but he wanted to know how much I, and Faye, knew.'

'Faye worked out what was happening to Ellie,' John said, a note of pride creeping into his voice. 'She telephoned Chief Superintendent Morgan and sent a nurse to the station house to get me.'

'Matron did the rest,' Ellie added. 'Getting Mr Philpott out of bed to open up the deep level shelters and mount a rescue mission.'

'And we rushed off into the shelters.' John's face grew serious. 'But Faye was already ahead of us. She knew there was another way in, via the platform level at Clapham South. She managed to persuade the guard there to let her go down into the station.'

'Lucky for me she did,' Ellie said. 'Otherwise I'd be dead.'

'Not lucky for her though,' said Reg.

'I know,' Ellie said. 'And I know what I owe your daughter, Mr Smith. I will forever be in her debt.'

The door to the waiting room opened and everyone turned in anticipation, but it was Beryl, carrying a bundle.

'Beryl,' Esme greeted the nurse with a tired smile, unable to hide her disappointment.

'Hello, Mrs S. Here, Ellie, I brought you some of your clothes.' She handed over the bundle. 'You should get out of those.'

Ellie looked down at her blouse and skirt, both encrusted brown with dried blood. They felt scratchy against her skin.

'Thanks, Beryl.' She stood, meaning to go and change in the washroom, when the door opened again.

Patrick Haverstock strode in, in full uniform.

'Ellie, my darling – what?' He looked at her clothes. 'Are you alright? What happened?'

'I'm perfectly fine, thank you, Patrick. How did you—?'

'I think you should be looked over by a doctor and at least get out of those clothes.' He made as if to take her in his arms.

'Pat, I'm fine!' She raised her hand to stop him.

'You're not yourself, you need to see a doctor and take a bath. I'll take a suite for you in a local hotel, you don't need to hang around here.'

'I'm staying. Get away from me.'

'I'm sorry.' Haverstock apologised to the room in general. 'She's not herself, I'll look after her.'

'Do you want looking after, Ellie?' John asked.

Haverstock looked down his nose at the police constable, his eyes hard and cold. 'This is my fiancée, Constable. I'll take things from here.'

'*Ex*-fiancée, Pat. Your fiancée no longer. And I don't want, or need, looking after.'

Haverstock flushed a shade of angry red. 'I'll be the judge of that.'

'No, you will not. That's the point!'

Ellie took a deep breath. Don't lose your cool, she told herself. Don't give him an excuse to intervene.

'I'm sorry, Mr and Mrs Smith, John, Beryl,' she apologised. 'Pat, this is completely inappropriate at a very difficult time. I'm going to change my clothes now; I don't expect you to be here when I return.'

Haverstock's lip curled when Beryl was named and he turned, towering over her, but the Scot didn't blink.

'So…' he began.

'D'you want any help, Ellie?' Beryl asked.

'No, thank you, Beryl. I can manage.'

'You're the… woman, she's been living with,' Haverstock said.

'Ellie rents my spare room,' Beryl answered. 'And you heard her, she wants nothing to do with you.'

'Beryl—' Ellie stepped in between the Scot and her former fiancé. Voices were rising.

'Listen here, you—' Haverstock raised his hand.

'What is going on here?' Matron swept into the room, taking in the situation. 'Nurse MacBride, are you on shift?'

'Yes, Matron. I called by to ask about Faye.'

'No news yet, best get back to your ward.'

Matron watched the nurse nod a goodbye to Esme Smith and leave. She turned to the officer. 'And you, sir, if you can't keep a civil tongue in your head and show some respect, then I suggest that you also leave.'

Haverstock put his shoulders back, drawing himself up to his full height and looked down at the diminutive figure in her navy uniform. 'I am Major Patrick Haverstock of the Royal Worcester-shire Regiment and I don't—'

'You, Major Patrick Haverstock, are in *my* hospital. If I ask you to leave you will do so, or you will be ejected, do you understand?' Matron spoke in an even voice, full of authority. 'And your colonel will be hearing about your misbehaviour.'

The major hesitated, then: 'Yes, ma'am.' He almost stood to attention, his face devoid of emotion.

'Good.' Matron was firm. She turned to Ellie and her demeanour changed. 'Go and get yourself cleaned up, Ellie. Use the nurses' common room facilities if you want.'

'Thank you, Matron.'

'Ellie, I'm not going anywhere,' Haverstock said and sat.

Exasperated, Ellie studied him for a moment. She shook her head. What was it going to take to make him understand?

Her godfather would be there later, she hoped. Maybe Phillip could have a word with Pat. Which reminded her about the drugs she thought she'd seen at the Black Cat Club. Did Pat know anything about them? Where had he, or his companions, got them from? Phillip would be interested.

And maybe that would be the way she could deflect Pat.

With that and clutching the bundle of clothes Beryl had brought, Ellie went off to wash and change.

60

ELEANOR

The hours ticked by slowly.

They heard the early morning sounds of the hospital; the kitchen clanging into life, the wheeling of the breakfast trolleys to the wards. As the day shift began, SLH staff looked in at the waiting room and each time Ellie gave a shake of her head. She had taken a chair opposite the door.

No news yet. No news is good news. Bound to be news soon.

To Ellie's relief, Pat Haverstock had left during the early hours. He'd said that he'd be back, but she hoped he'd think better of it.

'Was he really your fiancé, Ellie?' Esme had asked, and Ellie had assented. 'Are you sure you know what you're doing? Now might not be a good time to be making any major decisions.'

'I made that decision some time ago,' she'd answered and it struck her that, actually, she had, she just hadn't realised it. If she'd really cared for Pat there would have been no Hank and she couldn't have done what she did at the Black Cat Club. There would have been other, different decisions to be made, there might still be, but, either way, she wouldn't have gone home to Worcester. He, like her life there, was part of her past not her future. That was much clearer to her now.

Pat was the first born son of a wealthy family. He'd find someone else soon enough.

John had left for work, but returned half an hour later, saying he'd been told not to come in that day. A younger, taller version of Reg – another brother, Ellie surmised – had arrived with the dawn, wearing a bus driver's uniform and looking bleary-eyed.

'So, what's the prognosis?'

'We don't know, love. Have you been on the night bus again?'

'Yep. Time and a half,' he said, then glanced in her direction and said no more.

The money mattered, Ellie had realised. Phoebe's fees.

The door opened. This time admitting a white-coated doctor whom Ellie didn't know.

'Good morning, I'm Dr Webster. Are you the Smith family?'

'Yes,' Reg said as they all stood. 'How is she?'

'She's going to be alright,' said the surgeon. 'Though the operation was difficult and took more time than expected we've found and extracted the bullet. It didn't hit any internal organs.'

Esme subsided into her husband's arms weeping. John heaved a huge sigh of relief and sat again, putting his head into his hands.

His brother forced a smile.

Ellie felt light-headed. Things were going to be alright. She felt tears forming in the corners of her eyes.

Now was not the time to blub.

'When can we see her?' Esme asked eagerly.

'She's still in recovery and has been taken up to the ward,' the surgeon replied. 'But I should think she'll be ready for visitors this evening.'

'I'll go up and tell our Pheebs all about it,' John said. 'She ought to know what's happened. Her sister's in the same hospital as she is.'

'And there's the Lady Almoner…' Reg's voice tailed off.

'I can speak with her, if you want me to,' Ellie suggested, tentative. 'Not to arrange anything, that's your personal business,' she clarified as Reg looked about to interrupt. 'Just to explain that Faye's indisposed. Just in case she hasn't heard. Forgive me, but Faye told me that this month's fees were covered, so there won't be an imme-diate problem.'

'Oh yes, thank you, Ellie,' Esme said. 'That would be very kind.'

Reg narrowed his eyes but said nothing.

Ellie followed the Smith family as they made their way out of the hospital. The bus driver brother fell into step beside her.

'So you're Faye's new friend,' he said.

'Yes, your sister rescued me, showed me kindness when I needed it,' Ellie replied. 'Then she, quite literally, saved my life.'

'Sounds like our Faye.' He grinned. 'I'm Matthew, the annoyingly chirpy one.' He offered his hand.

'Ellie Peveril.' She shook it. 'I've met John already.'

'Ah, the dependable one. There's Vince, the already hen-pecked one and Ray, the invisible man.'

Ellie raised her eyebrows.

'He's always disappearing, never around when you want him.'

'Come on, Mattie,' Esme called. They had reached the front of the hospital.

'Mother calls.' With a rueful smile, Matthew lengthened his stride to catch up with his parents.

Parents.

She sighed, realising that she couldn't put it off any longer. She would ask to use the private phone in the office.

61

ELEANOR

'No, I'm living in a rented room in Clapham, south London,' Ellie repeated again. Her mother didn't seem capable of understanding. 'I stayed with Moira's parents until last Sunday.'

When she said it out loud, it seemed difficult to believe that her arrival in Clapham was only a week ago.

'But why? And when are you coming home?'

'Because I decided that I wanted to stay in London, be independent–'

'What about Patrick? What are you going to say to him?'

'I've already told him. Our engagement is over.'

'Well, I'm not surprised he's broken it off if you insist on launching out in this way. He's your fiancé!'

'Not anymore he isn't, and, for the record, I broke it off with him, not the other way around.'

'You...?'

Ellie heard her mother talking, her voice querulous, to someone else, then she heard her father's voice on the telephone.

'Ellie, what's going on? Your mother is very upset, she's talking about your running off and getting shot at. Are you still in Nuremberg? I thought you were in London.'

Ellie sighed. 'I am. It's a very long story, Dad. I've been trying to explain it all to mother.'

'Are you alright?'

'Yes, I've had quite a scare, but I'm alright now.'

'So you're coming home now?'

'No, that's it, Dad, I'm not,' Ellie said. 'My friend has been shot. She saved me from someone with a gun who wanted to kill me. She's the reason I'm still alive and she's in hospital. I can't leave now.'

'I see.'

'Oh, good.'

Ellie could hear her mother's voice in the background.

'Your mother's saying something about you ending your engagement to Patrick. Is that correct?'

'Yes, I've decided that I don't want to marry Patrick and I've told him so.'

'Why? You and he seemed so...? He won't be pleased, Ellie and he's every right not to be.'

Ellie gritted her teeth. Her mother had already tried her forbearance to its limits when it came to Patrick Haverstock.

'It's done, Dad. There's no going back.'

She heard his sigh.

'Well, you know what you want, I suppose.'

Suddenly she wanted to go home to Worcester. To explain everything to him.

'Phillip knows all about what's happened,' she said. 'He said he'll telephone you this evening. He's been very kind, Dad.'

'Good, I'm glad you've got someone with you.'

'And I've got a lot of new friends too,' she said. 'You'll have to meet them.'

She smiled at the thought of her father meeting Beryl and wondered how those two good people would find a way of accommodating each other.

'I'm going to have to go now, Dad. I'm using the hospital phone.'

'But you're not in hospital because you're hurt? It's your friend, the one who saved your life, who's in hospital?'

'That's right. Though I'm working here. Look, I'll explain later.'

'Alright, lovely. When will you telephone again?'

'Tonight, if I can beg the use of the telephone.'

'Try to avoid the early evening.'

He would be celebrating evensong. Her mind flew back to the huge cathedral, its nave of great columns, reaching upwards to form arches and yet more arches, then to separate out into the vaulting ribs of the roof so high above. The soaring voices of the choir caught in the net of stone and echoing back down to the congregation below.

'I'll try and telephone later, or, if not, then tomorrow.'

'Goodbye and take care, Ellie. We love you.'

'I know, Dad, I love you and Mum too.'

Ellie placed the telephone back on its cradle and wiped her fingertips across the damp corners of her eyes.

It was done. She felt relieved but also disappointed. Her new life had lost the sheen of clandestine adventure, it was back to reality now. There was a griping pain in her stomach.

She picked up the phone again and dialled Phillip's home number. She had to tell him what she'd done. The voice that answered was thick with sleep.

'Ellie, why aren't you asleep? Have you been up all night?'

'Yes. I've been waiting for news of Faye.'

'And?'

'She's going to be alright.'

'Good.' She heard an exhalation of breath. 'That was news worth waking up for.'

'And I've spoken with my parents. Father understands but Mother is still very confused. I've told them that you know all about it. But there's one other thing...'

'Ye-es.'

'You should also know that I've ended my engagement to Pat Haverstock.'

'Have you? But I thought I saw him outside the hospital.'

'You did. He turned up here, despite everything. He seems to doubt my decision. But I am quite decided.'

'Why, may I ask? Have you found someone else?'

'No. When I considered it, I realised that he wasn't the one for me. I think I've known for a while, actually, but didn't face up to it. Then I saw him in the Black Cat Club with another girl and–'

'The Black Cat Club?'

'It's in Soho.'

'I know where it is! What were *you* doing there?'

'It was Moira's last night before returning to her studies, so we went out. It was all innocent, Phillip, really. But Pat was there, he looked like he was there regularly, with his friends and this girl. I confronted him and ended our engagement there and then.'

There was a pause. 'Oh. I see.'

'I haven't told mother and father about that part, saving Pat's blushes, but I have told them that the engagement's over.'

'Right.'

'And there's one other thing.'

'Surprise me.'

'When I was underground, I was searching for matches in some storage cupboards and I found a stock of white powder in small sachets. I've still got it if you want it.'

'Ellie—'

'Thing is, I saw some of those sachets on the table Pat was sitting at in the Black Cat Club.'

There was silence from the phone for a few seconds, then Phillip spoke. 'That's very useful to know.'

'I thought you might say that.' She smiled to herself. 'And I mentioned George Packham, didn't I, Les Allen's accomplice, that should give you the two ends of the chain.'

'Ellie, has anyone suggested that you make a statement?'

'Only John, John Smith, Faye's brother, but he's probably asleep now.'

'Right, I'll come. Where is your rented room? Would your land-lady mind me arriving with my notebook?'

'It's Flat 40, Westbury Court, above the tube station and my landlady is Beryl MacBride. She's from Glasgow and I'd guess that she isn't a whole souled admirer of the police, but she's absolutely to be relied upon.'

'Is that the woman who was with Faye at the underground station and went and got the policeman brother?'

'That's her.'

'Right, go back to Flat 40. I'll be there in about an hour.'

62

ELEANOR

Ellie put down the phone. The pain in her abdomen was getting worse. It cut through her, sharp and piercing, as she rose from behind the office desk. She began to walk to the door, but stopped, doubled up in agony. Her lips stretched into a rictus of pain, tears squeezing from the corners of her eyes. There was a dampness between her thighs.

Was this her monthly? It wasn't usually so painful. Or...?

She had to get to the lavatories, otherwise she was going to be covered in blood again.

Ellie gritted her teeth, took a deep breath, straightened up and walked out of the office. The nearest lavatory was on the other side of the main entrance hall. Tension in every limb, she hurried across the marble floor.

At least the skirt Beryl had brought for her was a dark colour.

Inside the empty Ladies, she fell back against the inside of the door, then summoned up her energy and stumbled to a cubicle. It took but a moment to ascertain that she was bleeding very heavily. After six weeks, she realised, she was almost certainly miscarrying.

Ellie sat, knickers around her ankles, hands over her face, weeping silently. She hadn't wanted to be pregnant. She'd been terrified that she was and hoped, with increasing desperation, that she was merely 'late'. Again. The last few weeks had been marred by a constant low level of anxiety.

Now she wasn't anymore. So why was she so distressed? Why wasn't she relieved?

She wasn't in a position to look after a child and she certainly wasn't about to marry a man she didn't love because of it. There might have been something wrong with it anyway. Wasn't that what people said – that a miscarriage was nature's way of aborting an imperfection? Then she thought about the way the Nazis had treated those unfortunates who had not been born outwardly perfect and felt ashamed.

The babies who had been taken to the camps; the children who had been herded into the gas chambers.

She shook herself, she had to get home, to get to the flat. Phillip would be there in less than an hour and she had to get cleaned up again, take some medicine for the pain, sort herself out. Beryl would be able to help, she'd know what to do. Ellie pulled leaves of the hard, shiny lavatory paper from the dispenser to line her knickers and packed more into a pad, with some tissues from her sleeve.

The Ladies door opened, and she heard voices, two nurses chatting about the events of the previous night. Cubicle doors clunked closed.

'They say Les Allen was in love with Ellie from the canteen,' said one voice.

'I've heard that he was a villain, a real wrong 'un,' said the other. 'Tried to take her down the shelters to have his way and then kill her, like he did with Jane.'

'Really? Bloody hell! What happened?'

'Faye Smith went to rescue her, but Les shot Faye.'

'Is she going to be alright?'

'Death's door, apparently.'

'And what about Polly, then? Did she know how he was? Did he kill her as well?'

'Probably.'

'And the porters, what do they think now? They were with him every day; didn't they notice anything dodgy?'

'Dunno. Shouldn't think so, they were always going on about how great he was. They'll change their tune now.'

There was a small silence and then the sound of lavatories flushing.

'Have you seen that new picture at the Odeon yet?'

Ellie heard the nurses washing their hands and waited until they left before venturing out of her cubicle. She decided to make a dash for Westbury Court. Her greatcoat was, as far as she knew, still in the deep shelter and with it her key to the flat, but caretaker Ron would let her in. She hoped he wouldn't ask too many questions.

The entrance hall wasn't crowded and Ellie was able to slip out unnoticed and hurry down the ramp. She wrapped her arms around her chest, pushing her hands into her armpits as she hovered at the crossing, waiting for the traffic lights to change. It was freezing cold.

'Ellie, Eleanor!'

She turned to see Antoine Girard, hurrying towards her from the hospital, white coat flapping.

'You are alright, you are unhurt?' His face was full of concern. 'I heard this morning what happened. You were kidnapped?'

'Sort of, it's a long story.' Her teeth were chattering.

'And you will tell it to me, I hope.' He removed his doctor's coat and placed it around her shoulders. 'It's not much but... You are very pale. Are you going to Westbury Court?'

She nodded, not trusting herself to speak.

'Come.' He put his arm around her shoulders. 'You look as if you are about to fall over.'

'I've had a long night,' she whispered, leaning into him, grateful for the support. She pulled his coat more tightly around herself, then began to worry about bleeding on it.

Antoine delivered Ellie to a pasty-faced Ron, who accompanied her to the fourth floor and let her in to number 40. Beryl was still up and padding about in her slippers, pyjamas and an overcoat, looking wan and tired.

'I was wondering if you were coming home today,' the Scot said. 'Or if they were keeping you in.'

'No, nothing wrong with me,' Ellie replied, jaw tight. 'I was allowed to go...' She flopped down into the old armchair.

'You need to get some sleep by the look of you.' Beryl gave her a searching glance. 'Are you sure you're alright?'

'Yes, I... no, I mean...'

Tears sprang to her eyes and her shoulders began to shake. She tried to gulp back the sobs, but the floodgates opened and she wept, loudly and full of anguish and grief, doubling over and holding her head in her hands.

'Hey, hey, what's the matter?'

Ellie looked up to see Beryl kneeling in front of her, gently taking her hands.

'It can't be that bad.'

'It's bad enough! Being kidnapped at gunpoint, sure that I was going to die, then finding out for certain that I was pregnant by having a miscarriage.'

'Right.' Beryl closed her open mouth with a snap. 'I see.' The Scot got to her feet, a determined look on her face. 'Well, you'll need some pads and towels and something for the pain. Come on, let's get you cleaned up.'

Ellie raised her tear-stained face but didn't move. Suddenly her body seemed so heavy. 'My godfather's on his way, to take my statement,' she said. 'Chief Superintendent Morgan. He'll be here in about twenty minutes.'

'Well, he can make the tea. Come on, get up. You need a hot bath. Now.'

Beryl helped her to her feet.

'He mustn't know, Beryl,' she said. 'No one must know.'

'Yeah, yeah. What d'you think I am? Stupid? I didn't come up the Clyde on a scooter. Come on.'

MONDAY

63

FAYE

I t was cosy and comfortable and that's how Faye wanted to stay. She tried to ignore the voice, to snuggle back down into the warm darkness, but it wouldn't go away.

She opened her eyes. And immediately closed them again. It was much too bright.

She could see light through the pink of her eyelids. There were sounds. The squeaky wheel of a trolley, a hum of voices. Then the same voice again.

'Faye. Faye, you're coming round now. Don't be surprised if things seem a little shaky, a little woozy. That's normal.'

She blinked.

A nurse was bending over her, lifting her head up while she plumped the pillow.

'I... where am I?'

'Pankhurst Ward,' the nurse answered.

'How long have I been–?'

'Out? For about thirty-six hours after you came in.' The nurse stood and surveyed her handiwork. 'Mind you, you were in theatre for three of those.'

In theatre? Faye frowned.

Then she remembered. The stairs down to the deep-level shelters, the overheard conversation between Ellie and Les Allen. The tearing, searing pain.

'I was shot.'

'You certainly were. They couldn't find the bullet at first, rootling around in your insides they were, but they found it in the end. I think Matron's got it, to give to you.'

'The bullet—'

'The one you were shot with. My, you're all over the place, I'd better get my double ration order in now before you're back to your usual self. Ah, here are some visitors! I thought they'd be here as soon as you began to come round.'

Ellie and Beryl stood side by side at the foot of her bed. A contrasting pair, the tall and lovely English beauty, though looking somewhat pale, and the small and doughty Scot, who always looked ready for anything. Faye sighed in contentment. She was lucky to have such friends.

'We haven't brought anything for you,' Ellie said, looking apologetic. 'But it's rumoured that cook's been using large amounts of the hospital's ration of cocoa powder and butter and that truffles will miraculously appear soon.'

'I'm staying until they do,' Beryl added.

'Your mother and father will be here too, as soon as they hear you're awake. And your brothers,' Ellie said. 'So be prepared.'

'Aye and there's a certain Dr Nick Yorke who's been asking about you. Asking if a visit would be welcome,' said Beryl. 'I told him 'No'.'

Faye opened her mouth to remonstrate.

The Scot grinned. 'The look on your face! I told him that when you were awake and ready to receive visitors, he would be welcome.'

Faye subsided back into the pillows. There was a dull ache in her side and she closed her eyes against the pain for a moment.

When she opened them, Beryl had gone and Ellie was sitting by her bedside.

'You went away from us then. Beryl's gone to fetch Sister. To get you some more medicine for the pain.'

'Not cocaine, I hope.'

'No, something much less addictive,' Ellie answered. 'Faye, while I've got you to myself, I must thank you. Thank you for saving my life.' She held Faye's right hand, patting and stroking it. 'I would be dead now if it wasn't for you. Coming to my rescue like that…'

Faye watched her friend, as if from a distance, disassociated from reality. She looked pale, washed out and she'd been weeping… but she was speaking. Faye tuned in.

'…you were very brave.'

'But I'd be dead, if it wasn't for you,' Faye replied. 'Dragging me up those stairs, not letting me stop, making me carry on. If you'd left me, Les Allen would have finished me off. I'm certain.'

She recalled their flight and the overheard conversation deep beneath the ground. Had Ellie really said that she was pregnant?

'Well, maybe,' Ellie said. 'But you were only there to try and help me in the first place. The rescue mission was yours. You solved the case! Everyone's so proud of you.'

'Haven't had so much fun in ages,' Faye replied with a grin, then winced at the pain in her side.

'Your brother John thinks you're wonderful.'

'He always has,' Faye said, a smile creeping over her lips. 'It's because I'm like him, I like solving puzzles and mysteries, finding out things, like he does.'

Too clever by half. The phrase reverberated round her brain, but it wasn't a negative any more.

'My godfather will want to speak with you, to take your formal statement. He's already taken one from me,' Ellie said. 'I must say, he was mightily impressed with you as well.'

'Happy to see him. He listened, Ellie.'

'I'm very glad that he did. Look, here's Sister. I think she's going to throw me out. I'll come and see you later.'

'I'd like that. And Ellie, can you tell my parents that I'm alright?'

'They already know, Faye. They'll be here this evening, if not before.'

'Thanks.'

Beryl in her wake, Sister bustled up, holding a syringe and a swab.

'Out you go,' she said to Ellie. 'I'll take it from here.'

64

FAYE

The lights on the ward were dim. Patients were expected to rise and retire early, although reading lights were available for those who wanted them. Faye didn't. She didn't have the energy to concentrate on reading. Besides, she wanted to think.

She'd had visitors that evening, including her parents, which had tired her. It had cheered her too. She glanced at the bed-side table and the vase of yellow roses standing on it. Nick Yorke had brought them.

He had sat at her bedside and they had talked. About books, about the SLH and teaching, about Clapham, the deep level shelters and the common, about the changes it had seen over the last decade. About how things would change now, for the better. He'd been wanting to get to know her for some time, he said. Ever since he'd returned from the war. He'd been amusing and witty and caring. Faye's laughter had dragged at her stitches and she'd winced, closing her eyes in pain. He was solicitous and kind.

Even the arrival of her parents had failed to deter him. He stood and introduced himself as 'Dr Nicholas Yorke, a friend of Faye's'. If she hadn't already discovered how painful laughter was, she would have laughed out loud at the expression on her father's face, a mixture of suspicion, relief and protectiveness.

'Are you from Clapham?' Esme asked him.

'Not originally, but I've worked here since before the war. I'm a teacher at Morley College and Henry Thornton School. That's where I met Faye, at the Workers' Educational Association.'

Esme's mouth made an 'o' shape, though no sound emerged.

'And the war?' Reg asked, sticking out his chin.

'Navy, HMS Ajax.'

Reg nodded, deflating slightly.

'You never said,' Faye said. 'Though there's no reason why you should, I suppose.'

'That was yesterday, I'm more interested in today and tomorrow.'

'Good, so am I.'

'I'll be off now,' Yorke said. 'Let you talk with your parents. I'll be back – tomorrow?'

'See you then.'

He stood. 'Goodbye,' he said to her parents. 'Pleased to meet you.'

'Likewise, I'm sure,' Esme said.

Raising his hand to Faye, Nick was gone.

Reg harrumphed and his wife shot him a look.

'Well,' Esme said, taking her daughter's hand. 'So, when do they think you'll be up and about, love?'

'I don't know, Mum. I think it depends how quickly I heal.'

Esme nodded, none the wiser. She chattered on, telling Faye about the doings of their friends and neighbours, but sometimes coming to a halt and simply looking at her daughter. Reg said little.

'How much will all this cost?' he asked, eventually.

Luckily John arrived at that moment.

'Just what the patient needs!' he said, sarcastically. 'How are you feeling, sis?' He leaned over to kiss her cheek.

'Bearing up, as they say. And very glad to see you.'

'Happy sunbeam, me. Vince and Mattie are coming when they finish work. Ray said he'd be over too.'

'Blimey. Will Sister let you all in?'

'Oh yes. Heroine of the hour, you are. Nothing's too good for you. In this hospital and in my nick.'

'Don't encourage her, you.' Reg scowled at his son.

'God forbid you give your daughter some encouragement and praise.' John bristled, his anger very near the surface. 'For saving someone's life and plenty of other lives too given what that gang was up to. You should speak with Chief Superintendent Morgan about how the gangs organise and prey on people. Faye's done an amazing thing.'

'Stop it, both of you!' Esme kept her voice low, but it was sharp. 'Think where you are!'

'Sorry, Ma.' John looked chastened. Reg stared out of the window to the left of Faye's bed.

'Your sister's started on the drug trial.' Esme changed the subject. 'Dr Falconer told me about it when I went up to see Phoebe earlier.'

'Good. At least that's happening.'

'Because of you, sis,' John said.

'Stop it, you'll make my head swell.'

'Why not. You deserve all the praise you can get, in my book.' John shot a defiant look at his father.

'Did *you* know about this Dr Nicholas Yorke fellow?' Reg asked his son.

'No.' John looked at Faye, a quizzical expression on his face. 'Who's he?'

'Just a friend,' she answered.

'Who brings you flowers,' John said. 'I assume they're from him?'

'Roses in November,' Esme said. 'Must've cost a packet.'

To Faye's relief the arrival of Vince and Agnes curtailed any further discussion of Nick Yorke. The remainder of the visit, augmented by her other brothers, flew past.

'You're looking tired now, love,' her mother said. 'Had enough?'

'I am tired, Ma. It'll be a while 'til I'm back to normal.'

'We'll be going,' Matthew said. 'Chin up, sis. Everybody's saying how brave you were.'

'Well, she was,' growled Reg as he stood.

Esme bent over Faye to kiss her goodbye. 'He's very proud of you, really,' she whispered. 'And Nicholas Yorke looks nice.'

Faye had smiled.

Now she gazed at the yellow roses, which seemed to glow in the dim light. Where had he got them from? And when would he come tomorrow? Wasn't the Ajax involved in some famous battle or other? Her mind began to drift.

TUESDAY

65

FAYE

F aye stretched out her hand to hold open the lift door and Beryl steered the wheelchair through it. They were going down to the Nurses' Common Room, where Ellie, Matron, Miss Barnett, Chief Superintendent Morgan and the others waited. Faye said little and her friend, sensing her mood, did likewise.

Faye breathed in, deeply. She was determined to stay awake and sharp-brained enough to contribute to the discussion but was also bracing herself for another encounter with Miss Barnett. The hospital administrator had visited her in Pankhurst Ward that morning, sitting at Faye's bedside for over half an hour. The visit had not, Faye was certain, gone as Miss Barnett had intended it should.

'I must apologise to you, Faye,' Miss Barnett had begun in a formal tone. 'You saw something wrong was going on and tried, quite properly, to investigate it further. I was wrong to tell you to stop.' She paused.

Faye waited. She appreciated the apology, but she wasn't going to pre-empt any part of it. She remembered all too clearly how she had felt to blame and how much she had reproached herself, rather than considering that Miss Barnett might be at fault. She wanted to be gracious and understanding but wasn't about to assume responsibility for misplaced blame again.

'I responded... and acted... hastily,' Miss Barnett went on. 'I was wrong. It seems you understand rather better than I do what goes on in this hospital.' Her voice had grown sharp. Contrition didn't come easily to Miss Barnett.

Still Faye said nothing.

'I was disappointed that you hadn't bothered... hadn't responded to my offer. I thought that you would be surprised and pleased, would want to accept as soon as you knew.'

'I was,' Faye said. 'I was grateful for the opportunity, but I needed to consider how it would fit into my plans... and speak with my parents too, it affected their lives as well as my own.'

Even if it that was, ultimately, pointless, Faye thought.

'So you said, but you still didn't apply. Even though I reminded you. I stuck my neck out to create that post for you and this was how you repaid me. That's a strange way of being grateful!'

Miss Barnett pressed her lips together as if to hold her tongue.

'I would have still offered you the job you know,' she exclaimed. 'I only wanted to make a point. You should have responded more promptly.'

'You offered the office manager job to Ellie,' Faye pointed out.

'As you said yourself, she wouldn't have stayed long, she has other fish to fry.'

'I think you'll find that Ellie is staying now.'

'But I'm sure she'll make way when you're fit enough to return,' Miss Barnett replied.

'Why? Have you spoken with her about this?'

'She raised the subject with me, not I with her,' Miss Barnett said, glancing at her hands. 'She explained her position.'

Faye wished she knew what Ellie's position was. Standing aside was noble, but that might not be the best course for Ellie, or, given some of her more recent thoughts, for Faye.

'I see,' Faye said. 'But I need to consider mine.'

'I understand,' Miss Barnett said, but it was clear from her puzzled expression that she didn't.

'Thank you for the apology, which I accept, unreservedly. Someone acknowledging when they've been wrong is never easy and you have been very generous in doing so. But I need to consider my future.' Faye began to try and explain something she was only beginning to understand herself. 'Things have happened here and I must reassess, determine what I should do.'

'But you submitted an application,' Miss Barnett said. 'And the money must be useful, now that your sister's here. You're a heroine at the SLH, I don't understand this reluctance. Unless it's your way of getting back at me?'

'It isn't, Miss Barnett, I can assure you of that, really. I need to think.'

It was true. Miss Barnett had encouraged and helped her; she had given Faye opportunities and Faye *was* grateful, but she couldn't be condescended to forever, she wasn't a child and certainly not a surrogate one. In Miss Barnett's eyes she would always be her protégé, 'a local woman... who might not have had the sort of education available to others'.

Faye knew that she was more than that and she wasn't about to underestimate her own value again. Maybe she'd have to leave the SLH to do that, especially given it was she who'd exposed its lack of security. It was never comfortable being the one who brought others' shortcomings to light.

'Well, concentrate on getting better for now,' the hospital administrator went on, still puzzled. 'The hospital will cover your medical bills and sick pay. I'll assume that you meant your application until you tell me otherwise.'

'Thank you, Miss Barnett,' Faye said. 'That's very gracious of you.'

'It is, isn't it.' And, with that, Miss Barnett had left.

The lift stopped at the first floor and Beryl pushed the wheelchair to the Common Room. Nurses, doctors and others, stopped to congratulate Faye and ask after her health. The story of Saturday night had spread around the hospital faster than any contagion.

The SLH was an amazing place, Faye reflected, a special place. It felt like another home and she was very, very fond of it.

'Anyone would think you'd done something extraordinary,' Beryl said.

'Ye-es. Though what surprises me is how many people were suspicious of Les Allen all along. Pity they didn't tell anyone.'

The Scotswoman laughed as she backed her way through the door to the Common Room.

66

FAYE

'Seventeen people have been arrested,' Chief Superintendent Morgan said. 'George Packham talked, I knew he would; he likes his creature comforts. Not that there are too many of those in Pentonville.'

Now it was known that organised crime was involved, the chief superintendent had taken over the case. He sat, with the others, before a blazing fire. Beryl had placed the wheelchair close to the fire and Faye let the wonderful heat flow through her limbs. There was tea and cake from the canteen.

'The tunnel in the deep shelters has been a drugs factory for some time,' he continued. 'The gang mixed, weighed and bagged the drugs into sachets there. Each sachet contained a small amount, like the ones you found in the store cupboard, Ellie. We found scales, empty packets and utensils.'

'I check those tunnels,' Owen Philpott said, trenchantly. 'Not just the shaft heads, but all the main tunnels, every fortnight. How could I have missed that?'

'The deep shelters were a valuable base to the gang; they wanted to hold on to it. They'd have learned your routine and ensured your suspicions weren't aroused,' Morgan reassured him. 'The stores in that canteen looked like canteen stores, they made sure of that.

Even if you had reason to visit it, that side tunnel would look how it was supposed to.'

'I believe using the deep shelters was Les Allen's idea,' Faye said. 'He took patients there in forty-four and would have known the way the tunnels were laid out. After the war the shelters were unused and largely forgotten. Time moved on. It was the perfect place for illegal activity.'

'And Allen knew that the SLH had a key to the south entrance and where it was kept,' Miss Barnett said.

'Polly Brooks caught him trying to take it,' Ellie said. 'He told me. That's why he wooed her in the first place.'

'I should have taken more care of it.' The hospital administrator looked down at her hands and Faye felt a twinge of sympathy. Miss Barnett would feel mortified.

'He made a copy of the key to the drawer where it, and all the other hospital keys, were kept,' Ellie added. 'He told me he could get the deep shelter key any time he wanted it.'

'I think that was a boast,' Faye said.

'He couldn't have got it when I was in my office.' Miss Barnett's head snapped up. 'Or when Jean was there.'

'He couldn't,' Faye said. 'Though he'd have devised some diversionary pretext if he needed it urgently. That key was his passport into gangland and the illegal drug trade; the gang needed him so as to get into the tunnels. The SLH had forgotten it, so he could take it for long periods of time. I suspect he returned it only when he thought you, Owen, might ask for it, before you did your fortnightly check, for example.'

'I should have insisted it be returned,' Philpott said.

'Les was clever. Beneath that jolly, self-effacing exterior I think there was a warped personality,' Faye said. 'I suspect that the deep shelter key wasn't the only key in that drawer that he used. I think he enjoyed having the run of the SLH, a man among women. He took pleasure in the power that gave him.' Faye remembered their confrontations and his pressuring her in the office. 'People assumed he knew all the gossip because of his porters, but I think Les did some eavesdropping on his own account.'

'He said everyone had secrets and that he knew them all,' Ellie said. 'Maybe that explains some of his popularity.'

'You mean he was blackmailing people?' Beryl said. 'But he really was popular. Before the war, then during the Blitz when he organised the stretcher bearers. He seemed so courageous and such a good egg.'

'Maybe he was, or started out that way at any rate,' Faye said. 'He was an efficient organiser, a good team leader according to the porters. Perhaps the war changed him. It must have been humiliating to have to stay at home when all his peers were going to war, even a ne'er do well like George Packham. I suspect that he started stealing then, selling items on the black market.'

'He wouldn't be the only one who started out that way,' Miss Barnett said. 'And that could explain any number of things going missing.'

'The war has a lot to answer for,' Matron added.

'He was a practised liar who constructed a front behind which to hide his real self,' the chief superintendent said. 'Someone who appears to be like everyone else but has a psychopathic personality. He doesn't deserve any sympathy.'

'Most folk were taken in by him,' Beryl said. 'I was.'

'Faye wasn't fooled, were you?' Ellie said. 'You said all along that there was something odd about him and his "gossip".'

'Yes. He knew I was suspicious. He hated me for it.'

'I should have taken more care,' Miss Barnett said, again. 'All the locks will have to be changed.'

'At least the SLH key to the shelter has been kept out of the newspaper reports,' Matron said. 'Thanks to the good offices of Chief Superintendent Morgan.'

The policeman gave a pinched, uncomfortable smile.

'Chief Superintendent,' Faye began. She wanted to ask so many questions. 'Allen made Miss Lowell supply him with small quantities of cocaine, but Ellie saw equipment for processing much larger amounts in the deep shelters. Have you found the other sources of supply?'

'Not yet, though I have my suspicions,' the chief superintendent said, his face stern. 'I hope to get more information from those we've arrested. The SLH drugs were only the tip of the iceberg; most of the drug trade in south London was being run from those shelters. It was a stroke of luck that Ellie remembered seeing one of the drug packets at the Black Cat Club. It meant we could track distribution from the customer end of the process. Patrick Haverstock was most helpful.'

'Did you charge him?' Ellie asked.

'No. He claimed he hadn't purchased or taken cocaine and we couldn't prove otherwise. A good lawyer would've had the charge thrown out. But Major Haverstock will find that his regiment no longer has a place for him.'

'Good,' said Beryl with vehemence.

'By the way,' John chipped in. 'After Faye told me about the AWOL report made against the French doctor, I checked the station records. The report came from someone in the Royal Worcesters.'

'Patrick did that?' Ellie exclaimed.

'The report didn't say, but, if that was his regiment, I'd say he had something to do with it.'

'He hired a private investigator to follow me,' Ellie said. 'Presumably the man saw Antoine and reported back.'

'You're well rid of him,' John said.

'I agree,' Chief Superintendent Morgan said. 'And don't worry, Ellie, I've already spoken with your father about it. Something to tax even his belief in human charity.'

Ellie looked relieved.

'My unit will be taking on this case,' he continued. 'For now, we've managed to destroy their factory and their distribution network and scooped up a lot of the small fry in our net. I'm hopeful it will lead us to some of the sharks.'

'And the late Miss Lowell's involvement?' asked Matron.

'I think you should explain...,' the chief superintendent said, glancing at Faye.

'Polly came across Miss Lowell taking cocaine,' Faye began. 'She assumed that the pharmacist had filched it from hospital supplies, but Polly knew about the Register of Controlled Substances so she also knew that somehow the pharmacist must have accounted for it. Polly cross-checked patient records with Register entries and found that Miss Lowell had written prescriptions for imaginary patients. Once they knew this, it was easy for Les and Polly to blackmail her and, when she was in their clutches, they wouldn't let her go.'

'So that's what Brooks was doing when I caught her looking at the patient records!' Miss Barnett exclaimed.

'Yes, I believe so,' said Faye.

'When I was underground, Les Allen told me it was Polly who wanted to blackmail Miss Lowell,' Ellie said. 'For cash.'

'But her boyfriend saw a better way of using the pharmacist, getting her to order larger quantities of cocaine,' Faye continued. 'Then handing them over to him. Polly didn't know about that. Les told her he was blackmailing Miss Lowell for money as they had agreed and gave Polly cash.'

'Which explains why Polly was suddenly flush with money,' Beryl said.

'I followed Polly's trail and checked patient records relating to some of the entries in the Register and found that some of those patients didn't exist, that's how the cocaine was being stolen.'

'We must tighten up our procedures,' Matron said. 'Felicity.'

Miss Barnett acknowledged her remark with a tight little smile.

'We didn't discover what was going on because our systems don't cross check,' Faye continued. 'Miss Underwood, our new pharmacist, will make them more secure. This shouldn't happen again.'

'I understand that Polly Brooks' corpse was found in a chest in the shelter,' Owen Philpott said.

'I found her,' Ellie said, her face growing pale.

'Les Allen killed her and confessed to killing Jane, too,' Faye took up the tale. 'Jane believed something had happened to Polly; she hadn't just left. She confronted Allen with her suspicions and was about to go to the police.'

'That's when I heard her cry out,' Ellie said.

'Les Allen had to stop Jane reporting her fears about Polly,' Faye continued. 'Someone might have checked at Polly's home address and started asking questions at the SLH. It would have made things uncomfortable for him and his cronies, even if the police didn't believe her–'

'Like they didn't really believe me,' Ellie interrupted, indignant. She glared at her godfather.

'We haven't covered ourselves in glory with this,' he acknowledged. 'All I can do is apologise.'

'Why did Allen leave Jane's body near the door of the Clapham Common entrance?' Owen Philpott asked. 'He must have known I'd do my rounds.'

The Chief Superintendent looked at Faye.

'Allen took Jane to the deep shelters knowing that he was going to kill her, but he liked the idea of keeping her captive, making her do what he wanted. Somehow, perhaps when he came to the SLH to clock in the porters on Monday morning, she managed to find her way to the Clapham Common shaft head. When he returned, he searched the tunnels until he caught her and killed her, near the entrance. This would have been *after* you normally did your rounds, Owen,' Faye said. 'Allen couldn't get out of the Clapham Common entrance to dump Jane's body, he didn't have a key, so he left her there, assuming he'd have time to move the body later that day. Had you been checking the entrance at the normal time, Jane's body would never have been found. But, very unusually, you were late that morning, so you came upon it.'

'So Jane was still alive on Monday morning?' Beryl asked.

'Yes, I think so.' Faye frowned. 'She would have been able to hear the morning traffic on the South Side, might even have tried to call out, to attract attention. But she had no way of getting out.'

She remembered Jane's broken fingernails and bloody fingertips.

Had she been clawing at the door, hearing freedom so close by, as Les Allen came to kill her?

'It's fortunate for justice and everyone's peace of mind that Faye and Ellie were able to discover what was going on underneath our very noses,' Matron said.

'Faye was the one who worked it all out,' Ellie said. 'Just as well for me.'

Miss Barnett nodded in agreement with all the others, but her lips were tightly compressed.

'Time to consider a change of career, sis?' John chipped in.

'The Metropolitan Police are recruiting, we have a women's branch,' the chief superintendent said. 'It has a new chief superintendent, a former WAAF group captain, a flyer. She's very forward-looking.'

'Yes, John's told me about women police,' Faye said. 'Somehow, I don't think pounding the pavements is for me though.'

'We have women detectives now,' the chief superintendent said. 'A good thing, in my opinion. Women have a different perspective and we need all the help we can get. You're a natural and you're already used to wielding authority. I'm serious, you ought to consider it, I'd welcome you on to my team. You have a real aptitude for investigation. Here's my card. Starting pay is four pounds and nine shillings a week, plus benefits, though that increases rapidly once you've trained.'

'Male recruits get over five pounds,' Ellie said, sharply. 'I saw it on a recruitment poster.'

'They'd be doing a different job, Ellie,' the chief superintendent said. 'Well, if that's all your questions, I'd better be on my way.'

Faye put the card in her dressing-gown pocket.

'I'll show you out, Chief Superintendent,' Matron got to her feet. 'And you,' she pointed to Faye, 'should go back to your ward. This is all very exciting, but it'll tire you out and you need to husband your strength. Take her back, Ellie.'

67

ELEANOR

'Thank you,' Faye said as Ellie tucked in her bedclothes. 'Don't go. I've hardly had a chance to speak with you alone.'

Ellie hesitated. Her friend looked exhausted.

'Alright, if you're sure you aren't too tired.'

'What will you do now?' Faye asked.

'Go back to Worcester, I suppose...'

'I thought you wanted to stay in London, or has everything that's happened put you off?'

'It's not that. I've told my parents that I'm staying here, but I feel like I want a bit of cosseting...'

After the miscarriage she needed to rest. It would be pleasant to do so among familiar things and places.

'What about the baby?' Faye asked.

'The baby... Did Beryl..? No, she would never tell. How do you know, Faye?'

'I wasn't sure.' Faye looked amused. 'But I wondered, the first time I saw you in the canteen. Of course, I also overheard what you said to Les down in the shelters.'

'The first time...' Ellie marvelled at how Faye could have known before she knew herself. But maybe she had known, she just hadn't wanted to face up to the fact. 'I've lost the baby.'

Saying the words out loud was difficult, even though she had hoped beyond hope that she wasn't with child. Beryl had explained that she would be depressed and sensitive for a while, it was her hormones readjusting.

Faye reached out to hold Ellie's hand. 'I'm sorry,' she said. 'Even if you didn't want it, it's an emotional time. And you haven't 'lost' the baby', it isn't your fault.'

'You mean aside from getting kidnapped, threatened with a gun, almost killed.'

'You didn't exactly ask for that to happen.'

'I know, but I went into that yard, didn't I. When Phillip arrived at the flat, I was miscarrying.'

'I'm sure he's seen plenty of blood before.'

'He didn't see any then. Beryl and I made sure of that.'

'How did you get him to keep quiet about the SLH key?'

'That took a lot of persuasion, mainly to do with the way the police had ignored my warning and my involvement here at the SLH.'

'Which I hope will continue.' Faye raised an eyebrow. 'Miss Barnett has asked you, hasn't she? To cover for me in the canteen.'

'Yes, did she tell you?'

'No, but it was the obvious thing for her to do. I hope you said yes.'

'I said that I'd think about it.'

'But you are going to do it? You're not going back to Worcester permanently, are you? I'm sure it would be pleasant for a time, but then you'd find it suffocating. I… I'd be disappointed if you did.'

Ellie laughed. After everything that had happened, the friendship was still on offer. She found herself getting quite teary.

'I admit, I have quite taken to south London. It would be nice to see what Clapham's like when it isn't freezing. And there's a certain French doctor…'

'The common's lovely in spring and summer,' Faye said, looking out of the window. 'There's a funfair and the annual SLH Fete. That needs organising too, just the task for you.'

'Sounds like fun.'

'So, stay. Take the job. It'll tide you over at the very least and maybe it'll lead to something better. The pay's alright too. You could get a place of your own.'

'Alright,' she said. 'Though the job is still yours. It's there for you to come back to.'

'We'll see... I might not be coming back. I'm considering your god-father's proposition.'

'Really? To become a policewoman detective?'

'Why not?'

'It would mean leaving the SLH, leaving the place you've made for yourself.'

'I love the SLH and always will, but maybe I need somewhere new, like you did. The SLH is safe, at least for now, but it isn't the place for me anymore. I've always been a detective at heart and joining the police would give me a chance to get my own back for this.' Faye indicated her bandaged body. 'It was Les Allen who shot me, but it was the gang's business he was on. I'd like to help track them down.'

'It could be dangerous.'

'There'd be plenty of hefty policemen around to protect me.'

'Hmmm, what would Nick Yorke say about that?'

'So you'll stay?' Faye asked again.

'Yes, but I'll have to visit my old home, if only to explain what's happening.'

'Good, as long as you're coming back.' Faye gasped as she flopped back against the pillows.

'Now you really ought to rest.'

'Yes, I'm tired. Go tell Miss Barnett that you'll take the job, tell her we've talked about it.'

'I will.' Ellie rose. 'See you tomorrow,' she said.

At the door of Pankhurst Ward, she stopped and glanced back at her friend.

Faye was reclining, her face pale, her left hand on her chest.

With her right she reached out to the small bedside cabinet and picked up a business card.

THE END

AFTERWORD

The Midnight Man is fiction, a work of the imagination, but elements of it were (and are) real. From 1912 to 1984 the South London Hospital for Women and Children existed, offering health services to women and children in Clapham, south London. Part of it, the North Wing, still stands opposite Clapham South underground station. That building is now a large supermarket with apartments above. The South London Hospital gardens, which once won awards, are now the car park.

The SLH founders were Maud Chadburn and Eleanor Davies-Colley, two female surgeons who, denied the opportunities offered to their male colleagues, and seeing the huge demand among women to be treated by women, decided to set up the hospital. They and their friends raised the funds and purchased two large houses on Clapham South Side. The out-patient department opened in 1913 and the hospital proper opened in 1916, with the new North Wing in 1930.

Maud and Eleanor lived, together, in premises on Harley Street with their adopted children, the first of a series of remarkable women associated with the hospital. Maud is commemorated in the name of a road – Maud Chadburn Place – in Clapham, while Eleanor, the first female surgeon admitted to the Royal College, had a lecture theatre named after her at the RCS headquarters. Unfortunately, this was removed during the latest refurbishment.

Wandsworth Health Authority closed the hospital on grounds of cost efficiency in 1984, a claim strongly disputed at the time and that still causes blood pressure to rise among those who remember it. The closure was fought for several years and it became a cause cèlébre for many women's groups, locally, nationally and internationally.

I could not find biographies of the founders or of the hospital. The minutes of its management board show that it never suffered the shortage of nursing staff found across the capital in 1946, mainly because nurses, doctors and midwives, all female, wanted to work there. It must have been a special place and I hope, in a small way, to have given it an extra life, albeit as the backdrop to a crime novel.

Incidentally, a relatively recent Canadian study, widely reported in the press, suggests that, even in 2022, women have better health outcomes and are less likely to die after surgery if they are treated by women.[1] Historically, most surgeons in the UK were male, although parity is being achieved now.

The pill-box shaped buildings at the entrances to the deep level shelters at Clapham North, Clapham Common and Clapham South are still there and there are occasional tours of the shelters at Clapham South (where the list of Admiral's names is entirely different from that in the novel). The Balham Hill shaft head entrance has been incorporated into a new apartment block. The character of Owen Philpott is based upon Mr Copeman, the real guardian of the deep shelters.

Westbury Court still sits above Clapham South underground station, though many of the flats are now privately owned. The Odeon cinema at the top of Balham Hill is now a wine retailer and the police station house once found next to Westbury Court has been replaced by a luxury retirement complex. Cavendish Road police station was sold and converted into apartments (including the cells), but a blue police lamp still stands outside it.

The National Health Act was passed in November 1946. At a time when the NHS is being privatised by a succession of governments, while being consistently undermined and underfunded, I thought it useful to remember what life was like before it existed. Tuberculosis, the fatal disease referenced in the book, had, for many years, no cure and reached pandemic proportions at various times in its history. The drug trial in the novel, of the antibiotic streptomycin, took place in 1946 in London and was successful. I don't know if the South London Hospital took part.

The general election of 1945 elected a Labour government with a landslide; the first time Labour had been elected outright. The Attlee administration subsequently oversaw a reform of the state along the lines proposed in the *Beveridge Report* (1942). These reforms were hot topics at the time, prompting debate in all strata of society, which, I hope, I have reflected in the novel.

The Metropolitan Police Service was heavily criticised during and immediately after World War Two because of its failure to prevent a 57 percent rise in crime. The end of the war saw a huge recruitment drive, including of women.

Nonetheless, the prejudice and discrimination encountered by Ellie and Faye was common at the time. Women could vote, but were second-class citizens, unable, for example, to open a bank account without a male sponsor. Many forms of employment still operated a 'marriage bar' which permitted only single women to work. Abortion was illegal. A woman's role was to be a wife and mother, even after experience during the war had made it clear that women were capable of so much more.

I've tried to use the language and idiom of the period. This includes using pejorative terms that are, quite rightly, no longer used, such as the term 'crippled' for a disabled person, or 'simple'. I recognise that such language is offensive, but it was in common usage then, especially in a hospital setting. My choice is for authenticity rather than the more civilised terminology used today and I apologise in advance if this offends anyone.

There is one deliberate semi-anachronism (although there may be more unknown ones which I have failed to remove). Faye describes the massive increase in birth rate in 1946 as a 'baby boom'. The earliest *written* usage of this well-known phrase I can find is in 1949, but I have taken the liberty of using it anyway, especially as that is exactly what a hospital like the South London would have seen at first hand as it happened.

ENDNOTES

AFTERWORD

1. Association of Surgeon-Patient Sex Concordance With Postoperative Outcomes; Christopher J.D.Wallis, MD, PhD; Angela Jerath, MD, MSc; Natalie Coburn, MD, MPH. JAMA Surgery, December 2021.

ACKNOWLEDGEMENTS

I have been very fortunate, in writing *The Midnight Man*, to have received expert help and advice from several health professionals. Most notably, Juliet Boyd, Consultant Anaesthetist (Retired) at the South London Hospital for Women and Children in the 1970s and early 1980s, who supplied a goldmine of information, old photographs and hospital memorabilia from the 1930s onwards. She helped me create the ethos of 'my' SLH and I hope that it reflects how it really was.

Especial thanks also to Bernadette, a retired hospital pharmacist who helped me understand the internal processes of a hospital regarding the storing, dispensing and prescribing of drugs and how they are administered to the patient. She helped me develop the drug-theft plot. Both Juliet and Bernadette were good enough to read an early manuscript and comment upon it. As was Sue Norman, former CEO of the UK Central Council for Nursing, Midwifery and Health Visiting. Any errors made are mine, not theirs.

Thank you to Deborah Hughes, also known as @theundercover-midwife, who worked at the SLH as a midwife from 1981 4. Deborah is part of a Facebook group called South London Women's Hospital Occupation 1984–1985, which celebrates the occupation, by women, many of them the nurses who worked in the hospital, after it had been officially closed.

Many thanks also to the staff of Lambeth Archives, then at the Minet Library in Knatchbull Road, who suggested, when I explained what I was looking for, that I take a look at maps and architect plans. I found exactly what I needed. There was also a wealth of detail in the Management Committee minutes of the SLH and of other hospitals in south London at the time. I am also indebted to Alyson Wilson of The Clapham Society for her help and for her excellent article (with Derrick Johnson) on the Clapham Deep Level Shelters.

Thank you too to all the bloggers, podcasters and other online supporters and promoters of books – authors really appreciate you and your, often unsung, efforts.

As always thanks to those friends who are unfailingly supportive and have been since the start – Miv, Annette, Helen and Sue. Thanks, too, to Dick Garth whose chance remark about cocaine solution being readily available in hospitals not so long ago started my train of thought. And to Jonathan Burns and Dr Paul Gilluley for their support, plus thanks to Angustias Salgad for her friendship (and coffee). A final 'thank you as always' must go to my patient and long-suffering husband, Mark.

ABOUT THE AUTHOR

Julie Anderson is the CWA Dagger listed author of three Whitehall thrillers and a short series of historical adventure stories for young adults. Before becoming a crime fiction writer, she was a senior civil servant, working across a variety of departments and agencies, including the Office of the Deputy Prime Minister. Unlike her protagonists, however, she doesn't know where (all) the bodies are buried.

She writes crime fiction reviews for Time and Leisure Magazine and is a co-founder and Trustee of the Clapham Book Festival.

She lives in south London where her latest crime fiction series is set, returning to her first love of writing historical fiction with *The Midnight Man*.

Website: https://julieandersonwriter.com.

ALSO BY JULIE ANDERSON

THE CASSANDRA FORTUNE MYSTERIES

Plague, Oracle and the 2023 Crime Writers' Association Ian Fleming Dagger long-listed *Opera*

'Highly recommended.' Dr Noir (aka Jacky Collins)

'A thriller trilogy that calls to mind the joyfully clandestine dangers of Ian Fleming and John Le Carre.' Callahan Books

Whitehall thrillers with 'the sour tang of authenticity' AnneMarie Neary author of *The Orphans*

HOBECK BOOKS – THE HOME OF GREAT STORIES

We hope you've enjoyed reading this novel by Julie Anderson. To keep up to date on Julie's fiction writing please do follow her on social media or check her website https://julieandersonwriter.com.

Hobeck Books offers a number of short stories and novellas, free for subscribers in the compilation *Crime Bites*.

- *Echo Rock* by Robert Daws
- *Old Dogs, Old Tricks* by AB Morgan

- *The Silence of the Rabbit* by Wendy Turbin
- *Never Mind the Baubles: An Anthology of Twisted Winter Tales* by the Hobeck Team (including many of the Hobeck authors and Hobeck's two publishers)
- *The Clarice Cliff Vase* by Linda Huber
- *Here She Lies* by Kerena Swan
- *The Macnab Principle* by R.D. Nixon
- *Fatal Beginnings* by Brian Price
- *A Defining Moment* by Lin Le Versha
- *Saviour* by Jennie Ensor
- *You Can't Trust Anyone These Days* by Maureen Myant

Also please visit the Hobeck Books website for details of our other superb authors and their books, and if you would like to get in touch, we would love to hear from you.

Hobeck Books also presents a weekly podcast, the Hobcast, where founders Adrian Hobart and Rebecca Collins discuss all things book related, key issues from each week, including the ups and downs of running a creative business. Each episode includes an interview with one of the people who make Hobeck possible: the editors, the authors, the cover designers. These are the people who help Hobeck bring great stories to life. Without them, Hobeck wouldn't exist. The Hobcast can be listened to from all the usual platforms but it can also be found on the Hobeck website: **www. hobeck.net/hobcast**.

OTHER HOBECK HISTORICAL CRIME FICTION TO EXPLORE

Waking the Tiger by **Mark Wightman**

Shortlisted for a Crime Writers' Association John Creasey (New Blood) Dagger 2022.
Finalist for the Ngaio Marsh Awards Best First Novel 2022.
Longlisted for the Bloody Scotland McIlvanney Prize for Scottish Crime Book of the Year 2021 and shortlisted for the Scottish Crime Debut of the Year 2021.

Available in ebook, paperback and audiobook.

Chasing the Dragon by **Mark Wightman**

'A classy, and future classic, historical crime novel with all the nuance and intelligence of the best of the genre.' Natalie Marlow, author of critically acclaimed *Needless Alley*

Available in ebook, paperback and audiobook.